EAGLE'S DESTINY

C. J. Corbin

THIS IS A WORK OF FICTION. NAMES, CHARACTERS, ORGANIZATIONS, PLACES, BRANDS, MEDIA, AND EVENTS PORTRAYED IN THIS STORY ARE EITHER PRODUCTS OF THE AUTHOR'S IMAGINATION OR ARE USED FICTITIOUSLY. THE AUTHOR ACKNOWLEDGES TRADEMARKED STATUS AND TRADEMARK OWNERS OF VARIOUS PRODUCTS REFERENCED IN THIS WORK OF FICTION, WHICH HAVE BEEN USED WITHOUT PERMISSION. THE PUBLICATION/USE OF THESE TRADEMARKS IS NOT AUTHORIZED, ASSOCIATED WITH, OR SPONSORED BY THE TRADEMARK OWNERS.

This book contains content that may not be suitable for young readers under 17.

First Printing: November 2012
Second Printing: March 2016
Third Printing: May 2019

ISBN-13: 978-1480102811

Cover design by Scarlett Rugers

Berliner Bear Publishing
berlinerbearpublishing.com

DEDICATION

Mom, thank you for whispering, "*write the book.*"

Dad, thank you for pushing me along.

And to my girls, Debi, Nancy, Robin, and Jennifer
thank you for being there.

ACKNOWLEDGMENTS

So many people helped me on this journey.

Thank you to Debi Boniface for introducing me to Michael.

Thank you to Nancy Merola, Robin Walker, and Jennifer Sizemore for being with me every step of the way. You listened with infinite patience as I endlessly talked about plot points and character development. I will never forget the day Robin read a few chapters and said, "More!" Thank you, my sweet girls, Eagle's Destiny would not be here without your encouragement, friendship, and love.

Thank you to my beta readers, your validation and support gave me the confidence to see this book published.

Thank you to Cassandra Moss-Garofalo, my editor, for loving Eagle's Destiny as much as me.

Thank you to my cover designer Scarlett Rugers Design, you took my scattered vision of the cover and made it come true, twice!

Thank you, Dad, for believing in me.

And finally, thank you to the reader. Thank you for taking a chance on me. I hope you fall in love with Michael and Elizabeth the way I did.

"This is the stuff our life is made of; there is no part of the journey that is not important, each moment and each step whether planned or unplanned, played an important role in our fate."

Debi Boniface

CHAPTER ONE

It was an ending. I don't think I realized it at the time, and now wonder if anyone truly does recognize the event that starts an ending. Or is it when we look back, we are finally able to understand?

It was a dark and stormy night outside the Sacramento airport terminal. No stars were visible through the thick blanket of clouds. The air was humid and felt heavy. It had been a typically hot August day down in Southern California, and I had looked forward to getting back to the cooler temperatures up north. Since a downpour was imminent, I wondered if I'd make it home to my cabin before the rain started.

The skycap followed me out with two crates and luggage on a cart. He lifted each box and gently set it on the sidewalk. I clipped leashes on the wriggling cocker spaniels inside. My chocolate colored Topper jumped out barking, I think just to announce his arrival. Samantha, the smaller black and white cocker, came out stretching and then sidled up next to me.

Straightening, I turned to the skycap. "I'm going to pick up my car. I'll be back shortly for the crates and luggage. I appreciate your help."

The skycap nodded at me. "They sure are happy to be out of those crates."

I agreed. "Yeah, the short hour-long flight is easier than an eight-hour drive."

"I know just what you mean, my dogs hate the car too."

"Samantha, Topper," I called to the dogs as I set off toward the parking lot. "Come with mommy."

I found my twenty-year-old cypress green Range Rover quickly. It had belonged to my mother's sister, Ruth. It was a gas hog, but I loved it anyway. Don, my best friend's husband, had agreed to drive my tank down to the airport and park it for me since I expected to catch a late flight.

Chuckling before getting in, I gripped the bar under the seat to move it back. Don, who was several inches shorter than my nearly six-foot frame, always forgot to adjust it. I maneuvered the Range Rover around the airport and pulled up in front of the skycap. After all the bags and crates were loaded into the back, it was a relief to be on my way. I frowned as I checked my watch, I knew I wouldn't be home until after midnight, much later than initially planned.

I sighed audibly and mumbled, "What goes right when I plan something?"

The dogs were already snuggled down in the back seat. Settling myself in, I resigned myself to the drive. The headache that had threatened all day moved into overdrive. I just needed to relax, but as I relived the day's happenings, it was surprising the pounding in my head had not occurred earlier. I loosened the braid that held my waist-length auburn hair, hoping it would help. My hair felt tight like the rest of my body.

The plan had been to fly out of southern California early in the morning to avoid the late-night drive when I arrived in Sacramento. Before I left, a last-minute call from my publisher for an interview skewed my plans. The meeting was with none other than my ex-husband Kevin. He worked as a freelance writer for *Romance Magazine*, although he preferred to write more hard-hitting journalistic pieces rather than writing puff articles for what he considered a stupid magazine. Reluctantly, after much discussion, I agreed to an afternoon interview.

I wrote steamy mystery romance novels. The kind that started out with the mystery to solve and ended with the sizzle! My books sold well landing me on the critical best-sellers lists. They were a source of both my pride and independence. Too bad my own life never quite followed the lines of my novels. Kevin always complained he could never live up to my books, and that I was unrealistic in my expectations. I now considered that his problem, not mine.

We met for lunch at what had been our favorite bistro in Hermosa Beach. It was a cute little place, very French farmhouse chic. Its pretentiousness ended there. The food was good, and the service was attentive. He waited for me at the table when I arrived. I offered him my cheek, and he kissed it, lingering longer than was necessary. He looked good. He always did. We were the same height, and I always wore flats when I was with him. When I dressed before meeting him, I had debated on my choice of shoes and put the low-heeled ones on anyway not wanting to cause problems with him. He could become moody and angry when I would do or say things that pointed to his perceived shortcomings.

"You cut your hair?" I asked, surprised to see his dark hair cut so short. It was almost a buzz cut. He always took such pride in his hair.

"Yeah," he replied as we sat. "My hairdresser is on her honeymoon, and no one else can do it like she can," he chuckled.

I pursed my lips together remembering her. While we were married, I caught them together, in the romance novel way. Lucky girl, it sounded like she escaped him.

As we settled in to look at the menus, I noticed Kevin staring intently at someone. A redheaded woman in her twenties sat at a table behind me. I twisted around and noticed she had her eyes glued on him. He was returning her gaze. Turning myself back around in my chair, I shook my head and rolled my eyes.

"What?" he asked, fixing his eyes back on me.

"Nothing." I looked back down at the menu.

I wanted to get this interview over and be away from him. It did not surprise me that he received looks from women. He certainly did while we were married. He maintained his well-built six-foot body by regularly working with weights. When you looked up *abs of steel* in the dictionary, his picture was there. Always impeccably groomed, he appeared as if he stepped out of GQ Magazine.

I understood very clearly the magnetism he held for women. On the other hand, I might as well have been the placemat on the table for all the attention he gave me; nothing had changed. His infidelity was only one of the many reasons for our divorce.

After we ordered, he focused his attention back to me, but my hackles were already raised. I did not want to be with him any longer than necessary.

"So, what's this book about? Wait, let me guess." He leaned back in his chair with his arms folded behind his head. He had that look of self-confidence on his face because he knew that almost every woman in the place found him attractive. "Yes, I know." He bent forward toward me while his brown eyes challenged me. "Yes, a woman looking for love. Isn't that what they all want Liz?" His face wore a smirk.

I bristled at the name *Liz*. Kevin had persistently refused to call me Elizabeth during our five-year marriage. Why would it be different now?

"Didn't you bother to read it?" The frown on my face was evident. "That is also part of the job of writing the article."

He spread his hands out in front of him. "Come on. Your books are all alike."

"Why do you even trouble yourself if you're not going to take this seriously?" I asked, trying not to roll my eyes. "You know this is my livelihood, and I might add, yours too."

He flashed me a warning look, and a chill went through me.

"It isn't like real writing," he confronted me again, trying to provoke me into arguing with him. He liked our arguments since he felt they had always fueled our passion. My energy for these fights was gone.

He saw the change in my expression. "Okay Liz, I'll admit I didn't read it, but an underwater archeologist? How did you think of that one?"

Kevin took my writing as a fluke. My first book published just shortly after our second anniversary had him secretly furious. His public reaction certainly showed congratulatory hugs, but his compliments disappeared when we were alone. My books became a refuge for me. While I wrote they enveloped me completely and he did not exist in the world I created.

After finishing lunch and the interview, he walked me out to my car. As I turned to thank him, he stood very close to me. Too close.

"Don't I get a hug and kiss goodbye?" he said, already moving his arms around me.

At first, I didn't move because I was frozen with fear. Then, I tried to push him away, but he pinned my arms behind my back with one hand. Kevin pulled me against him and bent his head toward me, his mouth close to mine. With anger in my eyes, I wished for the courage to tell him my thoughts. As he leaned down to kiss me, I shifted my head, so he could only kiss me on the cheek, but he was too quick, and his hand came up to move my chin toward his lips. His kiss was not short, and he pressed harder. A little voice screamed inside of me.

Unhappy with my lack of response, he broke off the kiss. He looked me in the eyes. "Liz, you know you want it."

"No. I don't." Shaking my head, I wriggled to free my arms and pushed him away from me.

He stepped back. "I'll call you."

Defiantly I looked at him. "No Kevin, that would not be a good idea."

In disgust, I wanted to brush the feeling of him off my body. I did not look back at him though. I could tell he had turned around and started walking to his car. Snapping on my seatbelt, I looked up, and he was standing by his door, grinning at me. He had won. He had gotten the last move. As I drove out of the restaurant parking lot, I burst into tears.

CHAPTER TWO

Halfway to Mintock, it started to sprinkle and that brought me out of my thoughts and away from that dreadful lunch. By the time I arrived home was pouring. I parked in the rear of my cabin and was relieved to see that Don had left on the lights. While I gathered my purse, the dogs bounded out of the backseat and ran up to the back porch. For once, they did not run around the yard because they wanted to be out of the rain too. As I let myself in, I noticed the house next door had lights on. It made me happy to see it finally occupied. It had remained empty for so long.

I had been away most of the summer. The three months had flown by quickly. My house in Southern California was a convenient base of operations when traveling, but the cabin was now going to be my home. Even Topper and Samantha were acclimating nicely.

My cabin that once belonged to my Aunt Ruth was on the shores of Lake Mintock, located just north of San Francisco in the wine country. I appreciated the quiet of the area. Since it was the last house on a utility road off the main highway, I did not have to contend with the traffic and noise.

The single-story structure, although considered small in the area, was big enough for the dogs and me. The two-bedroom cabin had a rustic appearance to it with high polished pine floors and cabinets. The kitchen, dining, and living rooms were one large great-room facing the lake. Sunsets over the lake were dramatic in the late summer, and there were plenty of windows on the front of the house to enjoy the vibrant colors reflecting off the lake. Located near the front door was my writing desk. While writing, I spent many hours staring out the large picture window.

The vase on the desk, full of delicate pink mini-carnations, made me smile. The welcome home present from Don and his wife Debi touched my heart. Being at the cabin always seemed to increase my creative juices and could pull me out of any writer's block. My father and younger sister, who both had homes within three blocks of my house in Southern California, could not understand why I kept returning to this place.

After settling the dogs in with water and snacks, I took a shower and put on my white cotton nightgown. The bedside clock said one a.m. and my bones felt the late hour. The encounter with Kevin earlier in the day had zapped all my energy. I opened the window far enough to be able to hear the rain outside and to bring in some of the cool breezes. Listening to the rain at bedtime was a favorite because it would soothe me and help me sleep. Both Topper and Samantha were already on the bed when I crawled under the covers and snuggled into the down comforter with them.

I slept like a dead person, which was unusual for me. When I opened my eyes and looked at the clock, I could not believe it was already eight. I rarely slept in, preferring to get an early start to my day. As soon as Samantha realized that I was awake, she came bounding on top of me. We played this every morning. She would not bother me while I slept but open one eye and she was right there ready for cuddles and hugs. Topper was never far behind.

While the coffee brewed, I prepared the dog's breakfasts and silently thanked Debi for doing the grocery shopping for me. After eating, the dogs followed me out the front door. I sat in the big verandah chair on the front porch while they lay by my feet. Normally my routine included a jog with the dogs first, then coffee.

The crisp air from the rain the previous night was refreshing, but the day would warm up and turn humid and hot. Two young women from the house next door carried towels and baskets out to the small motorboat tied to the dock located between our two homes. A large terrier and a miniature German shepherd ran around them. Topper barked at the two dogs while standing safely up on the first step.

Both women were startled and looked up. The shorter blond woman started waving her arm, and shouted, "Hello!" She ran toward me with the two dogs and her companion following. As she came closer, I realized that she was young; definitely younger than the age of twenty.

I walked down the steps to greet them.

"Hi," I said when she reached me.

She was several inches shorter than me and beautiful. She wore her straight shoulder-length blond hair pulled up in a ponytail with her bangs brushed to the side. Her blue eyes framed a cherubic face with deep dimples on the corners of her mouth.

"Are you Elizabeth Sommars?" she asked breathlessly.

"Yes, I am. Do you live next door?" I pointed to the two-story house.

"Oh my gosh! I knew it. You look just like your pictures. Debi told me that you lived next door. I love your books. This is so exciting!" Her exuberance threatened to take her over.

When her companion reached us, it became clear that they were sisters. She reached out her hand to me, and I immediately noticed her long and delicate fingers with short trimmed nails. I would bet she was a piano player.

"I'm Katy, and this is my sister Tammy. We moved here about two months ago with our dad." Katy was slightly shorter and thinner than Tammy. Her face was longer, and her blond hair had more curl too.

While I was away, Debi told me a family had moved in after making renovations to the interior. The house, built in the twenties, was the first home in the cove and it had needed the repair badly. The previous owners used it only in the summers, and after their children grew, they let it fall into disrepair.

"It's nice to meet you. Would you gals like some coffee?" I asked.

Tammy responded immediately. "That would be great!" She came up the steps, and Katy and the dogs followed her. Tammy turned and looked at the dogs. "You two stay here."

"Oh, that's okay, let them in." I went into the house and tried not to trip over the four dogs moving around my feet.

"Your website said your new book is coming out soon," Tammy inquired as I pulled mugs out of the cupboard.

"The release date is in six weeks." I nodded and poured the coffee. "I have freshly baked coffee cake. Debi made it."

Tammy's excitement bubbled over. "I can hardly wait for the book. It's another Jessica story, isn't it?"

"It's a good thing you know the author." I winked and rummaged through my briefcase. I pulled out a book and laid it in front of Tammy. "This is a pre-publish copy, all for you."

She snatched the book up quickly. "Oh my gosh! Oh my gosh!"

Tammy held the book to her chest, her blue eyes sparkling. I thought she was ready to swoon. Katy and I both laughed.

"Tammy, get a grip," Katy admonished.

Tammy stuck her tongue out at her sister. "Oh, don't tell me you don't read them too!"

"Would you like me to sign it?" I offered.

Tammy thrust the book back at me. "Oh yes!"

While we drank our coffee and ate Debi's delicious caramel and pecan coffee cake, I learned more about my new neighbors. Tammy was eighteen and had just graduated from high school before moving to Mintock. In September, she planned to attend our junior college in Ashley, the town closest to Mintock, before transferring to UC Davis in January. Recently, she had decided to study veterinary medicine. The dogs certainly fell in love with her because they sat right next to her. It was either that, or she was dropping coffee cake to them.

Katy, two years older than her sister, was considerably quieter. She attended Julliard in New York and was on summer break. When she confirmed she played the piano, I smiled and nodded. The air about her was more composed and sophisticated.

"I know my dad will want to meet you when he gets back. He was interested in your boat when he saw Don parking it at the dock yesterday." Katy laughed. "Dad loves anything that goes fast."

I laughed too. "Yeah, it is a little too much for our lake. I like to water ski, and I wanted something fast. Is your dad away?"

Tammy piped in, "Dad's out shooting animals."

I was glad the phone rang at that instant so I could cover the horror her comment had brought to my face.

A wave of nausea came over me when I answered the phone. "Hello?"

"Elizabeth? I didn't wake you, did I?" The voice on the line hesitated.

"Oh Debi," I answered. "No, in fact, I have Katy and Tammy here, my new neighbors. We're enjoying your great coffee cake."

"So, you've met the Hoffman's?" she asked with curiosity in her voice. "What do you think?"

"Well, just the girls. Their father is away at the moment."

"Wait 'til you meet him. He is an absolute dreamboat. I mean he is freaking hot! He's someone I would go after…well… if I were still single."

I laughed. Sometimes she sounded like her teenaged daughter.

"Okay Debi," I said stopping her rave. "I'll see you in a bit." I could hear her giggle as I hung up the phone.

Katy and Tammy moved to get up as I replaced the phone in the cradle. They helped carry the dishes into the kitchen. With many thanks from Tammy for the book, they left to continue with their Saturday.

The walk along the lakeshore to Debi and Don's house was one of my favorites. On the other side of my new neighbors, there was the largest lot in the cove on which an empty cabin stood. It was about the same size as mine. Next was a large two-story old Victorian style home, belonging to my friends Angel and Lewis. Their kids were playing outside and came running when they saw me.

Angel walked down from her porch and reached up to hug me. "Welcome home! We missed you!"

Angel's face had a delicate bone structure with high cheekbones and full lips. She was a few years younger and a head shorter than me. Her hair was cut straight around her shoulders with full bangs and was a mixture of light brown and dark blond. Large chocolate brown eyes were the most dramatic feature to her face, and they could show a depth of understanding unlike any other.

"I missed you guys too. I heard about Lewis' knee, is he okay?" I asked while hugging her back. Her husband managed our baseball team and was the fire department captain for Mintock.

Angel bent over to pick up her youngest daughter and said, "Yeah, he's okay, but he's out for the rest of the season. The doctor said no more baseball for the year, although he is still able to manage us all. He was excited when he heard you were coming home. We desperately need you back because you know how he feels about my pitching." She groaned and then laughed.

I laughed too. Angel was better at third base. "I can't wait to get back to the game. See you tomorrow afternoon." I waved goodbye to her and the kids.

Finally, I reached Debi and Don's house at the start of the utility road.

She ran out to greet me. Her full round face and warm hug showed me how much she had missed me. "I have so much news for you! I'm glad you're finally back. I can't believe how long you've been gone."

She was substantially shorter, with the top of her head barely reaching my shoulders. She had her wavy dark blond shoulder length hair streaked with blond highlights. The area around her light brown eyes crinkled when she smiled.

Her hug took my breath away. It was always like that with us. Don came out of the house wiping his hands on a paper towel.

He gave me a hard hug too, almost crushing me against him. "Damn girl you cannot go away for so long again!"

I just laughed. "Oh, you two, stop it. I wasn't gone that long."

"Three months is way too long." Her voice sounded like a mom. I was glad to be home.

"Thanks for dropping the Range Rover off at the airport," I said to Don.

"Glad to do it. Jason came with me. He needed to pick up some schoolbooks at Stanford. School starts in a few weeks. You know he wants to get a head start on the studying," he said proudly.

Don was rugged from top to bottom. He owned the local garage and was responsible for keeping my Range Rover running after all these years. He was one of the most considerate men I had in my life. I always teased Debi that if she hadn't stolen Don away, I would have snatched him up for myself.

He was born and raised in Mintock. The town knew his family well. His father became the police chief twenty-five years ago when my Aunt Ruth first moved to Mintock. Don's mother, a Native American from the local Pomo tribe, was famous as a local artist. We had culled our friendship over many years, and he was more like the brother I never had. I spent many summers up here with my Aunt. My parents felt being in a small town would keep me out of trouble. Nothing had been further from the truth. Remembering some of the pranks we played, I was surprised we did not land in jail. Maybe it had been a good thing that his dad was the police chief.

Debi accompanied me to Mintock during the summers while we were in high school. When we graduated, she decided to move here. They had fallen in love. They married immediately and Jason, their son, arrived two years later. Their daughter Betsy, my namesake, followed three years after Jason. Both kids had taken on Don's Mexican and Native American darker looks instead of Debi's Southern California blond look.

After high school, our paths diverged. I went on to college in Southern California, and Debi concentrated on raising her family. While in our twenty's we kept in touch mainly by the phone and short visits a few times a year. After graduating from college, I went on to work at a magazine, not as a writer as I had dreamed, but in the production department working with the advertising.

While at the magazine, Kevin and I met and started dating. He was the writer, and I was enamored with him. Neither Debi or Don were fond of him. I should have taken that as a hint. Mostly they put up with him for my sake.

We went into the house while Don went back to the garage on the side of the house. Their home had a relaxing effect on me. It was comfortable, not fancy, but richly decorated. As I looked around the kitchen, the memories from all the knick-knacks and the pictures hanging on the wall flooded my mind.

She put mugs on the table in front of us and sat down. "So, Kevin trapped you again?"

I sighed and nodded my head. Taking a sip of tea, I said, "I really wish he would leave me alone. I don't know what to do anymore. I don't get it."

"It's a good thing you're up here. He'd have to have a big excuse to come here. He wants control over you like he had when you were married. You know it is not love. It's all a matter of making you bend to his will."

Don walked in through the back door. "Bend to whose will?" He sat down at the table.

Debi crinkled her nose. "You know, Kevin."

"Oh, that jackass?" He reached out and patted my hand. "Don't let him bother you. You want me to take care of him?"

I laughed and smacked him on the shoulder. "What are you going to do?"

He yawned and stretched. "You know, we mechanics can make many things go wrong."

"Don, don't even joke about that!" I admonished him.

"Well, if I can't help. I'm going to go out and work on Jason's motorcycle. I'd like to surprise him and actually get it running today." He stood and kissed Debi on the mouth. "Call me when lunch is ready, woman," he growled possessively.

"You got it, baby." She squeezed his butt.

I rolled my eyes. "You two want to get a room?"

He laughed and pulled on my braid as he passed me. "Remember you're in my house."

We heard the back-door slam, and Debi turned to me. "So spill everything!"

We talked about everything at length while she put lunch together. Their house was my second home. An invitation to lunch was a natural assumption. Filling her in about my afternoon with Kevin made me feel better about the situation. She was my rock during my divorce. She had been there with plenty of tissues. Not once did an *"I told you so"* escape from her lips.

More importantly, she filled me in on the local gossip, especially the happenings at the weekly town baseball games. Tomorrow our team would play one of the teams from Ashley, and everyone expected my pitching arm to be at the ready for the game. Pitching was probably in my blood since my Aunt Ruth had been a pitcher too.

Our conversation finally moved around to my new neighbors. Debi could not believe I hadn't met Katy and Tammy's father, but she assured me he would be at the game since he now played first base for the team. I pursed my lips, not admitting I was not going to be fond of someone who hunted. Kevin had gone big game hunting in Africa while covering a story there and each time I saw the pictures of the dead animals, waves of nausea almost overtook me. Debi had the overwhelming need to fix me up with someone even though I kept reminding her I did not need fixing because I was not broken.

As it started to get dark, I gave my thanks to both for the great day. Jason's motorcycle was running, and Don wanted to take it out for a spin, with me on the back.

"All you need to do is take me up to my cabin." I put on the helmet he handed to me.

"Aw come on. Let's take it for a real spin!"

Debi waved to us and as we took off yelled, "Have fun!"

I wrapped my arms around him. "Hey not so fast!" I squealed with delight.

The episode was too reminiscent of high school when his motorcycle was our primary mode of transportation. The brush of the cooling evening air felt good against my skin. He cranked up the speed as he headed for the highway. We drove to the edge of town, turned around and headed back toward home.

The jeep up ahead of us was not moving very fast and true to Don's character, he decided to pass the vehicle on the narrow utility road. The driver was polite and shifted over to the side to allow us to go by. We waved as we passed, and I caught a glimpse of the handsome man driving. At least he was smiling until we cut him off to make the sharp turn into my drive.

The car stopped at the house next door.

As Don pulled up in front of my back porch, I smacked him on the back. "Oh no! That was my new neighbor you just cut off!"

"Oh relax, he had plenty of room!" I handed him my helmet, and he gave me a big bear hug. "See you tomorrow at the game. Don't be late, and make sure you warm up first!"

I saluted him. "Yes, sir!" I gave him another hug. "Thanks for the ride!" He scooted off back down the road toward his house, driving at a considerably slower speed. As I watched my neighbor unloading his jeep, he caught me staring. Immediately I felt a blush creep on my face. He waved, and I waved back. I quickly let myself into my cabin.

CHAPTER THREE

Sunday afternoon in Mintock meant baseball. I had been on the Lakeside team for as long as I could remember. My fastball was a legend in Mintock and Ashley. Even better, I could hit the ball too. When not playing the other Mintock club we played the teams in Ashley. This was serious business because this was baseball. The weekly summer event was popular with the people of the town, and we even managed to draw our fair share of tourists too.

For me, there was a whole Zen thing to prepare myself mentally for the game. When Don told me to warm up yesterday afternoon, this was precisely what he meant. I followed the ritual carefully, from braiding my hair to making sure my socks were on straight and even. My uniform, purchased new at the beginning of the summer, was white and clean with no stains. I knew there would be stains covering most of it by the end of the day, and I wore them like a badge of honor because of their cost to earn.

Checking my reflection in the mirror, I placed my cap on my head. The pants were snug and clung to my long legs. With the shirt tucked in, I looked like all legs, and I was reasonably happy with what I saw. The curves were in the right places, and the jogging had kept me thin. That and forgetting to eat while writing.

I stuffed a pair of jeans, a tank top, and sandals into my sports bag for later. The team usually ended up at our local restaurant and bar after the game. Sitting around in a uniform never suited me, so I always changed clothes.

Stowing my stuff on the passenger side of the Range Rover, I glanced over at the neighbor's house. The jeep was already gone. Guessing they had already left for the game, I checked my watch to make sure I still had plenty of time. I rolled down all the windows of my old car. The warm summer air felt good and made it easier to get my mind into the game.

Arriving at the park with time to spare, I carried my bag over to join the group already gathered at the dugout. Lewis acknowledged me with a wave since he was deep in conversation with one umpire. The rest of the Lakeside team welcomed me with hugs and kisses all around.

Debi grabbed me. "Let me introduce you to your neighbor. Michael?" she called to the tall blond man standing with his back to us.

As he turned around, I stopped breathing. His eyes were the lightest blue, and his smile was broad showing his white teeth. There were the cutest little dimples at the corners of his mouth, and when he grinned, he had deeper dimples in his cheeks. His short-cropped hair was blond and curly. I was not used to looking up at someone since I towered over most people, but he was at least four inches taller than I was. With his square jaw and prominent Roman nose, he could have stepped out from the cover of one of my books.

Debi pushed me forward. "Elizabeth this is your neighbor. Michael this is Elizabeth. I'll let you two get acquainted." She turned and left us alone.

He looked down at me while his warm hand covered mine and held it a little longer than normal. "Hi Elizabeth, I've heard a lot about you," he said in a deep rich voice.

His sky-blue eyes sparkled. He filled out his uniform nicely with large broad shoulders that led down to a narrow waist. And, his pants… yes, he filled those out nicely too.

Even though I still was not breathing, I managed to get out a squeaky, "You have?"

"Yeah." He looked up and to the side as if compiling a list in his mind. "Let's see, I'm under strict instructions from Tammy not to call you Liz. She said your website said you don't like the name. Debi told me you are a great singer and you lead karaoke every week after the baseball game. And, everyone has told me you're an incredible fastball pitcher. So yeah, you have quite a fan club."

"Well, I…" I stammered looking down, feeling the blush rising on my cheeks. I took a deep breath and looked up again. "Just don't believe everything you hear."

Tammy came up from behind Michael. "Hey Elizabeth, you've finally met my dad. You have to see the pictures of the animals he shot yesterday! They are fantastic!"

I looked at her, I wanted to start shaking my head. Was this family nutty? Animals? There was more than one? I certainly did not want to look at pictures of dead animals. Yuck! I know people are into hunting but taking pictures of dead animals that you just killed. It made no sense to me. Michael picked up my expression and gave me a puzzled look.

Lewis limped up behind me, put his arm around my shoulders, and gave me a peck on the cheek. "Glad to see you're back. I thought Angel was going to have to pitch all summer. She's much better at third base." He handed me a ball. "Shouldn't you be warming up?" Lewis turned and shouted for Don.

After doing my warm-up pitches with Don, we started the game. Ashley had a good team, which made us evenly matched. In the beginning, I had trouble getting into my groove, but by the third inning, I pitched more strikes. Michael proved to be one of our strongest players at first base. We were ahead by one run in the top of the ninth inning, and their batter hit one squarely to me. I caught the ball, and I overthrew to Michael allowing the runners to advance on the bases. The classic bases loaded, go ahead runner at second base, with two outs.

Lewis called a time out. He and Don, who played catcher, walked out to me. Lewis waved to Michael to have him join us out on the mound. As the three men approached, I looked down kicking the dirt with the toe of my shoe.

Lewis spoke first. "Elizabeth, you seem a little distracted today."

Looking up, Michael's eyes caught mine and held them for the briefest of seconds. He was trying to look very serious, but I saw the grin in his eyes. How did I explain to Lewis that, yes, I was distracted today, and it was all the first baseman's fault? He had stared at me the entire game. Okay, yes, that was the job of the first baseman to watch the pitcher, but did he have to stare that way?

I looked back at Lewis. "So, are you going to give me some words of wisdom?"

"Yeah, strike out the batter." Lewis took the ball from Don and gave it to me. Both Lewis and Don patted me on the shoulder then turned to walk back to home plate.

Michael stepped closer to me and whispered, "Make him chase after it."

He turned to run back to first base. I took a deep breath trying not to concentrate on his tight pants and sexy butt and instead turned my attention back to the batter.

The first pitch was swung on and missed. Michael had been correct the batter was going to chase after the ball. The player knew there would be no walks with the bases loaded. I took a deep breath and threw a curveball. The batter almost fell over trying to swing at the ball. Don threw the ball back at me. I looked over at first base, and he nodded.

The crowd in the bleachers was on their feet and screaming, but I couldn't hear them. Lewis blew me a kiss, the fastball signal. I was in the zone. It was the ball, the batter, and me. A chill ran down my spine as I turned and looked at each base individually. Every runner was already inching forward. Closing my eyes, I stood on the mound in position. The wind-up and the pitch were perfect. The ball left my hand in one fluid movement. It crossed over home plate and straight into Don's glove without the batter even moving. The pitch had caught him looking. The home plate umpire called the strike and the third out.

I sighed and dropped my head. I had almost lost the game because I was more interested in the man on first base. Disappointment flooded through me.

Angel, who had been on third base, came up behind me and put her arm around my waist. "Good job Elizabeth." She squeezed me.

"I almost lost control. I almost lost the game," I said in a small voice.

She whispered, "He is charming. It's understandable."

I looked at her with surprise on my face and then felt the blush on my face. "Oh Angel, no, was I that obvious?"

She laughed, "Normally, you don't stare at first base all the time. Come on." She pulled me forward with her.

While we walked back to home plate, Debi and Lewis greeted us.

"Way to go girlfriend!" Debi said.

Lewis patted me on the back. "I knew you could do it."

Don grinned at me, and whispered, "Distracted huh?"

"Oh, you shut up!" I grimaced.

He laughed and touched my shoulder. "Elizabeth, I've known you too long!"

We started packing up our stuff. Most of us would meet right after the game at Viva Madrid our local restaurant since Sunday night was karaoke night. I noticed Michael talking with Tammy while handing her keys. She hugged him and left.

Debi saw me watching. "Tammy has been dating Jason. The kids think karaoke is boring. They're going over to the pizza parlor."

I nodded. "See you at the restaurant. Save me a seat."

My heart jumped when I turned to find Michael next to my car.

"Oh, hi," I said a bit breathlessly.

His smiled dazzled me. "Do you think I can get a ride to the restaurant with you? I gave Tammy the keys to my Jeep. She and Jason are going for pizza."

"Sure. Get on in," I said trying to keep my voice calm and even.

He threw our bags onto the back seat and slid into the passenger seat next to me.

"Do you mind if I push the seat back?" he asked.

I almost giggled. Debi had been the last person on the passenger side, and she was a foot shorter than he was. His knees pressed against his chest.

"No, go ahead. The lever is on the front of the bottom of the seat. Do you need some help?" The vision I had of me reaching between his long legs to help push the seat back made me blush.

Michael's look made me wonder if he could read my mind, which made me blush even further. "No, I think I have it," he said with a smirk.

He chuckled deeply and slid the seat back as far as it would go. It was still a tight fit for him. I tried to concentrate on breathing, but he was sitting so close to me. His presence overpowered the aura around us.

"How tall are you?" I managed to get out.

"I'm six-four. My Jeep is specially retrofitted because of my height," he said as he buckled his seat belt.

I backed out of the parking space and saw Debi waving at me and blowing me kisses. Her car was full of passengers. I guessed she was responsible for sending him my way.

"Good game today. You lived up to your reputation," he said.

I tried to keep my eyes on the road and to focus on inhaling and exhaling, which were no longer automatic. "I appreciate your help … you know … at the end. Don't know what happened to me." Breathe in. Breathe out.

"You were still good today. Ashley is a good team. We would have lost without you."

Yes, his breathtaking eyes were looking at me. I felt at a loss for words. Why was it so hard to breathe? Why was he sitting so close to me? When I stole a side-glance at him, he looked relaxed. Maybe it was just me. Okay, think normal conversation.

"I'm going to be sore tomorrow."

"Your shoulder from pitching?" he guessed.

"No, it's from sliding into home plate during the fourth inning."

Michael laughed with me. "Yeah, Lewis can be a brutal manager. He wants it all." We were silent for a moment, and he shifted in his seat bringing his body closer to me. "Tammy showed me your book last night. She was very excited. It was nice of you to give her a copy."

Oh! I suddenly remembered page seventy-five in the book, one of the more colorful and sexually explicit parts. Was she mature enough to read that section? Would he be angry with me for giving her the book?

"I was glad to find a fan. Maybe she can help me out when I get stuck."

"I know she'd be thrilled," he replied.

We stopped at a light in town.

I took a deep breath and finally had to ask, "So, you go hunting?"

He looked over at me with a bewildered look on his face, his brow furrowing deeply. "Where did you get that idea?"

I pulled forward slowly when the stoplight turned green. "Tammy told me."

"She told you I went hunting?" His voice sounded incredulous.

I nodded. "She said you were out shooting animals."

He burst out laughing. "Oh, Elizabeth." He shook his head back and forth.

"What? You don't shoot animals? She distinctly asked me if I wanted to see pictures of the animals you shot," I said with conviction in my voice. If he was a hunter that was his own business, but I certainly didn't have to condone his hobby.

"No, I mean, yes, I'm a photographer, but I don't kill animals. They are usually alive when I take their picture and alive when I leave them. I'm a wildlife photographer." He continued to chuckle.

"Oh," I said simply. How did this misunderstanding happen? Great, now he probably thought I was crazy.

"I have to tell Tammy to be careful in the future when she's describing my profession."

"Don't you dare!" I looked at him with a spark in my eyes. "Not everyone needs to know how stupid I am. It's plenty with just you."

"Okay, I promise." He held up one hand laughing. "I won't tell anyone. It will be our secret." He grinned at me. "Better?"

I grinned too. "Well okay, I guess it was funny. I'm glad you don't hunt though, you don't do you?" Oh! Maybe he was a hunter too. Did I just insult him?

"No, I promise I don't hunt. I only take pictures." Michael held up both hands as if to surrender.

We pulled into the restaurant's parking lot.

"Then, I'd like to see your pictures sometime. I'll see you inside. I'm going to change clothes," I mentioned as we went inside, and I headed for the bathroom.

The bathroom was quiet, and it was a relief to be alone for a few minutes. Having Michael in my car made me feel electric. I don't know why. I hadn't been attracted to any men for so long that I was used to not feeling anything when I was around one.

I changed into my jeans and top. Looking at myself objectively in the mirror, I was not too bad for thirty-eight. Loosening my hair from the braid, I shook it out and the waves framed around my face. After pulling a brush through, I tucked my hair behind my ears and let it lay down my back. Wrinkling my nose at my reflection, I was all legs. Well, all legs and boobs.

I bent over to stuff my uniform into my bag, two women I didn't recognize walked into the restroom.

"I told you he would be at the game," the first woman said as she came through the door.

Her companion agreed, "Oh my god, he is so hot. He has a totally gorgeous butt in his uniform, like a blond Greek god!"

When they saw me, they stopped speaking immediately. There was no need for me to guess who the subject of their conversation was. I grinned and zipped up my bag. As I left the restroom, I could hear them continue their conversation in whispers. My neighbor was definitely the center of attention in our little town.

The restaurant was crowded. Debi waved me over to their section. I looked around for Michael and noticed him surrounded by women. He caught my eye, and I raised my eyebrows and smiled.

Lewis called to me from the Karaoke stand, "Hey Elizabeth, do you feel lucky?"

I laughed, and yelled back, "Yeah, that's a good one!"

Debi handed me a glass of sangria as I sat down. She whispered in my ear, "Looks like Michael already has a fan club."

I nodded and whispered back, "Two women were in the bathroom raving about his cute butt."

"You know what I say, if you've got it, bring it out!" She laughed throwing her head back.

"Why didn't you save him a seat?" I asked seeing our already full table.

"So now you're interested?" she said with a glint in her eye.

I looked back over my shoulder and noticed that he was still chatting up the women around him. He caught me looking, and I quickly averted my eyes.

"We got some things straightened out in the car on the ride over," I commented.

"Like how I maneuvered that one?" She leaned over to Don and whispered, "I think Michael needs to be rescued from that group of women."

Don looked over at him and laughed. "He doesn't look like he needs rescuing to me."

"I think you need to get him and have him join us." She pushed at him.

He peered at me. "Is this your idea?"

"Don't look at me." I spread my hands out in innocence. "I think I'm being called, my number is up."

Lewis stood up on the small stage. "She's back! Elizabeth feels lucky tonight, let's give her a big hand."

I made my way up to join him. "Okay, here's Mary-Chapin Carpenter's, "*I Feel Lucky,*" and I think we all feel lucky tonight after today's game!"

After hamming it up through the song, I made my way back to the group. Sure enough, Debi managed to get Michael to our table. He stood up and scooted his chair over to make room for me between them.

As I squeezed in next to him, she whispered, "You owe me." I shook my head in disbelief at Debi and her maneuvering.

The next karaoke singer started, and Michael whispered, "Is everything okay?"

I smiled at him and nodded my head. When I reached for my sangria my shoulder brushed against his chest. The close contact sent tingles through me.

"Great singing," he mouthed.

"Thanks," I mouthed back.

He laid his arm over the back of my chair. His body was close enough to me. I could smell his cologne. I took a big gulp of my wine. It wasn't often a man made me feel petite, and he made me feel that way. My shoulder and arm kept brushing him, and I could feel the warmth from his body. Was it the wine or our close proximity that made me feel so heady?

When the waitress passed by in between singers, we ordered tapas, salads, and paella. It had been quite a while since lunch. I needed to eat, or I would end up collapsing, and it would not be pretty. Our food arrived quickly, and we all dug into the appetizers. The couple who owned the restaurant made every effort to be as authentic as possible. The tapas were so flavorful. The cheeses, tortillas, olives, sausages, chicken, and bread were all delicious.

Michael matched our healthy appetites and complimented the food. He mentioned that he had lived in Spain for several months working at the Rock of Gibraltar's monkey sanctuary. Debi, Angel, and I shared our memories of our girl's trip to Madrid. Our vacation had been shortly before my marriage to Kevin eight years ago. Kevin had been furious that I had gone without him. Just thinking about it made me smile again.

After the karaoke, Mr. Sanchez, the owner of the restaurant, started playing flamenco guitar. The sangria, the music, the food, and the company were making an incredible evening for us. We sighed heavily when we realized it was late and needed to make our way home. None of us wanted the fun to end.

In the parking lot, I didn't wait for Michael to ask. Giggling and shaking the keys at him, I invited, "Can I give you a lift home?"

"Thanks, I appreciate it. I don't want the wrath of Tammy if I interrupt her date." He'd already picked up my bag in the restaurant and tossed it in the back seat. "Would you like me to drive?"

"Why?" I giggled again. "Do you think I've had too much Sangria?"

The moment I finished my sentence Don walked up behind me and kissed me on the cheek. "Yes, darling girl, the last thing we need is to have my dad pull you over, we'd never hear the end of it." He took my car keys out of my hand and tossed them to Michael. "Get her home safely for me."

Both Don and Michael chuckled together as they tucked me into the passenger seat. They offered to help me with my seat belt, but I slapped their hands away.

"Okay, I'm not that tipsy boys, I think I can buckle my own seat belt."

Don waved goodnight to us, and Angel and Debi were waving at me from their cars as Michael backed out of the parking space.

"That was a fun evening," I sighed and stretched on the seat.

Stealing a glance over at him through my eyelashes, I almost stopped breathing again. He was so big and masculine sitting in the driver's seat.

We took the road back through town and were both quiet as he drove. When the highway turned curvy, I held tightly to the car door handle.

"Could you slow down? I think I'm going to be sick," I whispered.

Dinner, drinks, everything was at the back of my throat ready to make an appearance. I rolled the window down to let the fresh air hit my face.

He looked over at me with concern. "Really?"

Immediately pulling over to the side of the road, he stopped the car.

"Now I know why I drive home, and I don't drink. Yuck," I said with my hand over my mouth.

I opened the door quickly and hurried away from the car. Michael was next to me instantly.

I put out my hand toward him to stop his approach. "I'm going to puke my guts up. I don't think you want to be around me."

He didn't answer. He reached down and held my hair back for me while I retched into the bushes. Afterward, he disappeared briefly, and when he returned, he gave me a bottle of water and a paper towel. I felt grateful to rinse my mouth. When I finished, he put his arm around me. He led me back to the car and helped me into the seat.

I leaned back. "I'm sorry. This is so embarrassing. You hardly know me."

He examined me closely. "Why are you embarrassed? You had a little too much fun tonight. Are you okay?"

"Yeah," I sighed weakly. "Drive slowly, okay?"

A few minutes later he pulled up behind his house and parked the car. "You are coming in, and I'm going to make you some tea. It will quiet your stomach."

There was no argument from me. He helped me ease out of the car, and we entered his house through the back porch. When I heard the piano playing, I guessed Katy was home. Michael showed me the guest bathroom and gave me a washcloth and towel. Impressive, most men I knew did not have two towels that matched. After splashing cold water on my face, I peered at myself in the mirror. My face was chalk white. Oh boy, what a beauty I was!

I wanted to go home and crawl into bed with my dogs. Michael was trying to be kind though, and I would tough it out. After about ten minutes, there was a soft knock on the door, and I heard Katy's anxious voice on the other side of the door.

"Do you need some help Elizabeth?"

I cracked the door open slowly. "No," I whispered. "I'm okay."

She took my hand and led me into the living room. Katy had turned off most of the lights, and just one small lamp glowed by the couch.

"Dad's making your tea." She patted a couch cushion. "Sit down and get comfy. He is good at making sour tummies feel better."

Smiling halfheartedly up at her, I sank into the massive black leather couch. Leaning my head back, the smell of leather enveloped me. I closed my eyes.

Katy spoke again with a soft voice, "I'm going to take the dogs upstairs and go to bed so they won't bother you. I hope you feel better."

I nodded and murmured a quiet, "Thanks."

A short time later, Michael padded into the room with silent footsteps. He had taken his shoes off and changed into jeans and a black t-shirt. As sick as I felt, watching him cross the room made me feel warm. He wore his jeans low on his hips, and the bottom of his t-shirt barely reached the top of his pants so that when he walked a hint of skin showed. Sitting down next to me, he handed me a steaming mug of tea. I breathed it in deeply. I could smell peppermint and another ingredient that I did not recognize. He lifted my legs up and put them on the couch. Any other time I would have protested, but I knew he was trying to help. He sat at the other end of the sofa and put his feet up on the coffee table. Looking at me with concern on his face, he didn't speak a word.

I took a small sip of the tea. "This is delicious. Thank you."

"Drink it slowly but as hot as you can," he instructed.

"Old family recipe?" I asked holding up the cup.

"Oh yeah," he said smiling, "Great-me-ma."

We both were quiet as I sipped the tea. I noticed the décor in the house was for him and not his daughters. Everything was masculine, the dark leather furniture, the gleaming hardwood floors, and the small black baby grand piano in the corner of the room. And the pictures, they were everywhere on the walls. All were photographs of animals, polar bears, brown bears, dolphins, sea turtles, whales, otters, and each picture carefully placed.

"Are they all yours?"

He grinned broadly. "Do you like them?"

"Oh yes, they are magnificent!"

He was obviously proud of his work. I set the mug of tea down on the coffee table and walked over to a floor lamp next to the piano. When I switched the lamp on it filled the room with warm light. Michael watched me from the couch. I looked at each picture, not speaking.

I leaned over one of the polar bear photos. "I thought so. Imagine that, I have this one as a framed poster in my bedroom. You'll have to sign it for me."

He stood up, carried my tea over to me, and handed it to me. "Drink," he ordered. "I'll get you a real print. Would you like a tour?"

I turned to him, and he was standing very close. I was glad my stomach was feeling better so I could concentrate on my breathing.

"Yes, I would. Lead the way," I answered.

He smiled. "You saw the guest bathroom." He led me into the kitchen and switched the light on. The kitchen had warm colors with cherry wood cabinets, and the brown Spanish tile floor was bright and cheery. There was a small cherry wood kitchen table with four matching chairs in the middle of the room. All of the major appliances matched the cabinets.

"Do you do a lot of cooking?" The number of appliances on the counters indicated there was a chef in the house.

"Out of self-preservation. My ex-wife was a terrible cook."

Oh! This was the first time Michael had mentioned his ex. How long had they been divorced?

He guided me into the dining area. Like my cabin, the dining room combined with the living room as a great room. The dining table was long, and it could comfortably seat ten people, it almost seemed excessive for a family of three.

He pointed to the staircase. "The girl's bedrooms are upstairs. Katy is leaving for New York next month to go back to school. It will be Tammy and me until January. She decided to go for a semester to the junior college and then transfer over to the university. Since we moved here, she has been working at the animal clinic in Mintock."

"It sounds like she's taking after you, and your love of animals," I commented.

It was apparent when he spoke about his daughters that they were a big part of his life. He just about screamed parental pride.

Michael had a wistful look on his face. "Yeah, I'm glad. The last room is my bedroom, do you want to see?"

"My stomach is feeling much better. I think I can take it." I let out a giggle.

His bedroom, like mine, faced the lake. Michael flipped the wall switch, and the lamp by the bedside lit up. I stopped at the doorway because the size of the room surprised me. It was at least as big as the living room. Two large windows and a sliding glass door led out to the front porch. Large scatter rugs done in gold and black covered the floors. His bed was huge, the covers matched the carpets.

"This is custom made, isn't it?" I pointed to the bed.

He nodded. "I got tired of my feet hanging over the edge."

Again, photos covered the walls. This time, however, the images were of his daughters, at all different ages. Not only were there color pictures, but black and white ones, and sepia tones too. He watched me intently as I walked around the room looking at all the photographs. A large black and white photo caught my eye. It was of the young girls on a school ground merry-go-round, hanging upside down, as kids will do.

"I like this one," I said as I pointed to the picture.

The next picture included Michael and the two girls. He wore his curly hair down below his shoulders.

"Oh my gosh," I exclaimed, "when was this taken?"

He shrugged his shoulders. "A couple of years ago. I alternate between short and long. Look closely I think I'm wearing my earring in that one."

I peered at the picture carefully and could make out a small diamond in his left ear. "Yep, it's there. Do you still wear it?"

"I usually have it on, but definitely not when I play baseball," he replied.

I moved down further, and there was one small photo of a woman holding an infant and a child leaning over peering at the baby. "Is this your wife?"

He pursed his lips together. "Ex-wife," he corrected.

Michael volunteered no additional information. I was not going to pry. Interesting. He had a picture of his ex-wife, on the wall ... in his bedroom. What should I make of that?

The tea in my mug was gone. It was time for me to go home. "I'm feeling much better, thank you for taking such good care of me. I think I better hit the road."

Accompanying me to my car, he handed the keys to me. He stood on his back porch until I waved at my back door and went inside my cabin.

I greeted my dogs, fed them a snack, and got ready for bed. The shower felt good. After examining my leg in the mirror, I noticed there would definitely be a bruise from the slide into home base. Lewis knew I hated sliding, but with him, you gave your all for the game.

After dressing for bed, I opened the blinds and the windows in my bedroom. There was a good view of Michael's house. I could see the light on in his bedroom. I shook my head and admonished myself. I was becoming a peeping Tom!

The tea had relaxed me and my stomach. I lay in bed thinking about the last few hours. The sick scene kept playing in my mind. I could not believe that I vomited in Michael's presence. The blush on my face probably glowed in the dark. Nevertheless, he was gallant about the whole episode. What could he do? Runaway? Drive away? I giggled at the thought. He was driving my car. Still, oh yuck!

I turned over and cuddled with the dogs, happy sleep finally won.

CHAPTER FOUR

Monday started my first full week home. Before breakfast, I took the dogs for a run down the lakeshore. It was shortly after dawn, and there would be no one out this early except a few people fishing. I put on my earbuds and selected Muse from the playlist. Dressed in a pair of old baggy sweats and my hair pulled up in a ponytail, I started out in a slow jog. As I passed Debi and Don's house, I could see someone running toward me. Yes, it was Michael. I could not believe it. No one ran this early … well … except me.

He slowed as he neared me. He looked me up and down with a big grin on his face. "Nice outfit," was his only comment. He waved as he passed me and continued with his jog.

His sweats looked older and baggier. "People in glass houses shouldn't throw stones," I retorted running past him.

I ran another mile and turned around to make it back to the cabin. The dogs and I could have gone farther, but my curiosity got the best of me. I would have expected more conversation from him. Admittedly, my performance on the way home last night certainly was not appealing. My cheeks colored red just thinking about the episode. He had seemed understanding. Perhaps now he had a chance to think twice about my poor manners. He had an effect on me, but I had just met him, how was it possible? I never drank after baseball and never lost my confidence during a game. What was it about him that rattled me so much?

As I approached my cabin, Michael was sitting on our common dock with his back toward the shore. His shoes and socks were off while he dangled his feet in the water. I could hear the click of the camera as he took pictures of the ducks near the dock.

The rich aroma of the brewed coffee hit me when I entered the cabin. I grabbed two mugs from the cupboard and poured coffee into both, then took a couple of pieces of bread from the refrigerator. "Mommy is going to be very bold," I said to the dogs.

I walked slowly down to the dock trying not to spill the coffee from the full mugs. The dock gently rocked when I stepped up, and Michael turned around.

I lifted up one of the coffee mugs in his direction. "Coffee?" He smiled and made a move to get up, I shushed him back down, handing him the cup. "Hope it's okay that it's black. I didn't know if you take cream and sugar."

"No, this is perfect. How did you know?"

"Well," I laughed, "you don't look like one of the health nuts who drink water after a run."

"Actually, I am one of those health nuts." He chuckled. "But I have to admit, coffee sounds good right now."

The ducks saw me and started swimming closer to the dock.

He looked surprised. "Now why are they coming closer?"

I sat down next to him and showed him the bread in my hand. "I'm usually a regular out here in the mornings. You had better pull your feet out of the water. The ducks will dive and nip your toes, especially if they know bread is coming."

As I made the comment, he pulled his feet out quickly. "Ow!" he exclaimed. "They really do!"

I handed him a piece of bread. "Here, you help. They'll remember you and then when you sit out here the ducks will pose for your pictures."

We were quiet for a few minutes while we fed the ducks. The sun was making a nice dawn and Michael started shooting pictures again.

I finally broke the silence. "I'm sorry for getting sick like that last night."

"Don't worry about it, it can happen." He turned toward me, focusing quickly, and snapped a picture.

"Oh! Don't take my picture! I look horrible!" I buried my face in my hands.

"Why is it women are so paranoid about having their picture taken?" He chuckled and leaned over to knock my shoulder with his.

He had changed the subject of my late-night illness. Either it disgusted him so much, or he was trying to spare my feelings. To stop torturing myself, I decide to go with the latter.

"So, how did you get into photography?" I asked.

"Do you really want to know or are you just being polite?" He turned to me sitting cross-legged.

"I would never ask unless I wanted to know, remember, I'm a writer. I have this ridiculously inquisitive mind."

Turning toward him, I mimicked his posture. We were sitting close. Our knees were not quite touching. I had a mad thought to launch myself into his lap but managed to control myself. Was it the rising sun making me hot, or him? I giggled to myself and was glad that he could not read my mind.

As he launched into his story, I pulled my sweatshirt off and tugged my tank underneath down. He paused and looked at me for a moment. I thought I saw him swallow hard, but if he did, he managed to recompose himself and continue his story.

Michael's love of photography happened early in his life. He joined a camera club during high school. His father had given him his first camera, an old used 35-millimeter Kodak, with an automatic light meter. It was not until he attended UC Santa Cruz that his talent truly developed though. His parents insisted he major in courses where he could find a real job that paid real money. Compromising, he majored in marine biology, but he also managed to squeeze in photography classes as well. As he finished college, a lucky break of an internship, and then a paying position at the newly built Monterey Bay Aquarium, presented itself.

At the aquarium, he became a fixture with his camera around his neck. Pictures of marine life started to adorn the office walls. The aquarium used his candid shots of the visitors interacting with the aquatic animals in their advertisements. Soon his photographs of the otters became the top seller in the gift shop. Slowly he became less of a marine biologist and took over the role of the official aquarium photographer.

He explained that his time at the aquarium had been fortunate. Not only was he paid, but he could develop his skills as a photographer in his chosen environment. It was not long before National Geographic, and other magazines focused on him and extended opportunities to him.

His sky-blue eyes sparkled, and they became animated as he spoke about his past. "I started traveling, spending more time away from the aquarium. They understood when I finally broke from them and I'm still invited to cover their important events."

"So, do you go back?" I asked.

Michael nodded. "If my schedule permits, I always try to be there."

"Are they still selling your otters?"

He grinned. "Yeah, those pictures are twenty-three years old and are still their best sellers, especially on the t-shirts and sweatshirts. He leaned back on his arms. "It's great because they make a lot of money from the merchandise they sell, and I'm glad I can support the aquarium in that way. I signed the photographs over to them very early on."

"The aquarium owns the photos?" I asked.

"Working there was a great experience for me. So, yeah, I'm happy that the aquarium received something in return. Now, how about you, did you always write?"

It was my turn to gasp, but I'm thankful I did it silently. Michael pulled his sweatshirt over his head. His broad chiseled chest had a smattering of curly blond hair. His tan was even, and it was evident that he often went without a shirt. The blush started creeping on my cheeks when he caught me gaping. I hated being so obvious. Leaning back again on his hands, his flat stomach and narrow waist showed to his advantage. I tried to look everywhere but at him. It was difficult. I took a deep breath and then blew it out slowly, hoping the color on my cheeks could be mistaken for the warm weather. Most likely not.

Launching into my story was easy. I started writing short stories in high school. Although I had taken journalism classes in both high school and college, I enjoyed the creative writing classes the most. My college magazine regularly published my short stories. After college, full of hope, I convinced myself that I was just one step away from the great American novel. Reality set in quickly. I found a job at a magazine in Los Angeles, not writing, but working in their production department. The job was not glamorous, but at least it paid my bills.

I continued to write even if it was only for friends and family. The editor at the magazine took me under her wing and started to read my narratives. She agreed I had no talent in journalism, but she recognized my flair in creating a story. She helped me with my composition and editing. She also invited me to her parties. These invitations allowed me to connect with other writers, agents, and publishers.

At one of the parties, I met Nancy who became my agent and subsequently a close friend. When we met, I had recently finished my first book and hesitantly showed it to her. She literally grabbed it out of my hands. Apparently, my talent lay in the fluffy prose of romance.

"The romance queen was born!" I concluded with a flourish.

Michael sat up and applauded. "Tammy certainly loves your work. She waits in anticipation for every book. Although with some of the book covers I wasn't sure if I should let her read them." He winked.

My face grew red again. "The books have adult material in them, though the early ones were harmless. The covers can be dramatic, but it's to draw in the reader, so they pull it from the shelf and buy the book." I laughed. "Most of my books talk big to build the anticipation, but it always ends, '*the next morning*.' And Tammy is just the kind of fan every writer wants, a reader who waits in the book store for the next release."

"So you're good at building the anticipation?" he asked, looking at me with a wide grin.

I rose to stand up. "I'm excellent at building the anticipation, but like I said it's always 'the next morning' in the end. Speaking of books, I better get to work." Bending over to pick up the coffee cups, he caught my hand as I straightened up.

"Elizabeth, will you have dinner with me Saturday night?"

I cocked my head at him unsure whether he was serious. "Ah…" I answered slowly, "Yes, okay."

"Good." Michael smiled. "Thanks for bringing the coffee." He squeezed my hand then let go. He stretched out his long legs on the dock.

"I'll see you then." I moved toward the dock steps.

"I'm looking forward to it." He smiled again.

Walking toward my cabin, I turned around to look at him, and sure enough, he was watching me walk away. My face reddened. I waved and continued to walk to my cabin furious with myself because I was blushing again.

I fed the dogs their breakfast and then jumped into the shower. The phone rang as I shut off the water. I heard Nancy's voice on the machine in the living room and ran into the bedroom to pick up the receiver before she finished her message.

"Hello!" I said breathlessly.

"Hi Elizabeth, I'm so glad you picked up. I sent you an email a few minutes ago. The book tour cities are changing. Berkside decided to start the tour in Miami. They want a beach-like opening to the tour since the book is about an underwater archeologist. I've sent the entire schedule to you. It's the same two weeks, but they've turned it all around."

I put the phone on speaker and started to dress. "I don't care, as long as it's no longer than two weeks."

"I know," she answered. "But they have us flying all over. Man, I'm feeling the jet lag already. So, now that you're up in the country how is everything going? How are you doing on the new book?"

Sitting on the bed, I put on my sandals after buttoning my jean shorts. "I'm stuck. I'm having real difficulties getting past the beginning. I still don't know what it's going to be about. Something will come, I know…but I have my own news."

"Do tell?" Nancy said.

I could almost hear her grinning over the phone.

"I have a date!" I pulled my pink tank on over my head.

"What? A date? When did that happen?" she asked with excitement in her voice.

"He's my next-door neighbor. I've known him for one day!"

"Well Elizabeth, I am impressed. You haven't had a date in... what has it been … two and a half years? You meet some guy, and after knowing him one day, you're going out with him already?" She laughed.

"I know, totally out of character for me. But, he's charming and yummy looking."

"Okay, give me some background. What does he do and how much baggage does he have?"

I briefly filled her in on what I knew of Michael's history. "His photography is amazing."

"What did you say his name was?" she asked.

"Michael Hoffman." I heard clicking noises as she quickly typed on her laptop.

"Whoa!" Nancy exclaimed. "Have you checked out his website?" I heard clicking noises again as she was typing again. "Wow! I would say you scored major girlfriend. Michael is famous in the world of wildlife photography. He has three…four, no five coffee table books. I wonder if he needs an agent?"

"Nancy!" I exclaimed. "It is just a date for dinner."

"And yes, he is definitely delectable looking. Look at that wonderful long hair!"

"His hair is short now." I heard more clicking noises.

"Yes, here's a picture with it short. Short…long, he is still cute. So when is the date?"

I started to braid my hair. "Next Saturday night."

"After you've worked on your book today, you definitely need to check out his web site. Very nice."

I laughed. I loved her enthusiasm. I loved her encouragement. "Okay, I will."

"I've got to get back to work, and so do you. Listen, I'm sorry Berkside had Kevin interview you. I told them under no circumstances was he to be the writer, but some stupid assistant screwed it up."

"Don't worry about it, everything was okay," I said, not wanting to drag Nancy into the ex-husband saga anymore. She had supported me through the entire episode with my divorce. I needed him out of my life and continuing to talk about the situation did not help.

"I want to hear all about the date on Sunday," she said with emphasis as she wrapped up our conversation.

After agreeing to call her, I sat at my desk like a good little writer. Unfortunately, my writer's block did not break. I surrendered and ended up watching a movie on the Lifetime channel during the afternoon.

It was a relief when Debi called to invite me over for dinner. I needed to fill her in on my time with Michael after we had left the restaurant and, of course, the date invitation.

The sun was beginning to set on a hot day as I started out for Debi's house. I met Katy and Tammy coming up from the dock.

"Hi girls, did you spend the afternoon out on the lake?"

They both nodded their windblown faces.

"There were a lot of people on the lake today," Katy said.

"Yeah, this is the height of tourist season. Sometimes I wonder where they all stay at night. I'm glad our cove is so quiet," I said.

"Dad said the campgrounds are full. There was trouble in town yesterday, and he's gone up to check on the eagles that are nesting on Mt. Mintock," Tammy added.

"Do you know what kind of trouble?" I asked. The occurrence of eagles on Mt. Mintock was a new one for us. They had arrived and began nesting at the beginning of the year.

"No, he didn't say. But, he's been going up the mountain to watch them all summer. They really are cool to see. You can see them flying over the lake all the time," said Tammy.

"I was thinking of taking my boat out tomorrow. Do either of you ski?"

Katy's face grew enthusiastic as well as her voice. "Do we? We love it!"

"Do you want to come with me?" I offered.

In unison, they said excitedly, "Yes!"

We agreed to meet in the afternoon. I continued on to Debi and Don's house. Don greeted me at their front door. He gave me a hug and let me into the house. "Debi's in the kitchen." As I passed by him, he whispered in a singsong voice, "Somebody's got a new boyfriend."

I tried to hold back a smile and put a grimace on my face. I shouted, "Debi! I'm going to kill you!"

Don laughed as Debi came out of the kitchen drying her hands on a towel.

"What did I do now?" She batted her lashes at me with innocent eyes. She saw my face. "Oh that. Don just has big ears." Debi swatted him with the dishtowel.

Don's father got up from his chair in front of the television and hugged me. "Mija, it's been such a long time! Did you just get back into town?"

I loved that Frank and his wife Annie called me the Spanish word for daughter.

"Hi Frank, I arrived on Friday night. I was surprised you weren't at the game yesterday?" I smiled.

"Oh, once in a while I have to pull weekend duty, just to remind them how valuable the chief is to the town." Frank sat back down and turned off the television. "There was some stuff going on with some of the tribal high school boys on the other end of the town. At first, we thought it was some tourists, but it is some of our kids getting out of control."

"Everything is okay now, although I don't feel good since they had guns," Debi commented.

"They had guns?" I asked with shock on my face.

"They said it was for target practice out on the range. We confiscated the guns anyway and had a severe talk with them and their parents. They probably won't be any more trouble, but we'll keep our eyes on them," Frank explained.

I just shook my head in response. Debi pulled me with her into the kitchen. She called out to the men, "Dinner will be ready in 10 minutes."

"What can I do to help?" I picked up some celery from the cutting board and started munching.

"Nothing, just sit and keep me company." She stirred the spaghetti sauce and popped the garlic bread into the oven. "You didn't really vomit last night, did you?"

"Oh god, you would have to remind me of that!"

"You were always the one with the sensitive stomach. Never got sick in Mexico, didn't matter what you ate there, but a little twisty road and too much sangria and you're tossing your cookies."

I laughed. "I'm not that bad. Michael was sweet last night. I was surprised when he asked me out. I hope he doesn't think because I went over to his house last night that I'm…" I trailed off looking for a word. "I mean I just met him."

Debi looked at me over her shoulder as she drained the pasta at the sink. "Elizabeth, it's a date. Don't let the romance writer in you get ahead of yourself. You're not going to sleep with him when you go out Friday night are you?"

"Debi!"

She snickered. "Okay, simply asking." She put the pasta into a bowl and carried it into the dining room. "Could you pull the garlic bread out of the oven?"

She was right, how many times in the past had I jumped ahead of myself? I didn't want to repeat the same mistakes again. My romance with Kevin had been quick, and I put so little thought into where we were heading. Before I knew it, we announced our engagement and I was walking down the aisle. Now, I wanted to be careful and not get ahead of myself. I wasn't sure if I wanted to be in a relationship with someone. It was time for me to face the facts. I did not have a good list of accomplishments when it came to relationships with men. Looking objectively at my marriage, our relationship was doomed from the beginning. We were total opposites. He was outgoing and gregarious, and I was introverted.

Being in the public eye was difficult for me, and I had to feel safe before I could come out of my shell. My first few book tours were miserable for me. I worked very hard to be extroverted in meeting my fans and doing interviews. People who did not know me were surprised to hear me sing karaoke. I could only guess when friends and family surrounded me, I felt secure.

CHAPTER FIVE

The next day, after my run, I settled down at my desk to work on my book. Frustration began to plague me after writing only a few pages, and there was no clear vision for the book. My writer's block had never been so bad. Usually leaping from the ending of one book smoothly into the next one was normal for me. Something was different this time around. Fighting the urge to visit the internet, I still had not looked at Michael's website. I found myself staring out the window for chunks of time, and even sitting outside did not help.

I was happy when the clock on my desk clicked to one thirty. I quickly switched off the computer and changed into my favorite swimsuit. The back of the black suit was open down to my bottom, and the French cut made my legs look even longer. The front covered in a see-through mesh material pretended to be modest but did not leave a lot to the imagination.

The girls knocked on the door as I finished pulling towels out of the linen closet. They followed me down to the dock, and we set off for the ski area of the lake. I had purchased the boat new when I decided to make the cabin my permanent residence. Since my family had always lived on the ocean, I grew up enjoying all water sports. It was not unusual for the family to spend the whole weekend boating or spending our time on Catalina Island. My sister and I learned early on how to water ski, and we were like fish in the water.

As the three of us made our way out to the central part of the lake, I acquainted the girls with all the safety features of the boat. It was a fast boat and handled well, but I would not ski until they felt comfortable driving her.

The late summer view of the lake butting up against the mountain was especially picturesque. The bottom half of Mount Mintock was filled with pine trees and California scrub brush turning dark and golden. By August, the colors were toasty brown. As I looked higher, large boulders replaced the scrub brush, and more pine trees were on the top of the mountain.

For a Tuesday, even with the tourists, the lake was not too crowded. After an hour of working hard at waterskiing and wakeboarding, we pulled into a small cove and quickly dug into the refreshments and drinks I brought along for us.

Munching on a handful of almonds I asked, "So Tammy, how long have you been dating Jason?"

She blushed and smiled. "A couple of months, since we moved here. I met him right away and things sort of clicked."

Katy rolled her eyes as she leaned over to grab another handful of almonds. "The two of them have been inseparable and insufferable since we moved here."

"It sounds serious," I said.

"Well," she hesitated, "Jason will be going to Stanford next month, and I'll be at UC Davis in January. We don't know what's going to happen. It's not practical for us to be serious." She looked down at her Coke can and took a sip.

"It sounds like your dad has been talking to you," I said.

"Yeah." She nodded slowly still staring down at her soda. "I mean, I understand what Dad is saying, but it's hard because we want to be together all the time."

"Well, my advice is to enjoy the summer!" I leaned over the edge of the boat and splashed both of them with water. We giggled together. "So, Katy, how about you, who'd you leave behind in New York?"

She giggled. "Too many boys! Although there is someone special, Dad isn't happy about it."

"Really?" I asked.

Tammy cut in, "Because he's much older!"

Katy frowned at her sister. "Paul is not that much older, he's thirty."

"Okay, I'm not going to touch this one!" I laughed. "I won't have your dad mad at me for giving you the wrong advice."

Katy laughed. "Coward."

"Yes, that's me," I said nodding.

"How about you? You're divorced, right?" Tammy asked.

I nodded. "About 3 years ago."

"What happened?" Tammy asked again.

"Let's just say in the real world sometimes happily ever after doesn't really exist. Now I'm changing the subject. Looks like we all have our problems and all I can say is we have a beautiful lake here, and the skiing is fantastic, so why should we be worried about men?"

Both girls nodded their heads in agreement. I started up the boat again, and we drove out to the main lake for more skiing. It was late afternoon and getting chilly by the time we motored back to the dock. Michael greeted us as we tied up the boat.

"Hold it right there!" He aimed his camera toward us and started clicking pictures. The girls began striking crazy poses, and I wanted to hide behind a towel. He called out to us laughing still taking photos, "Okay Vogue!"

The girls started to cling on me and force me into poses. We all ended up in a heap on the dock laughing hysterically.

"Oh, let me up," I said giggling. "Please!"

Tammy and Katy both started tickling me. I rolled over and started tickling them back. All three of us cried uncle at the same time.

Michael walked over and helped the three of us to our feet. His silent appraisal of my bathing suit did not make me feel uncomfortable, but I did wrap a towel around my waist. He winked at me without either girl noticing. I glanced away not commenting.

"I think I got some great shots of you waterskiing. I saw you on the lake while I drove through town. Quite the three beauties!" he quipped.

"The next time you'll have to go with us," I invited.

"Oh Dad, Elizabeth's boat is so fast. You would love it!" Tammy exclaimed.

He smiled. "I'll just have to do that, the three beauties and the beast. What is the top speed on her?"

"I've pushed it to fifty-five, but then the marine patrol comes after me. You know, the sirens are embarrassing," I joked.

He looked around the boat. "She's twenty-two feet, isn't she? Nice wakeboard tower too. It's a sweet boat Elizabeth."

"Thank you. Like I said, you'll have to come with us next time."

Tammy and Katy started gathering their stuff. I picked up the picnic basket from the boat and Michael said, "Here, give that to me."

I handed the basket to him. "How are the eagles?"

He took the skis from me. "They're good."

"Good. Leave the skis on the porch, and I'll put them away later."

"I'll put them away, where do you keep them?" he asked.

"Back in the garage, let me open the garage door."

The dogs trailed after me. He knelt and petted both dogs.

"Nice neat garage. I like it," he commented.

"Thanks. My dad always pressed me on the importance of the garage."

The garage was large enough to fit my Range Rover. After I inherited the cabin from Aunt Ruth, I made a few changes to the interior of the cabin. I upgraded the kitchen with modern appliances. The new air conditioner and the heating system brought needed relief, and I redid the garage. Adding the drywall, cabinets, and new flooring, made Don faint with envy every time he visited.

The girls joined us.

They both thanked me, and I suggested we go again next week, with their dad invited. Everyone nodded in agreement, and they set off toward their house.

I went back inside my cabin and fed the dogs their dinner. After a quick shower, I sat down at my desk in front of the computer with a cup of tea. I was ready to write. For some reason, maybe spending the day with the girls had started my creative juices flowing again. The day had turned out fun, and I was happy to have found two new friends.

I wrote into the night, only rising from the chair to stretch. By midnight, I had written several chapters. The writing flowed smooth and easy, and it surprised me. The dogs were sleeping by my feet. I finally shut down the computer and padded into my bedroom. Topper and Samantha sleepily followed me and jumped on the bed. They lay down in their places. Slipping the nightgown over my head, I peeked out the curtain. Michael's bedroom light was still on. I wondered what he was doing up so late at night. Shaking my head in disbelief, I felt silly.

"Oh Elizabeth, you're in trouble," I said to myself.

Samantha looked up at me and then lay her head back down. She was used to her silly mommy.

CHAPTER SIX

The book took my time and attention for the rest of the week. I ran with the dogs early in the morning and was usually at my desk by seven. Nancy called me daily to check on my progress and was happy to hear that the writer's block was behind me. Each day she asked me if I had checked Michael's website. I had not because I did not want anything to jinx my writing and distract me. She agreed, but still thought I was nuts.

Debi knew to stay away too. She was aware that I was deep within my writing, so she left me alone. Instead, she sent Betsy each afternoon with a care package containing dinner and snacks. Food was the last thing on my mind when I wrote. I usually would keep nuts and water on my desk just to keep my energy level up, but cooking was never on the agenda.

By Saturday morning, I was happy with the progress I had made on the book. Deciding to take the day off from writing, I planned to spend the morning on the lake. Burying myself so deeply during the week, I had not seen any of the Hoffman's.

After putting on my black bikini, I pulled a couple of towels out of the linen closet. The weather was typically hot for August, and the lake would be welcome. I could pull into a shady cove and read someone else's book for a change. Drinks and ice filled a small cooler. As soon as I pulled the doggy life vests out of the closet, Samantha and Topper's little tails started wagging furiously. They knew it meant they were coming along. I packed a bottle of water and a bowl for the dogs.

As the dogs and I walked down to the boat, we met Michael finishing his jog. He waved and ran up to me. Not even a bit out of breath, he said, "I hope we're still on for tonight? I thought I'd pick you up at seven?"

He looked delicious even as the perspiration ran down his chin and dripped onto his chest. This morning he was only in sweat pants, and his chest and shoulders were shiny with his exertion. His sweats rode low on his hips. There was a small trail of blond hair that led from the middle of his chest to his belly button and then disappeared into the waistband of his pants. I had a maddening thought wondering if his hair was blond all over and just the thought alone made me blush and almost topple over.

His eyes failed to notice my blush and perusal of his body since he was eyeing my bikini as he roamed from my face down to my feet stopping in between at my chest, waist, hips, thighs, and legs. Michael gave me a great big grin when he saw that I noticed him giving me the elevator look. His smile was not the least bit apologetic either and reminded me of the dogs when I caught them staring at their cookie jar. Yes, I confirmed to myself, there was some mutual drooling going on.

"Yeah, that sounds good. Where are we going?"

"Do you know Mama Rosa's in Ashley?" he asked.

"They have great Italian food. That would be terrific."

"Good, see you then." Michael smiled and turned to go back to his house. He turned around again and called out, "Very nice bathing suit!" He winked at me.

I just laughed. "Thanks." Of course, the blush again started creeping up my cheeks. I shook my head in disbelief. "Knock it off okay?" I called out to him.

Michael laughed and waved. He turned back toward his house while I finished loading up the boat.

The day out on the lake proved to be relaxing. I enjoyed listening to the breezes blowing through the trees in my favorite cove. Even though I tried not to think about Michael, he was foremost on my mind. My thoughts kept drifting to him and our date. Would he try to kiss me at the end or would it be a staid handshake? Would we have wine, or would he shy away from alcohol because of my past wretched performance? Memories of being sick on the side of the road made me feel embarrassed all over again.

I wondered if he would try to hold my hand? I loved the look of his hands, and still remembered the enveloping feel of them when Debi first introduced us. Would we dance? Mama Rosa's had a live band on Saturday nights. I wasn't a great dancer, and as it was I was certainly out of practice, but the idea of Michael having his arms around me was definitely appealing. As I lay in the boat thinking of him, my stomach began to feel nervous and started to do flip-flops.

I concluded that it must be hunger. The fresh air made me hungry. I maneuvered the boat quickly back to the cabin. After lunch, I lay down to take a nap, and the dogs cuddled up with me. This was one of my favorite Saturday afternoon activities, especially if I had plans for the evening. Since I usually woke early in the morning, because I could not stay up past ten. As far as I was concerned naps were good, and if I was asleep, I could not worry about the date. Nevertheless, lunch and the snooze had not cured the nervousness in my stomach either.

After showering and blow-drying my hair, I faced the big decision of what to wear. It had been a warm day, and would probably be a warm evening, so I decided on one of my favorites, a dark blue spaghetti strap dress. The bodice was tightly fitted with boning, no bra was necessary. The ballet-length skirt was full and flowing, and it was perfect when I slipped on a pair of dyed to match sandals with three-inch heels. My hair fell down my back, and my curls were soft and relaxed. My appearance in the full-length mirror made me smile. There was a very feminine woman looking back at me. The knock on the back door just as I was slipping small gold hoops into my ear lobes brought me quickly into the present.

As I opened the door, Michael stood in the doorway. My heart skipped a beat, my knees felt weak, and my stomach started the flip-flops. My mother often told me about the same reaction on her first date with my Dad, and I always thought she was exaggerating.

He looked more than yummy. Dressed in a black shirt open at the neck, he had rolled the cuffs of both sleeves up showing off his muscular forearms. The black dress pants that fit him well all the way down to his black loafers. In his left earlobe, he wore a small diamond stud. I suppressed the urge to reach out and touch the earring. He was one incredible looking man. With my three-inch heels, I could finally look him directly in the eyes.

Michael's eyes showed an equally appreciative expression. He did not have to say wow because I could read it in his face.

"I see that you are ready." He smiled with his deep dimples showing.

When he took my hand in his, my heart was singing its own song of happiness since one of my fantasies for the evening was happening at that moment. My hand was in his. His hand was big, his fingers were long, and he held mine firmly. My heart was not only singing but doing a dance too.

"You might want to check out what we're going to drive in."

He led me to the back porch. Parked there was a fully restored classic dark blue Mustang convertible.

"Oh, wow!" I said as I turned my attention away from his hand to look at the car. The white top was down and showed the blue and white leather interior. "This is beautiful. It's a '66, isn't it?" I walked slowly around the car admiring each feature.

Michael smiled. "You know Mustangs."

"One of my book characters had a '65 Mustang. I always do a lot of research. Wow, wow, wow. Did you restore it yourself?" I asked.

He looked proud. "It took me ten years, and it was a labor of love."

"Let me go get a scarf and sweater."

"I can put the top up if you prefer," he suggested.

"Are you kidding? And miss the thrill of riding in a convertible, I don't think so."

I went into the house to find a long white scarf and the little white cotton sweater covered in sequins that I didn't have much occasion to use. I quickly joined him back outside.

He opened the car door for me. I felt his hand on the small of my back as he guided me into the seat. His touch sent electrical charges through my body. I wrapped the scarf around my head and let out a deep breath realizing that I needed to get myself under control or I would end up whirling into outer space.

He slid into the driver's seat next to me. The seatbelt was only a lap belt.

"This is definitely pony," I commented.

Michael chuckled shaking his head. "You know all the jargon too!"

"Like I said, I'm thorough with my research. I love this car." I ran my hand over the dashboard.

"I'm glad you like it." He was obviously thrilled with my reaction. He started the engine, and it roared to life. "Ready?"

"Let's do it!"

The ride was exhilarating. He accelerated as we approached the highway, which connected Mintock and Ashley. It felt like we were flying. The people in the cars we passed were checking out the Mustang, and we received thumbs-up signs from them. Michael was in his element as we waved to the passing cars.

We arrived at the restaurant quickly. I wanted the ride to go on longer, and I think he did too. He parked the car near the front entrance, and I sat still allowing him to open my car door.

I took off the scarf while I waited. As I stepped out of the car, I asked, "How is my hair?"

He grinned and pushed it back off my shoulders onto my back. "Perfect. You are beautiful."

I concentrated on not blushing, and this time I was able to keep the redness down. "Thank you for the great ride. I loved it."

"You're welcome. It was one of the three things I fought for during my divorce." As he looked down, a shadow crossed over his face.

"And the other two were your girls?" I asked quietly.

He answered just as quietly, "And I would have given up the Mustang."

He took my elbow and led me to the entrance of the restaurant. Since it was Saturday night, the restaurant was busy.

The owner greeted us, "Miss Elizabeth? Mr. Michael? You are together?" He spoke in a wonderfully accented Italian voice.

I gave Michael a surprised look. "How often have you been here, you've only lived in Mintock for two months?" Mama Rosa's was one of my favorite restaurants, and I had known Caesar for years.

He shrugged, and Caesar saved him. "Oh, Mr. Michael comes in many times with his lovely daughters. I have a perfect table for you, but it is not ready yet. A few minutes more. Please go into the bar. We have a new band, and they are good. Dance. I will come and get you."

Michael found an empty table for us in the bar. The cocktail waitress came over quickly and took our drink order.

"Sorry I was a little melodramatic in the parking lot." He smiled softly.

"Don't worry about that," I said. "I understand completely. I've been through it too."

"I forgot, Tammy told me you're divorced."

"Almost three years. I'm still paying him alimony."

"Really?" he asked. "How long were you married?"

I sighed. "Five very long years. I wrote my first three books while I was married to Kevin."

"I take it you are a bit more successful than your ex-husband."

"You can say that." I rolled my eyes.

After the waitress set our drinks on the table, I took a small sip of the white wine. My nerves were jittery. The band was playing.

"Would you like to dance?" he asked.

"Sure." I smiled in anticipation.

We joined a few other couples on the dance floor. The band moved into a ballad. He smiled his quirky smile bringing out his dimples. He pulled me close, and we started dancing to the music. Michael holding me provided an overwhelming experience. I felt my insides melting and hoped I would not pass out. I recognized his cologne. It was one of my favorites by Chanel. I breathed in and quietly sighed. His mouth was next to my ear, and I could feel his warm breath.

It sent tingles down my spine when he whispered, "I'm glad you wore such high heels. It's nice not to have to bend over."

I leaned back to look at him and laughed. His left arm wrapped around my waist and he pulled me close again. The song was over too quickly, and when we made our way back to our table, Caesar was waiting. He led us to a table in a secluded spot. The lighting was subdued as most of the restaurant had only candlelight, which reflected off the white tablecloths. A very romantic first date Michael had selected.

After telling us about the evening's specials, Caesar left us with the menus. I breathed in the aroma surrounding me and could feel my hunger rapidly rising. I ordered the smoked chicken ravioli, and he chose the gnocchi. Both of us selected the garden salad. He ordered a delicious dry Riesling, which would go well with our white cream sauces.

"Well I'm impressed," he commented in disbelief.

"About what?" I looked at him over the flicker of the candles, and his blue eyes were sparkling with the reflection.

"Most women would never order a cream sauce on a first date. I expected you to pick at a salad." His eyes continued to sparkle, and I noticed it was not only the glow of the light. There was mischief in his eyes.

"I like food, but I don't eat a lot while I'm working. I think you're going to notice that I'm not like most women."

"Oh, believe me, I've already discovered that. I haven't figured you out yet, but Elizabeth you are unique."

I gave him a little smile. "And are you planning on trying to figure me out?"

He laughed and leaned across the table. "Are you willing to let me?"

"That's where the anticipation comes in." I winked.

He reached for a breadstick and took a bite. "You are wicked. I think you enjoy teasing me."

The waiter arrived with our salads, and we dug in. I encouraged Michael to tell me more about his daughters, and his face lit up when asked. His pride in both girls was evident. The girls' personalities were like day and night. Tammy was his tomboy. She liked to roughhouse and would chase the dogs around the yard for hours. She always had animals, and the larger she got, the larger the animals. He was surprised they did not have a horse already, although she had hinted at it several times. Tammy loved to go hiking and camping with him, but the photography part didn't interest her.

Katy, the more sophisticated of the two, was perfectly happy living in New York. She enjoyed city life and everything it offered. Katy took to music very early on in her life and unbelievably her piano lessons were never forced. She was the one always wearing the dresses and enjoying her dolls. Exceedingly patient, she would look at her dad's photographs offering praise and criticism.

"I can't believe that you let Katy move to New York all by herself," I said as the waiter was placing our dishes in front of us.

"No way in hell would I have let her go there alone," Michael said emphatically and then added, "My sister Christina, who we lived with for several years after my divorce, moved to New York two years ago. When Julliard accepted Katy, it was a natural decision. She lives with Christina in Manhattan, although she doesn't advertise that she lives with her aunt often."

I smiled. "What about tall, handsome, and thirty?"

Michael pressed his lips together. "Oh, him. Christina promised she would keep an eye on the situation, but then I don't totally trust my sister either."

"Why don't you trust her?" I took a bite of my chicken ravioli. "Mmm …this is yummy."

"Christina is somewhat of the loose cannon when it comes to dating."

I raised my eyebrows in response. "Sometimes love takes all forms."

"Not with my daughters," Michael said as he took a forkful of gnocchi.

I laughed, taking a sip of wine. "You sound just like a dad! Wait until you meet my dad, you will have met your match."

He laughed with me. "Is he tougher than me?"

"Oh yes, and then some. He's a retired L.A. police detective. He would greet my dates at the door holding a gun and then interrogate them in our living room. I'm surprised that some of the guys even bothered to call me for a second date."

He raised his eyebrows. "I'm not that bad."

I giggled. "You say so now, but wait, one of these days you're going to meet Mr. Thirty."

Caesar came by our table to check on us. He beamed. "Ah, Mr. Michael, you now have three of the loveliest ladies in the area. You must not take them all. I have not seen Miss Elizabeth look so happy in a very long time."

At that moment, it would have been acceptable if the earth cracked open and swallowed me whole. I did not even try to stop the blushing. I looked anywhere but at Michael. Caesar gave me a wide smile.

Michael laughed and answered with his own compliment, "It was easy to lure them here with your delicious food and wonderful ambiance."

"Mr. Michael, you know you are most welcome here!" Caesar took my hand and pressed a quick kiss on the back. "And my beautiful Miss Elizabeth, you had my heart from the beginning."

I giggled. "Don't you let Rosa hear you say that, or she will be after the both of us!"

He suppressed a laugh. "I am fortunate because my Rosa is always after me! Enjoy, my friends. It is good to have you here."

As he left us, I commented, "He's such a cutie."

Michael looked at me, and his eyes were sparkling again. "You like that romantic old-world charm."

"Remember, I am a romance writer."

"That I have not forgotten," he answered, with a raised eyebrow.

We lingered over the rest of the meal and wine. Caesar tried to sway me with his tiramisu dessert, but I was too full. He even had to pack half my dinner to go.

Leaving the restaurant, Michael took my hand and said, "I'll be glad to put the top up."

"No, I'll be okay."

Helping me with my sweater, his hands lingered on my shoulders, and the heat of his fingers warmed me through. It seemed as if he was going to lean down and kiss me, but the moment passed, and he opened the car door. I slid in and put the scarf over my head. The air was warm, it was a perfect summer evening, and I was out with the most delightful man. I sighed aloud.

He sat next to me. "What?"

I looked at him and smiled. "Nothing."

I leaned back in the seat and closed my eyes. The engine roared on again and off we went.

We did not drive home as quickly. There was no traffic, but it felt like he was taking his time. I relaxed in the seat, reveling in the sky. The stars were out, and it looked like a full moon tonight. Caesar had been correct, I had not been happy like this in a long time. Michael was smiling too. I was curious about his thoughts, but this time, I would let it go.

We pulled up in front of my house, and he shut off the engine. He quickly jumped out to open my door.

"It isn't too late to come in for coffee," I invited softly, hoping for a yes because I didn't want the evening to end.

He took my hand and helped me out of the car. "I'd like that."

My heart leaped up, and I wanted to do a high five!

We walked together up to the door. I slipped the key into the lock.

"Why are all your lights on?" he asked.

"I don't like coming home to a dark house," I answered simply. I did not want to explain to him about my ex-husband, not tonight. "Would you like a tour? It's not as grand as yours, but I like it."

Michael smiled. "I like what I see." He stood very close to me with his hand at the small of my back. That little touch made my stomach start the flip-flops again.

I pointed out the kitchen, the guest room, and great room. "And what's in there? Is that your bedroom?" he asked, his hand almost guiding me in that direction.

I nodded. "Yep."

"Can I see? I showed you mine."

"It's not like yours. It's just a regular bedroom." I was relieved I had made the bed and tidied up after dressing this afternoon. "Okay." I led him into the bedroom.

"I wouldn't have taken you for a sled bed person."

He pointed to my bed with the enormous dark cherry wood head and footboards. The walls and floors in the bedroom matched the rest of the house. The bed looked fluffy, covered with a large feather comforter and six big pillows. Higher off the ground, a normal height person would have had to take a running leap into the bed. For me, it was a small hop. Being tall had its benefits.

"Remember, romance writer," I answered.

"And the steps?" He indicated to the steps next to the bed. They matched the dark cherry wood on the head and footboards.

"For the dogs. The bed is a little high for them to jump."

He sat on the bed. He did not have to hop. "See it's not too high for me."

As if by cue, both dogs jumped on the bed and rubbed up next to him for petting, which he obliged. I almost expected Michael to pat the spot next to him for me. I was not going to take the bait even though I wanted to. He sat on my cream-colored feather comforter grinning at me. The vision burned into my memory. I shook my head and slipped out of my shoes.

As Michael looked around, he zeroed in on the framed polar bear poster on the wall next to the bathroom door and walked over.

"I need to get that print for you," he said tapping the glass in the frame.

We both looked at ourselves in the full-length mirror which stood along the wall next to the polar bear poster. Putting his arms around me from behind, he rested his chin on the top of my head.

"I don't mind you being shorter too." Gently pulling my hair off my shoulders and letting it fall down my back, he murmured, "Your hair is beautiful. It's very sexy when you wear it loose."

His lips were close to my shoulder, and his warm breath on my neck sent shivers down my spine as it had while we were dancing. Our eyes met and held in the reflection of the mirror.

I stopped breathing. What was he expecting? What was he thinking? I was inclined to push him over to the bed where we both could just let ourselves go. Our mutual attraction was obvious to us… well, to everyone. The little internal voice I always tried to ignore began shouting again, *"No!"* This was not like me. Why was he having this effect on me? Normally I could hold onto my dignity when encountering a good-looking man.

He whispered again, "Breathe Elizabeth."

I caught my breath, and my rational thinking returned. "Coffee."

Michael pressed his lips together and nodded in agreement. Clearing his throat and letting go of me, he replied, "Yes, coffee. Decaf?"

When we were back in the kitchen, I pulled the decaffeinated beans out of the freezer and started grinding the coffee.

"I see you're a purist."

I grinned. "Coffee is like my baseball, serious business."

He chuckled. "I like that about you. You put everything you have in the things you do."

"I think that's where you and I are a lot alike."

He strolled over to the entertainment center on the wall opposite the kitchen. He scrolled through the playlist, and Frank Sinatra started singing.

"I would never have taken you for a Sinatra fan," I called from the kitchen.

Michael laughed. "Back at you." He moved around the room turning off all the lights and left the two lamps on by the couch.

"I grew up with music playing in the house all the time. My mother majored in musical history in college. She was definitely of the hippy generation. I'll never know how my parents ended up together. When I was young, Dad was ultra-conservative. I'm surprised how far to the left he has moved."

"Do your parents live up here?" he asked.

"No," I said as I brought the coffee tray in and set it on the couch table. "Dad lives down in Torrance where I grew up, and we lost my mom a few years ago to cancer. There's a picture of my parents by the television."

He picked up the photo. "They were a handsome couple. Your mom was beautiful. You two look a lot alike. I'm sorry to hear you lost her." He picked up the picture sitting next to my parents. "Who's in the other picture with you?" he asked as he sat in the middle of the couch.

"That's my perfect sister Lisa. You know… gorgeous husband, two-and-a-half children, and a house with the picket fence."

He laughed. "Two-and-a-half children? How did that happen?"

"Oh, you know, if she could figure out a way, it would happen."

We sat together and listened to Frank Sinatra. The evening wound down slowly, and after finishing the coffee, he stretched.

"I should let you go to bed. We have baseball tomorrow afternoon, and I still need to edit some pictures for my Monday deadline."

He turned to me before leaving and said, "I had a great time tonight Elizabeth."

"I did too. Thank you. And I loved the car."

Michael put one arm around my waist and pulled me into him. He looked down into my eyes. "May I?"

Smiling, I nodded. "Thanks for asking."

He leaned down and gave me the softest kiss on my lips. It was almost as if a feather had touched them. I felt myself melting against him. His strong arms wrapped around me and it was good he held me. Otherwise, I would have collapsed onto the floor. There was no hesitation on his part, only an inviting touch and his body pressed against me. The heat building between the two of us was evident as he pulled me into a tighter embrace and I wrapped my arms around his shoulders. Tucking his hand under my chin, he pulled my face up to his. Our second kiss had more substance, yet it was still a soft warm kiss, which was not too intrusive but left me the feeling of bigger things to come.

I could not resist this time and pulled his ear lobe with the earring. "I like your diamond," I whispered.

He chuckled, hugged me one last time, and we broke apart. "Well, there's baseball tomorrow," he said with a low note to his voice. "Can I give you a lift to the field?"

I leaned against the doorframe not trusting my voice and nodded.

"I'll see you tomorrow."

I nodded again.

"Elizabeth," he laughed softly. "It's okay to breathe."

CHAPTER SEVEN

The next morning, I made a batch of box brownies for the baseball game. This was the only baking I ever attempted. I carried the extras over to Michael's house thinking they would enjoy them.

Katy greeted me at the door and invited me inside. "Dad and Tammy are out. They'll be sorry they missed you, especially since there won't be any more brownies left!" She laughed wickedly. "They went up to check on the eagles. There was a report of trouble up near the nest again. They'll be back before baseball this afternoon."

"I'm sorry I interrupted you, it looks like you were practicing," I said noticing the piano covered with sheet music.

"There's always time to take a break." Katy took a bite of the brownie. "Oh yum! This is delicious. Thank you so much. I love the powdered sugar on top too. Where are my manners? Would you like some coffee?"

"That would be nice."

I walked around the room admiring Michael's pictures once again. In the daylight, and without him peering at me, I could see far more of the detail. He had been able to capture the essence of each animal. It was remarkable, the photos were so lifelike. The antics of the polar bear cubs climbing out of their winter den were in complete opposition to the mother bear ever alert for predators, staring directly into the camera. The otters sleeping, eating, or grooming themselves went about their business, ignoring the disruption of the camera. Each photograph showed the care and respect he felt for these animals. In all of the pictures, Michael had been able to convey a depth of emotion to the viewer. It was evident why he was such a successful photographer.

She carried out mugs of coffee and sat next to me on the couch. "So, how was the date with Dad?"

Of course, I started blushing. "I had a nice time."

Katy laughed. "Elizabeth, you are cute when you blush. I can imagine Dad loves it. He always loves to get a rise out of Tammy and me, and that probably goes for you too."

"Yeah, I have the impression your dad is a tease."

"He is a tease, it drives us nuts. He lets you back yourself into a corner." She leaned forward almost conspiratorially. "We were surprised he took out the Mustang. He was definitely trying to impress you. Dad certainly doesn't take it out for us."

"I have to admit it was thrilling. So, when are you going back to school?" I said, changing the subject.

"Next month." She stretched, and one of their dogs climbed into her lap. As she petted her, she continued, "It was a nice break, and I liked being with Dad and Tammy, but I'm lonely for Paul. And I miss school too."

"Paul is your boyfriend?"

"Yes," she said rolling her eyes. "He's the thirty-year-old monster. I don't know why Dad is so upset. How many years are between you and Dad?"

"I don't know how old your dad is, but it's not the same thing. First, he is not my boyfriend. You have a nine-year difference. It may not be a lot between thirty and forty, but between twenty and thirty, there is a lot of living to do. Has your dad ever met Paul? If he hasn't, maybe he would change his opinion of him if he did," I offered.

"I didn't think you were forty!" she said it as if forty were ancient.

I couldn't believe how she kept turning the subject around to me. Katy definitely was clever. "I'm not forty. I'm thirty-eight."

"Well, then Dad is forty-five. So, you and he are seven years apart."

"But he's not my boyfriend," I countered.

She laughed, and it reminded me of Michael. "Okay, I can see the acorn doesn't fall from the tree. You're a terrible tease too!" I said.

"I'm sorry." She laughed again but looked contrite enough. "I've been trying to get Paul to come out for a small vacation, but he's been swamped at the office. Besides, with the type of reception he might get, I can't blame him for not being too enthusiastic. My aunt really likes him too. I know Dad would like him if he would just give him a chance."

"Just keep working on Paul. I'm sure you can convince him to come out for a visit."

"Maybe you could talk to Dad for me?"

"If the moment presents itself. I'm not going to make any promises. But nothing will work if Paul doesn't come for a visit. Besides I'd like to meet this guy too."

She grinned. "It's a deal!"

I left to prepare for the baseball game. Michael knocked on my back door promptly at one-thirty. He stood in his baseball uniform and grinned when I answered.

"All ready to go?" he asked as he picked up my bag, which sat by the door.

I nodded and followed him out. He opened the door to the jeep, and I hopped in.

"What's in the box?" He pointed to the box on my lap.

"More brownies," I said. "How are the eagles? I was surprised to hear Tammy went with you."

"She likes to go. She enjoys hiking and being outdoors. I think that she wanted some TLC from me. Katy is the one who doesn't really care for the outdoor life. We found some shotgun casings near my tree stand, so I called in the park rangers. They'll investigate." He pulled the jeep out onto the main road behind our houses.

"The girls aren't coming with us?" I asked.

"No, Katy is working on her music. And, Tammy went with Jason."

I glanced over at him trying not to be noticeable. It looked like he had gotten sun today because his cheeks were a little pink. I almost sighed aloud thinking that he certainly filled out his uniform nicely. Michael had strong muscular thighs, and a blush started when I remembered the vision of his rear end from last week.

He gave me a quick look, and I was sure he could see the blush. "Penny for your thoughts?"

I shook my head. "No, nothing, just enjoying the drive." I looked straight ahead trying to get the thoughts of his butt out of my mind. It wasn't easy.

I shifted my body so that I could look at him. He was smiling, and the partially opened window was blowing in his hair. He looked so darned cute.

As we stopped at the light, our eyes caught, and the flash in his told me he may have been thinking along the same lines as me. I didn't know what to do with him. Certainly, I had men interested in dating me, but I always made it difficult for them to crack my surface. I did not date much before Kevin, and my marriage with him had soured me on any new relationships. Michael definitely intrigued me. Was it his openness? He was different from my ex-husband who had a hidden agenda for everything he did. Kevin always had to win to feel superior. At first, it was a challenge for me, but then the games tired me. He was all about the angle, so the motivation of Michael's interest stumped me.

Plenty of women in the town were aware of our new resident. We pulled into the parking lot and made our way over to the dugout, it was apparent there were more women in the bleachers than usual.

"You seem to be collecting quite the fan club." I pointed to a group of women sitting up in the bleachers.

He leaned over and whispered, "What makes you think they're here for me?"

I pulled my glove out of my bag. "Because we've never had so many women at a baseball game! Besides, I heard them twitter when you walked by. You know it's the sound that a group of excited women make when a handsome man walks by," I teased.

He leaned over and whispered again, "I thought that sound was called panting. Did you just call me handsome?"

Debi walked up behind him and put her arms around his waist. "Michael, did you get a look at your fan club."

He slipped his arm around her shoulders and gave her a squeeze. "You too? Those women are not here for me."

Don walked up laughing. "Hey, making more moves on my women? Wasn't stealing Elizabeth enough?"

Michael winked at me. "I don't think Elizabeth has been captured yet."

Debi caught the look in my eyes. "Oh! Look Elizabeth brought brownies."

Our team did well, and I managed to keep it together. The small group of women yelled every time Michael came up to bat and with every out at first base. It was clear they were throwing his timing off, and he looked embarrassed with each scream. Our team did not make it any easier as we all ragged on him in the dugout when we were up at bat.

After the game, a few of the bolder women came down to speak with him. I recognized two of them from the restaurant last Sunday. News traveled fast in a small town. Even though Michael did not consider himself a celebrity, he was still a well-known photographer, and he was cute. He shot me a look that pleaded.

I watched the women with Debi. "So, should I go over and save him?"

"Is he a good boy?" She laughed.

"Yeah, pretty good."

"Well, then you better hurry before he goes with them." She laughed again.

When I walked over to the group, the women barely moved for me. I had to push my way through to Michael. "Okay ladies, sorry, this one's mine. You need to give him back to the team now."

He took my hand and grinned at me. A few of the women gave me killing looks. I ignored them.

He slipped his arm around my waist. "Nice to meet you, ladies." He waved as we walked back over to the team. "Thanks for coming to the game." When we were out of earshot, he leaned over. "So am I really yours?"

"Debi thought you needed saving."

"I think I owe you my life." He kissed me on the cheek before he released me.

I blushed. The entire team looked our way.

While in the car on our way to the restaurant he leaned over and brushed my shoulder with his.

"I enjoyed our date last night," he said.

"So did I, it was fun. Thank you again."

I shifted in my seat to be able to look at him directly. He had a beautiful profile, and when he grinned, I could see the little dimple at the corner of his mouth.

"I thought maybe if you'd like we could go out again next Saturday, you know, if you don't have anything else to do?"

It wasn't like him to stumble over the words. It was sweet to hear he could be a little nervous with me too.

"I'd enjoy that. Are you going to be able to come out waterskiing this week?"

When we stopped at the stoplight, he turned to look at me. His eyes looked like a liquid sky. "Yeah, if you let me drive the boat."

I smiled. "It's a date then."

He pulled into the restaurant parking lot. "It's a date."

I reached into the backseat to get my bag as he opened my door.

"I'm going to go change. Could you make sure Debi has saved us a seat? It would be just like her to make me sit with that group of forlorn-looking women that were following you around today."

He flashed a grin at me. "Don't worry I'll take care of you."

I popped inside the women's room and entered the handicap stall. As I started to change my clothes, three women came through the main door of the restroom. I recognized the voices of the women who had been talking to Michael earlier. They were loud and boisterous. I hadn't known them as being from Mintock. Most likely they were from the neighboring town of Ashley. I was glad to be hiding in the stall.

"He is so gorgeous. What a body, I couldn't get over the tight baseball pants," said the first women.

"Who was the tall chick who dragged him away?" the second woman questioned.

"Who knows? She certainly wasn't around a few weeks ago," the first woman responded.

The third woman piped in, "I saw them leave together, to come over to the restaurant."

I tried not to giggle and to dress as quietly as possible.

The first woman spoke again, "There was nothing on his website about being married, so it's probably not his wife. Hey, is there someone in the handicap stall?"

I unlocked the door and stepped out. They were surprised to see me. I figured they would just let me pass by them. I was wrong. It was too reminiscent of high school.

The tallest woman who first spoke stepped in front of me. "Hey, are you the girl from the baseball game? You know the one with Michael?"

I pulled my bag onto my shoulder. "Excuse me I need to get through." Fortunately, she stepped aside as did the other two women. Glad that they did, I was not sure what I would have done had they not moved. I looked back with my hand on the doorknob. "He's a friend of mine. I'll let him know you're interested."

As I walked out of the restroom, the first woman had the last word, "Tramp!" she called after me. I let it just roll off me. At first, they did frighten me, but then I got a good look at them and smiled. I grinned knowing that there would be no interest in them on his part.

I joined Michael, Debi, Don, Angel, and Lewis at our table. Michael stood when I arrived. The effort endeared him to me. I sat next to him, and he casually slipped his arm around my shoulder and leaned over.

"What took so long?" he asked.

I whispered, "I met your fan club in the bathroom." He gave me a puzzled face, and I answered, "You know the gals from the bleachers."

"Oh," he nodded.

"They seem to be quite enamored with you."

"Does it make you jealous?" He looked me straight in the eyes.

I glanced away, and the blush came anyway. I decided to answer truthfully, "Yes."

"Okay, I like that."

The waitress came by, and we quickly ordered. Since I had eaten so much the previous night, and the brownies today, I only ordered a small salad with cheese and olives. Michael ordered the gazpacho soup with bread and cheese.

Debi waved her wine glass at me. "No sangria, Elizabeth?"

I must have turned a couple shades of green. "No, I think I'll pass this week."

Michael grinned at me. "Are you sure? I'm driving."

I pursed my lips together. "No, I think I'll stick to just the salad."

He was such a tease, but at least he knew when to stop. Usually, the teasing with Kevin pushed me to the edge, and it ended up in an argument.

It was good to be with my friends, and we always looked forward to being together on the summer Sunday nights. Our group was a special one, and we never stepped out of bounds. I wasn't sure if I could ever explain to Michael the comfort and safety the group gave to me. I hoped he would be able to see for himself and understand why I felt free to be myself in front of my friends.

Before we called it a night at the restaurant, our group made plans for the bonfire party on the following Friday. I explained to Michael that our bonfires were usually grand affairs. We built a large fire on the beach in front of my house because it was the last house in the cove. The party included plenty of food and all of the neighbors in the area were invited.

As we drove home together, he brought up the women at the game again.

"You know they are not my type at all," he said as he took my hand and squeezed it.

"Really, and what is your type?" My heart beat a little faster.

He laughed as he pulled up in front of my back door. He turned off the jeep and looked at me. "You are." He pressed my nose with his finger. He leaned over and kissed me on the forehead.

I felt the heat rising on my cheeks and was glad it was dark so he couldn't see I was blushing again. "Would you like to come in for coffee?"

His voice was reluctant. "I would love to, but tonight I have to turn in early. I'm due in San Francisco tomorrow for a meeting, and there will be traffic in the morning." He got out, and I sat in my seat waiting for him to open my door. Normally I would never have stayed, but I could tell he wanted me to, so I did. He opened the door and then reached for my bag on the backseat.

"Don't forget waterskiing this week," I reminded him while walking up to the back door.

The dogs ran to the door with their usual exuberance, and I could hear their snuffling under the door.

"I wouldn't miss it."

I turned to him. "And we have the bonfire on Friday."

His smile was amused. "And we have our date on Saturday. So yes, I think we have our week sewn up."

Relief washed through me, and it must have shown because he leaned down and kissed me softly on the lips.

"You are too sweet," he whispered softly, all the amusement gone from his voice. His arms wrapped around me pressing me against him. I felt the deep rumble of a sigh in his chest, and my own heart started to pound. "I need to go home, but I really want to come in," he said following with another kiss, which was deeper, harder and lingered longer. His sigh was full of regret. "I have to go."

He released me and took my keys from my hand to open the door.

It took everything I had not to pull him into the house as I stepped inside. "Goodnight Michael," I said turning to face him again, and his expression confirmed that he did not want to leave.

"Go inside before I change my mind." When he reached his jeep, he turned while I stood in the doorway and he called wistfully, "Goodnight Elizabeth."

I smiled and shut the door.

CHAPTER EIGHT

I stretched languorously when I awoke Monday morning with thoughts of my time with Michael. No detail was too small to replay in my mind as I scrutinized each one repeatedly and realized our date had been perfect. Remembering his kisses made me blush. Kevin told me at one time that I kissed horribly, and after that, I always wondered about how other men felt. I certainly did not get much practice after my marriage, and I questioned if Michael felt the same way Kevin did? We only shared two, not enough to judge a performance, but I thought as I snuggled down into my pillows that he was an excellent kisser.

Nancy called early prodding me with questions about my date and the baseball game. She squealed with delight in all the appropriate places. Our conversation made me think of high school and my first dates when I would go through every word and action in excruciating detail. These were stories I could not share with Debi or even my sister since they were married and somehow the wedding ring made you forget what it was like to be single. They would laugh at all the silly fine points we unattached girls would chew over for hours.

"You should be glad I wasn't in the bathroom with those women yesterday," she said with a heated tone. "I would have given them what for!"

"Nancy, I'm glad you were not there. I can just imagine it, a cat fight in the bathroom."

She laughed heartily. "Girlfriend, I will always have your back."

I laughed with her. The comment was especially true since her negotiation skills with my publisher were legendary.

"It definitely sounds like he is interested in you. He appears to be quite the tasty morsel."

"He has invited me out next Saturday, and I think he wants to spend the day with me. He mentioned it while we were driving home last night." I couldn't control the excitement in my voice.

She paused a moment. "That's a good development. It sounds like he is wooing you and not just trying to get into bed with you."

"I think last night he was close to it though."

"I'm looking forward to meeting him." She sighed on the other end of the phone. "I can't get up there before our road trip, darn it."

"You'll just have to wait then and trust me that I'm handling everything."

Nancy roared with laughter. "Elizabeth, that is not a skill I associate with you."

I frowned at her comment but giggled anyway. "Okay, knock it off. I may not be as silver-tongued as you are, but I do okay."

She contained a giggle. "Okay, I'm sorry. Yes, you are one smooth operator."

The rest of the day I spent squirreled away with my writing. By the end of the day, cabin fever started. Jason had already delivered Debi's homemade goulash for dinner. The dogs looked lethargic, and I needed to stretch my legs too. Their ears perked up when I whistled to them, and they followed me out the back door quickly. Jason's motorcycle took the place of Michael's jeep by their back porch. Michael would be either late or staying the night in San Francisco. I had been curious about the reason for his trip, but he had not volunteered any information.

I found Snow Patrol on my playlist and walked to the lakeshore. The sun was starting to set. In a few weeks, the tourists would be gone, and the lake would belong to us again. I could actually feel autumn coming in the air. The leaves on the trees in between the houses would soon be turning their familiar burnt orange, yellow, and red colors. This was my favorite time of the year, even if it included raking leaves.

It was hard to realize that it had only been a week since I had arrived. Being in Mintock usually meant quiet time, a time to get away, to concentrate on my work, and enjoy friends. Instead, the past week had been a whirlwind all surrounding Michael. He was a man that took a lot of energy, but then so did Kevin. I shook off the thought. I did not want Kevin to invade my thoughts again. There would be no good coming from that direction.

Caesar had been correct. I was happy. In one week, I became happy. Had Michael done that? My book was on its way, and my writing was streaming forward. The happiness seemed to overflow to the other areas of my life.

The dogs and I turned away from the cabin. We started a slow jog. Angel came out on her porch and waved. I waved back but continued to run. I was not in the mood for conversation tonight.

After arriving back home, I popped the goulash into the microwave oven and heated up the homemade rolls in the oven. Not too pathetic of a cook, I made my own salad. After feeding the dogs, I ate at the dining room table, reading the paper. I continued to write through the evening. It was well after midnight by the time I shut the computer down. While taking out the trash, I noticed Michael had not yet returned. Jason's motorcycle was still parked by the porch. My eyebrows raised, and then I chastised myself for being a nosey neighbor. Tammy was over eighteen and what she did was her own business. I was not her mother.

The next evening, when I took the dogs for their jog, Michael's jeep had returned. Seeing the car made my heart leap a little. I rolled my eyes. Why would seeing his vehicle make me happy? I was silly. The run with the dogs tonight was lighter and taken at a brisker pace. I looked forward to seeing all three of my next-door neighbors tomorrow. I realized that I had missed interacting with them. Maybe I was a little lonely too. Yes, that was it. The cabin had held me captive too long. It was definitely cabin fever. Of course, the remedy was simple if that was the cause, I could visit Debi or Angel. I did not want to.

I awoke early Wednesday morning with a sense of excitement. The day was ready to break. I put on my sweats and decided to take the dogs on my jog. I wanted to run. The morning was still cool, and the wind against my face felt good. I ran faster than I normally would, and the first two and a half miles came quickly. When I turned to go back home, I slowed down to my regular pace.

Michael was sitting on the dock facing toward me. It appeared that he was waiting for me and I smiled at the thought. He lifted up his thermos when he saw me and waved me over. The dock swayed as I walked up to him.

"You ran fast. I almost couldn't make the coffee in time," he said as he poured a cup for me.

"Thanks," I said as I sat down opposite him. "This is a nice surprise."

"I like to watch the dawn too. Especially out here, it's so quiet."

"Are the girls up yet?" I asked, taking the mug he offered.

"No," he said with emphasis, and he leaned back against the pylon with his legs stretched out. "They usually don't see much of the dawn. Especially when they are on vacation, they are very much alike when it comes to that."

He wore an old San Francisco Giants t-shirt and jeans torn at both knees. Both had seen better days. He looked incredibly sexy with his day-old beard and disheveled hair as if he had just crawled out of bed. His feet were bare, and I found myself looking at them. His feet, like the rest of him, were long. I had the strangest urge to play "*this little piggy*" with his toes. It made me smile.

Michael asked, "What are you grinning about? My feet?"

I blushed and shook my head. "Nothing."

"No, it was something. It was about my big feet. You know what they say, big feet…," he trailed off with a big grin on his face showing his deep dimples.

I answered him, "Yeah, big shoes." I laughed, still blushing at the innuendo even though I tried not to.

He laughed with me. "Oh, you've heard that one."

"Yes, I've heard that one." I tried to change the subject. "So how was your appointment in San Francisco?"

"Good, actually better than I thought. I met with my ex-wife, our lawyers, and a judge," he answered.

Deciding to pry, I asked, "Nothing too serious I hope."

Michael's face looked disgusted. He took a drink from his coffee mug before he replied, "No, she only wanted more money. We agreed that I would support her until Tammy turned eighteen. Then the support would stop. She wanted to change the agreement. She felt it was too harsh to simply turn off the money."

I wrinkled my forehead. "So you had custody of the girls, and she didn't pay you support?"

"No, that was one of the stipulations of me getting the girls. Maggie received it all, the house, and alimony, everything except the girls. I agreed to pay her support for 6 years, to help her go back to school and get herself set up." He smiled quietly. "I figured I received the best of the deal. My lawyer got me exactly what I wanted."

I looked at Michael with surprise on my face. His devotion to his daughters was so strong that he gave up everything for them.

"It was difficult for the three of us when we first started on our own," he admitted. "I was astonished Maggie could cut herself off so completely from the girls. Her visits and calls became less frequent. I tried to be there for them, but I know it must have hurt them deeply." His voice grew softer and filled with pain, and the ache showed on his face.

"What did you do? I mean, you had to make a living, especially if you had to pay your ex-wife," I asked. My voice filled with incredulity. I wanted to reach out, to hold him if just to wipe the hurt from his face.

His voice became bitter. "Yeah, especially when she regularly threatened me that she would take the girls back if I didn't pay her on time. My little sister rescued us. She is a saint. Christina is financially well off. She had a big house in Oakland, and she let us move in with her. She'd recently divorced too and said she was lonely. I don't know what we would have done without her."

I thought he wanted to tell me, so I pressed him to continue. "How did you work trying to raise your two girls alone?"

Michael's face brightened. "Very creatively. I took shorter trips.

Christina was there in the evenings when I was gone. I worked on my books more. I took the girls with me when they had breaks from school. My sister actually went with us too." He laughed, and his eyes sparkled again. "Remind me to tell you those stories sometimes. Christina is not the most graceful of campers."

I was glad his mood started to lift again. "So, what happened yesterday? Did your ex-wife get what she wanted?"

He shook his head laughing. "No, just the opposite. The judge thought she was trying to grab more money, which she was." He shrugged his shoulders. "He told her if she didn't drop it, he would recommend that I go for back child support. That took the puff out of her sails."

"Well good." I smiled at him. "I'm glad it turned out right."

"So am I." He grimaced. "Though Maggie did threaten, or should I say promised, to visit Tammy." He rolled his eyes upward. "That's all I need, having to deal with her."

"I'm sure Tammy will be glad to see her."

"She will, even though she would never admit it to me. The fact that Maggie is no good for her, I know she still needs her mother."

"I'm glad you brought that up." Inside my mind was screaming not to get involved, but then, when did I listen to myself, so I continued, "Michael if this is too intrusive, let me know okay? Is Tammy taking birth control?"

His look showed the surprise on his face. "Is there a reason why you ask?"

I grimaced but plowed forward. "I noticed Jason's motorcycle parked at your house very late Monday night, and well, I wondered."

He closed his eyes. I could not tell if he was angry or confused, or maybe a little of both. He finally let out a sigh. "You know I didn't think to ask her. I just assumed that she would take care of that sort of thing herself."

I sighed too. "Generally young girls won't just take care of it. They still deny the possibility that they will have sex and then it is too late. Would you like me to talk to her?"

"I hate to ask you to do that Elizabeth, but would you? I'm afraid I'm not very good with those types of talks. Her mother would give her all the wrong advice too."

I smiled gently. "I don't have much experience with those types of talks either, but I guess it might be easier coming from me than from you."

The relief showed on his face.

"I don't mean to cut this short," I said while standing up, "but I've got to feed the dogs. Let's meet at one for our water skiing. Okay?"

He stood up and slipped his arm around my waist while we walked back to our houses.

"Yeah, that's good," he answered. "I'll tell the girls. They're really looking forward to skiing. In the meantime, I'm going to have a talk with Jason."

We stopped in between our two houses and stood together.

"Just don't kill him, okay?" I said laughing.

"You know what I mean Elizabeth, they are way too young," he said.

I nodded. "I know, but I also remember when I was eighteen. It's not easy, suddenly faced with all that freedom."

I stood up on my toes, put my hand on his shoulder, and kissed him softly on the cheek. "It will be okay."

He smiled. "Thanks."

I wasn't sure if he was thanking me for the kiss or the talk with Tammy, or both. I would take both.

"See you later," I replied.

After feeding the dogs and showering, I sat down at my desk, and stared out the window, looking at nothing. Michael had distracted me. Our conversation on the dock kept replaying in my mind. His willingness to discuss his ex-wife and take me into his confidence surprised me.

The knock on the door startled me. A quick glance out the window revealed Tammy at the front door. I took a deep breath. I had gotten myself into this discussion, and it was time to face the music.

"Hey," I said answering the door. "Come on in."

The dogs greeted her with jumps, and she bent down and cuddled with both of them.

She straightened up. "Dad said you wanted to talk to me?"

"Uh, yeah, I guess so. Sit down, would you like a cola?" I asked.

She shook her head. "I'm fine. Thanks."

The dogs jumped up and laid on her when she sat on the couch. She petted them and looked at me expectantly.

I sat at the other end of the couch. "So, Jason was over pretty late night before last, wasn't he?"

She looked at me, and her eyes grew wide. Redness crept slowly on her face. "We didn't do anything, really. He just stayed a little late. Dad knows, doesn't he?" Tears started to well up in her eyes.

I scooted next to her and put my arm around her shoulder. "Tammy there is no reason to get upset." My own emotions were getting to me. I felt fury with her mother. She should be here with her arm around her talking her through this. "Have you slept with Jason?" I asked softly.

She buried her face in her hands. "No. We're not doing anything like that."

I tried to modulate my voice, so it would be even and not accusatory. "Do you think you might?"

She looked up at me, and her face was beet red. "Elizabeth, I don't know. I really like him, but I know he's going away to school and I'm probably going away to school. It's all very complicated." She clasped her hands tightly in her lap.

Memories of my own talk with my mother flashed back to me. The mortification I felt when she first talked to me about going on birth control. I was Tammy's age and in much of the same situation. Had my mother felt the same as I did now? It was awkward as heck and never in a million years did I ever expect to be having a talk like this.

I blew out a deep breath. "When you're with him, how do you feel?"

She looked down again at her hands in her lap. "What do you mean? I like to be with him."

I wasn't sure how to phrase it. I looked up at the ceiling and prayed my mother would give me the right words. I knew one thing, in the future, I'd keep my mouth shut and not offer advice.

"How do you feel when he kisses you?"

She giggled and looked at me with a shy look. "My stomach gets all crazy. How about you?" She giggled again. "You know... when my dad kisses you?"

I laughed and then grimaced. "Okay, you got me. My stomach gets all crazy too." I shook my head. "You know what I mean." She laughed with me. "Okay, straight, you should probably go on the pill, you know, just in case."

"You really think so?" She looked at me seriously. "I'm really not planning on sleeping with Jason."

"Tammy, it only takes once. He's cute, and it would be easy to give into the passion of the moment, especially when he stays late." I frowned trying to give off an older wiser sister look.

She pondered what I had said for a moment, and I remained quiet. Finally, she looked back at me. "Would you go with me? I mean to the doctor."

It was my turn to look relieved. "Yes, I have a great doctor in town. She's good."

Tammy nodded her head too. "Okay, I'll go. But this doesn't mean that I'm going to sleep with Jason."

"Of course not," I replied. "But it will make your dad rest easier, not that you having sex is going to make him happy."

"Well, tell him I'm not!" she said emphatically pointing at me. "By the way are you on the pill?"

"Tammy, your father and I have no intention of sleeping together. We are just friends and neighbors, nothing more."

"I don't know," she giggled. "What about the heat of the moment?"

"I'm not sleeping with your dad, and we shouldn't be talking about this." I took a breath and exhaled slowly. "Besides, I can't get pregnant."

"Oh," she said, "I'm sorry. Is that why you and your husband didn't have kids?"

I looked straight ahead trying to focus and felt the sadness wash over me. "Yeah, that's why. I don't think Kevin wanted kids anyway. He certainly wasn't unhappy when it was confirmed that I couldn't get pregnant." I looked back at her. "Enough about me. I'll make an appointment for you, okay?"

We finished the conversation with big hugs. She looked like she was going to cry again when our hug ended, but I rose from the couch and went over to my desk to give her a little time to compose herself. My writing was finished for the day, so I switched off the computer and invited her to stay for a pizza and salad lunch. Katy came over to join us, but Michael was on a conference call and said he would meet us at the boat when we were ready to go skiing.

After we finished eating, we changed into our bathing suits. I was in the mood to entice him after our morning coffee. My one-piece black suit adorned with small red dots was almost backless. The material just barely covered my butt, and the French cut legs rode high up to my hips. On the front, a V plunged down my middle exposing my belly button. If I tied the halter tightly around my neck, my breasts would remain covered while I skied. If not, then everyone on Lake Mintock would be in for quite the show.

The girls helped me carry the skis to the boat. Michael met us out on the dock. He was shirtless and wore his bathing suit. Suddenly I was happy I would be able to stare at his bare chest all afternoon without anyone thinking there was anything odd about me. While we loaded the boat, the towels came up missing, and the girls made a quick trip back to the cabin to retrieve them.

Standing on the dock, he handed his sunscreen to me. "Would you do the honors?" he asked pointing to his back. The blushes were rising on my face, and he grinned.

"Yeah sure, turn around," I said, squeezing out a small amount of the sunscreen into my palm and touching his back. He hissed with the coolness of the cream. "Sorry," I said. "Should have warmed it up in my hands first."

I smoothed the lotion on his back. I was about to swoon. His back was smooth under my hands, and his hard muscles were responding to my touches. Michael wore his suit low on his hips like he wore his jeans. I could almost see myself wrapping my arms around his waist, closing my eyes, and resting my cheek on his shoulder. I didn't succumb to the vision. He stood very still while I rubbed his back. I wished I could see his facial expression.

"Okay," I said, since I couldn't draw the moment out any longer and handed the tube back to him.

"How about you?" he asked softly when he turned around.

I cleared my throat. "Okay." I swiveled and stared at the lake.

Michael lifted my ponytail off my back. I reached back and pulled my hair forward. He rubbed the sunscreen on his hands before he touched my back. His hands moved very slowly. As his strokes moved down, I closed my eyes. My knees felt weak, and my stomach was doing flip-flops again. His hands slipped between the edges of my suit and my skin. Then, he wrapped his hands around my sides and pulled me against him.

Michael leaned forward, nuzzled my neck and whispered in my ear, "Breathe Elizabeth."

I heard the girls make their way to the dock. His hands withdrew from my suit, and I immediately turned around dropping my ponytail down my back. His face was inches from mine. With intense eyes, he kissed me tenderly on my lips and backed up.

Tammy's voice was first. "Hey, what are you guys doing?"

He turned around and held up the sunscreen. "Want some?"

Both of them shook their heads and answered in unison, "Already done."

We finished putting the rest of the stuff into the boat. Michael wanted to go to the center of the lake. I sat in the back just looking at him trying to slow down my pulse. If either girl noticed my beet-red face, they were polite enough not to say a word.

The day was perfect for waterskiing. Both the air and water were warm. Even though it was the middle of the week, water skiing tourists filled the lake. This close to Labor Day everyone tried to squeeze the last drops out of the summer. All of us took turns skiing. When Michael skied, I watched his movements closely. I wanted to memorize everything about him. He piloted while the girls skied. His joy was evident, and he told me several times how much he liked fast boats.

We took a break from skiing and moved into one of the coves. I hadn't done much skiing and wanted to swim to cool off. The girls wanted to tan and stayed in the boat. He followed me into the water. I couldn't touch bottom, and we swam over to the shallow end of the cove.

"So where are we going on Saturday?" I asked.

Michael swam up next to me. "I thought we'd start in Calistoga for breakfast and then go where the road takes us." He slipped his arms around my waist and pulled me close. "Elizabeth, you are gorgeous in this bathing suit."

He nuzzled my neck as he had done on the dock. His lips trailed up my neck to my chin and then to my lips. My arms went around his shoulders. His kiss was tentative at first and then more urgent as I parted my lips. We explored each other's faces, necks, and mouths. Lifting me up with his hands, he wrapped my legs around his body never letting his mouth leave me. As he did this, I gave a small gasp of surprise. Even with the cool water, it was evident that his body was happy to have me close.

This brought me back to my senses. "Michael, your daughters can see us." I pulled back from him.

He looked at me with desire in his eyes. "No, they're busy tanning themselves. Relax Elizabeth."

Before I realized what he was doing, he reached up and loosened the tight knot in my halter. My breasts fell forward into the material of my suit.

"What are you doing?"

Amusement filled his laugh. "Just giving the twins some breathing room. I kept trying to figure out while you were water skiing, why you didn't fall out of your bathing suit. Now I know why you had the poor things smothered in there." He bent down, nuzzled me on my neck, and worked his lips lower.

We both heard the splash of water behind us. The noise sobered us both, pulling us apart. I turned with him toward the boat and saw Tammy swimming toward us.

He muttered quietly under his breath, "Damn."

I laughed and looked back up at him. The spell wasn't quite broken just a little damp. His moves this afternoon certainly startled me. His reaction probably would have been the same if I had been wearing a gunnysack, but there I was trying to entice him, and look where it got me. I wasn't going to try that again. Or was I?

We skied the rest of the afternoon. His eyes were on me the entire time. When I sat next to him, he would squeeze my hand or my shoulder. Michael definitely was a physically demonstrative person. I had noticed how affectionate he was with his daughters. There was a warmth and protective feeling he conveyed, and I could feel it drawing me in. I wanted to lay my head on his shoulder and simply let him take care of me. These feelings of inclusion beckoned me, but my mind, mired in doubt, kept repeating, was this all my imagination?

CHAPTER NINE

Early Friday morning, after a short jog with the dogs, I dressed in a pair of navy blue shorts, a red tank top, and my sandals. A small matching blue ribbon complimented my braided hair. I wanted to make sure my outfit was uncomplicated because the day would be a busy one with all the preparations for the neighborhood bonfire. A grand affair that took place at my house.

Lewis, Don, and Michael were supervising the actual fire itself, as they considered this *man's work*. I asked dryly why the fire was more important than the food, which they believed to be *women's work*, but the boys ignored me and rolled their eyes. We had been doing the bonfire for years on the Friday before Labor Day, and it was always done near my cabin since mine was the last home along the lake in our cove.

Neighbors set up tables and chairs in my front yard. Volunteers constructed a small dance floor in Michael's front yard. We also commandeered his refrigerator to store food. The food tables had large ice chests to accommodate all the soft drinks. And since we women were in charge of the food, there was plenty to eat. So they could be supervised, my front porch held the beer kegs and bar. Katy and Tammy converted Michael's front porch into a stage to hold musical instruments and speakers.

Debi and Angel arrived around three. Both of their pickup trucks were full of trays of food. We stuffed the food into the refrigerator in my cabin and the extra one in my garage. Then, Jason and Tammy helped carry food over to her kitchen. The actual barbequing was a couple of hours away, so we had a little while to relax.

Debi, Angel, and I made margaritas and sat on my front porch observing all the activities. Katy had a recording of steel drum music playing from the stage. It was our own little piece of Jamaica. We spied Michael, Lewis, and Don sitting on the dock drinking beers. They had finished building the bonfire, and all three of them had their feet dangling in the water.

Debi, ever direct, looked over. "Hey, so what's happening with you and Michael? Anything interesting? You both looked very chummy last Sunday. How was the date?"

I smiled looking up from my margarita. "Do you ever take a breath?"

Debi laughed, and both she and Angel looked at me expectantly.

I continued, "He's sweet. We went waterskiing on Wednesday with the girls. We had fun." I giggled inside. Fun was an understatement as far as I was concerned.

Debi peered back at me. "Uh uh, I don't think so, you're not going to get away with that explanation."

Angel piped in, "I think she means to say that we want the details, you know, kiss and tell."

"There isn't that much to tell," I explained. "I'm enjoying being with him." I leaned forward. "And, wow, he is a great kisser!"

Debi clapped gleefully. "I knew it!"

Angel looked at Debi, her sunglasses slipping down her nose. "And what is it Miss Debi that you knew?"

"Oh, you know what I mean." She laughed. "Look at those lips…absolutely scrumptious."

I tilted my sunglasses down on my nose too. "Just how much have you had to drink Miss Debi? I think we're going to have to cut you off early tonight."

She sat back, cackled, and took a long drink from her margarita glass. "I did think it was great when Michael paid a visit to Jason yesterday."

"You are kidding, he actually did it?" I asked.

Angel looked confused, and I filled them both in on the conversation I had with Tammy. Debi told us that Michael had approached Don and her first.

She waved her hand. "I said have at it. We've talked about it, but I thought maybe it would be good for Jason to have a menacing dad after him."

"Was Michael menacing?" My brow wrinkled with worry.

She shook her head. "Does he look menacing to you? Michael is a big pussycat. No, but Jason told us they had a good conversation."

"Tammy agreed to go to the doctor with me next week," I added.

Angel nodded. "That's nice of you to do Elizabeth. Where is her mother in all of this?"

I sighed. "Their mom isn't very active in their lives. It's sad. When I think how close my mom and I were."

Debi laughed. "Yeah, and boy, your mom hated Kevin."

I stood. "Another one?"

She nodded and gave me her glass.

"Everyone hated him," I replied.

Angel handed me her glass too. "He was a real stinker."

Our conversation continued as I mixed new drinks for us. "That was the thing, I didn't find out what a stinker he was until after I married him. He hid many of his really worst traits from me until I said the '*I do.*'"

Debi shifted her chair closer. "I can't believe you still have to pay him alimony!"

Angel's eyes widened. "You're paying him alimony? I thought he was more successful than you?"

I smirked while cutting up the lime and then rimming the glasses with salt. "You'd think that with the way he talked. However, no, I actually made a lot more money than he did. My books sold well right away. When we split up, I gave him most of the money and an agreement that I would pay him alimony for three years."

"And the three years are almost up, and then you can tell him to kiss off." Debi wiped her hands together as if she was brushing off crumbs.

"Yeah, at the end of November. It will be my Christmas gift to him."

Debi shook her head. "I kick myself every time I think about it because I should have been more adamant about you not marrying him."

"Well," I sighed, "who knew that I would start writing? Maybe I needed to go through hell with Kevin before I got the urge to write."

"Bull!" Debi said vehemently. "You wrote in high school and college, it was always there! That pipsqueak did not bring out anything in you. He tried to destroy you!

"Okay!" I held up my hand. "Let's drop Kevin. I do not want to ruin my day thinking about him. Besides look what's coming toward us, far more handsome and loveable."

I pointed to our men who were making their way up from the shore. Michael was dressed in knee-length jean shorts and a navy-blue t-shirt. He looked delectable enough to eat.

Debi danced the cha-cha down the porch over to Don and hugged him. She danced around him and bumped her butt against his back. He yelled over to me, "Okay, who has been giving this woman alcohol?"

I raised my hand. "Guilty!"

He laughed and hugged Debi. "Give her some more!"

Debi pulled him up on the porch with her, she looked at me, and I nodded my head slightly. Both of them disappeared into my cabin. I smirked.

Angel walked down the steps and took Lewis' hand. "I think we need to light the barbeques."

Lewis laughed. "Oh, that will keep us busy!" They walked off arm in arm toward the barbeques.

Michael climbed the porch steps with a puzzled look on his face. "Okay, what happened? Why is everyone disappearing? Where did Don and Debi go?"

I laughed and sat with him on the porch swing. "They disappeared into my guest bedroom, and if I had only one guess, they are probably going to do the big nasty with each other."

"What?" he asked with surprise on his face. "They're not really…" he paused, "in your house?"

"Relax. They do it all the time, I mean, when I'm not here. It gives them somewhere quiet to go that is not too far away. The kids can't walk in on them. Their house is tiny."

"I can't believe it!"

"Michael, stop it, it's not like they're having an illicit affair. They are married after all. After what you and I were doing on Wednesday afternoon I wouldn't have taken you for such a prude."

He shook his head and laughed. "I'm not really. I'm just surprised they're so blatant."

I frowned. "What's blatant? It's not like they announced it to the neighborhood. They just quietly went into my cabin."

He put his arm around my shoulders. "So, would it be that easy with you?"

I looked at him and batted my eyelashes. "Would what be that easy with me?"

"You know the big nasty," he said squeezing me.

"No, I'm not interested in doing the big nasty with Don."

He lowered his arm down my waist and pulled me closer. "You know what I meant. I have a guest bedroom too." He raised his eyebrows.

"Oh great, I'll let them know, they can use yours next time."

Michael laughed and shook his head. "You were right, it's the anticipation."

Over along the shore, a boat arrived at the dock. Grabbing his hand, I pulled him up. "Don's parents are here. Let's go meet them."

We walked down to the shore and greeted Frank and Annie. She was a tiny slim woman, just an inch over five feet, wearing a pair of black jeans and a red cotton blouse. Her long-braided salt and pepper hair hung down her back. She hugged me tightly and then shook Michael's hand.

"So this is your new man." Annie didn't as much as ask the question as she stated a fact. She peered up at him and apparently, he met with her approval.

"Yes, this is my new friend. Michael, this is Frank, who is the Chief of Police, and Annie who is the chief of everything else. They are my second parents."

Michael grinned. "Frank and I have already met."

Frank nodded. "Good to see you again Michael." He shook his hand, then turned his attention, and hugged me. "Michael helped me round up the boys that were giving us some trouble in town."

"Come on up to the porch and let me get you something to drink," I offered.

Annie slipped her arm around Michael's, and they walked ahead of us toward the porch. The two of them walking together was a sight with the disparity in their sizes.

She turned back around and looked at me. "Where are Debi and Don?"

I just nodded at my cabin.

Frank shook his head. "Those two are worse than rabbits."

"Shush Frank. We should be happy they are so happy." While looking up at Michael, she said, "I am of the Pomo tribe."

"The Pomo are especially artful basket weavers," I included. "Annie is well known for the beautiful baskets that she makes."

Annie patted his arm. "Debi has told me you are quite the photographer. I would like you to take pictures of my baskets. The Smithsonian contacted me. They want to display some of my baskets in their new Native American exhibit in Washington DC," she said proudly.

They both settled themselves into chairs when they reached the top of the porch.

Michael responded, "I would be honored to take pictures of your baskets."

She smiled and leaned forward to touch him on the knee. "Good that's settled then. Thank you. I've heard that you are interested in our eagles. When you come and take pictures, I will tell you about the Pomo tribe. The eagles on the mountain are sacred to us. We believe that before we lived here, bird people lived on our mountain, and the eagle is what is left of them."

"I'd like to hear the stories," he said.

I was happy to see him be so respectful to Annie. Without my mom around, she filled a very empty spot in my heart. We sat on the porch and shared stories from past bonfires. Katy, who seemed to be in charge of the music, changed the music from the steel drums to Native American flute music. I don't know how she knew how appropriate the choice had been.

Just as Lewis came to get Michael and Frank to start barbequing the meats, Debi and Don came strolling around from the side of my cabin. They looked as if they had been on a long walk. I smiled appreciating the love they had for each other.

The afternoon activities began to wind down. As the sun commenced its slow descent, we lit the torches and put the food on the tables. The boys had the barbeques well underway, and people were milling around talking. Katy and a band started playing on Michael's porch.

When the food was ready, we sat down with our overladen plates at a long table filled with our friends. The air was electric, and you could feel the anticipation for the bonfire. I looked around and saw happy faces, eating, laughing, and joking. I smiled and sighed.

Michael put his arm around me and squeezed me. Leaning over he whispered, "Penny for your thoughts."

I smiled again and dabbed at the corner of his mouth with my napkin. "Mustard."

He took a bite of his burger and kissed me on the cheek. Dabbing at my cheek with his napkin, he replied, "Ketchup."

Tammy accosted us from behind by putting her arms around our shoulders. "Someone has a girlfriend!" She looked at her dad and teased.

Michael turned, grabbed her, and started tickling her. "You mind your own business."

She screamed with delight as she giggled and squirmed around. She reached out for Jason who was behind her. "Jason, help me!"

He backed away laughing. "No way am I getting in the middle of this!"

Debi who sat next to me, winked and said, "Oh yes, I think we should teach him a lesson."

Both of us jumped up and tackled Jason. I sat on his legs while his mom did the dirty work of tickling him.

"Oh Mom, stop!" Jason laughed. "Please Aunt Elizabeth, tell her to stop."

Debi laughed. "This will teach you to always come to the aid of your girlfriend."

We both rolled off Jason and picked each other up. The laughter felt good. Michael had let Tammy go, and she ran over to rescue Jason.

Michael called out to them, "Have you learned your lesson?"

Tammy giggled. "I give."

Frank looked over at Jason and pointed to Annie. "If you don't behave yourself I'll send your grandmother over!"

Jason rolled over. "I give too!"

After we finished eating, it was dark enough to start the bonfire. Everyone spread blankets around in a circle. We stood back as Lewis did the honors and lit the fire. There was an appreciative hush as the flames rose.

A hush fell over the gathering. Annie walked toward us from the beach and tapped the small drum she had in her hand. She spoke in the traditional Pomo language, and even though I didn't speak the Native American dialect, I knew what she said because I had heard it so many times before. It was a time-honored prayer of thankfulness.

She circled us still beating the drum and then continued in English. "We thank you, Mother Earth. You are our provider. You have returned our precious daughter Elizabeth to us and have brought us a new family, Michael, and his daughters, Katy and Tammy. We are thankful for the continuance of our lives. You have brought the eagles back to us, which began our tribe. We are blessed."

After she finished, she took her place next to Frank. Michael had his camera and took pictures of the fire and our radiant faces. We stood there mesmerized as the red glow warmed us. Through the silence, we heard the crackling from the flames and the tide rolling up on the shore. In the midst of the quiet, Katy started the recording of the Native American flute music again. Everything was perfect.

As we sat around the fire, Michael approached me from the rear. I patted the empty spot next to me. Instead, he sat directly behind me and stretched out his legs on either side of me. It was a shocker to have him so close. Wrapping his arms around my shoulders, he pulled me back against him.

"Relax," he whispered in my ear, "I promise not to ravish you tonight."

I relaxed and leaned back into his body. "Okay," I said, "but know I can always fetch Annie if you don't behave."

He chuckled and murmured, "She doesn't scare me. However, she might get after you if you're not nice to me. I think she likes me."

I giggled with him. "I think you're probably right."

I closed my eyes and listened to the music. It felt warm and secure to be in his arms and, for once, I wasn't concerned about what the people around me were thinking.

His lips brushed against my ear. "Can I take your hair down?"

I opened my eyes and saw Frank and Annie sitting the same way we were. Frank was unbraiding Annie's hair. I nodded and closed my eyes again. Michael's fingers worked through my hair gently, weaving from bottom to top to untangle my braid. The combination of his fingers, the music, and the fire made for a very sensual experience.

When my hair was loose, he pushed it forward, and I felt his warm lips against the back of my neck. He wrapped his arms around my waist. I didn't want to open my eyes and destroy the spell he was weaving.

Gradually conversations started again. I began to hear voices over the music and the sound of the tide from the lake. After sitting a while, I shifted in his arms so that I could lay my head on his shoulder.

I looked up at him with my head still on his shoulder. "Are you okay?" I said softly.

Michael grinned, and his voice was deep when he replied, "For the pure pleasure of holding you tonight, I would say I'm more than okay."

"Are we going in the Jeep tomorrow or the Mustang?" I referred to our date tomorrow.

"We're definitely taking the Mustang. I enjoy taking you out in it, and it's meant to be driven not garaged away."

"Good, I agree with you. What time?"

"I thought we could head down to Calistoga about nine for breakfast?" He asked it as a request.

"That sounds good to me."

We all spent the evening dancing, talking, laughing, eating more, and enjoying the festive atmosphere we had created. We broke up a little before midnight, and everyone worked together to load up the vehicles. Michael, Tammy, Katy and I waved good-bye to Don and Debi as their truck pulled away from my back porch. Tammy and Katy both yawned, and we hugged before they trouped off next door.

Michael pulled me close as we stood in the kitchen all alone now. "Do you need any help in the house?"

"No, Debi helped me clean up everything. It's all back to normal."

Wrapping my arms around his shoulders had started to feel very natural to me. He ran his fingers through my hair and pressed his lips into my forehead.

"I love your hair down like this."

He lowered his lips to mine and gave me a slow lingering kiss that made my stomach start the flip-flops. As the kiss became more intense, his hands pressed into my lower back pushing me solidly into his lower half. When I didn't pull away, his hands moved lower cupping my butt. My body responded with a lot more than flip-flops as my knees felt weak and a powerful need flooded through me.

He smiled when he broke the kiss. "I look forward to seeing you tomorrow."

"Tomorrow," I replied breathlessly.

His finger touched my lips as we parted. "Breathe Elizabeth."

CHAPTER TEN

The next morning the engine of the Mustang came to life with a roar. Standing on Michael's back porch, I watched as he put the top down. He was dressed in black jeans and a black polo shirt, and the muscles in his back flexed while he wrestled with the roof. I simply admired the rear view.

Michael opened the car door for me, and I put my sweater on the back seat next to his jacket. When I dressed this morning, I pulled my hair up in a ponytail. As much as he would have preferred me to wear it down, the convertible played havoc with my hair. I wrapped a red scarf around my head and put my sunglasses on. I was ready to go.

Michael slid in on the driver's side next to me. He leaned over and kissed me on the lips. "Good morning. I didn't get a kiss yet."

I smiled, ran my finger down his cheek, and kissed him again. "Good morning."

He cleared his throat. "You know we don't have to go," he said winking.

I pointed to the road ahead. "Drive!"

Laughing, he put the car into gear. "We look like twins today!"

Michael referred to my outfit. I carefully planned my clothes today, and I chose them with him in mind. I dressed in tight black Capri pants paired with a new thin black cotton sweater. The sweater's neckline plunged and was short enough to show off my midriff. A flat pair of leather slip-ons completed the look.

"Hey, I have my red scarf. Where's your color?" I noticed his jacket was black too.

He simply laughed and pulled out onto the road. The morning air was cool and crisp. The weatherman predicted hot weather for the day. This was normal; it was merely another hot September day in California. Settling into his seat, he squeezed my hand and then held it gently. We entered the freeway and headed toward Calistoga.

"Did you bring your camera?"

He nodded not taking his eyes from the road. "I usually try not to leave home without at least one camera. You never know. It's in the trunk."

Even though today's date with Michael had me keyed up, I had slept well. Tammy volunteered to take all the dogs on a long walk later in the day, so I could sleep in. I skipped breakfast because Michael promised me a great one in Calistoga.

As we entered a residential neighborhood, I wondered where he was taking us. He pulled into the driveway of a small bungalow style house. Tall rose bushes surrounded the lawn in the front yard. The garage door was open and parked inside was a small passenger car. An older version of Michael walked out of the garage. He looked pleased and not at all surprised to see us.

Michael called, "Dad!"

He got out of the Mustang and hugged his father. His dad was a head shorter, and except for the eye color, the resemblance between father and son was uncanny. I got out of the car and walked around to them.

Michael took my hand and introduced us.

I shook his hand. "Hello, Mr. Hoffman. It's a pleasure to meet you."

He smiled at me. "Call me Steve." He looked back at Michael. "Your mother and grandmother are in the house waiting with breakfast, you're late, and there's hell to pay."

"Thanks for waiting for us," Michael said as he walked through the front door.

I gave him a look that said I wanted an explanation. He silently pulled me inside the house with him. I followed, even more confused. He led me into the living room, which was a small room with a television in one corner next to the window and a corner-group couch against the opposite wall. An easy chair completed the room. On the walls were framed photographs of family members in graduating caps and gowns. I spotted Michael's high school graduation picture easily. He had short hair and looked clean cut. I smiled when I saw his college graduation picture with long hair and I was sure I could see an earring peeking out.

A tall thin woman with short blond hair rose from the couch. "Michael there you are! You really kept your grandmother waiting. When you said breakfast, I thought it would be much earlier."

"Hi, Mom." He hugged her. "I'm sorry. I didn't want to make it too early. I know grandma sleeps late. I didn't know you and Dad would be here too." He leaned over to the older woman sitting in the easy chair and kissed her on the cheek. "Hi Grandma, I'm sorry we're so late."

"When your grandmother called me to let me know you were coming with someone, well, I knew we should not miss the occasion," his mother said dryly.

Michael's grandmother hugged him back and patted his cheek after she kissed him. "You're not late my dear." She spoke with an accent that I couldn't place. "Are you going to introduce me to your friend?"

He reached for my hand and pulled me forward. "I'm sorry Elizabeth, you're probably wondering what is going on."

Steve came into the house and stood behind us. I nodded my head.

He continued, "I thought it would be a nice surprise for you to meet my grandmother Helen while we were in Calistoga. Breakfast was her idea."

I shook his grandmother's hand. "Thank you for inviting me."

She smiled at me and rose from the chair. She patted my hand. "Yes, breakfast was my idea." She laughed. "I thought you should get some food into you before you two start drinking all that wine at the wineries. Besides Michael never brings his lady friends to see me which tells me that you're special."

I could feel the blush rising on my face and actually had the thought to run away.

His mom reached for me as if she could read my mind and knew I was ready to dart. "I'm Candace, and it's good to meet you Elizabeth. Both Tammy and Katy have mentioned how nice you are."

Steve headed toward the kitchen. "Are we going to eat?"

Candace laughed. "Yes!" She pushed us forward.

The kitchen-family room was around the corner. The room, done in blue and white, faced the back yard. There was a small Greek flag hanging in the kitchen. I concluded his grandmother was definitely from Greece, complete with the accent. The family room held the large round dining table. A couch lined the opposite wall, and a television was in the corner. On the wall above were two large framed photographs. They were Michael's shots of dolphins and sea turtles. The blue in the pictures went well with the blue and white motif of the room.

"Let me show you Michael's awards," his grandmother said as she pointed to the far end of the room.

Proudly displayed were large bookcases filled with trophies, plaques, and framed award certificates. I guessed that this was the family's central repository of awards.

"Oh, Grandma." He was actually blushing.

I followed her to the display and there in the middle were his awards. At first, I expected to find his high school awards, and then I found that these were far more recent. First prize photo awards from World Press, BBC Wildlife Photographer of the Year, National Geographic Society Masters of Photography, and additional photographer of the year awards from magazines like Time, Life, Natural History, International Wildlife, newspapers, and corporate sponsors. Then I realized that he alone took up an entire bookcase, not just a shelf.

I stood there amazed. "Michael I had no idea."

He rose and grinned. "This is my grandmother's bragging area."

I could tell however by the tone of his voice that he was pleased to be able to show them to me.

"That's an award from Life Magazine!" I picked up the plaque. "Wow!" I said with both astonishment and amazement.

His grandmother laughed and clapped her hands. "That is my Michael. We are so very proud of him."

He pulled me away from the bookcases. "Come on Elizabeth, let's have some breakfast."

In the middle of the table was a platter of sliced oranges, a pot of honey, a large bowl with yogurt, and a smaller bowl next to it with strawberry preserves. Candace and Michael went into the kitchen. I sat with Steve and Grandmother Helen at the table.

Candace pulled a platter out of the oven. He took the tray from his mother.

"These are medallion pancakes, or they're called *tiganites* in Greek," he said as he placed the platter on the table.

I nodded and said, "They smell wonderful!"

Candace started to whip up what looked like an omelet in a large black frying pan. "This is a potato and feta cheese omelet. Normally Greeks don't eat much for breakfast, maybe some bread and cheese or yogurt. But this is a special occasion, and Michael, don't forget the coffee."

I smiled. "Good, I like coffee."

She answered, "Good. Michael, are you making the coffee?"

"Mom, I think she likes American coffee. I don't think Elizabeth is going to like Greek coffee."

He began scooping a dark finely ground coffee into a small open pot with a long handle. I suppressed a grin. He looked about seventeen standing next to his mother.

"Oh, nonsense." She looked over at me waving a spatula. "Elizabeth, you're going to try our Greek coffee?" She phrased it as a question, but I knew it was more of a statement.

I quickly nodded my head. I was not about to say no to her. I didn't think she would listen to me anyway.

She pointed the spatula at me again. "See, she's going to try it. Give it to her sweet, it might be too strong otherwise. Make sure she has a glass of ice water too." When the omelet was finished, she slid it onto another large platter and brought it to the table.

He stayed in the kitchen. It appeared he was boiling the coffee. My eyebrows raised, this was going to be strong coffee. Candace sat down next to Steve leaving the spot open next to me for Michael. She put portions of the omelet on everyone's plate along with a few pancakes.

"Just a little for me," I requested when she came to my plate.

Candace didn't look up. "Nonsense Elizabeth, you're thin. Besides, it is almost lunchtime." She put a large spoonful of omelet on my plate and handed it to me.

Michael brought the small cups of coffee and my glass of ice water out and set them on the table. "Mom, stop bullying Elizabeth." He turned to me and pointed to the small cup in front of me. "Let the coffee grounds settle to the bottom of the cup first."

She looked up from the platter of eggs. "Elizabeth, am I bullying you?"

I shook my head afraid to say anything else.

Looking smug she said, "See, I'm not bullying. Sit down, Michael."

Steve, who had been reading the paper, looked over the pages at her and he cleared his throat. "Candy."

A message, I couldn't quite decipher, went between his parents. Steve folded up his paper, bowed his head, and everyone followed his lead as he said the blessing. They all crossed themselves when he finished.

Grandmother Helen put a few of the sliced oranges on my plate then she drizzled a little of the honey over them. "Try this," she said. "It is one of Michael's favorites."

I took a bite of the orange with the honey. "The honey tastes of sage," I said surprised. "It's good. May I try the coffee now?" Everyone nodded, and I picked up the small cup. I took a small sip. The coffee was thick, sweet, and very strong. All eyes were on me. I smiled. "I like it."

Grandmother Helen patted my hand. "You would make a good Greek girl."

I guess I passed the coffee test. Everyone started eating, and the conversation began to flow more naturally.

"Tell us about the books that you write," Grandmother Helen said.

I looked at Michael.

"I already told them that you're a writer." He answered my unspoken question.

I nodded. "I write mystery romance novels. I've been writing them for the past seven years."

"You mean the books with the big handsome men on the covers?" Grandmother Helen asked, her eyes sparkling. I saw where Michael's eye color came from; she had the same sky-blue color.

I laughed. "Yes, those types of books."

"Tammy brought some of your books to the house so I could read them, but it's hard for me to see such little words. My grandchildren come by and read to me, but they get bored. Maybe you could come with Tammy, and we could read them together?" she suggested.

I squeezed her hand lightly, it was not frail, as I had expected. "Yes, I would like to do that if you would like me to come." I looked around the table, and I was surprised to see everyone very intent on our conversation. I felt like I was passing a series of tests.

It appeared Michael felt the same way, and he straightened up in his chair. "Mom and Dad were high school teachers before they retired. They live in Oakland."

"Oh! So was my sister Lisa. What did you teach?" I asked.

We spent the next half hour sharing information about both of our families. On his mother's side, he had two aunts and a multitude of cousins living in Calistoga. His father had two brothers and a sister living in Oakland. He had a huge family.

The mood was suddenly broken because the third test walked through the front door.

"Hello?" called several voices.

Before I could turn around, there were Michael's two aunts, his uncles, and assorted cousins standing in the family room. I suddenly felt very claustrophobic. At that moment, if the earth swallowed me, I would not have minded. We stood as everyone shook my hand. He slipped his arm around my waist and pulled me close to him. His body tensed as mine had. This encounter was not enjoyable for him either, and the worst was yet to come.

He tried to herd me toward the door after the introductions were completed. Grandmother Helen walked over to me and took my hand in hers. She looked me straight in the eyes. I didn't quite know what to expect. Her hand pulled me down toward her, and I knew she wanted to whisper something to me.

"You don't have any babies at home do you?" she asked very quietly. The whole room stopped jabbering, their attention focused on the two of us.

I shook my head softly. "No, Grandmother Helen, I don't."

"I see two babies for you." She said it solemnly as she squeezed my hand tightly and then let go.

I blinked and looked at her. "Okay," I said in a small voice.

There was a collective sigh around me, and it was if everyone started breathing again. I swear I almost heard bouzouki music playing in the background. I shook my head in disbelief because this was too surreal even for me.

Michael had a look on his face, and he knew he had to get me out quickly. He pulled me forward. "Mom, Grandma, thanks for breakfast. It was good seeing everyone. We really have to go." He kissed both of them. He continued to lead me to the door.

One of his aunts spoke up. "What? You're not staying for lunch? We just got here. We want to get to know Elizabeth more."

He looked firm, and we walked outside. "Sorry Aunt Tia, we have to go."

She called to him as everyone stood on the front porch. "Then come back for dinner. We'll barbeque some lamb."

He opened the door for me. While I put on my scarf, he called to them, "Some other time. I'll see you soon!" He waved and quickly backed the car out of the driveway.

Everyone stayed on the porch and waved madly at us. As we drove down the street, he started apologizing to me. "I am so sorry Elizabeth. I didn't expect this to happen."

When we were a couple of blocks down the road, I turned to him. "Pull over."

He slowed the Mustang down. "What?"

"Just pull over now." He did as I asked. I unbuckled the seat belt and got out of the car.

He tried reaching for me, but I was already out and standing under a nearby tree. I paced back and forth hugging myself with my arms. He left the car and walked over to me. Pulling my scarf off my head, I bunched it up in my hand. He stood next to me with his arms by his side.

With tears in my eyes, I blurted out with force, "Don't ever do that to me again!"

Michael again reached out, but I backed away from him. "Elizabeth, I'm sorry. We were only going to drive by my grandmother's house. She suggested breakfast, and I didn't see any harm in it. I thought it would be a nice surprise."

I kept pacing. "Here I am meeting your parents, dressed like this." I spread my arms out pointing to my clothes.

"I don't see anything wrong with what you're wearing. You look cute and sexy."

"That's just it. Sexy is not an outfit to wear to meet parents, especially your mother."

He touched my shoulder. "My mother doesn't care about what you wear."

"Then you don't have a clue about mothers." Even though I stood outside, the feeling of claustrophobia was still overwhelming. How did I explain to him how trapped I had felt? One of my biggest fears was the scrutiny I had just experienced and top it all off his grandmother had to express it aloud to everyone.

"Something else is bothering to you. You wouldn't be so upset about what you're wearing." He put his hands on my upper arms, his eyes searching my face. "What is it Elizabeth? Is it what my grandmother said to you?"

I looked down and nodded. He pulled me closer. "My grandmother is an old woman, and she likes to play the role of the psychic, besides she's actually accurate sometimes."

I looked up at Michael. I couldn't hold the tears, and they started streaming down my face. "Well, she isn't very accurate about me."

He put his arms around me completely. "What is it Elizabeth?" he repeated.

Pushing my face into his neck, I started sobbing. He held me tightly and let me cry.

"Tell me," he said softly.

I pulled back slightly and tilted my head up at him. His eyes were worried.

"I can't have babies!" I wept.

As soon as the words were out, my face pressed into his neck again, and my shoulders were shaking with the tears.

Rubbing my back, he tried to comfort me. "It's okay. Maybe she just meant your dogs. You have two of those, and you treat them like babies."

I sniffed and said slowly into his neck, "Do you think so?"

"It's got to be that. Remember if my grandmother was right all the time, she'd be living in a much bigger house," he reasoned logically.

I giggled and nodded my head.

He tilted my head up. His eyes still showed concern. "Do you want me to take you home?"

I thought for a moment and then shook my head. "No. I want to spend the day with you."

He smiled. "I want that too. Can we put this behind us?"

"Promise never to spring a surprise like this on me?"

Michael chuckled. "Yes, I promise where my family is involved never, ever to do that again. They even scared me. Believe me?"

I nodded. "Okay." He helped me back to the car. "So you're Greek?" I asked.

He laughed as he got into the driver's seat. "Yes, but only half. I'm half-German too. If you thought the Greek's were crazy, wait until you meet the Germans!"

We were quiet as we headed toward Napa. The sun was bright, but with the wind hitting us it wasn't too hot yet. I turned in my seat to face him and didn't speak but watched him drive. His intentions had to be innocent with this morning's breakfast fiasco. I was completely familiar with the realm of crazy families. My family was nuts in its own way. As Nancy had told me after my divorce, "Normal is only a setting on the washer."

I studied his profile while he drove. His hair was getting a little longer than when I had first met him. He had wisps of curls barely over his ears and down around his collar. I wondered aloud what his family thought of the earring.

Michael looked over at me. "What did you say?"

"What does your family think of your earring?"

"Oh that," he said, "I've worn it so long I don't think they even notice it anymore. I had my ear pierced in college. There was some discussion when I first came home with the earring, but my grandmother Helen loved it. My grandfather thought it meant I was gay. My parents are liberal. We lived in Berkeley when we were young, so it blew over. What didn't blow over was my divorce."

"Catholic?" I asked.

"Greek Orthodox," he answered.

"The same here. I left Kevin shortly before my mom became sick, and even though they didn't like him, my parents weren't happy."

"Catholic?" he asked.

"Yeah. Of course, it didn't help that my sister had the perfect marriage."

"That's where I had it easier. Christina took the brunt of the criticism because her divorce was first. She didn't have children though. Man, did I hear that one over and over again." He shook his head.

He reached for my left hand almost as if he was testing the waters. I smiled as he gave me a squeeze and pulled it over to his leg. He was watching the road ahead and absently playing with my fingers, interlacing his with mine. This act alone started my heart pumping faster, and with my hand placed on his thigh, I thought I would pass out. I have a thing for male thighs. I don't know, maybe it all started with the baseball uniforms. There's nothing like a guy in baseball pants.

I finally moved my hand up to his curls. I tucked them behind his ear and then left my hand resting on his shoulder. This was better and far less dangerous for my hand because if I left my hand on his thigh, I knew for sure it would have a mind of its own. The game did not end there. He moved his right hand down and rested it on my bended knees. My eyes did not leave his profile, and Michael only concentrated on the road ahead.

He eventually turned and asked, "A penny for your thoughts."

I laughed. "Oh, I don't think I'm going to share what I was thinking with you."

He smiled. "This has to be good. What were you thinking?"

"No." I shook my head. "Not gonna tell."

Rubbing my knee, he moved his hand up my thigh. "Come on. I think it's really bad if you won't tell me."

I laughed again and squirmed away. "That's right. It is really bad." I blushed and knew that there was no way I was going to verbalize the scene that was happening in my mind involving him and no clothes. "Hey, isn't this our exit?"

"Don't change the subject." He flipped on the signal light and exited from the freeway.

The first winery we visited was very close to the freeway. After he pulled into the parking lot, he helped me out of the car and pressed me gently against it. His arms wrapped around me and he leaned in to kiss me.

"You know, you and I were probably thinking the same thing." His mouth lingered at my lips.

I smiled and gazed into his sparkling eyes. "Mine was probably better." I giggled.

He kissed me again quickly. "If you won't tell, I guess we'll never know." He let me go and took my hand to lead me to the door of the winery.

Something between us had been changing. I noticed it for the first time today. He held my hand when we walked, and he pulled me closer. There were times when we would simply look at each other in silence. I felt a comfort level with him and knew he shared it with me. Most importantly, I had stopped blushing every time he spoke or looked at me.

After the third winery, I began to feel the effects of the wine. Michael had tasted the wine and spat out the samples, which was the proper way. I thought that method was a waste of good wine. He knew far more about it than I did. He showed me how to taste the wine by rolling it in my mouth, observing the color, and sniffing it in the glass. Still, he could not get me to spit it into the bucket. We had several cases in the trunk and on the back seat, all his purchases.

At the fifth winery, Michael helped me into the car. I was giggling and finding everything quite amusing. Sitting in the driver's seat, he looked at me and raised an eyebrow. I simply sat there with a big grin on my face.

"I think I need to get you home," he declared.

I giggled again. "Okay."

I leaned back against the seat and waved my red scarf around. He rolled his eyes.

"Hopefully the drive home will sober you up." He laughed.

I giggled and wrapped my scarf around my head as he started the car. Putting my head back, I was fast asleep before we were on the freeway. I awoke shortly before we arrived home.

"I must have fallen asleep. Sorry."

He laughed. "You snore."

I protested, "I don't!" Then I blushed. "Do I?"

Michael kept laughing. "Buzz-saw city."

"I'm sorry. I didn't realize how tired I was," I said.

"Don't apologize. You're cute when you sleep."

Straightening myself out, I sat up. "We're almost home?"

He nodded. "The Giants and Dodgers are playing tonight. Do you want to watch it together?"

"Real cross-state rivalry. You know I bleed Dodger Blue."

He chuckled. "Somehow I am not surprised. We'll watch it at your place."

"Okay. Want to invite the girls?" I asked.

"No." He answered with firmness in his voice. "They are not invited. Besides its Saturday night, they're probably going out." He pulled up in front of my house. "I'll take my car home, and I'll be back shortly."

I got out of the car. "Don't you need help carrying the wine in?"

"No. I got it. I want to garage the Mustang."

I greeted the dogs, and quickly took a shower. I didn't wash my hair but wanted to get the road dirt off me. I pulled on a pair of shorts and a tank top. When I came out of my bedroom, Michael was already in the kitchen. He changed clothes too, wearing a pair of blue jeans and a t-shirt. Even with a loose pair of jeans on, he still had the best-looking butt. I saw his shoes by the back door, and that meant he was barefooted.

Leaning over him I asked, "What are you doing?"

He straightened up, pulling a few containers out of the refrigerator.

"I'm trying to put some dinner together for us. Aren't you hungry?"

"I'm starved. There should be some left-over's from the bonfire."

"I think I have everything we need." He had brought over several ingredients from his house. He handed me a brick of cheese. "Here, cut this up in small chunks please."

I pulled a knife and cutting board out from the drawer. "How big do you want the chunks?"

"Dice sized," he answered. "Tammy told me she fed the dogs about an hour ago."

"Yeah, I figured. They weren't dancing around me for food. Was she home?"

He started washing small grape tomatoes in the sink and put them in a bowl.

"Yeah. She wanted to come over, and I said no."

"Oh Michael, you didn't?"

"Yes, I told her we wanted to be alone." He put the cheese chunks in the bowl with the tomatoes.

"What did she say?" I blushed again.

He laughed as he sprinkled balsamic vinegar and olive oil over the tomatoes and cheese. "I told her we were going to make out and that she would probably get bored watching us."

"Oh great." I rolled my eyes. Now my blush was in full force. "I told her last week nothing was going on between us."

Wrapping his arm around my waist, he kissed me. "So far nothing has."

He opened the container of pasta salad from the dinner last night. After a quick bite of the salad, he added it to the tomatoes and cheese mixture. Then, he threw black and green olives, cut up mushrooms, and a jar of artichoke hearts into the mix. Next, he added some garlic, onions, and ground some pepper over the top. Michael took a big spoon and offered me a taste. The combination of flavors was delicious.

"Yum," I murmured.

He opened one of the bottles of wine he had purchased today. I pulled two glasses out of the cupboard, and he sliced up a loaf of French bread.

"Can we eat on the couch?" he asked.

"Absolutely," I answered, already carrying the food over to the couch table and turning the television on. The baseball game had not started yet.

He sat on the middle section of the couch, and I sat in the corner. He poured us both a glass of wine, and he handed mine to me.

He held his glass up and looked at me. "To us."

"To us," I said, as we toasted.

The wine was one we had tasted earlier in the afternoon. It tasted of wild berries with a hint of orange. After our tours, I appreciated the flavors even more.

When we finished eating, I leaned back into the corner of the couch. Michael lifted my legs and laid them across his lap. The game was boring, and the Dodgers were losing. Far more interesting were his hands moving up my legs. He started nonchalantly tracing circles softly on my knees and proceeded to travel slowly up my thighs until he reached the bottom hem of my shorts.

He leaned over me to turn off the lamp. The room was dark with just the glow of the television.

I looked at him. "You weren't kidding, were you? We really are going to make out?"

He chuckled low and cleared his throat. "Those were my plans. I usually make smoother moves and don't announce it in advance."

I moved my arms up around his shoulders. "Oh, you're plenty smooth enough for me."

Michael did not answer. Fortunately, the big couch accommodated us both when he stretched out next to me. While his arm wrapped around me, he traced the line of my jaw with his other hand. Touching my mouth softly with his lips, he delved into mine, and I could taste the wine we had shared. While our kisses explored, his hands were on their own expedition around my body. His large hands gently kneaded my hips and waist and awakened a deeply buried passion in me. A well-hidden excitement inside of me I had not felt in a long time started to grow. If his kisses could elicit these types of responses from my body, I could only imagine what it would be like when his hands actually touched naked skin. I expected him to pull back after we kissed. Instead, his lips trailed to my neck, and then they went lower on my chest. His mouth stopped slightly above where my tank top started. He raised his head and looked at me. His free hand moved under the bottom of the tank, and he touched my bare stomach.

I breathed in. I wanted him to go higher, and I wanted him to go lower. There were also those parts of me that said no and stop. My body tensed, and he felt the change. He looked up at me with questioning eyes.

"Too much?" he asked.

I nodded. "I'm sorry Michael. Things are just moving kind of fast."

He removed his hand from under my top and laid it around my waist. He smiled at me. "You know that wasn't my intention, you are hard to resist."

"You are too. You're not going to leave, are you?"

I did not want to know the answer because I was so sure he would answer yes. Disappointment started to fill me. Once again, I had messed up a good thing by being cautious.

"Do you want me to?" he asked.

My eyes grew big, and I could not believe that tears were forming my eyes. I closed them, and I shook my head. "No. But…" I trailed off opening my eyes again.

Michael laughed. "Oh, Elizabeth." He sat up and pulled me up into his lap. "I'm not going anywhere." His smile was inviting and warm, and not the least bit angry. "At least not right now, later I'll have to go home and take a cold shower."

I whispered into his neck, "I'm sorry."

He bent to kiss me again. "I don't want to rush you. When you're ready, you'll let me know."

CHAPTER ELEVEN

I had drawn the line, and Michael did not attempt to cross it again. We sat on the couch watching the game and kissing, but it was all tame in comparison to the earlier event. He left me with a goodnight kiss after we cleaned the kitchen and a promise that we would go to the baseball game together the next afternoon. I lay in bed Sunday morning long after I awoke. I wasn't interested in my usual coffee. There I was just staring at the ceiling, thinking.

He confused me and at the same time excited me. He was a man that would not deter easily. I knew this, and yet I still didn't know why he was so attracted to me. I was certainly attracted to him. He was handsome, intelligent, caring, fun to be with, and definitely sexy. I giggled aloud at that thought. There were no bad sides, or at least none had seen the light of day. What was it that I offered him?

I was so boring. I waited for life to come to me and rarely chased after it. Michael, on the other hand, seemed to pursue life, capturing the excitement with every step he took. I was simply a writer, living vicariously through my characters.

I sighed and spoke aloud, "Even they have more exciting lives than I do."

Samantha, after hearing my voice, rose from her spot and laid on my stomach. I petted her soft head. "Mommy is feeling sorry for herself, isn't she? Are you both hungry for breakfast?" I pulled myself together and threw back the covers. The dogs happily followed me into the kitchen.

While I made coffee the phone rang, and I wasn't surprised to hear Nancy's voice on the other end. I had been neglecting my writing, and she yelled at me for a few moments. She was far too interested however in what had transpired yesterday between Michael and me.

"Girl, he has it bad for you. I'm surprised he didn't rip off your clothes and have his way with you," Nancy teased me.

"You know I've never been one for casual sex, and I'm not going to start now," I retorted.

She laughed, her voice was low and easy. "How long are you planning on dragging this out? The poor man, how many showers are you going to force on him."

"Nancy," I said, my voice taking a serious tone, "all kidding aside, I know he is interested in me, I'm just not sure why. I don't want to get into a relationship with someone only for sex, because I'm not looking for that in my life. It wouldn't be fair to him or to me."

"Then Elizabeth, what is it that you want? It certainly isn't fair for you to string him along."

"Do you think I'm doing that? We've only known each other a few weeks," I asked worriedly.

"Girl, this is not one of your romance novels, this is your life. You need to figure out what you want, and when you've decided, then you need to figure out if he fits into the plan." Even though Nancy was younger than me, she started to sound like my mother. "Michael obviously likes you. Look, he introduced you to his grandmother. What man does that? I say go for it."

I paused so long that she had to ask if I was still on the line. "I'm here. I think I'm afraid, you know of being hurt all over again."

She snorted, "Well my dear, welcome to the club. None of us wants to be hurt, ever. Nevertheless, how are you going to enjoy the mountains if you have never been in the valleys? Hurt is intrinsic to relationships. Of course, you can be stupid and marry someone like Kevin the wonder boy."

"Exactly my point, I don't want to make another mistake like him."

She laughed. "Oh, I doubt you will. He is one in a million. You just got lucky."

"Some luck," I whispered.

I had plenty to think about after our conversation. I sat at my desk and started on my book. A commotion outside drew my attention. Michael and the two girls were playing with a Frisbee. When one of them missed it, their dogs were on the scene to pick it up and run.

Their laughter was contagious, and I found myself laughing with them. I walked out to the porch. All three of them saw me at once. My dogs went bounding down the steps to join them, and I followed.

"Catch Elizabeth!" Michael snatched the Frisbee out of Tammy's hands and threw it at me.

I caught it with one hand.

Tammy yelled, "No fair Dad! Throw it to me Elizabeth! Dad and Katy are cheating!"

I laughed and looked at each one of them. "I don't think so! It's mine now." I shielded the Frisbee. Michael and Katy ran toward me, and I quickly threw it to Tammy. They rapidly turned and ran toward her. She threw it back to me.

Michael jumped up and caught it in the air. He was so close to me as he came down he pulled me with him. We lay there in a heap with our dogs surrounding us. He breathed heavily from the exertion as he waved the Frisbee up in the air.

"I win!" he shouted victoriously. He was back on his feet and pulled me to my feet in two fluid movements. Putting his arm around my waist, he planted a kiss on my forehead. "Thanks for helping!"

I was a little surprised that he did not kiss me on the lips, but I shrugged it off. "I wasn't trying to help you win!"

Michael laughed. "It's all the same!" He did a little victory dance. "Have you had breakfast?" When I shook my head, he said, "Come and join us. I made quiche, and we've got some strawberries that Katy bought yesterday while she was out with her friends."

The table was already set for four. Someone had planned to invite me. The idea comforted me.

"What can I do?" I asked looking for a task.

Michael quickly replied. "Sit."

The three moved around me like a well-oiled machine. They had performed this drill many times before and were well used to their roles. The table reminded me of the setting at Grandmother Helen's house. Plain yogurt and preserves were on the table. Tammy added the baguette and cheese to the table, and she sat next to me. Bringing in the strawberries, Katy sat opposite to me. He brought the quiche to the table and sat between Katy and me. This time when he gave the blessing over the food I was waiting for it. He took my plate and put a big portion of quiche in the middle.

"Way too much," I said.

Tammy poked me in the ribs. "Wait until you taste it, it is really good."

I took a bite. I could not believe the taste. The quiche was a wonderful blend of different types of cheeses with broccoli, spinach, onions, and roasted peppers.

"Oh my gosh!" I exclaimed with another bite in my mouth. "This is incredible!"

Michael smiled, and Tammy whispered, "See I told you. Dad is a fantastic cook."

His face had a slight blush. "It was out of necessity," he said humbly. He continued to heap quiche on the remaining plates.

"You're not kidding on that one," Katy replied matter-of-factly. "Mom is a terrible cook. Her idea of cooking was a frozen dinner for us and then she would eat out."

"It isn't that bad Katy," he objected.

So, his ex-wife did not cook either, at least we were even on that score. I smiled to myself, and he caught my grin. He looked puzzled but let it pass.

We continued the brunch with a lively conversation around the table.

Afterward, both Katy and Tammy begged off the dishes, and they left the house. We carried everything into the kitchen, and I helped him load the dishwasher.

Michael turned to me as he put the last dish in the washer. "Would you do a favor for me Elizabeth?"

"What?" I asked.

"I'm going to Louisiana tomorrow to start a job. It's been planned for a while," he explained.

"Oh? What's in Louisiana?" I asked. This was the first time I had heard about an assignment in another state, but his work had not been an extensive topic of conversation for us.

"Alligators," he said giving me a broad grin.

My eyes widened. "You're going to photograph alligators?"

He laughed quietly, closing the dishwasher door and pressing the buttons to start the cycle. "Yep. National Geographic is doing a special photo expose' on Louisiana, you know, after Hurricane Katrina. There is a biologist who is trying to rebuild some of their habitats in the bayou."

I laughed too. "So you want to know what shoe size I wear?"

He chuckled. "Elizabeth, shame on you! No, I want you to keep an eye on the girls."

"Oh, you mean to spy on them for you?" I joked.

"No, well, yes. No, I mean no. I don't want you to spy on them. I want to make sure everything runs smoothly in the house, with Jason and the other boys. So there are no wild parties going on."

"Don't you trust them?" I asked raising my eyebrows.

"Of course I trust them. I just want to make sure there is a mature adult around in case they have problems."

"Gee, what a compliment Michael. A mature adult."

He grabbed me around the waist. "You know what I meant. Stop giving me such a hard time."

I laughed and expected him to kiss me. When he did not, and he just released me, it made me pause.

"Well," I said, "I need to get home and prepare myself for the baseball game. What time do you want to go?"

"Yeah, about the game today." He broke off for a second. "We can drive together, but I'm coming back to the house right after the game. I need to pack and get my gear together. I'm meeting up with a new assistant, and I want to have everything ready to go. Do you think you can get a ride home with Debi and Don?"

My heart sank. I knew it. Michael was rejecting me. I would not sleep with him, and now he was not interested in me anymore. I wanted to cry, but I held back the tears.

"Oh, okay. Well, come by and let me know when you're ready to go."

"Okay." He picked up the newspaper from the kitchen table, and we both walked to his back porch. Topper and Samantha followed me down the steps while he stuffed the paper into the trashcan. "I'll see you in a little bit."

I did not turn around. I was afraid that he would see the tears running down my cheeks. Two days in a row, I had cried over him, and I was more confused than ever now. The more I told myself not to think about it the more I did.

I went straight to my bedroom. Laying down on my bed with the dogs snuggling up to me, I held my pillows tightly and cried.

Time went by, and I knew that I had to get up and put my uniform on. I did not want to play baseball, and I was in no mood to see anyone. Dreading the ride over to the park, I hoped there wouldn't be an uncomfortable silence. I thought about taking my own car and almost called him.

My eyes were puffy from crying and holding a cold, wet washcloth against them did nothing to alleviate the puffiness. I sighed and resigned myself to wearing my sunglasses until the game started. No one would really be able to see me when I was on the mound.

Michael knocked on the door, and I grabbed my stuff. I opened the door with full hands and no chance to put my sunglasses on. He was standing in front of me, and I knew he saw the appearance of my eyes.

"Are you okay?" He hesitated and then softly touched my cheek. He quickly removed his hand as if he had done something wrong.

I cleared my throat and swallowed. "Yeah. Fine."

Not wanting to fabricate a story, I offered no further explanation. He moved out of my way when I walked toward him. I slipped my sunglasses on and waited at the car for him to open door. Michael slid into the driver's side and started the engine. Anything was better than sitting in the car in silence.

I poked my brain for something to say. "Did you get started on your packing?"

He nodded as he moved out into the traffic. "Yeah, I'm leaving at about seven tomorrow morning, and there is always a lot of preparation before a shoot. I'm working with a new assistant from the university, so I'll be breaking him in too. My biologist friend sent me a ton of informational material discussing the new habitats. Tonight I'll be doing a lot reading about alligators and their behavior, so I know what to expect."

"How long are you going to be gone?" I tried to keep the emotion that was building in me out of my voice."

"I should be back late Thursday."

"You know I'm taking Tammy to the doctor on Wednesday."

"I really appreciate your helping Tammy. I don't know if I could do it."

"It's not something she should do alone, at least the first time. I don't mind." Thinking to myself that it was more important to go photograph some stupid alligators than go to the doctor with your daughter. I inwardly huffed to myself.

Michael let the conversation drop, and we drove in silence after all. When we arrived at the park, I looked for Don since I needed to warm up my arm.

He started throwing the ball to me. "Hey, Miss movie star, are you going to take your sunglasses off?"

I had not forgotten that I was wearing them. I put them in my bag and knew immediately that he could see my puffy eyes. His face changed to concern, and his arm slipped around my shoulders.

"There is something major wrong Elizabeth, what is it?" he commented.

"Nothing." I choked back a sob.

"Do you want me to get Debi?" He led me to a bench, and we sat down.

"No. I'll be alright." I was going to lose it quickly if the questions continued.

"Is it Kevin?"

I shook my head. "No. Really, I'll be okay." I tried sniffing back a tear.

"I'm going to find Debi." He stood up before I had a chance to object and strode off looking for his wife. Poor Don, he never did well when I cried. Well, whenever anyone cried. I sat on the bench waiting and was glad the park was not full of people.

"Hey, darling." Debi came up behind me and put her arms around me. "Don told me you're in a world of hurt." She took one look at my face. "Oh damn, what has Kevin done now?"

I shook my head and started crying. "It's not him."

"Well, those are man tears," she said and then paused, "Michael? Debi asked slowly, "What happened?"

I explained his change in attitude toward me. She looked as perplexed as I felt.

"I don't get it Elizabeth, you two were quite cozy Friday night at the bonfire."

"And we had a great day yesterday and last night, even after I put the brakes on the make-out session. He is just not interested in me anymore because I won't sleep with him. So I guess that's all he wanted."

She took my hand in hers. "I just can't believe this. I don't know Michael as well as you, but he doesn't seem the type. Especially with all the women around here after him. Did you see his fan club is here again? If all he wanted was to sleep with someone, there are plenty of women to take him up on that offer."

I turned to face her. "What other explanation is there? He's turning a cold shoulder to me, and he'll pursue someone else." My tears were coming faster. "Could you take me home right after the game? I don't want to drive home with him."

"Sure. Let me get Don so you can warm up. Wear your sunglasses, and no one will suspect you've been crying."

The game was horrible. I avoided Michael as much as I could, and both Debi and Angel huddled around me when we were in the dugout. My pitching was terrible, and Lewis made several trips out to the mound to talk with me. Finally, I told him that I was not feeling well, and he replaced me with Angel.

At last, Debi drove me home.

"Did you tell Don why we were leaving?" I asked.

She nodded her head. "Yes. Let me warn you he didn't look happy."

Shock registered in my voice, and I turned to look at her. "He wouldn't say anything to Michael, would he?"

"You know he would do just about anything to right a wrong if it concerned you. Both of us would."

I turned back in my seat and was quiet the rest of the way home. Once inside and alone, I undressed and climbed into bed. Sleep took me quickly. The knocking on the front door and the dogs barking woke me up. The clock showed 5:30. The only person who would knock on the front door would be Michael, everyone else would be at the back door.

There was no way I was prepared to face him. I lay in bed until he walked back down the front porch. The phone rang not more than 5 minutes later. My answering machine could take that one too. I heard his voice over the speaker wanting to know if I was okay. No, I was not okay, and I did not want to talk about it either.

I moved into the living room and plopped down in front of the television. I wasn't in the mood to write. After two movies, I fell asleep on the couch and woke to a dark house. I switched on a light, and the clock showed two a.m. The answering machine was still blinking from the message he had left earlier in the evening.

Entering my bedroom, I looked out the window. Michael's bedroom light was on. It was strange for him to be up so late and I had the immediate urge to call him. Truthfully, I was growing angry about the whole episode. I had enough of the misery and thought we should get it out in the open.

My fingers were dialing his cell number before I thought clearly about what I was doing. The phone rang a few times before he picked up.

He answered with worry in his voice, "Elizabeth, are you okay?"

Why did everyone keep asking me if I was okay? No, I was not okay. I was tired of answering that question.

"Why are you up so late?" I asked abruptly.

"What?" he asked with surprise in his voice. "How did you know I was up?"

"Your bedroom light is on," I answered. "I can see it from my bedroom window."

"Why aren't you asleep?" he asked me.

"Never mind about me. Please come over here. I want to talk to you."

He hesitated. "Why do you want to talk?"

"I don't want to talk over the phone. Please just come over here."

Michael sighed, his voice sounded tired. "Why don't you come over here Elizabeth? I'll make us some tea."

"Okay, I will come over to you." It surprised me how determined my voice sounded.

"I'll wait on the porch for you."

I threw on a robe over my nightgown. By the time I opened my back door, he had his porch light on, and I could see him leaning against the railing. He looked surprised to see me in my robe. He followed me silently into his kitchen. A kettle was already heating on the stove.

Sitting at his kitchen table, I watched him prepare the tea. He wore only sweat pants in that sexy way he had. Molly padded into the kitchen and lay down next to my feet. Her long tail thumped against my legs. I bent over and petted her head. It was deadly silent in the kitchen.

He finally set the mug of hot tea in front of me and took a seat on the other side of the table crossing his arms over his naked chest. "Let the tea cool down first."

I nodded. He looked at me expectantly.

"Why the change Michael, or are you just mad at me because I won't sleep with you?"

He grimaced at me across the table. "Is that what has been upsetting you today?"

I could see evidence of a slight smile on his face as he looked at the ceiling lights shaking his head in disbelief.

"Yes," I replied. "What is so funny? I don't think this is very funny."

He sighed. "No, it's not funny, but it is a comedy of errors." He stood and took my hand. "Here, come with me."

I stood up and followed him. "Why? Where are we going?"

He flipped the kitchen lights off. "My bedroom. We need to talk, and I don't want the girls listening in."

"Well, I don't think we need to talk in your bedroom. I'm quiet."

"The girls are very nosey when it comes to us." Michael led me into his bedroom. The room was messy with clothes, papers, and his laptop strewn on the bed. A suitcase sat open in the corner on a small table. Beyond the table, a door leading to another room was open. Max, his other dog, was lying on the folded bedspread at the end of the bed and Molly joined him as we entered. He closed the door behind us.

Turning to me as I leaned back against the wall, his hands cupped the sides of my face, and he tilted my face up. His thumbs rubbed across my cheeks and up underneath my eyes.

"Promise me that before I make you cry again, you'll always talk to me first." His voice was softer than a whisper. "I'm sorry, I thought I was doing the right thing."

His lips found mine, and he gently kissed me. One arm went around my waist as he pulled me closer. He held the back of my head, and our kiss intensified while his fingers stroked my hair. His back felt strong against my hands when I tightly embraced him.

The kiss broke, and we stood wrapped securely together not wanting to part. His eyes burned as he looked at me.

"Elizabeth, you know I want to make love with you." I started to interrupt, but he continued, "However, I know I have to wait. I don't want to force you to do anything you're not ready to do, and I thought I needed to step back to give you some breathing room. It looks like I stepped back too far."

"Is that all it was?" I searched his face for some other sign.

"That's all it was," he confirmed.

"I'm glad." I snuggled my head against his shoulder and neck. As I kissed his inviting neck and trailed my lips up to his jawline, I felt him shudder in my arms.

Michael cleared his throat. "Babe, I need to get ready for my trip. Seven o'clock is going to come early."

I stepped back nodding my head. "I'm sorry."

He tilted up my face. "Don't be sorry. I love kissing you. Do you want to stay with me and keep me company while I get ready?"

"Okay," I murmured.

With quick movements, he cleared off half of the bed. I slipped off my slippers and sat cross-legged on the bed. His laptop displayed an article on alligators. While he packed his suitcase, I turned over on my side to watch. Pulling out a pillow from the top of the bed, I snuggled into it and closed my eyes.

When I awoke, the room was dark. It took me a minute to realize I was still in Michael's bedroom. He had pulled the bedspread up to cover us. He lay sleeping on his back next to me. I pushed the pillow away and cuddled close to him, laying my head on his chest. Turning toward me, I felt him kiss the top of my head, as he wrapped me in his arms.

When I awoke again light filled the room. I was alone in bed. The house was quiet. The nightstand clock showed eight o'clock. A folded note lay next to me on the pillow.

"Babe, I couldn't bear to wake you this morning. I'll call you when I get to New

Orleans. Please keep an eye on my girls. Michael. P.S. Thank you for staying with me last night. We should do it more often!"

I refolded and tucked the note into the pocket of my robe. I made the bed and noticed the door at the end of the bedroom was still open. Curious about the room behind the door, I peeked around the corner and found a small room with a desk, a light table, and bookshelves. It was Michael's office. Did he leave the door open on purpose? Was it okay for me to go inside the room? I was nosey but stood at the edge of the doorway a little afraid to cross the threshold. The window was covered with a black shade that would block out all the light if needed. The desk was neat, but when I turned to look at the light table, I saw the photographs he had taken of the girls and me over the past three weeks covering the entire work surface. It was touching that he had them printed. On the bookshelves lay three worn copies of my books. I grinned and wondered if he'd read them.

The sight of the room and the photographs comforted me. Not wishing to intrude into his privacy any further, I opened the bedroom door quietly listening for sounds within the house.

Tammy was in the kitchen eating cereal. I didn't see her at first but heard her voice instead. "Good morning Elizabeth." Her tone was slightly disapproving.

Her voice had startled me. "Oh, hi. I didn't think you were up."

"I usually try to get up with Dad when he's going on a trip. I like to say goodbye to him. There's some coffee left, Dad made it for you." She pointed to the coffee maker. "The mugs are in the cupboard above." She didn't make a move to get one for me.

I crossed into the kitchen. Both dogs were under the table wagging their tails when they saw me. I poured myself a cup. Luckily, I liked it black because she was not volunteering any additional instructions.

I sat next to her. She found her cereal bowl interesting and did not look up at me. I touched her shoulder. "Tammy what's wrong."

After a pause, she looked up at me with disappointment in her eyes. "So you and Dad had a sleepover. You told me nothing was going on between the two of you. You lied to me."

My brow knitted because I was not expecting her pouty reaction. I would have thought she would be happy to see her dad and me together. "No, we did not have a sleepover, not in the way you think we did."

Her look was incredulous. "Why should I believe you, because you didn't believe me?"

"You know I believe you." How did I get myself into this type of conversation? Better yet, how was I going to get myself out of the discussion?

"You're only going to hurt him like his other girlfriends." As she said the words, the real reason for her anger became clear.

"It's not my intention to hurt your dad. For goodness sake, Tammy, your dad and I are just friends." I had not yet concentrated on her use of the word girlfriends in the plural. This would probably strike me later on in the day. "Instead of talking to me about this, shouldn't you talk to your dad about it?"

"I tried," she replied. "But he told me that it wasn't any of my business and to stay out of it."

I thought, how typical of a man. What a way with words he had.

"It appears your dad and I will be more than casual friends. I don't have a crystal ball, and I don't know how this will end or what will happen. I'm hoping that it will turn out well, but let's face it, your dad and I don't have good track records. Both of us have been divorced, so that means we aren't very good in the relationship department, but we're trying. If your dad wants to share, it's up to him. He does deserve his privacy as do I, and so do you. So, I hope you allow us to stumble around making whatever mistakes we make without your input." I swallowed down the remaining coffee and rose from the chair.

Tammy stared up at me with a look of surprise on her face. "Okay." She said quietly. I walked to the back door, and she called out to me. "Are you still taking me to the doctor on Wednesday?"

I turned around before opening the door. "Absolutely." I smiled at her and then walked out to the back porch closing the door behind me.

As I turned around to go down the steps, Debi drove by with her car. When she saw me, she pulled up by my house and climbed out of her car to wait for me. Rolling my eyes, I couldn't believe my good fortune. My day was getting better and better.

CHAPTER TWELVE

She followed me up to the back door. "That's an interesting jogging outfit you're wearing this morning Elizabeth. Or is it the walk of shame you're doing?"

"Shut up Debi. Come in and make some coffee while I feed the dogs. I'll fill you in."

She knew her way around my kitchen. She started the coffee maker while I prepared breakfast for the dogs. As the dogs ate, we sat down and drank our coffee.

"You look a lot better than you did yesterday," she said.

"I took your advice. I talked to Michael." I drew little circles on the table with my fingers and then looked up at her. "You were right. It was a misunderstanding."

"So, I conclude by your attractive outfit this morning you finally gave it up?" She smirked at me.

I shook my head. "Why does everyone assume that we've had sex?"

Debi looked with wide eyes. "Who do you mean by everyone?"

Laughing, I told her about my conversation with Tammy.

She took my hand. "I think Mr. Don can top that one."

"What do you mean?" I asked suspiciously.

It would be just like Don to get involved in my private life. He had been rescuing me forever, and of course, he wasn't always successful, evidenced by Kevin.

She hesitated, then laughed, knowing that somehow it was well intended. "Well, after the game he told Michael he would do him great bodily harm if he hurt you."

I laughed loudly. "Michael must have laughed at that threat. He's at least six inches taller than Don and probably has fifty pounds on him."

Debi laughed with me. "Hey, my Donny is scrappy!"

"I know. I love him too because of that character trait. I hope he doesn't have to follow up on his warning."

"You and me both." She chuckled.

We spent the next two hours talking like the two old friends we were. We poured over the note Michael had written to me and analyzed every word. We laughed and admitted we were terribly silly. Debi had always accepted me the way I was with no pretense. She made me promise to come for dinner, and since I was responsible for the girls, I was supposed to bring them with me.

When I arrived at their house, Tammy was in the kitchen baking cookies. The kitchen looked like it had exploded in flour with baking pans scattered from one end to the other. She smiled and seemed to be in a better mood than this morning.

She stood by the stove with bright red oven mitts on. "Hi Elizabeth, cookies will be ready soon. Would you let Katy know."

I smiled. "The cookies smell delicious. We're supposed to go over to Debi and Don's for dinner this evening." I silently hoped that the kitchen would be clean before Michael came home on Thursday, but I had my doubts.

"Yeah, Jason called to let me know about dinner."

"Have you heard from your dad?" I asked trying to keep the emotion out of my voice.

Tammy nodded her head. "Yeah, about an hour ago. He said he arrived safely and was on his way out to start shooting the alligators."

I looked at her and then she laughed, teasing me, "But you know only taking their pictures, not killing them!"

I chuckled and nodded my head as I left the kitchen. "Yeah, yeah."

The answering machine did not have a blinking light when I walked into my kitchen. Disappointment hit me immediately since Michael had already called Tammy. His note said he would call. What would it take to stop me from worrying? The answer was simple. All it would take was a call.

I changed into shorts and a t-shirt and called the dogs. Needing to burn off the excess energy, I decided on a run. Normally it was not my routine to run so late in the afternoon, but it had been a cool day for September. Being too close to the phone was driving me crazy. Still, there was no message when we returned home, and after my shower, I rechecked the machine.

The phone rang suddenly as I was dressing. I nervously picked up the receiver. It was Tammy letting me know it was time for dinner. I hung up the phone and frowned. I was not going to be able to take much more.

Arriving back home after dinner I was again disappointed to see that Michael hadn't called. Maybe he forgot I told myself. It was already midnight in Louisiana, and I knew the call would not be coming tonight. I threw on a t-shirt after undressing for bed. The dogs were already in their places.

I turned off the light and slipped under the covers. Topper crawled his way up to me to snuggle. As I petted the top of his head, we were both jarred with the ringing of the phone. My heart jumped into my throat when I answered the phone.

"Hey, Babe." Michael's voice was clear, but he sounded tired. "Are you in bed?"

I cleared my throat and tried to put my heart back into its proper place. "Yeah, I just got home from dinner."

"I figured. Tammy called me to let me know that both she and Katy were tucked in safely."

"So you arrived safely?"

"Yeah, I went right to work." A noise on the other end of the line sounded like he was situating himself in bed. "I wanted to call you before you went to bed so you'll dream of me tonight."

The comment made me laugh. "Hey, the next time you leave in the morning, make sure you wake me up, I wanted to say goodbye to you."

"So you're promising there will be a next time?" His voice sounded dreamy and smooth, and it made lower parts of my body react to him.

I giggled and turned over on my side. "There is an excellent possibility of that happening." I paused for a moment and then continued. "I peeked in your office this morning."

"Did you see anything you liked?" he asked.

"Yeah, I was surprised to see my books on your bookshelves. Have you read them?"

"Of course I read them."

"And?" I asked.

"They told me a lot about you."

"You think so?"

Michael paused thoughtfully. "Yes. Jessica has a lot of you in her. Not everything, but I could see the similarities. The erotic parts were great too."

I laughed. "Oh, you liked the sex? You didn't think it was too over the top or too much fantasy?"

He laughed with me. "No, I thought it was all doable. That is why I can see us together. You created the stuff in your books."

I was quiet. "Well, that doesn't mean I've done all the stuff that's in my book. My editor prompts me on some of it."

He chuckled. "Then with the next book, you can tell the editor you're writing from experience."

I could feel the blush immediately on my face. I had no comeback for that comment.

"You're blushing aren't you?" he asked.

"You can tell over the phone?"

"Not too difficult to tell."

I filled him in about the day's events with the girls, including the conversation I had with Tammy early in the morning.

"She told me about it too." He added, "I told her that my relationship with you was none of her business and that she needed to stay out of it."

"That's kind of harsh don't you think?'

"Sometimes with Tammy you have to be direct. She'll be okay now. I know she really likes you, so I can't understand what it is all about."

"Michael, she's afraid that you'll be hurt again."

"Really?" he responded with wonderment in his voice. "My baby girl is growing up and wants to take care of her dad."

"She does, and I think it's sweet."

As we spoke, he told me his trip was extended another day until Friday, but I tried not to let the disappointment appear in my voice. I would have stayed on the phone with him all night, which is one of my faults. I never knew when to say goodbye. He finally said goodnight.

He was right. He filled my dreams that night.

CHAPTER THIRTEEN

Tammy and I arrived at the doctor's office on Wednesday shortly before her appointment time. Her nervousness spilled over to me. I could remember my first visit and understood her feelings.

When the nurse called her name, she grabbed my hand. "Please come with me." Her eyes pleaded.

"Are you sure you want me there?" I asked her.

"Please? I don't want to go alone."

I smiled and stood with her. We both followed the nurse into the examination room. Doctor Helga joined us shortly after. The doctor was surprised to see me.

"Elizabeth? Hello?" She checked her chart.

"I'm here with Tammy for support." I filled in the blanks for the doctor.

Doctor Helga had been my doctor for years. I started seeing her just after I inherited the cabin and started spending the majority of my time in Mintock. In her middle sixties now, she always wore her grey hair tightly rolled back in a bun and was known for her no-nonsense, putting everything straight style. She insisted that everyone call her by her first name. She said it was a better alternative than the names she was called by women in the throes of childbirth. When Kevin and I had first married, she had worked with me on my conception problem. After the problem eluded her, I saw a doctor down in Southern California who very adroitly pointed out the problem was not Kevin's, but mine.

Doctor Helga performed the examination on Tammy quickly. She squeezed my hand so tightly I thought I would have lost all feeling in my hand. She stared at me, and her face was beet red.

I leaned over and whispered in Tammy's ear. "It's almost over. Everything will be okay." I kissed her on the forehead.

After the examination, we met the doctor in her office. While she was writing the prescription for the birth control, she went into a lengthy commentary about the responsibilities of taking the pill and the responsibilities of having safe sex. Tammy blushed through the entire discussion. I was glad it was the doctor and not me doing the talking.

Doctor Helga handed the prescription to her, which she hurriedly stuffed in her purse.

As we walked to her office door, the doctor called back to me. "Elizabeth, stay for a moment, I'd like to talk to you. Tammy, you can wait in the waiting room, Elizabeth won't be long."

She nodded and closed the door behind her. Doctor Helga pointed to the chair opposite her desk.

I sat and asked worriedly, "Is there a problem with Tammy?"

"No, this has nothing to do with her, but it is you I wanted to talk about." She walked around the big mahogany desk and sat on the corner closest to me. Doctor Helga looked down at me over her glasses. "I've heard that you have a new boyfriend."

I sighed. "News certainly travels fast."

She laughed. "You know this is a small town. Michael created quite the stir in town when he moved here. First, he redid the house and then when we found out he was a famous photographer. Well, you know how this town gossips. So, are you having protected sex?"

Surprised filled my face. "What makes you think we are having sex?" I sputtered out.

"You're not? The stories made it sound like you are very cozy. Especially last weekend at the bonfire."

I looked at her in amazement, and here I was the fodder for gossip. "Well, we're not."

"Okay." She nodded her head. "When it does happen, what are you planning on doing? Are you going to go on the pill, use condoms, what?"

"Doctor Helga, you know I can't get pregnant. I already went through this with Kevin."

She nodded and sat down in the chair next to me. She put her arm around my shoulder. "I know, I remember going through it with you. However, if you recall, I was clear when I said that I couldn't find anything wrong with you. I believe you can get pregnant."

"The other doctor I saw in Southern California told me it was my fault." Tears welled in my eyes. "He very clearly told me I was to blame."

She leaned back in the chair. "Do you remember what the diagnosis was? Maybe we can contact him?"

"I don't remember who it was. Kevin kept all those records." I shook my head.

"Well, to be safe, why don't we just put you on the pill?"

I stood. "No, I appreciate your concern, but, I know I'm not going to get pregnant. If something happens between us, we'll use condoms." I walked over and opened the door. "Thanks, Doctor Helga."

CHAPTER FOURTEEN

Friday could not arrive soon enough for me. I must have checked the window at my back porch ten times before I saw Michael's jeep parked behind his house. Tammy called to invite me to their Friday pizza night.

I knocked on their lakeside door promptly at six o'clock. The dogs barked and rushed to the door. Katy opened it wide trying to hold Max back. Molly greeted me with her tail wagging. As soon as the door was closed Max was there sniffing at my pants and giving me kisses all over.

Michael looked up from his laptop. "Max, get down! Sorry, Elizabeth. Tammy, can you control him?"

Both he and Tammy, who had been reading the newspaper, tried to pull Max off me.

She gave me a big hug. "Sorry."

"He's okay. I don't mind, I know he can smell my dogs," I said, pushing Max down again.

Michael put his arms around me and kissed me softly on the lips. He whispered in my ear, "I missed you, Babe."

I smiled at him. He made me melt.

He released me. "Do you want to see the new pictures?" he asked excitedly.

I nodded. "Yes, I do. I want to see what you were up to!" I gave Katy a hug. "How are you doing?"

"Hi, Elizabeth, I'm just putting the finishing touches on my new piece," She replied walking back over to the piano.

He picked up the phone and waved to us. "Okay, what do you want?"

Both Tammy and Katy shouted, "The works!"

Michael nodded at me. "You two I know, Elizabeth?"

"I'm okay with anything."

He frowned. "Elizabeth?"

"Okay, Okay," I gave in, "anything without meat. I don't like meat on my pizza."

He ordered two pizzas, one vegetarian with extra cheese, and one with everything. The pizza parlor was on the edge of town. Although it was relatively close to us, it would be about forty-five minutes before the food arrived. I helped Tammy make a salad while we waited for the pizza. She poured colas for herself and Katy. After Michael poured us some wine, he sat back down and motioned for me to sit next to him on the leather couch. Friday pizza night was a very casual affair.

We huddled together as he started the slide show on his computer. The shots of the alligators were magnificent, showing them sunning themselves on the shore or in the water with only their eyes showing. He even had action shots as they scrambled after food.

"I can't believe you took these."

He beamed at me. "I have to go back next week. I ran out of time."

I tried to keep the unhappiness out of my voice. "Next week? Will you be gone all week?"

"Probably. There are only so many nighttime hours, and the alligators are the most active then. We also ran into some eagles, and I want to photograph them too."

I frowned. "Oh."

He looked at me. "What's wrong?"

"Oh, nothing. It's okay," I said.

He appeared to accept my explanation. I didn't want to remind him I would be starting my book tour the following Friday and would be gone for two weeks.

Tammy picked up the newest National Geographic sitting next to Michael and flipped it open to the middle. She handed me the magazine

"Have you seen Dad's new spread? He shot these photos last spring in Hawaii."

"Wow, these are incredible." The underwater photos contained a family of dolphins. I started turning the pages.

He looked up from his laptop. "This shoot was interesting. The article is all about how dolphins have learned how to go through elaborate measures to prepare their food. The researchers observed the dolphin group teaching their young and using tools. It was amazing."

As he leaned forward to look at the magazine on my lap, he moved his arm around my waist. His hand traveled up my back, rubbing and caressing me. I wanted to melt into him. All I could do was swallow hard and look over at him. He stared directly into my eyes, and it was as if I was soaring through the sky.

I cleared my throat. "These are so cool. Is that you?" I said pointing to a picture taken of a swimmer with an underwater camera.

As his hand moved down my back, I quivered, and he quietly chuckled. "Yeah, they thought it would be funny to take a picture of the photographer. I never thought they'd publish it."

Michael's hand moved underneath the bottom of my tank top, and he started making small circles with his fingers on the small of my back.

The picture of him was almost as breathtaking as the dolphins. His broad, well-developed shoulders and chest were evident, as well as his long and muscular legs. It was all very yummy. My stomach started to flutter, and lower parts of me tightened. I realized he was watching me look at the picture. My cheeks turned hot as I closed the magazine quickly and sipped my wine.

"I'd love to go on a photo shoot sometime," I said hurriedly.

"Actually, I am going to work with the eagles tomorrow. I know the girls don't want to go."

Katy did not interrupt her playing on the piano.

"I've wanted to get back up to look at the nesting pair of eagles we have north of the lake. It is an overnight trip. You could come along," he said casually, still with his hand caressing my back.

All I heard were the words overnight and alone. Something constricted my throat as the words continued to roll over in my mind… overnight and alone. It was true that Michael and I had spent the night together just a few nights ago, but that was different, the girls were around, and I knew nothing would happen.

I immediately started thinking of all the reasons not to be alone with him. Before I was able to get out at least one excuse, Tammy beat me, "Oh Dad, that's a great idea. Elizabeth you can use my sleeping bag, and I'll be glad to take care of Topper and Samantha. They can stay here with us!"

I was surprised at her response. Where was her anger from early this week? She seemed to have given up on the argument.

"I haven't been backpacking in ages." My last camping trip to Yosemite a few years back with my friends had been a disaster. "I'm afraid I'd slow you down."

Katy finally looked up. "Don't worry about that, I hate camping and Dad drags me along anyway."

Tammy laughed. "She really doesn't help at all!"

Katy threw a dirty look in her sister's direction.

"Well you don't!" she said. "Besides it's just a short hike to the eagle stand, and Dad will usually camp there."

While this was going on, my thoughts were in a jumble. I kept replaying the words alone and overnight. In the meantime, Michael had kept up his ministrations on my back, moving his hand further and further up. I wouldn't have been surprised to see a puddle underneath me because I definitely was melting with his touches.

I looked back at him and decided to be brave. "Okay, it sounds like fun. Will we be back in time for baseball on Sunday?"

"Absolutely, we can't miss the last game of the season. We'll leave around eleven tomorrow morning. Do you have hiking boots?" He quickly wrote down a short list of clothing items I would need and handed it to me. "I'll bring everything else. We'll be dry camping so everything we bring in we'll take back out again."

I scanned the list. "Okay boots, jeans, sweatshirt, and jacket. I don't need to bring anything else?"

"Not unless you want to carry it," he said. "Really Elizabeth, we're not crossing the plains in covered wagons."

The dogs started barking again. The pizza deliveryman was at the back door. The pizza smelled delicious, and I was more than hungry by this point. We sat at the dining room table and filled our plates with pizza and salad. Michael took a slice of the vegetarian pizza.

"No meat on your pizza either?" I asked.

The three laughed, and Tammy answered because he had already stuffed a bite into his mouth. "You know Dad's a vegetarian. He's tried that stuff on Katy and me, but we're not biting."

I looked at him incredulously. "You're a vegetarian? You can't be a vegetarian. I've been out to eat with you several times." I pictured all the times we had eaten together and could only think of the one time I saw him eat meat. "Wait a minute. You ate a burger at the bonfire. I saw you."

He laughed again and shook his head. "That was a veggie burger. Remember I was helping with the barbeque. I'm surprised you didn't see them in the freezer."

"I can see I'm not going to win this one. So, no meat?" I questioned.

"I do like eggs, cheese, and once in a while, I'll eat fish. However, I just don't care for the taste of meat. I do like pizza!" He grabbed another slice and took a large bite.

The man sitting next to me was amazing. Every time I spoke with him, he became more complicated. Where I thought I had peeled a layer away, another layer appeared.

He looked at me, and his eyes softened. "You are not getting away with eating just one slice! You need to fill at least one of those long legs."

I felt my face turning red again at the reference to my legs. "Okay, one more piece." I rubbed my stomach. "I guess I'll have to pack it in somehow."

Tammy rose from the table and picked up the Monopoly game. "Elizabeth, you owe me a rematch."

I grinned. "So losing two times wasn't enough?"

"That was only against Katy and me, you'll have Dad to contend with now," she said opening the box and setting up the game. "He's the world's best Monopoly player!"

"Oh, it looks like the challenge is on!" I nudged him. "The world's best huh?"

"You haven't seen all my moves yet." He laughed and nudged me back.

That is what I was afraid of, his moves. I had already seen some of his attempts, and I was not thinking only about Monopoly.

As the girls cleared away the leftovers and the dishes, we finished setting up the game. Both of us argued over who was going to use the little dog piece, and he finally conceded it to me because I was the guest. He was sitting too close to me, and I had too much wine to concentrate on the game. At least that was the excuse I was giving to myself. After he thoroughly beat the three of us at the game, he made us all hot chocolate, and we munched away on Tammy's freshly baked sugar cookies.

I yawned. "I better get myself home."

Michael insisted on walking me back over to the cabin. He put his arm around my shoulders as we strolled together.

"So give it up. Why did Tammy all of a sudden get all friendly with me again? She sure changed her tune after you talked with her."

"What do you mean?" He looked at me with a faux-shocked expression. "I merely explained why she should be more gracious."

I knew that was not the reason. What was it that she was so excited about when we drove over to the doctor's office? It suddenly hit me.

I stopped and turned to him. "You bribed her!" I said it with surprise in my voice. "You bribed her with a new car!"

He chuckled. "It worked, didn't it? Besides I was going to get her a new car for school anyway. This was simply convenient."

He kissed me quickly, and we continued to walk toward my front door. We climbed the steps to the front porch.

"So do you want to come in for a while?" I turned around and rested against the door.

He smiled, his arms were already around me, and his hands traveled lower to cup my butt. He leaned into me and started to kiss my lips. My hips pressed against him while my stomach started the flip-flops again.

He broke the kiss. "I better not come in. I'm tired from the trip. I need to go home and take a cold shower too."

Michael lifted me up against him, and I could feel the reason why he needed a cold shower. A need rushed through me straight to the area between my legs. He nibbled on my jaw and neck as I wrapped my arms around him tighter, running my hands over his back and shoulders. When he pulled back from me, I felt a strange aching void in my body, and it made me struggle for a breath.

"I'll see you tomorrow morning," he said.

I only nodded. He hesitated a moment and then turned around quickly.

I wanted to reach out to him because the ache in my body was so sharp. I wanted him to take the pain away.

"Goodnight Elizabeth." He walked down the steps. "Breathe Babe," he called back to me.

I leaned back against the door, trying to remain upright, my mouth falling open. "Goodnight Michael," I gulped for air. How was I ever going to make it through tomorrow night?

I let myself into the cabin. Topper and Samantha greeted me eagerly by the door.

"Oh boy, Mommy had quite the evening!" I said out loud.

His embrace kept coming back to me in waves. He smelled so wonderful, a mixture of pizza, wine, and his aftershave as a lingering scent. When he kissed me I had not felt a beard, so he must have shaved this afternoon. The thought made me smile. He had prepared for my visit. His hands had been warm on my body and his lips so soft and tender. Climbing into bed, I felt ready to swoon. My knees were not steady. Replaying the scene in my mind, my heart started racing. It looked like sleep would be difficult to find tonight.

Topper and Samantha lay down next to me, and I reached out and petted both of them.

"Yes, Mommy has a very yummy man."

CHAPTER FIFTEEN

The alarm rang at seven the next morning. After my shower, I braided my wet hair in one long braid down my back. My hair was uncontrollable enough without having to worry about an overnight stay.

I sat at my desk and started my laptop. I had to get some writing done. Robin, my editor, had already emailed me twice about my book. She wanted to see the pages I had written before my visit to Southern California. The neighbors were proving to be quite the distraction, especially Mr. Hoffman. Remembering the feel of his body next to mine, I shivered and could feel a blush creep up my face. Would the blushing ever stop?

After working several hours, I glanced up at the clock. I shut down my computer and stretched. The dogs started barking before I heard the light knock on the door.

Tammy was at the door. "I'm not too early am I?" she said, bending to pet the dogs.

"Come on in, I'm getting ready. Do you want a muffin? There's some on the kitchen counter."

She picked up a muffin and nibbled on the top. She stood at my open bedroom door while I sat on the bed putting on my socks and boots.

"Dad has been up since five-thirty, he seems a little excited about going on this shoot," she said between bites.

"Really?" I tried to sound nonchalant and attempted not to blush. "Why do you think?"

She smirked while popping a piece of chocolate muffin in her mouth. "I can't remember the last time he's taken a date on location, especially overnight. That would usually be way too much trouble for him." Tammy added, "Dad mostly wants to concentrate on the photography."

"Maybe your dad feels I won't be much of a distraction," I offered. "Besides, I'm not a date. I am the next-door neighbor, another professional just like him. I want to go for the experience." I finished tying my bootlaces.

She looked straight at me and frowned. "Elizabeth, don't try to feed that to me anymore. I know how Dad feels about you, and it is obvious how you feel about him. He asked me to stay out of it, but I know better. He doesn't kiss all the neighbors like that either."

"I certainly hope not. Okay, honest?" I rose from the bed and put my arm around her shoulders. "I really like your dad, and I'm glad that he wants to spend time with me."

She grinned and squeezed me around my waist. "Okay, that's much better."

"I heard about your car," I said as we walked out to the kitchen together.

"Isn't that totally cool?" she said excitedly. "I'm trying to talk him into a truck. We'll see how far I get."

We reviewed the feeding routine for the dogs. Topper and Samantha already loved Tammy so they would be just fine in her care. I put on a dark blue sweatshirt over my tank top and jeans since the weather was unpredictable this time of year. Michael's jeep pulled up to the back door.

"Grab the back door while I get my jacket," I called out.

Back in my bedroom, I pulled my leather jacket from the closet, and then tucked my digital camera, a pen, and a pad of paper into a little bag with some toiletries, and a spare pair of panties.

Hugging the dogs and kissing Tammy, I said, "You three take care of each other!"

I walked out to the porch where Michael stood and handed him my little bag. The roof was on the Jeep, and the back was loaded with equipment. He looked great as usual. His jeans and black t-shirt made him look exceptionally rugged today. Seeing him made my knees go weak again. He tipped his sunglasses down on the bridge of his nose, and the look was complete. I hoped I was not drooling. I was sure he knew the effect he had on me.

"Ready?" he asked. I nodded, and he helped me into the passenger seat of the Jeep. As he slid into the driver seat, he called out to Tammy, "Behave yourself and take good care of the dogs."

She just nodded with a broad grin on her face and made the okay sign with her fingers. We backed out of the driveway while I waved madly at her.

Glancing at the storage area of the Jeep, I said, "That's a lot of stuff."

He looked at me through his sunglasses, and it was disconcerting that I could not see his eyes. "Don't worry, the girls were teasing yesterday, the stand is only a fifteen-minute hike from the road."

My curiosity got the best of me. "Why the overnight stay?"

Michael kept his eyes on the road. "I like to get shots during different times of the day because the lighting is different. These are not zoo animals. You can't predict when they will be in the nest. Sometimes it can be mind-numbing sitting there hour after hour hoping your subject will come home." While waiting at the stop light, he turned to grin at me. "Besides, you're not scared of being alone with me are you?"

"Oh don't be silly!" I laughed and turned away pretending there was an interesting scene going on across the street. I could feel the redness creeping up my face. He reached over and tugged at my braid chuckling softly.

Our trip through Mintock took about twenty minutes. We stopped in front of the diner.

"Let's have some lunch first. This will be our last real meal, and I can't promise you're going to rave over dinner," he said, unbuckling his seat belt.

"Did you make it? I'm sure it will be fine. But lunch is a good idea."

Michael opened the restaurant door and followed me inside. Karen, who was on Mintocks's other baseball team was behind the counter. She wore a look of surprise on her face when she saw the two of us enter together.

"Hi, Karen." I gave her a small nod.

"Hey, guys!" She grabbed two menus and led us to a booth.

We slid in together across the bench. She raised her eyebrow to me while his head was turned. I pretended not to notice.

"I'll be right back for your orders. What would you like to drink?"

We both responded in unison, "Just water please."

I was determined not to let her disturb me. After my visit with my doctor, I understood it was common knowledge in town that we were dating.

Even though I knew what I wanted to order, I was ever hopeful there would be a surprise inside the menu. There never was.

Karen came back with our waters and took our order. After she left, I leaned back into the corner of the booth.

"We're going to be all the gossip at the baseball game tomorrow," I sighed.

"I don't have a problem with it, do you?" He looked at me earnestly.

I melted within his eyes.

"Of course not," I answered. "Though it makes me feel strange to be talked about."

He chuckled and moved closer to me. Michael caressed my cheek with his fingers and then kissed my lips. "Let's give them something to talk about."

I giggled. "You always say the right thing." I kissed him back.

Our food arrived, and Michael dug into his veggie burger and fries. He gave me a bite of his pretend burger, and I wrinkled my nose. I ate the chicken on top of my Cobb salad. I was too nervous being so close to him to eat properly. I chewed on the cheese toast while he polished off the rest of my bowl.

Karen called to us as we left the diner after we finished. "See you at baseball tomorrow?"

We both turned and nodded. Michael whispered in my ear, "Remember let's give her something to talk about tomorrow." As we walked out, he wrapped his arm around my waist, nuzzling and kissing me on the neck.

As the door closed behind us, I laughed and whispered back, "You're very bad!"

He laughed with me and then drew me into his arms while we stood by the Jeep. Kissing me and looking at me seriously, he said, "I want the whole town to know about us Elizabeth."

I smiled in response. As soon as I had the opportunity, I needed to think about his statement.

When we merged onto the highway, it became almost impossible to speak in a normal voice in the jeep. I looked around the car, and it had a comfortable, well-worn look. I was not sure how old it was, but the Jeep had been around the block a few times.

"No radio?" I pointed to the empty area on the console.

"I got tired of having to replace the radio, it kept getting ripped off." He leaned over to tell me. "If I want music I use an iPod."

I nodded in agreement letting him know I understood. He turned his eyes back to the road. "We'll be getting off here in a bit, sorry it's so noisy."

"That's okay," I shouted.

Michael turned off the highway about ten minutes later, and the Jeep started to climb a small ancillary road that took us into the forest. The narrow utility lane was not well traveled. The fir trees surrounded us and blocked out the sun. It was markedly colder in the shade, and I was glad to have my sweatshirt on. After a few minutes, the road ended suddenly, and he parked the jeep.

"We're walking from here. Are you okay?" He got out of the jeep.

I nodded and opened the door. He was already in the back pulling equipment out.

"It's a short hike, about fifteen minutes." Grabbing the little bag I had packed, he stuffed it inside a small backpack which had Tammy's name embroidered on the outside. I guessed her sleeping bag was inside. He handed the backpack to me. "I'm going to make a couple of trips."

"I can carry more than this backpack," I offered.

He looked at me as if to size me up. "Okay, you can carry my tripod, and some of the food." His voice trailed off as he started pulling items out of the back. "Okay, my tripod." He handed me the large tripod. "And the most important item." He grinned as he gave me a canvas bag.

I could hear the clink of the two bottles, and I peered inside the bag. "Wine?" I laughed. "I don't think I know what I'm getting myself into."

He laughed with me. "Remember if anyone asks, they're a housewarming gift for the eagles. The rangers would have a spasm if they knew." The huge backpack Michael pulled out had to be at least twenty times the size of the bag I carried. He leaned it against his legs and quickly swung it on his back. Slamming the back door of the Jeep, he indicated to the path in front of him. "Are you ready?"

"Lead the way."

The pines in the forest were thick, and the needles that covered the ground crunched under our feet. We walked for fifteen minutes and came into a clearing. I was astounded when I saw the lake far below us. I had not realized that we had climbed so high in the Jeep. Our walk had been relatively flat. "Wow! How far up are we?"

"Only about twenty-five hundred feet." He pulled off his pack and leaned it against a tree. Michael took the tripod and my pack from me. I held onto the bag with the wine, and he laughed. "You're not going to give that one up, are you?"

"Hey, as far as I know, this is the only nutrition you brought." I pulled the bag closer to me. "You'll have to fight me for this." As he stepped nearer, I thought better of my challenge, but he only leaned over to pull my braid again.

"Will you be okay?" he asked. "I'm going back to the Jeep for one more pack."

"I wish I could help more, but I'll be a good girl and sit right down and wait." I sat and waved as he left.

As he started toward the path, he called out over his shoulder, "Watch out for the rattlesnakes!"

"What?" I jumped up from the dirt, found the nearest boulder, and stood up on it. I could hear him laughing. I sat gingerly down on the rock looking around at the ground.

The scenery was exhilarating, the air was fresh, and the sun felt good on my face. This was a great opportunity to think about how crazy all this was. I questioned my sanity for being here. The last thing I wanted was to get into a relationship. I was too busy. I had a book to write.

On the other hand, admitting to myself, I was attracted to him. Who would not be? His face was perfect, his body was yummy, he liked to cuddle, he was smart, he was sensitive, and most of all he was waiting for me. No woman in her right mind would give a gift away like that. Passion, or maybe lust, was definitely brewing between us, especially after our kiss last night. Did I need passion in my life? I thought I was doing okay, but of course, all of my friends disagreed.

It was getting warm sitting on the rock. I pulled off my sweatshirt over my head. Retrieving my notebook and pen out of my jacket pocket. I started to take notes about my surroundings. I liked to capture different places on paper and then later, when I needed some scenery for a book, I could check my notes and remember my impressions. There were mixtures of trees on the edge of the clearing. A rope ladder hung from the tree where he had left his backpack. Halfway up the huge tree, a platform stood on the sturdier looking branches. The platform was small, but it looked like it could fit two people. I gathered this was the eagle stand.

The sky was light blue with large white puffy clouds. I stared up at them imagining different shapes. Then I saw the bird. It was closer to the lake, and its wide wingspan was unmistakable. I took a sharp intake of breath. The eagle was magnificent soaring over the lake. Watching it fly, the tears welled up in my eyes. The view touched me deeply; its flight looked effortless as the wings beat. Then it gracefully floated over the lake. The eagle dipped down and then flew upward again finally flying out of my line of vision.

The sound of Michael setting down his backpack startled me. I stood up and turned around. He looked at me and saw the tears.

Alarm showed immediately on his face as he took my hand. "Are you okay, what happened?"

"Oh, I'm sorry, no I'm okay, I just saw an eagle flying." I wiped my eyes with my hand.

His smile was bright. "They are glorious aren't they?"

"It was so unexpected, and it was so beautiful. I don't know, I guess I got caught up in the moment."

He pulled me toward him and gave me a hug. He looked down at me with his eyes matching the color of the sky. "Babe, you are just a softy."

As he held me, my stomach started fluttering. Every time he used his new nickname for me, my body heated. I was sure I was going to pass out as his other arm came up around me. His hands moved down my back and came to rest around my waist.

He whispered, "I like softies." He bent and kissed my eyelids gently. Moving down to my lips, he gave me a tender kiss, and then he very gently released me. "Breathe Elizabeth." He touched my nose and then my lips with his fingertip.

I stood there speechless.

He pointed up to the trees right across from the clearing that were coming out of a deep ravine. "While I'm setting up our camp, look across there for what looks like little white golf balls in the trees."

"White golf balls?" I asked looking confused.

"Yeah, the eagle's head is white. When they are in their nest all you see from down here is what looks like a golf ball," he explained.

I turned to scan the trees, but nothing was visible. "Are you sure I can't help? You don't have to do everything."

He teased, "You're enough of a distraction already."

Michael was very efficient in his camp set up routine. The small tent went up quickly. He stuffed his large sleeping bag inside followed by Tammy's small thin fluffy pink sleeping bag, which looked like it would not provide much protection from the cold. Next, he set up a table and two chairs. Then a small cook stove went on the table. When he finished the setup, he pulled out several camera bodies out of his bags and proceeded to check them.

I sat back down on the rock glad for a few moments of silence. The electricity was building between us, and I wasn't sure if my reaction to him was a sign that I was ready for a relationship or if it was simply lust. I reminded myself that he had not even mentioned having a relationship with me. He had been quiet on the subject of his intentions. Okay, it was clear his plans were my seduction. Long term though, it was unclear. He had already told me that once Tammy went off to school, he was looking forward to beginning his life. What he didn't say was whether I fit into those plans. For now, I was only concentrating on my seduction.

I felt a light touch on my shoulder and looked up. He stood behind me pointing to the trees he had shown me earlier. "Look, see the golf ball?"

"Is that an eagle?" I asked with excitement in my voice.

"Come on, it's time to get up in the stand." He pointed behind him to the tree with the platform.

I looked at the rope ladder and the height of the platform. "Oh, you have fun up there."

"No, you're coming along." He pulled me to my feet and led me over to the tree. "I'll help you up."

"Michael," I tried explaining, "I have a fear of heights."

"Elizabeth, I will be right behind you, I won't let you fall. Just try it. I mean you play baseball," he challenged.

"What is that supposed to mean?" I flashed at him.

"You know, girls don't play baseball." He grinned.

"Okay, I know what you're trying to do." I grabbed the rope ladder and lifted my foot onto the first rung.

He steadied the ladder. "Look up and try not to look down. I promise this will be worth it."

I lifted each foot, slowly moving up the ladder. He called to me, encouraging me with each step. "Easy does it Elizabeth." When I reached the platform, he instructed, "Take hold of the railing on your right and step up."

I was so relieved when I stood out on the stand. I leaned my back against the tree trunk and tried to breathe evenly. "Hurry up!" I called down to him.

He grabbed his camera bag and tripod. Michael scaled the ladder quickly.

"Are you okay?" He touched my arm and looked down at me.

I brushed my bangs out of my eyes. "As you said I do play baseball."

He attached one of his cameras to the tripod. The camera had the longest lens I had ever seen. He bent and looked through the viewfinder. He turned the focusing rings, and then I heard clicking noises, one after another.

I pulled out my little digital camera from my pocket and looked through the viewer. "All I see is two of the little white ball things. Can you see anything? I mean it is way across the clearing."

"Do you want to see?" he asked and then pulled me in between the camera and him. "Look through here." He pointed to the viewfinder. He put my hand on the focusing ring of the lens. "Focus here."

I gasped when I saw the image. Two eagles were sitting in the tree as clear as if they were perched right next to me. "Oh! They're so beautiful, I can't believe it!" I looked up to see the real image and then bent over again to look through the viewfinder. With all of this happening, I was still very aware of pushing up against him, and I tried to keep my breathing normal.

Michael had his hands on my hips, and that was not helping the situation. He leaned over and placed my hand on the shutter button. "Press here to take the picture, and then move the lens back to get a different view. The big one is the female, and the smaller one is the male."

After taking a couple of shots, I was losing the battle trying to breathe normally. "I better let you get back to work," I said, making a move to step to the side.

He still had his hands on my hips. "I don't mind teaching you." He grinned at me when I looked over my shoulder.

"I'm sure you could teach me quite a few things," I said. I quickly sat on the stand and pulled out my little notebook. Leaning back against the tree, I started writing.

He bent to see my notebook. "What are you writing? Are you working on your book?" he asked.

"When I go someplace new or have a new experience, I like to capture it on paper. Sometimes these little notes give me inspiration. They help me picture a scene in my mind. I see little movies in my mind when I write."

He turned back to his camera. "If you see a movie that means you're visual. You would make a good photographer. Will you let me read what you've written when you're finished?"

I nodded yes, but more than likely, he did not see me. He was already in photographer mode. We were silent for the next hour. I glanced up at him periodically and watched him work. His work completely absorbed him. He changed lenses, used different cameras, and moved the tripod into different angles. A couple of times he spoke to the eagles as if trying to coax them into different poses.

The stand had only a small area, and I tried to give Michael as much room as possible. I stretched my legs when I stood up. My movement caused him to look up from his work.

"I'm going to go down to earth, can I get you anything?" I asked.

He frowned. "I'm sorry. I haven't been a good host, I get wrapped up in my work."

"You're not supposed to be a host, no apologies necessary. I've enjoyed watching the creative photographic experience. However, if I don't move my legs, I'm afraid I'm not going to be able to climb down." I stretched for the ladder.

Michael reached for me. "Here, let me help you down. I'll go first and steady the ladder for you."

Over my objections, he quickly climbed over me and down the ladder. Going down the ladder was much easier for me than climbing up.

"Would you like me to make some coffee for you?" he offered when I reached the bottom.

His arms were on the rungs of the ladder, capturing me in between him and the ladder. Standing very close, I had a difficult time steadying my breathing, and it was not the exertion from climbing down the ladder.

"Now you're in your host mode? No, go back up and get to work," I said as I pushed him toward the ladder.

He grinned back at me as he moved up the ladder easily. When he reached the top, he called down to me, "It will only be another hour. I'll lose the light soon. When I come back down, I'll start a fire."

"Good idea," I yelled back up to him.

It was getting a little chilly as the sun was moving to the west. I picked up my sweatshirt from the rock I had occupied earlier and pulled it over my head. It was warm against my cold skin. Next, I rummaged around in the backpacks, found a bottle of water, and drank it down. I leaned back against the rock as I sat down and closed my eyes. It had been an incredibly peaceful afternoon. The quiet was so welcome. The remaining sun was warm on me and relaxed me even further. Eagles filled my mind as I drifted off to sleep.

I woke to the smell and sound of a campfire, and the vivid red, pink, and purple of the setting sun just above the crest of the mountain. Michael kneeled down next to me and handed me a cup. I smelled the deep rich aroma of red wine.

"I guess I must have fallen asleep, too much eagle overload."

"Come closer to the fire." He took my hand and pulled me up to my feet. Wrapping his arms around me, he pulled me in. Soft lips nibbled at my mouth.

He murmured, "Mmmm…, I love kissing you. I don't think I'll ever get enough of this."

Michael had made a nice spot next to the fire for us with a blanket so we would not have to sit on the ground.

I took a sip of the wine. "Yum, this is good."

Sitting down next to me, he took the cup from my hand and set it down.

"But this is better," he said as he continued the kiss where he left off.

"Mmmmm… I agree."

We kissed and cuddled on the blanket. His kisses and gentle caresses made my body respond to him by aching to move closer. I enjoyed touching his face and neck with my kisses. When we surfaced for air, we grinned when we both reached for the glasses of wine.

"I'm actually not supposed to have alcohol with me. We're on the reservation, but it is also a federally protected park. The rangers are cool with me and will usually look the other way, so if the ranger visits just remember you brought the wine in," he joked.

"So that's why you made me carry the wine?" I grimaced with a fake frown.

He laughed. "I'm honest if nothing else."

"Do the rangers visit often? Do you need a permit to be here?"

"No and yes. I have the approval from the tribal council to be here and actually have a special grant from the federal government. The government removed the bald eagle from the endangered and threatened species list only a couple of years ago. I've been working on a book about bald eagles." He took a long drink from his cup and turned to lie on his back. "I work mostly in Alaska, but this pair here has intrigued me. Bald eagles mate for life. Unfortunately, this pair did not have any eggs this year. It happens, but we don't know why."

Surprised I asked, "They mate for life?"

I looked down at him. It was either the wine or him working a spell on me. When he lay down, his t-shirt rose a bit above the waist of his jeans revealing his firm hard abdomen. The muscles in his upper arms bulged as he moved his arms to the back of his head. In addition, his thighs, well, didn't they just fill out his jeans? And, his jawline…didn't I want to nibble there?

"Yeah, and they can live up to 30 years in the wild. That's a long time together."

I nodded in agreement. "That's amazing."

I was having a hard time finishing the sentence. My mind would not focus on my words because I was concentrating on Michael's body. I drained my cup of wine and looked around.

"More?" I said wiggling my cup in his direction.

He moved to get up. "I'm sorry, Elizabeth. Let me get it."

I pushed his chest back down. "No, no, I'll get it. Just wanted to know if you want more?"

I tried to be graceful getting up, but at almost six feet, grace was not my middle name. My family often referred to me as *Legs,* and it wasn't a compliment. He was watching me intently, which made my lack of coordination even more apparent. A grin formed in the corner of his mouth.

I picked up the bottle and made my way back to the blanket and the fire. Reaching up, he took the bottle from me as I sat back down. He poured wine in both of our cups and handed my cup back to me. The sun was almost gone, and it was getting dark. The fire gave his face a warm contemplative glow. The darkness made me realize that we were very much alone tonight. Alone and overnight. I concentrated on my two vocabulary words. Both the wine and the fire were making me feel quite warm and toasty. I took another gulp of wine.

"Doesn't it make you curious about the natural instincts of the bald eagle to mate for life?" I asked.

Michael started laughing as he ran his hand through his hair. "Oh my god, Elizabeth, aren't you the professor tonight?"

"Don't laugh at me, I mean doesn't it make you wonder how that happened?"

"No, I hadn't planned on thinking about the mating habits of bald eagles tonight. I was thinking of the mating habits of a completely different species." The grin he gave made me blush. "Come here." Pulling me down against his chest, he softly said, "Relax."

My head rested against him. I took a deep breath and exhaled which did not help my spinning mind. "You make it very difficult for me to relax."

"Why is that?" his voice sounded surprised. He picked up my hand from his chest and intertwined his fingers with mine.

"I mean, well, here with you tonight …alone… well," I stuttered trying to express my thoughts. "I just don't… well… understand."

"Don't understand what Elizabeth? That you're a smart, sexy, beautiful woman and I want to spend time with you?" He squeezed my hand. "Now, let's watch the stars come out."

The darkness surrounded us quickly. The only sounds we heard were the crickets chirping and the crackling fire. I turned over onto my back and leaned my head back down on his shoulder. We lay together watching the stars slowly peeking out. There was no moon tonight, which added to the darkness.

"Can you name the stars?" I whispered.

"Yes," he replied. "Can you?"

"Of course. That's part of a romance writer's repertoire."

"Okay." Michael pointed up to the sky. "What's that one?"

I giggled. "You silly boy that's not a star, that's the planet Venus."

"Oh?" He rolled over to his side and looked down at me. "Is that the planet of love?" He traced my chin with his hand and then brushed his finger across my lips.

CHAPTER SIXTEEN

Our eyes met and locked. We lay there, not moving or speaking for what seemed like an eternity. The world had disappeared, and we were alone. All the glances, the touches, and the kisses had led to this moment. His lips met mine in an unbroken kiss, and suddenly I knew that this was right. Everything was right. Michael and I were right.

His lips moved down my face to my neck, and we locked into an intimate embrace. The core of my being was quickly becoming molten lava and the need inside of me to have him closer became overwhelming. He explored as far as my sweatshirt would allow. I moved to pull it off because I wanted to feel his skin on mine.

His voice suddenly deep, he whispered, "Are you okay?" As he helped me remove the top layer of my clothing.

"Yes," I hissed, and the desire we both felt whirled around us.

His kisses continued where they had left off. My hands stroked his soft hair as his kisses slowly moved down to my chest. I closed my eyes when I felt his hands move my tank top up to expose my breasts. My nipples stiffened and puckered as the cold air hit them.

When his tongue lapped at my sensitive skin, my back arched toward his mouth and a soft, "Oh!" escaped from my lips.

The area between my legs tightened with anticipation, and feeling his erection straining against his jeans made my excitement even more palpable. With every tug from Michael's mouth, an electrical charge raced from my nipples to my center. The need he created was so foreign, but I didn't want him to stop.

He sat up on his knees and pulled his t-shirt over his head. By the light of the fire, I could see his sculpted chest with the familiar blond hair smattered across his chest, the sexy trail that disappeared into his jeans, and the large rigid bulge below.

His eyes did not leave mine as I pulled the tank over my head. When my fingers reached for the button on my jeans, I could hear his sharp intake of breath. Neither of us blinked.

His voice was rough and deep when he spoke. "May I do that?"

I nodded. My skin felt so heated that I no longer noticed the coolness that surrounded us. Michael knelt between my legs. His fingers unbuttoned my jeans and then slowly unzipped them. Still not breaking our eye contact, he tugged at the top of my pants. Then, slowly, he moved them off my hips and down my legs removing my boots and socks along the way. I had stopped breathing, and his had slowed.

"You are so beautiful Elizabeth," he growled as he placed kisses on my stomach, slowly trailing them up to my breasts again.

He continued to tease my nipples, and when his teeth gently grazed them, I moaned in pleasure.

Feeling his skin against mine made my hips start to move with him. The thin material of the thong I wore did not offer much protection against the friction I created as my body came into contact with his jeans.

When he moved up to kiss my lips, his erection angled directly over the center of my body. All of the sensations his movements made built up the delicious pressure inside of me. I wanted to feel all of his skin against mine.

The pleasure I felt slipped from my lips, and I cried out, "Oh, I want you."

Our eyes met again, and I nodded in confirmation. He stood up above me and slipped out of his boots. Then very slowly, as if he was teasing me, he pushed down his pants and briefs until they dropped to the ground.

My lips formed the word *oh,* and then I said in amazement, "Wow!"

He grinned as he stepped out of his pants and socks. His lips grazed the inside of my thighs, and I could feel the stubble of his beard rubbing against my sensitive skin. When his tongue lapped at the material covering my sex, my hips bucked toward him.

I heard him softly chuckle and he knelt up again. He whispered, "I think I am only going to get to tease you for so long. I don't think either of our bodies will take much more abuse. You are so beautiful Elizabeth, and so sexy. I've wanted you so much." He hooked his thumbs under my thong and slowly dragged it down my legs.

My eyes held his even as I felt him place his palm on my mound. He was right. I was coiled so tightly now, and I was afraid I would explode with merely a wave of his hand. Michael's body was more than exquisite, and feeling him, his skin on mine, made my body respond in ways I had never experienced.

I found my voice. It too had dropped several octaves. "Then take me."

He reached for his discarded jeans, and he pulled a small packet from the pocket. In a quick sure motion, he slid the condom on and lifted me up into his lap, straddling me against him. Our bodies molded together. His hard erection was positioned amid my soft, slippery warmth. Lifting my hips with his hands, I felt him slowly enter me, my body stretching to accommodate his size.

We sat motionless for a moment lost in each other and then the need won out. The languorous climb of sensations began. At first, our pace was slow and steady, building the desire inside my body. Our breathing accelerated, and I felt that elusive fire lick around me. Kisses became less kissing and more of just mouths and tongues dragging across our skin. There were small words spoken, but no sentences were articulated. Every nerve in my body was on alert, and the world consisted only of him and me. Then, there it was.

As my body snapped, I uttered one word, and Michael held me tightly as my nails raked into his back and shoulders. The orgasm slammed through me as my body bucked against him, and a heartbeat later, I heard his guttural cry while he released himself into me. We moved together as one as the rush crashed through us, convulsing our bodies in waves.

It took a while for us to still. We did not move and held in that tight embrace. Feeling the after effects of the tremors as they slowly dissipated, our lips met in a kiss. Our eyes slowly opened to see each other.

Michael was the first to speak. "Wow."

I smiled. "Yeah, wow."

He kissed me again. The night around us was silent except for the crackle and pop of the campfire. When we slowly pulled apart, he reached over and picked up the extra blanket next to us. Wrapped in it, we sat holding each other while we stared at the campfire.

My stomach growled, and we both broke into giggles.

"I better feed you!" He moved to get up.

I didn't want him to leave me. "It's okay, I'm not starving."

He leaned over and kissed me. "It's all done, Babe. It won't take more than a moment."

He stood up and handed the second bottle of wine to me with the bottle opener. As I worked on opening the bottle, I watched him walking around apparently unconcerned that he was naked. He stepped on a rock and hopped around on one foot as he pulled out a small cooler from his backpack.

"Ow, ow, ow!" he exclaimed.

His dancing put me into a fit of giggles as he landed back down next to me. "Hey! No fair laughing at the naked guy!"

I grinned. "Sorry."

He kissed me. "You don't look sorry."

I giggled again. "Oh, but I am. Now, what delights have you brought for me?"

"Normally I don't have actual food with me, but I didn't want to put you through the freeze-dried hell. Tonight we're living it up!"

I pulled the cork out of the bottle with a pop and filled our cups. He laid out several sandwiches and several small bowls. Pointing to the first sandwich, "Gruyere, avocado, and sprouts." He indicated to the second sandwich, "And this one is brie, tomato, and sprouts. I like sprouts, makes the sandwiches crunchy. This one is everything!" He pointed to a large roll cut in half. Michael quickly snapped off the lids to the bowls. "Pasta salad, bean salad, and rice salad."

I took a sip of wine looking at all the food. "Who is going to eat all this food?"

"You're the one with the growling stomach."

I chose half of the brie sandwich and took a bite. The brie was perfect, creamy with a rich flavor. "Yummy, you make good sandwiches."

He picked up half of the sandwich with everything and took a big bite. "You see being a vegetarian can be good. I'm starving!" he said with emphasis and a wink. "You wore me out!"

I giggled and of course, blushed. "Did I?"

He grinned and kissed me.

We sat quietly munching our sandwiches. The salads were flavorful too. I leaned back and sighed when I finished the brie sandwich. "Oh, I can't eat anymore! I'm so full." The wine was having quite an effect on me. My head was swimming a bit, and I felt very relaxed.

"Save some room for dessert." He grinned.

"Desert, oh no, I can't!" I moaned. I glanced sideways at him. "What's for dessert?"

"A family and a campfire favorite," he said with glee. "Smores! My girls love the way I make them."

"What's your secret?" I leaned toward him, and I could see the firelight reflected in his eyes.

He leaned toward me and said conspiratorially, "It's all in the thinness of the chocolate. The hot marshmallows have to melt the chocolate."

Michael finished eating the sandwiches on his own. We toasted the marshmallows and assembled the desert. The combination of the chocolate and the red wine was heavenly. Afterward, he cleaned up the food and put everything back in the pack. I refilled our wine cups, and he sat next to me.

He smiled and brushed his finger above my lip. "Chocolate." He licked his finger.

I wiped my hand over my mouth. "Did I get it all?"

"Not quite," he said as he leaned over and brushed his lips against my upper lip. Then his mouth was on mine fully. "May I take your hair down?" he whispered softly in my ear. "I've been waiting to do this all day long."

I slowly nodded. His hands pulled my braid forward and deftly removed the band from the end. Michael loosened the braid gently. I closed my eyes as his hands moved through my hair. His lips were against my neck after he splayed my hair around my shoulders. Finding my mouth again, he kissed me deeply. We broke apart, and our eyes met.

"Elizabeth, you are so incredible."

I smiled and kissed him back. I settled back in between his legs with my back against his chest and his arms wrapped around me. My fingers played a small pattern on his upper thighs. He pulled me tight against him and cleared his throat.

"I have some exciting news," he said.

I half turned to look at him. "You do?"

He nodded. "The aquarium is having a charitable benefit, and I'm one of the guests of honor."

"Wow!" I exclaimed. "That is exciting."

"They're having a formal dinner ball at the aquarium at the beginning of October, and I thought, well, I'd like you to attend it with me."

"Oh, Michael, I would be thrilled to go with you." I turned again in his arms and touched his face. "That would be really nice."

He kissed me. "Thanks."

"Is it sexy formal or conservative formal?" I asked with a query on my face.

He laughed. "Only you would have two different types of formal. I suppose it would be conservative formal. Why do you ask?"

I turned back to lean against him. "There are sexy formal dresses and conservative formal dresses. I need to know what to wear."

"I don't want you to be too sexy. Someone might try to steal you away, and I'll get jealous. Besides I won't be able to keep my hands off of you," he murmured in my ear.

He ran his hands down my thighs and then back up to my waist. I shivered at his touch. The fire was beginning to die, and the temperature was dropping.

"Are you getting cold?" he asked.

"A little."

"I think it's time we turned in. It's going to be chilly tonight." He reached for my boots and slipped them on my feet. "I don't want you to have to do the naked dance to the tent." He laughed. "But then again…" Pulling me up to my feet, he wrapped the blanket around me. "Okay, go get into the sleeping bag while I put out the fire." He handed me a small flashlight.

As soon as I moved away from Michael and the campfire, I could feel the cold. I crawled into the tent and smiled. He had Tammy's sleeping bag rolled up for use as a pillow. There was never any doubt in his mind that I was going to sleep with him. Folding the blanket, I slipped quickly into his sleeping bag. I giggled. Now, I had three words… overnight, alone, and naked.

He crawled in through the opening and turned around to close the tent flap. "Are you okay?"

"Yeah." I tried not to let my teeth chatter. It was cold.

He removed his boots and placed them at the end by the door. He climbed in next to me, "Babe you are ice cold! Come here, you'll be warm in a minute," he said while pulling me close.

"Michael?"

"Yes, Babe?" His voice muffled in my neck.

"Thank you for today. I enjoyed watching you work."

His squeezed me. "My pleasure. And Elizabeth?"

"Yes?"

"Thank you for tonight."

I giggled, and in between his kisses I said, "My pleasure."

I had no trouble falling asleep quickly. The fresh air of the day, the wine, the food, and our tender lovemaking had done their jobs.

I awoke a little while later with him pressed tightly up against me, spooning me. His hand had moved underneath me cupping my breast. He was definitely naked as I felt his erection pressing against my back. We were definitely alone. Yes, I was using my vocabulary in complete sentences, so I knew I was not dreaming. He was not sleeping either, because his thumb was brushing lightly against my nipple. The simple stroking of his thumb made my entire body yearn for him.

I turned around to face him. The darkness did not allow me to see much, but I knew that he was happy with my decision. No words broke the silence of the night. Pulling me close, his mouth located mine. I felt his hardness pressing against my stomach. My arms wrapped around his neck and shoulders as we kissed. His tongue probed my mouth, and I returned the favor. His kisses moved down my neck to my breasts. I pressed his head to my chest. Sucking and teasing my already sensitive nipples, he brought flashing sensations to me, reminding me of the aching need inside. My legs moved apart, and his leg slipped between mine. I leaned my head back because his tongue and mouth were making my head spin.

"Oh, Michael." I broke the silence by whispering his name.

While his mouth was busy, his hands massaged my stomach and thighs. His hand slipped between my legs and found the silky wetness.

"I want to touch you," he hoarsely whispered. I could hear his need in his voice.

My hips automatically arched toward his fingers as they slowly stroked my sensitive nub.

A groan slipped from my mouth, and I pushed my hips up toward his hand. "Oh," I cried out.

His tongue plunged into my mouth again, and his kisses pressed harder. My mouth separated from his and I ran my lips and tongue down his neck to his chest.

My hands explored his body. His stomach was firm and hard, and I lightly trailed my hand down his body from his chest, past his abdomen, following the thin line of hair under his navel. I caressed his hardness gently, moving my fingers slowly up and down his length.

He moaned deeply. "Babe, I can't control myself tonight, I want you too badly again," he said softly.

I nodded slowly, understanding and moved my caresses to his hip. I was lost in the feelings he was creating in me. His fingers were nudging me closer and closer to the cliff edge.

I pressed myself against him, my leg moving over his hip. My breathing accelerated. "Oh, Michael."

He replaced his fingers with his own hardness. I gasped as he slowly entered and filled me. I could feel him moving over me and through me. With his urging, he pushed my body further and further to the edge. I dove off the cliff and soared like an eagle. Our names were on the other's lips as we both ascended into the heights.

We lay together fighting to slow our breathing and our racing hearts. He pulled me close as he rolled over.

"I knew it would be you," he softly whispered, and then covered my face with kisses. He kissed my lips. "Sleep, my love."

Closing my eyes and secure in his arms, I fell into a deep sleep.

CHAPTER SEVENTEEN

I awoke trying to figure out where I was and then remembered and slowly stretched. Alone in the sleeping bag, I knew Michael would be taking pictures. Searching for my clothes, I realized my panties from yesterday seemed to have disappeared. I smiled remembering.

After dressing, I stepped outside of the tent. The air was a little brisk, and I pulled my sweatshirt over my head.

He called down from the stand. "Good morning sleepy head. I made some coffee for you, it's in the thermos."

Looking up at him, I lost all thoughts. He looked wonderful. There was the man who loved me last night. My knees went weak, and my stomach started flipping again. I looked him up and down, and now I knew exactly how his body felt against my skin.

He grinned at me, and I wondered if he could read my mind. "Bring the thermos up, and let's have some coffee together."

I nodded fighting the blush rising on my face. I picked up the thermos and climbed up the rope ladder to where he was poised on the edge of the stand. He took my hands and lifted me onto the platform. As soon as his hands touched me, I felt a rush between the two of us, and it made me take a deep breath.

His hands caressed both sides of my face as he pulled me in front of him. His day's growth of beard felt wonderfully masculine against my face as he slowly kissed me. Since I needed something to steady my shaky legs, I backed up against the trunk of the tree.

"Did you sleep okay last night?" he asked.

I smiled softly. "Yes. How about you?"

I looked up again and found him studying me. His eyes were the color of the morning sky.

He wrapped his arms around me. "I haven't had a sleep like that in many years," he murmured

His lips found mine again and left a trail of kisses from my mouth to my neck. Both hands slipped underneath my sweatshirt and tank caressing my back. One hand slid to the front of my body while he continued kissing me. His hand found a breast, and he gently kneaded it, brushing his knowledgeable thumb over my nipple.

A small groan escaped from my lips. The sensation of heat hit between my legs. My hands, which had been embracing his back, slipped down lower. I was glad he wore his jeans so loose that I could slide my hands down his back under his jeans. He wasn't wearing briefs under his jeans. I giggled.

Barely breaking our kiss, he whispered, "What is funny?"

My hands were still on his butt. "You're not wearing underwear." I smiled and kissed him.

"Sometimes I don't." He teased, "Babe, don't tell me you're a prude."

"How will I know when you're wearing underwear and when you're not?" I teased him back.

He grinned at me. "You won't unless you're willing to stick your hands down my pants, or you can undress me."

Suddenly we heard a voice below us clearing his throat, "Ah…" the voice trailed, "Hello?"

We pulled apart, and he leaned over the platform. I wanted the tree to swallow me.

"Hey Ranger Tom!" Michael called to the man below us. "This is a nice surprise."

"Hi Michael, do you have a few minutes? I'd like to talk to you about the shotgun shells you found."

"Yeah, sure, I'll be right down." He started climbing down the ladder.

I tried composing myself. I knew my face was bright red. Why wasn't Michael embarrassed?

He looked straight at me and grinned. "I'll hold the ladder for you as soon as I'm down."

I nodded and followed him down the ladder. Michael introduced us, and we sat on the rocks. Tom was a tall young man in his early thirties. He seemed very serious and uncomfortable that he had found us kissing and doing other things up in the stand. Michael on the other hand just grinned widely like he was proud to be caught.

After we spoke for a while, Tom relaxed. He informed us that the rangers had been up here last week and found another set of shells around the stand. Someone was probably shooting at the eagles. Although considered part of the reservation, the park rangers still patrolled the area.

"We're going to put a barrier up at the start of the ancillary road that leads up here. You'll need to let us know when you're coming then we can move it for you. If we block the entrance we're hoping whoever is coming up here will be put off by the long hike," Tom explained.

Michael nodded. "Not a problem."

Tom leaned over and looked at him thoughtfully. "Do you still carry your gun?"

He nodded again. "Always."

I looked at Michael with surprise and shock on my face. "You carry a gun?"

He encircled my waist with his arm, and his look was somber. "Only for protection Babe."

Tom rose. "I'll let you get back to what you were doing."

Even though he was not smiling when he said it, I thought I caught a glint in his eye as he looked at Michael. I remained silent.

As the ranger walked away, Michael followed him, and I buried my face in my knees dying of embarrassment. He returned to me after Tom was out of sight.

I stood up. "So, should we break camp?"

He pulled me up into his arms. He had the same glint in his eye that Tom had. "No, we don't need to yet. It's still early."

He led me toward the tent. He held the tent flap open for me, and I went inside. Kicking off his boots, he followed me in. He slipped his t-shirt over his head and threw it in the corner.

"Now where were we?"

I took a sharp intake of breath at the vision of him standing in front of me. It had been so dark last night that I had no chance to feast my eyes on him. Grinning, I knelt down on the sleeping bag, and he matched my position. I moved to take my sweatshirt off, and he caught my hands in his.

"No, let me," he said, and in one motion, he pulled both my sweatshirt and tank off over my head. "I want to look at you."

I followed the trail of his eyes. Next, he deftly loosened my braid. As I stayed kneeling in front of him, he lifted my hair, so it cascaded down my back. His audible sigh directed my attention back up to his face. His smile was for me only, and his gaze seemed to encompass me completely, which almost made me stop breathing.

I sat back on my heels and slowly danced one hand up the length of his chest to his shoulder. I traced over his nipple, and it immediately responded to my touch by tightening.

Gasping when I saw the red scratch marks on his shoulders, I asked, "What happened to your shoulders?" My fingers traced over them, and my eyes flew to his face. "Did you get tangled up with an animal?"

Michael chuckled as he pulled my other arm to his shoulder. "Yeah, that's my new Hellcat."

"Your what?" I was puzzled, and then I realized he was referring to me.

I remembered using my nails on him last night. "Sorry," I said hanging my head down and blushing.

Michael lifted my head up slowly with his hand and kissed me softly on the lips. "I consider it my merit badge. Come here."

He laid me back into the sleeping bag, and his hand trailed down from my throat to between my breasts coming to rest on my jeans button. I quickly reached up, unbuttoned my jeans, and drew the zipper down.

He laughed. "Well, you are my Hellcat."

I started wriggling around because there was no way I was going to get my jeans off without help.

"Off," I said.

He helped me kick my jeans off and throw them to the end of the tent.

"Oh, I like this," he said, "I can see so much more."

His fingers trailed around my belly and slipped tentatively under the band of my spare pair of panties. My lower half immediately tightened with the feel of his fingers.

Shifting my weight around, I pushed him on his back and sat up on my knees spanning his hips. "So you want to see more?"

I was happy his face wore a surprise. I took both of his hands in mine and put his palms to my lips, kissing one and then the other. I rubbed his knuckles against my breasts. His lower half responded to me by filling his jeans, and I could feel his erection straining against the material.

Michael pulled me down over him so he could kiss my breasts. I rested on my elbows on either side of his head while his hands and lips teased me. My hair tumbled around my shoulders and brushed against his chest. He bit lightly on one nipple, and I threw my head back as a moan escaped my lips. Slowly, I scooted back to my previous position over him and leaned down for a kiss on his lips. My lips trailed down his chest, and I stopped to tease his taut nipples. It was his turn to groan.

I continued down his chest and over his stomach. My tongue stopped just below his belly button. He watched me with great interest in his eyes. I sat up and straddled his legs. My hands fluttered lightly over his zipper. He leaned up on his elbows. Reaching down, I slowly unbuttoned his jeans. His eyes closed. I waited for him to open his eyes again and then touched the zipper.

"We need these off, don't we?" I asked.

I turned my attention to what lay just below my reach. I slowly inched his jeans over his hips. The evidence of his excitement was there for me to touch.

He moaned deeply, "Oh, Babe."

I stroked his length with my fingers and leaned over to take him in my mouth. My tongue teased him as he struggled to keep watching. He lay down flat, his hands pushing my hair away from my face as I continued to pleasure him. The sounds he made coursed through me and I wanted to rub myself against him. His breathing deepened and became more labored.

Michael pulled at me. "Come here."

I inched my way up to him while he slipped the rest of the way out of his jeans. The jeans landed in a pile with my clothes. His lips were against mine as he pushed my mouth open. Our tongues probed each other, and our hands were busy removing my panties.

Once free of them, I wrapped one leg around his hips and pressed myself to him. I had never wanted any man as much as I wanted him. His body felt wonderful against me, and I tried to maneuver myself to bring him closer. He laughed low as he watched me, and he placed his hands on my hips to still my movements.

"We are not anywhere close to that yet," he softly spoke into my ear.

I stared into his eyes, which were twinkling with amusement. "We're not?" I asked.

He shook his head while he pressed me lightly onto my back. "Oh no, my little Hellcat, not even close. I'm not done looking."

His lips again traveled down my neck and stopped at my breasts. His tongue teased me to hard peaks, and his actions caused the heat to rise from the center of my body. Responding to the involuntary movement of my hips, he stroked the inside of my thighs as I parted my legs for him.

My groans were audible when I arched my back up to make sure his mouth stayed in contact with my breasts. His lips continued to travel down my body, and I fell back against the sleeping bag breathing roughly.

Michael repositioned himself with his shoulders between my legs. His lips kissed the inside of my thighs where his hands had been only moments earlier. I felt his tongue move closer to the very center of my being as the movements of my hips encouraged him.

My eyes flew open when I realized his goal. "Oh, you don't have to do that." I touched his head with my fingers.

His mouth barely broke its rhythm to answer me. "But I want to taste you."

"It's okay Michael, you don't have to…" I trailed off and was barely able to speak when his tongue lapped at my super sensitive button. My mind broke free from my body while he created waves of pleasure in me all centered in that one tiny spot. Were the sounds I heard coming from me, or from him? I didn't know the answer. I only knew that I did not want him to stop while the heavy intensity built inside of me.

When I felt his fingers inside of me, stroking me, I knew I had to have all of him, now. My hips pressed against him hard and he moved up over me. I gasped when we joined because his size surprised me again.

"Are you okay?" he whispered.

I nodded as I caressed his face. "You're kind of big."

Michael chuckled. "Big feet too."

I giggled remembering our feet conversation. "I know."

He groaned as he moved inside of me. "So tight, so small."

His movements took my thoughts away as my hips met his rhythm. The force of his passion built inside of me again. I could feel the wave building as if I was surfing and waiting for the waves to swell. Whoosh, my body exploded, and wave over wave of intensity came crashing over me.

In between my roaring force, I could hear him calling me by my pet names. I felt his body stiffen as he shuddered and released inside of me. We lay tangled together for a few moments and then gently moved apart. Our breathing was rough and ragged, and our bodies glistened with our exertion.

His eyes looked like pools of clear blue water when they opened. His hand reached up to caress my face. "You are amazing!" he said.

I smiled and kissed his fingers.

He pulled me over so I could lay my head on his shoulder. I curled my fingers around his chest hair while he stroked my back.

"Can I ask you something?" I said, finally breaking the silence.

He took my hand and laced his fingers with mine. "What?" he asked while kissing my forehead.

"Last night after we made love you said you knew it would be me. What did you mean?"

I scooted up so that I could look at his face. His eyes told me that he hadn't realized he had spoken the words aloud.

Michael smiled. "It's a little silly. Do you really want to know?"

"Only if you want to tell me."

He turned on his side while my head was still nestled in his arm. "I don't mind telling you." He pulled me closer, and I slid my leg up and over his hip to settle us together.

Kissing me, he began his story. "When I first divorced, I was a little wild." He chuckled. "Truthfully I was a lot wild. I chased after every woman who would have me, and I wasn't very discriminating either. Maggie and I did not have a very loving relationship. After Maggie, as the song says, I was looking for love in all the wrong places."

While I watched him tell his story, I could tell he was picturing it all in his mind. I giggled. "So you were the man's version of a loose woman."

"Yes, I was very much that. I noticed though as the weeks went by I became more choosey in who I brought to the house. The girls had the ultimate veto, if they didn't like the woman, I would stop calling her."

I feigned shock. "You were absolutely heartless."

"I was also stupid. The women were smarter than me."

"That's always the case."

"You're right," Michael agreed. "They got wise to me, and they started pandering to the girls, hoping that would lead them to me. It worked for a while until I figured it out. I was disgusted mainly with myself when I finally did figure everything out. I decided just to be a dad and stop dating. I concentrated on the girls and promised that I would do so until Tammy graduated from high school."

"Oh my! How long was it?"

"The last five years. I've been out a couple of times, mainly blind dates that I was forced to go on, but, I've been celibate since then."

"No fooling around?"

He smiled and kissed me again. "Not at all."

"So what was with the comment you made to me?" I asked.

He laughed. "If you would stop interrupting, I'll finish the story."

I reached down and pinched him on the butt. "Okay, mister. Now finish the story."

He laughed again and pinched me back. "Hey!" I cried, and teased, "Knock that off!"

"Okay, okay. I don't want to get into a pinching contest. So, then when I moved to Mintock, I heard about this incredibly sexy next-door neighbor I was going to have."

"And?" I said, fluttering my eyelashes.

"And, I even looked up your website, and you were amazingly beautiful. I was really looking forward to meeting you. You have quite the salesperson in Debi too."

I laughed, happy to cuddle against him. "I'll have to thank her some time."

"Then Tammy met you and told me how nice you were and that you had given her a copy of your new book, the alarm bells went off in my head. I immediately thought another woman was being nice to my daughter to get to me."

"But, I hadn't even met you yet," I protested. "I barely knew that you existed. Although Debi did quite the sales pitch on you too."

"Remind me to thank her. Tammy pointed out to me that you were not like the other women. Then I met you at the baseball field. I wanted to lay you down on the bleachers and have my way with you right then and there. You looked so sexy in your tight uniform. You were hot."

"So was it then that you knew that I would be the one that would break your celibacy?"

Michael shook his head. "No, not then. It was later, when we drove home that night, and you…"

I finished the sentence for him, "Oh great, when I got sick all over you."

"You didn't get sick all over me, but it was when you showed the most vulnerability. You were the big baseball pitcher, romance novelist, and singer when I first met you. But when you were in the car, you were a very normal fragile person. I saw a woman who would let me take care of her."

"Oh!" I said surprised. "That's nice. I like that."

"Good, that's my story, and I'm sticking to it." He slapped my bottom playfully. "Okay my Hellcat, we need to get up if we're going to make our baseball game today."

We packed up the camp and made our way back to the jeep. Even though I insisted, he would not let me carry one of the large backpacks, and he made two trips to the car. I waited at the stand and made the second trip with him. It was difficult for me to believe that less than twenty-four hours had passed since we had arrived. The time felt more like a week to me. I was almost sad to be leaving the eagles and this peaceful place.

The day was warming up, and I wore only my tank top and jeans. After we loaded the jeep, both of us were warm from the hard work.

Leaning against the car door, I took a deep breath and let it out slowly. "Whew! I'm going to need to get into better shape if I want to keep coming out here."

Michael walked up and opened the car door for me. He put his arms around my waist and planted a kiss on my lips. "I'd say you were in pretty good shape." He squeezed my bottom. "The altitude is what is taking your breath away."

"Oh, I don't know. I think you're doing a pretty good job of that on your own." I put my arms around his neck and pulled him down for another kiss.

The corners of his mouth turned up in a small smile. "Did you have fun?"

Nodding, I put my head on his shoulder and murmured, "Did you?"

His hands slipped under my tank, and he rubbed my back. "It was like heaven," he whispered.

We held each other just enjoying the closeness. This was the happiest I had been in many years. The exhilaration I felt when I was with Michael surprised me. After my life with Kevin, I was adamantly against any further relationships. Being with my ex-husband had hurt me deeper than I could have imagined. Thinking of it now while Michael held me almost brought tears to my eyes.

He must have felt the tension go through my body as I thought of Kevin. He lifted my chin to look into my eyes. "Hey, are you okay?"

I nodded mutely trying to cast the thoughts of my ex from my mind. Michael kissed me again. It was not like the passionate ones we shared earlier, but a gentle, sweet kiss. The kiss was not chaste either, and it held the promise of passion coming later. When he pulled back, I could almost feel myself collapsing. He opened the car door, and my legs gave out, so I literally plopped onto the seat.

He chuckled making his way around the car. I pulled my feet in and buckled the seat belt. Everything was moving in slow motion. As he pulled out onto the highway, we didn't speak. He took my hand and squeezed it, and the touch sent a jolt through me. He was smiling as I glanced over at him. How could this man elicit these feelings in me? What had happened to me?

We were quiet on the drive home. Both lost in our own contemplation. His face gave me no clues of what his thoughts contained. The jeep pulled up in the back of his house. All four dogs and Tammy rushed out of the house to greet us.

CHAPTER EIGHTEEN

"How are the eagles?" she asked by way of a greeting.

Her father smiled and kissed her on the top of her head. "They were great, and they say hello. I see all the dogs are doing okay."

She nodded and started to help unload the car. "What did you think Elizabeth?"

I bent to pet all the dogs.

"It was amazing," I said truthfully, but I referred more to what Michael and I had shared.

He flashed me a private smile. "Go on home Elizabeth. I know you're dying for your shower. Tammy and I will get all this unpacked." He handed my little bag to me. "I'll pick you up in an hour for the game."

I nodded as he bent down to kiss me quickly.

After my shower, I braided my hair. I looked at my face closely in the mirror. Michael's stubble had done a number on my face. It looked wind burned at best. I touched my swollen lips with a grin. I didn't mind the after effects at all.

Before I knew it, he was knocking on the door. I called for him to come in while I prepared dinner for the dogs. He came up behind me, wrapped his arms around me, and planted a kiss on my neck. I grinned. He had shaved and smelled deliciously of soap.

"Is Tammy coming with us tonight?" I asked.

"She and Jason are planning on having dinner at the house with Katy too," he replied. He placed dog food bowls on the floor. "Ready?"

I rinsed my hands. "Yeah, let's go and play some baseball."

Even though we arrived at the field early, the parking lot was still packed. It looked like everyone in Mintock had turned out for the game. It wasn't unusual. A crowded town was the rule for the entire week following Labor Day. I looked forward to the end of summer when sleepy little

Mintock would go back to normal. Michael insisted on dropping me off while he searched for a parking space. Debi snagged me before I traveled ten feet.

"Hello darling, how was your visit with the eagles?" she asked and then looked me squarely in the face and laughed. "Oh dear, you've had your horn honked haven't you?"

"I don't know what you mean?" I frowned.

"Yes, you do." She linked her arm with mine as we walked toward the field. "Your face looks like it has rug burn, your lips are all swollen, and you have that cross-eyed look to you."

I could feel the blush from the roots of my hair down to the tips of my toes. "Is it that noticeable?"

"Only me and your close friends will notice." Debi laughed again. "Okay, it's not that bad."

"Really?" I looked at her earnestly.

Debi shook her head, but I didn't know whether to believe her or not. I pulled my hat onto my head and pushed the brim down hoping that the shade would hide my face a little. I warmed up with Don. He was a gentleman and did not mention anything to me. He had known me the longest of anyone at the field, and I knew he had put two and two together.

When Michael joined us, I appreciated that he did not hang all over me. I was not ready to declare to the world that we were involved any more than just dating. I needed time to acquaint myself to the idea first.

The game was over quickly. The other team from Mintock was no match for us, and we breezed through the game without much effort. It was the last game of the season, and we were happy with the win. I asked Michael to drive me home so that I could shower again and change clothes before we met the team for dinner.

He dropped me off at the back of my house. As I got out of the car, he grabbed my hand.

"Do you want some company in the shower?" He grinned and looked like a teenager.

"I think I have that one covered. Are you changing clothes?"

"Yeah."

"Well, when you're done, come on over. I'll leave the door unlocked."

"Oh?" He raised one eyebrow.

"No. You can keep me company while I get ready. I'll see you in a bit."

I entered the cabin and stripped off my uniform in the bathroom. The shower was hot against my skin. My body was sore from sleeping on the ground the previous night as well as, I was sure, from last night's activities. The water pounding on me felt good. Steam filled the bathroom, and I wiped off the mirror. My skin was pink from the hot water. I wrapped my hair in a towel and wrapped another towel around myself.

A blast of cold air hit me when I opened the bathroom door, but that wasn't what made me gasp. Michael lay on my bed with his head propped up on one arm.

"Hi," I said after I took a breath.

He grinned at me. "Sorry, I didn't mean to scare you."

"No, you didn't scare me, just surprised me."

I was glad I had decided to wrap the towel around myself instead of walking out nude the way I usually did. Really, what difference it made I don't know, he had already seen me naked. He sat up with his legs dangling over the edge. He reached out for me and grabbed the side of the towel.

"Come on over here," he beckoned.

Since he had a hold of the towel, it was either lose it or move over to him. The latter seemed like the best choice. His hands encircled my hips, and he looked up at me.

"So, are you going to show me what's under this?" His eyes teased me.

Placing my arms on his shoulders, I leaned down to whisper. "I think you already know what's under here."

He grinned. "That I do."

He caught my face between his hands and kissed me. When I straightened up, he took the opportunity to pull me closer in between his legs. His hands loosened the front of the towel, and I let it drop to the floor.

"Are you going to let me come over tonight and make love to you?"

I softly answered, "Yes." My knees started to go weak at the mention of tonight.

"Good. In that case, then…" He stopped to kiss my stomach while his hands reached around to caress the back of my thighs. "I can give you a little sugar now to tide us over." Pausing again, he bent to kiss me lower while his fingers trailed between my thighs.

I closed my eyes as his words sank in. When I realized what he was going to do, I opened my eyes wide. I would have taken a step back, but he was holding me too tightly. "No Michael. You don't have to, I can wait for tonight. I know men think that's icky, you don't have to."

He stopped when I said no. He looked up at me with a puzzled face. "What is icky?" He looked at me and then smiled with understanding. "You mean kissing you here." He bent down and planted a noisy kiss low on my belly. "And using my tongue here." He ran his tongue just below where he had kissed me.

I was torn, but his hands moved up my thighs, and I wanted to part my legs for him further, but how could I when I told him to stop?

"You don't have to. I know guys think it's…" I stopped. Was I repeating myself, had I already said that?

He laughed and trailed his tongue and lips further and further down my belly. "Just because your ex-husband did not want to kiss you like this, that isn't going to stop me." He looked up at me. "I like to give you pleasure. I like to see which movement you like the best, which one makes you gasp, and which one will make you moan." He stood up and removed the towel around my hair. My wet hair fell down around my shoulders and back. "Now I can't make love to you both now and later, so I'll wait for later for myself. But you're not going to deny me this little delight I can have now by giving you enjoyment are you?" His voice was so silky smooth and so reasonable. Michael made perfect sense.

His eyes engulfed me, and suddenly the sky surrounded me. I shut my eyes and whispered, "Yes."

"You are my little Hellcat," he softly spoke as I surrendered myself to him.

It was the first time I had ever had joy given without any expectations. He led me on a path that was slow, fast, exciting, teasing, and every moment with every movement, the momentum built within me. He took his time and did not rush the journey. When the surge finally racked through my body, he was there at the end holding me tightly against him. I could not talk or think clearly in the moments after and lying in his arms made me feel warm and protected. Knowing that I had to break apart from him to get dressed made me miss him already.

"When are you leaving for Louisiana?" I asked while I was still in his embrace.

Michael kissed the top of my head. "I'm leaving at seven in the morning. Katy is coming with me to the airport. She starts school next week. When do you leave on your book tour?"

I rose up on my elbows to look at him. "I thought you had forgotten about my tour?"

"No. I'm very much aware that tonight is all we have for the next three weeks."

"I wish I could change it. I'm flying down to Los Angeles on Thursday. I have to take care of some business things first. Nancy and I are leaving for Miami on Sunday," I said as I nuzzled up to him again and kissed his neck.

He cleared his throat. "Babe, you better get up and get dressed. Otherwise, I'm going to make you stay in this bed with me."

I giggled. "I wouldn't mind that you know."

He watched while I dried my hair. I did it in the nude, and when I flipped my hair back over, it had never felt more sensual as it cascaded down my back. While I dressed, I tried not to be self-conscious. Dressing in front of someone is far more an intimate act than I had realized. I put on a matching set of grey silk panties and bra. Then I added a pair of black thigh high hose. He studied my every movement, and when I stepped into my black cocktail dress, he was behind me in an instant to pull up the zipper.

He dragged me back against him and almost growled in my ear, "I get to remove those panties tonight, but we're leaving on the thigh highs and the shoes."

He stepped back as I slipped into black four-inch stiletto heels. The sleeveless cocktail dress was plain with a V cut out in the back. The front had a rounded neckline. It was tight and very short.

"You are all legs in that dress. I like it a lot," he said appreciatively.

I blushed when he had me pirouette for him. When he started the wolf whistling, I pushed him out of the bedroom.

"You're going to make me late!"

We stepped outside, and I was touched to see the Mustang parked at the back of my cabin.

"We're riding in style." I flashed a smile at him.

Michael opened the door. I sat on the seat, keeping my legs together, and slid them into the car.

"Very nice, you've done this before," he commented.

I laughed and shook my head when he joined me in the car. "You're a silly boy." I leaned over and kissed him.

"You know I'm not going to be able to keep my hands off of you at the restaurant." His eyes gleamed at me while he ran his hands up my legs under my dress.

"Hey, that's enough of the pawing," I protested lightly. "How would you like me to paw you?"

I ran my hand as he had done to me, along his thigh and then I rested it in his crotch. I was surprised to find him hard under my fingers. Grinning, I squeezed him through his pants.

He flashed me a grin and held my hand against him. "You are an evil and wicked woman, Elizabeth."

He let my hand go, and I reached up to kiss him again.

"You bet. Let's go, I don't want to be late!"

It was dark by the time we arrived at the restaurant. Debi had saved us seats at their table. After we ate, we lingered over our coffee.

Michael laid his hand on my thigh and leaned over to whisper, "We're waiting ten minutes, and then we're leaving."

"Why?" I whispered back.

He whispered back to me, "Because I need to remove that article of clothing I mentioned to you earlier."

I could see his desire for me in his eyes floating on the surface.

As soon as we could, he rose and explained that we needed to head for home because he was catching an early flight in the morning. I needed no urging from him to leave the restaurant. My level of excitement matched his. He joined me in the car, and I immediately put my arms around his neck and started to kiss him. He responded quickly to me and eagerly. His hands roamed under my dress, and he began to pull at my panties.

Michael breathed out roughly. "I need to get you home, or I'm going to take you right here in the car."

I giggled and let my breath out slowly in his ear, "The car is okay."

"No, it's not. I have something else in mind entirely."

I snapped the seatbelt on, and he pulled out of the restaurant parking lot. His right hand continued to rest on my thigh under my dress, and I casually laid my palm over his crotch.

He grinned. "You're really pushing it, aren't you?"

Turning in my seat to face him, I put my arm around his shoulder and leaned over to nibble on his ear lobe while my hand made small massaging circles over the stiffness in his pants. He didn't utter a word, but his hand under my dress matched the motions I was making.

He turned onto the road behind our houses. He abruptly removed his hand from me and put it on the steering wheel as he pulled up to the back of my house.

"It appears that you have a visitor," he said with a puzzled tone.

My head turned to the front, and I had a difficult time focusing at first. I had left the porch light on, and Kevin was sitting in one of the chairs on the back porch.

"What is he doing here?" I asked as I unbuckled my seat belt.

I waited for Michael to come around and open the door for me. He helped me out of the seat and took my hand as we walked up the steps.

Kevin rose from the chair. "Hey Liz, it's great to see you." His tone contradicted the words he spoke.

He gave me a once over look, and I knew he was noticing the short dress and the four-inch heels. Then he looked at Michael with an unwelcoming face. He was not pleased to see I was with someone.

I introduced the two men. Kevin reached out his hand, and I knew he was happy that Michael was on a step below him. It made them almost even in height.

"And you know Liz how?" Kevin asked with a sneer on his lips.

The question did not faze Michael in the least. "Elizabeth is my girlfriend."

I smiled at his response. He could have introduced himself as the next-door neighbor or as a friend. The girlfriend answer was the one I liked the most.

Kevin barely acknowledged the answer. "Well Liz, I need to talk with you." He glanced at Michael. "Privately."

Michael turned to look at me. I nodded and touched his arm. "Let me talk to Kevin, and I'll call you as soon as he leaves, okay?"

He leaned over and kissed me. "I'll be waiting." He turned and went back to his car.

I unlocked the back door and let Kevin in behind me.

CHAPTER NINETEEN

"Wow, you've done some great things to our cabin," Kevin commented as he walked around.

I ignored his comment and petted the dogs. They weren't happy to see him either, and surely, they were detecting my uneasiness.

"Why are you here Kevin?"

Kevin ignored my question. "So you wore this dress for him?"

I straightened up. With the heels, I was taller than Kevin was. "Yes, I did."

He smirked. "Maybe if you would have worn that with me it would have saved our marriage."

"No, Kevin, I don't think a dress would have saved our marriage." I slipped off my heels and stood in my stocking feet. The way he stared at me in my dress made me suddenly uncomfortable. "So, Kevin, why are you here?"

He stood close to me, and his voice became quiet. "I don't have good news for you."

I looked at his face, and he was serious. I steeled myself. "Okay?"

"I wanted you to know that my dad passed away." He turned his face away from me.

"Oh, Kevin, I'm sorry." In the old days, I would have wrapped my arms around him to try to take some of the pain away. Tonight I didn't want to hug him, but I did take his hand. "Let's sit down."

I caught Kevin by surprise, and I knew that he expected me to hug him, but he followed me to the couch and sat. I took a seat at the other end. I had not liked his father. He had always called me Liz even though he knew I hated the name, and he was continuously pinching my bottom. I had put up with him only because he was my father-in-law and I had not seen him since the divorce.

"Will there be a funeral?"

"We already had the funeral last week," he said matter-of-factly. "I knew you probably wouldn't want to come anyway since most of my family doesn't like you since you divorced me."

Now I was confused. "Okay, Kevin, why did you come up here? You certainly could have called me about your father."

"I thought, that since my dad was gone now, we could see about getting back together again." He put on his sincere face.

I looked at him incredulously. "What difference could that possibly make? You are not making any sense."

He inched closer to me on the couch. "Look, I know you, and my dad didn't get along. I thought that maybe now that he was gone, we could rekindle our relationship."

I stood. "It wasn't that your dad and I didn't get along. You and I didn't get along. We are over. Period. Finished."

He moved closer on the couch to where I was standing. "Come on Liz, you know what we once had, we were great together." He took my hand.

I shook his hand off, but he seized it again roughly and pulled me down on the couch. "Ow! Kevin, you are hurting me. Look, I think you need to leave."

He quickly let go of my hand. "I'm sorry. I didn't mean to hurt you." He was almost sitting on top of me. I had my back squeezed up against the armrest of the couch. "Don't throw me out. I'll be good. I don't have anywhere to go," he pleaded and looked at me with his large brown eyes.

"I'm sure you can find a hotel room," I retorted.

"Not during a holiday week."

He looked at me again, this time with the look that had worked on me many times. Complete innocence and non-culpability spread all over his face. He had my number, and he was correct, he would never find a hotel room tonight. Damn.

I squeezed myself out and stood up again, holding up my hands. "Okay. Okay," I surrendered. "Sleep in the guest room. But, I want you out of here the first thing in the morning." I did not know how I was going to explain to Michael that my ex-husband now ruined our wonderfully planned evening. "I have to make a phone call." I walked toward my bedroom.

Kevin called out to me, "Are you going to call your boyfriend to let him know I'm staying and we're spending the night together?" A dark look passed through his eyes, and it gave me a chill.

"Don't push it or you will find yourself out on your ass," I called back as I angrily slammed the bedroom door. The dogs had run into the bedroom ahead of me, they were not great fans of him either. I paced for a moment and then picked up the phone to call Michael's number.

He picked up the phone on the first ring. "He's not gone yet." His tone was tight and clipped.

"No. He is spending the night in the guest room. All the hotels in the area will be full. It's still the Labor Day holiday week," I explained.

His voice turned very low, his anger was evident. "I can't believe this."

"Michael, I can't just throw him out. He came up here to let me know his dad passed away."

"Couldn't he have phoned you with the news?" he derided.

I could not believe I had to deal with two moody men tonight. "I'm just as disappointed as you are. I'll talk to you tomorrow morning before you leave."

I was furious with Kevin, and I was not very happy with Michael at that moment either. After I changed into a long nightgown, I opened my bedroom door a crack and stuck my head out. The living room was empty. I snuck quietly out to the kitchen. I made a snack for the dogs and myself. Just as I turned to go back into my bedroom, he was leaning up against the wall by the guest bathroom. He stood there in only his briefs with his arms crossed over his chest. He had not lost any of his physique. I knew what I had first seen in him, and then, he opened his mouth.

I frowned at him. "No pajamas?"

He opened his arms wide. "You always preferred me like this before we went to sleep."

"Yeah, well now I prefer pajamas on my overnight guests," I snapped back.

"I'm not a guest. This used to be my place too."

My lips pursed, and I spoke with a low even voice, "This was never your place. Ever."

Kevin changed the subject. "Did you make me a snack too?"

"Here." I handed him my plate. "Don't get crumbs all over the place."

He snorted. "You always hated the crumbs. Guess you still do."

I walked toward my bedroom.

He called out to me laughing, "I guess your plans got canceled with your boyfriend. That's too bad. But, if you need a good roll in bed, you can call me."

I fought against turning around, but I did, "And then who would you call to do the job?"

He glared at me. I walked into the bedroom and slammed the door. I blew out my breath. I know I should not have said anything, but I have a big mouth. That big mouth used to get me a beating. He was good at hitting in places that most people could not see, though he did give me a black eye a couple of times. He was infamous for catching me off guard, usually in the dark, which was one of the reasons I always kept lights on in the house at night.

I gave the dogs their biscuits. I turned all the lights out except a small night light and checked outside the window. The only dim light I could see next door was probably from Michael's laptop. I smiled. Not all was lost. We would talk in the morning. I climbed into bed and snuggled into my pillows thinking about the last time I had been in my bed. It had been a long day, and I was tired.

I awoke with light streaming through the windows. Michael was spooned against me with his arm wrapped around me. I wriggled my hips back against him. He was not ready yet, but I would change that condition quickly.

"Let's make love," I whispered.

"Liz, I knew you'd come around."

Something was wrong. Why was Michael calling me Liz? Why did his voice sound so funny? Why was the hair on his arm black?

I screamed and pushed Kevin away from me.

"What are you doing in my bed?" I shouted.

I could hear the dogs barking in the living room. Why were the dogs in the living room? I backed further away from him. My head still was not clear. I was still wearing my nightgown, which was a good thing.

"Get out of here."

Kevin lay back down. "Come on Liz, you know you want it. You even said it." He pulled the covers away from his body and stretched. He was naked. His excitement was becoming more evident. "Let's not waste a good thing." He stretched again and rolled over on his side. He stroked himself, and his erection began to grow larger.

I was not going to watch this performance. I turned my head away, and this was my undoing. He moved so fast, and I did not see him coming. Wrenching me by the hair, he had me quickly pinned underneath him. I struggled, and even though we were the same height, I did not have the added benefit of his extra weight and muscles. He straddled both of my legs to keep them still. Forcing both of my arms above my head, he pinned them down with just one hand. In the scuffle, my nightgown had risen above my hips. At that moment, I wished I had worn underwear because it would have made it more difficult for him.

Clearly, I knew what was coming. "Kevin, please don't." He was not listening to me. His free hand was frantic under my nightgown. I cried again. "Don't!" He pinched my breasts hard, and I cried out, "You're hurting me."

He growled at me, "I know how you like it."

He pinched me roughly again and moved one leg between mine to force my legs open. When I resisted, he backhanded me across my face. The hit made me gasp, and even though he did not break the skin of my lips, the pain felt almost as bad as a punch. He knew a blow would have left a mark. His knee dug into my thigh to keep my leg still while he pushed my other leg further apart. I could feel the hot tears running down my cheeks.

"No, you're hurting me. Please stop," I begged and continued to struggle. I could not think. He was not going to stop. I knew if I complied it would go a little easier for me, but I wanted to fight. I did not want this to happen. "Kevin, I'll tell…"

He interrupted me, "What you'll tell Don's dad? It's your word against mine. I'm your ex-husband. You invited me to spend the night. Everyone saw you in the slut dress and shoes yesterday. No one would believe you."

"No, I'll tell my dad," I said it with finality. I knew what he was going to do to me. I would not be able to fight him off now.

It took him a moment to think. My father was a retired cop. My dad had friends who were cops. He also had other friends. Those were friends who had gone straight. But were still fearsome, and he knew it. He uttered a profanity, and then he let me go. I scrambled up quickly and ran to the other side of the room.

"I want you out of here now. I do not want to see you again, ever. Do not contact me again. Nothing. Do you understand?" The tears were still streaming down my face.

"God, you're a touchy bitch." He got up and sauntered toward the door. He turned once more before he reached the door. He had gone soft again, and he reached down to handle himself. "You'll never know what you missed."

I just went into the bathroom, closed the door, and locked it. I sat on the toilet stunned.

Ten minutes later I heard his car engine, and I crept out of the bathroom. I tiptoed out into the kitchen and checked the back window. His car was gone. I let out a sigh of relief.

A quick glance at the microwave clock showed ten minutes past seven. I ran into my bedroom and quickly pulled on my jeans and a shirt. There was no worry about underwear. As I ran through the house and sprinted out the back door, I prayed that Michael would have gotten a late start. The jeep was gone.

I knocked on the back door, and Tammy answered it quickly, she must have been in the kitchen.

"Tammy," I took a breath. "Did I miss your dad?"

"Elizabeth, they just left. You missed them by just a couple of minutes."

"Oh no," I said leaning against the doorframe with my eyes closed. My head started to hurt from Kevin pulling my hair.

"Yeah, Dad talked to your ex-husband for a few minutes. Then after your ex-husband left, Dad ordered Katy into the car, and they left. Dad was really angry."

"What? … Tammy can I come in, I'm not feeling very well." She moved from the door and followed me into the kitchen. She poured me a glass of water while I sat at the kitchen table. "Kevin talked to Michael?"

"Yeah, I didn't hear the entire conversation, but he told Dad that the two of you spent the night together last night and decided to get back together again. He said that he was looking forward to being our neighbor." Tammy paused, looked down at her hands, and then back up at me. Her eyes looked hurt and betrayed. "I can't believe you would hurt my dad like this."

I tried to take her hands, but she pulled away from me. The tension between us was thick.

"Tammy, whatever Kevin told your dad, it was a lie. I am not getting back together with my ex-husband. I did not spend the night with him. Well, he did stay in the house, but that is all. Your dad knew he was staying at my house because I called him last night." I shook my head and covered my face with my hands. My head started throbbing now, and it was making me nauseous. "I've got to go home and try to reach your dad to clear up this mess. Are you still coming over for pizza tonight?"

She looked at me, trying to see the truth in my eyes. I do not know what my eyes showed. "Do you still want me to come over? I mean now that you're back with your ex-husband. Will he be back tonight?"

I closed my eyes and sighed. "Yes Tammy, I want you to come over tonight. Kevin will not be there, he will never be there again. We are not getting back together. He was lying. I don't know why?" Well, I actually did, but that was a more complicated explanation than I could handle now.

My head was pounding when I walked into my kitchen. I took two aspirin and then picked up the phone. I dialed Michael's cell phone. It rang and went directly to voice mail. I wanted to talk to him, not to the voice mail, but I had no choice.

"Michael, it's me, please call me back. I need to talk to you."

That was the best I would be able to do for now. I stripped the sheets in both rooms. I wanted to burn them, but my practicality got the better of me. I washed the bedding in hot water. Twice. Then I took a shower, as hot as I could stand it. My headache had lessened, but it was not gone completely. I remade my bed and put on a pair of shorts and a t-shirt. I looked at my cell phone. Damn! How had I missed the call?

The voicemail was from Michael. It simply said that we would talk when he got back from his trip. Had he forgotten that when he got back, I would be gone for two weeks? I called his cell phone again. The voicemail picked up immediately which meant his phone was off.

"Michael, we really need to talk. Tammy told me what Kevin had told you. He lied to you. We are not getting back together. Please call me back, I need to speak with you."

I lay down to take a nap. My head started to hurt again, and I did not feel like doing anything else. When I awoke, the headache was gone, and I felt better. I was hungry too, which was always a good sign. I checked my cell phone, and there was another message. How was I missing these calls?

I listened to the message, and it made me angry. He repeated that we could talk about our relationship when he got home. I called his phone again, and the phone rang four times before it went to voice mail. Was he screening my calls? I could feel the irritation building inside of me.

"Michael, this is Elizabeth. It appears you really don't want to talk to me." I ignored the fact that he had been returning my calls and that my phone had gone to voice mail too. "We won't have the opportunity to see each other face to face for another three weeks to discuss our relationship." The way I said relationship sounded as if there were quotation marks around the word. "What really gets me though is your jump to believe Kevin without bothering to talk to me first. So maybe we don't really have a relationship to discuss. Furthermore, perhaps our intimacy was a mistake since we don't have a relationship."

I ended the call and turned the phone off. I was not prepared to talk to him but wanted to get the last word. I was like that when I was angry.

After I made a peanut butter and jelly sandwich, I plopped down in front of the television with the dogs. Both dogs helped me by eating the crusts while I ate the soft interior. We watched a romantic movie on one of the women's channels.

I felt like crying, but the tears would not come. I was fuming at both Michael and Kevin. This morning had been more than Kevin had ever done to me. His sex play had always been rough which I had never enjoyed, but this morning there was a mean nastiness that was frightening. He had used the violence to excite himself. Had I not used the dad card, he would have forced sex on me. My father scared him. I am sure somewhere along the line my dad had a talk with him because Kevin had always cut a wide circle around him. What had he said to Michael that made him so angry? It made me sad Michael had believed him.

It was late in the afternoon, and the ringing house phone made me jump. I heard his voice on the machine, "Elizabeth it's Michael. Please pick up the phone. I know you're home." I frowned. So much for screening my calls. Tammy had probably told him I was home. I picked up the receiver on the table next to the couch.

"Michael?" I answered, not sure of my own voice. My body began to tremble.

"Elizabeth, I tried reaching you on your cell phone. You must have it turned off because it is going straight to voice mail."

I was so happy to hear his voice. His voice sounded only tired, not angry. "Oh Michael…" I trailed off because the tears started coming down my face. "It was awful, really awful, and then when Tammy told me that Kevin had spoken to you, he lied to you…" I stopped short again because I could not talk and cry at the same time.

"Babe, what's wrong. Elizabeth, tell me what happened." The concern in his voice took over the tiredness.

"Michael," I snuffled, but the tears were continuing to stream down my face, "tell me you're not mad at me."

"Babe, I'm not mad at you. Elizabeth, you're worrying me, can you stop crying to tell me what happened?"

I wiped my eyes and blew my nose on my t-shirt. I started to explain what had happened with Kevin this morning and stopped short of finishing the story when he interrupted me.

"Oh shit, Elizabeth, did he rape you?" The anguish in his voice was unmistakable.

I started crying again. Reliving the episode just brought it back to me in waves. "No." My voice shook. "No, he stopped."

"Elizabeth, I can rearrange my schedule here. I'm coming home to be with you."

"No. You don't have to do that. I'm okay. I'm just a little shaky." I gave him the rest of the story including threatening Kevin with my dad.

"Oh, babe, I'm so sorry. When he spoke to me, I jumped to the wrong conclusion. I should have stayed and talked to you first, but damn," he paused and then continued softly, "he handed me your panties from yesterday and told me you had sent them over as a souvenir. I couldn't believe it. I just exploded when I saw them."

"He handed you my panties? Oh Michael, no wonder you reacted the way you did. Kevin could not have possibly known what that underwear meant to the two of us. It was just a lucky chance on his part."

His voice became serious. "Are you going to press charges against Kevin?"

I hesitated a moment. "I just can't."

"Why not?" he questioned me.

"What I said about my father was true. My dad would seriously hurt Kevin if he ever found out. I'm not protecting him, but I am protecting my dad. I don't think he meant to do what he did to me this morning. I doubt that he will bother me again."

He sounded unconvinced. "I don't know after what he pulled with me. I think he's capable of anything. At the very least you should get a restraining order against him."

"I'll think about it, okay?" I promised.

"Okay. I'm sorry Babe. I should have better control of my temper. I was glad I had the plane trip to think things through, and I realized what an ass I had been."

"Are we okay now?" I asked.

"Do you forgive me?"

"There is nothing to forgive," I said softly. "By the way, what did you do with my underwear? It is part of a matching set."

He laughed. "They were my souvenir, weren't they? I have them in my carryon bag."

I exclaimed giggling, "Michael you didn't?"

It was good to hear him laugh. "I didn't know what to do with them. Truthfully, now I'm glad I have them."

"Oh?"

"Yeah, Tammy lent me your new book, I especially like page seventy-five. I think we should try it."

"Page seventy-five?" I hesitated a moment and then giggled. "Oh, page seventy-five. I don't really think that's physically possible, you know, creative license."

He laughed low. "Trust me I'm working it out in my head."

I was happy we had gotten to the easy part of talking with each other again. I felt refreshed, and the tension that Kevin had caused was slipping off my shoulders.

"Do me a favor, call Tammy and let her know we're okay again. She gets a bit possessive of her dad, especially when she thought I had hurt you."

"I will," he said. "Is she staying with you tonight?"

"Yeah, she should be over in a little while."

"Thanks for keeping an eye on her for me. Since Katy is gone, I'm glad she has some company. It was lucky she didn't hear the entire conversation I had with Kevin. Tell me, did he ever hit you, besides today?"

"Yes." My voice became quiet. "But, it wasn't all physical. Most of it was mental and emotional."

"I'm sorry Elizabeth," he said softly.

"It's over. I need the pain to be behind me so that I can get on with my life."

"I know."

As we reached the end of the conversation, I asked, "Call me again tomorrow night, okay?" I knew my voice sounded hopeful, but I could not contain it.

"I'll call you every night Babe," he promised.

When I hung up the phone, my heart was lighter. He had left me with a warm, happy feeling. My problems with Kevin were behind me.

CHAPTER TWENTY

The dogs started barking while I was changing my t-shirt. Tammy had called, and she was on her way over. When I answered the door, she looked like she was ready for a sleepover. Both dogs were with her too. Since she would be caring for Topper and Samantha while I was on the book tour, we wanted all the dogs to be as comfortable as possible with each other. We put her stuff in the guest room and agreed on the pizza ingredients. The pizza would be half vegetarian and half meat.

Tammy groaned when I ordered a salad to go with the pizza. "You're as bad as my dad making me eat salad!"

I smiled at the comparison, liking the compliment. "Do you miss Jason yet?"

She frowned and threw herself on the coach in drama queen fashion. "Miss him? I've thought of nothing but him all day long," she said with emphasis. Jason, Don, and Debi had driven down to Palo Alto since he would be starting at Stanford the following Monday. She frowned again. "He's not answering any of my text messages either." She waved her phone at me.

I handed her a soda and sat down next to her on the coach. "Give him a chance to get settled, he'll call you."

"You think so?" She smiled brightly at me.

The smiled reminded me of Michael. Her dimples were the same as her dad's. Just thinking of him made me miss him. I shook my head silently and wondered if I had a teenage crush like Tammy.

"I'm sure of it. It's not like he's going to be gone forever, he'll be home on the weekends."

"I know," she answered. "But, it's not like having him nearby. Besides, when I go to UC Davis, we'll be on different schedules. We won't have any time for each other." She drew a heavy sigh. "Dad told me that if our relationship can't stand a little time apart, then it's not a real bond."

"You know he's right. School will be so exciting for both of you. You are both taking on big challenges, and you're young, you will change a lot. Don't stress out about it now. Email and cell phones make it much easier to communicate than when I went to school."

Tammy flashed me a look and then giggled. "Oh yeah, I forgot, you and dad are ancient. Did they even have phones when you went to school?"

I smacked her with a couch pillow. "Watch it, or all the pizza will be mine, and I'll make you eat just the salad!"

"Okay, not fair." She giggled. "So can I ask you something?" Her face turned serious, and she blushed."

"Ask away."

"Okay, please don't think this is stupid, okay? How old were you the first time you did it?" She blushed and did not look me straight in the face.

"Did what?" I asked with puzzlement on my face. I paused while she pressed her lips together. "Oh, you mean that!" I tried not to blush myself when I finally figured out that she was talking about sex. "You really want to know?"

I knew only two reasons she could want to know. That she had already slept with Jason, or she was about ready to, and wanted to compare her actions with my own.

Tammy nodded her head. How do I answer this question? What is the right answer? My mother always answered me truthfully, so I decided on that tactic.

"I was eighteen, about the same age as you, but for each person it's different."

"Was it what you thought it was going to be?" She looked down at her hands, again not wanting to look me in the face.

I lifted her head up with my hand and looked her in the eyes. She had answered my question without having me ask it, she had already slept with Jason.

"Tammy, what are you trying to ask me?"

"Well, were you disappointed by, you know…" she trailed off. She kept looking at me, her eyes searching mine.

"Yes, it definitely was not worth all the hype. It could have been better if one of us had some experience. He was my high school sweetheart, and we had dated our entire senior year. Shortly before we left for college, we decided to commit to each other. His parents had gone on a trip, and we found ourselves alone in his house. One thing led to another. It wasn't something I had planned. We fumbled and stumbled through it."

"What happened to the two of you?" she asked.

"We both met other people in college, and we drifted apart. I saw him once or twice after that, but I didn't sleep with him again."

Tammy did not start crying even though she looked like she was going to burst into tears. "Jason and I slept together Saturday night while you and dad were with the eagles."

"And you were disappointed?" I questioned.

She nodded and again pressed her lips together. "It was just like you said, a little stumbling and fumbling around. Then all of a sudden it was over, well, at least for Jason."

I slipped my arm around her, and she rested her head on my shoulder. "Are you in love with Jason?"

"Yes, I think so," she answered.

"Would you understand if I said what happened to me is not necessarily what will happen to you and that it does get better with practice?"

She giggled. "I hope so. Everyone makes such a big deal about it."

"When you love someone and want to spend time with them the intimacy that you share becomes very special. The times you are together then become wonderful, and that leads to greater fulfillment," I explained. "Give it a bit."

Tammy gave me an uncertain look. "You won't tell my dad, will you?"

I shook my head and squeezed her. "Absolutely not, you're an adult, and you're not doing anything illegal. It's none of his business, and it's just between us girls. Okay?"

"Thanks, Elizabeth. You are easy to talk to, and I appreciate it. So do you love my dad?" she asked with a serious look on her face. She certainly had been listening to me.

A knock on the back door interrupted us. All four dogs rushed to the door. For me, it was the proverbial saved by the bell. The rest of the night we had a real girl's night, we ate our pizza and salad, much to the distaste of Tammy. We laughed and giggled at the chick flick we had on television. We argued about baseball. It turned out she was a Giants fan, like her dad. Finally, we parted ways to our bedrooms.

The next morning I could smell baking cinnamon, and another sniff told me there was brewing coffee. It was quite a difference from yesterday morning with Kevin in my bed. I rolled over and glanced at the clock. I could not believe I had slept so late. The dogs were with me, so I assumed that Tammy must have let them out. I threw the covers back and got out of bed. Slipping on my robe, I poked my head out of the bedroom door.

"Mmmmm, it certainly smells good out here."

Tammy peeked her head around the kitchen wall. "Good morning Elizabeth! I figured the coffee smell would wake you up. The coffee is finished brewing, and I just pulled the cinnamon buns out of the oven. I thought we could use a treat this morning."

"Where did you find cinnamon in my house?"

"You had coffee and sugar, which was the total sum of your ingredients.

The rest came from my house."

"Whew, you had me worried," I teased her. "If I have spices, someone is sneaking stuff into my kitchen."

"You don't like to cook?"

"When I was younger I cooked with my mom and sister, but my sister was much better at it, so I gave up. I do other things better, probably just like you and your sister."

"Are you still competitive with your sister?" She paused cutting the cinnamon rolls to look at me.

I had to think about the question for a moment. Were we still competitive? No, not really, but we certainly had some unresolved issues. It had worked out that I was closer to our mother and she had become closer to our dad. Mom and I had shared more interests.

Moreover, quite frequently, I had trouble seeing the world from my father's perspective. Lisa saw the world more in the black and white of our dad, the world of law enforcement, right and wrong, good and evil. Even though I did not do anything with my music, as my mother had wanted, she had been proud when I had chosen to write.

"No, we're not competitive any longer. We just chose very different lifestyles."

"I guess that will happen to Katy and me too. Everyone thinks we're a lot alike, but we're not. She is way too serious, and she doesn't like to have fun."

"Katy does like to have fun, but it's different than the type of fun you like to have," I countered with a different viewpoint.

Reaching up, I retrieved two small plates from the cupboard. "Coffee is done!" We put the cinnamon rolls on the plates and carried them to the table with the coffee mugs. I inhaled the cinnamon bun deeply. "This is too incredible for words. Thank you!"

She beamed. "They are Dad's favorites too. He has a big sweet tooth."

"Does he?" I asked.

"He has to replace meat with something." She giggled.

Just the mention of Michael made my heart skip a beat somewhere deep in my chest. I wondered what he was doing at that moment. It made me feel good just to think about him. All of a sudden, I realized Tammy had been talking to me, and I had not heard a word. I frowned inwardly and chastised myself. I would need to pay attention and stop being a silly teenager.

We enjoyed our day together. We took my boat to the lake. She read, and I worked on my laptop. It was a relaxing day. We went to the local diner for dinner. Afterward, Tammy decided to turn in early. She had too much fresh air today and had woken very early. I sat at my desk trying to finish the chapter I was working on earlier.

When the cell phone rang, I almost jumped out of my skin. I had not been expecting a call tonight, and then I remembered Michael said he'd call me. How had I forgotten?

"Hello?" I answered quietly.

"Hey Babe, how was your day?" he asked.

The sound of his voice gave me a thrill. My face immediately lit up with a smile. "Great. I enjoyed Tammy's company today."

"She told me she made cinnamon rolls for you, and you didn't have any of the ingredients in your house."

"Guilty as charged," I said. "How was your day? Did you take lots of pictures?"

"Yeah, I'm in picture heaven. I'm glad I made the second trip down here. We traveled a little further into the bayou, and it certainly has been worth the time."

"Good, then I'm glad you went."

"Yeah, but I miss you."

"That's good too, but it's only been two days. I'll be gone for two weeks when you get home."

Michael blew out a deep breath. "That thought is killing me too. The wife of the biologist I'm working with is a big fan of yours, and she tried to talk me out of the copy of your new book. But since it is Tammy's book I couldn't give it away. Besides, it makes me feel like I have you with me."

"How did you find that out?" I asked wondering how he could find one of my readers.

"She saw the book in my camera bag and almost came unglued. When I told her that you were my girlfriend she almost passed out and told me the book I had would not be out until next Tuesday."

Hearing his description of me as his girlfriend had my head spinning. Was that what I was? I could feel my heart pounding in my chest. I liked the description a lot. I tried to even out the tone of my voice, it was difficult because hearing that made me want to jump around the room and celebrate.

"Tell her that I'll be in New Orleans at the end of next week and if she comes to the book signing, I'll make sure she gets a special copy from me."

"You are so sweet Elizabeth. I'll be sure to let her know. She is going to be thrilled."

"I have to take care of the fan base you know."

"So what are you and Tammy going to do tomorrow?" he asked.

"We are going to visit your grandmother. It was Tammy's idea. She told me that you go at least once a week and your grandmother would miss you. We'll go to lunch and maybe catch a movie."

"Like I said, you're too sweet. You know she could go by herself, she has Katy's car."

"I know, but I want to go. I enjoy Tammy," I said.

"I'm going to have to do something special for you." His voice took on a deeper tone, and it made me shiver.

"You already have," I said quietly.

"The pictures we took of the eagles came out very good. I have to take you with me more often, you're my lucky charm."

Remembering our first night together made my body react, and his voice was sending lightning strikes through my body. I cleared my throat wondering if I would be able to speak. "I enjoyed the trip too. I'd love to go again. It was exhilarating."

Michael laughed at the double meaning. "I'll say it was exhilarating."

I blushed and knew he could hear the blush over the phone. "You know what I meant. But, yeah that other thing was wonderful too."

His voice became quiet. "You mean when we made love? You know it is okay to say that aloud. And you're blushing aren't you?"

"Stop teasing me," I said with mock indignation. "I don't say things like you do, I can't."

"You do in your books," he teased.

"That's different. Those are characters, they are not me."

"I don't know about that," he continued to tease. "I think Jessica is very much you, now that I've read more."

"Oh, I know what you're getting at, you are still hung up on page seventy-five."

"Okay, you caught me. That section of the book is a zinger."

"Just wait until you get further, I'm going to have you drooling."

"Is that a promise or a threat?"

"Both!" I giggled.

"Hey, no fair, you're getting me all hot over the phone, and here I am alone, all by myself. You better behave yourself."

"I'm sorry." I giggled again. "No, I'm not!"

We both laughed together, and it felt good to be able to share and laugh with him even though we were miles apart.

"Do a favor for me? Would you let me read the notes you wrote while we were watching the eagles?" he asked.

"If you really want to read them, sure, I'll be glad to write them up for you. Can I ask you why?"

"I have something in mind, but I'm not sure yet."

"Okay, I'll email them to you."

I wondered what he had in mind, but did not press it any further. Talking another few minutes, he promised to call me the next day, and we ended our call. As soon as we hung up, I missed him more than I had the whole day. Michael had a way of brightening my outlook. I felt more complete after speaking with him. It was going to be a tough two weeks while I was on the book tour, but his continuing calls would help me through. What would he think if he knew how dependent I was becoming?

I awoke before Tammy and took advantage of the early morning to go for a run with all four dogs along the lakeshore. I had dreamt of both Michael and Kevin and needed to clear the cobwebs out of my head. More often than not Kevin was threatening or chasing me in my dreams, and this one was no exception. This time though Michael was trying to save me. I could just imagine what my therapist would have concluded from the dream. She would have thought that once again I was looking for rescue. I let it mull over in my mind while I ran, but by the end of the run, no reasonable answers had surfaced.

Tammy was up when I got back to the house. While she fed the dogs, I showered and dressed. Since we were visiting her grandmother, I decided to dress more conservatively this time. A pair of crisp white linen slacks, a navy cotton blouse with short sleeves, and my flat white sandals completed the outfit. My hair went into a ponytail with a red scarf.

"Elizabeth, you look really nice," she commented when I exited my bedroom. She wore her standard jeans, t-shirt, and sneakers. "Dad keeps telling me I should go out and buy some new clothes, but it is way too much effort. I could never look as good as you because I look like an elephant."

I frowned at her. This was not the first time she had made remarks about a negative self-image. I slid my arm over her shoulder. "First of all, you are not overweight. I don't know where you get that idea. You're perfect for your height."

She grinned. "I'd be even better if I was as tall as you."

"Believe me, I did not grow into these legs gracefully. I was a tall, gangly, lanky teenager. For years, my nickname was Legs. I always stuck out of the crowd. Even today I tower over most people, including most men. As far as dressing, I've always dressed like this. I wear solid colors and very few prints. You will develop your own style. You're not Katy, and you are not me, and you will come into your own. I'd be happy to go shopping with you."

"I'd like that. When you get back from your book tour, we can go into San Francisco."

"Sounds like a good plan." I smiled with her. "So, shall we get on the road?"

We took my Range Rover. Tammy gave me directions to her great-grandmother's house in Calistoga. I was relieved when we arrived at the house and found only Grandmother Helen there. I almost expected the entire family to be in wait for me. Maybe since it was the middle of the week, or perhaps it had gotten around to the family that I had been uncomfortable with what seemed like an assault.

We spent the first hour trying to talk her out of making lunch for us. Finally, she agreed to let us take her out. She had dressed up for our visit, and her excitement was evident. The stories of her adventures arriving in the United States as a young girl with her parents were delightful. It was unmistakable where Michael received his sense of humor. The resemblance between her and Michael was clearer the more time I spent with his grandmother. I felt drawn to her as I felt drawn to him.

Arriving back at the house after lunch, she had Tammy pull out the photo albums, especially the ones with Michael. We had the books spread out over our laps on the couch and Grandmother Helen was pointing out the pictures to Tammy and me regaling the old stories to us.

"This one is our Michael next to his cousin Alex, they were 4 years old." Grandmother Helen pointed to a picture of a blond boy, and I could immediately make out Michael's features. Certainly, he always had the dimples, and it appeared as if he was always tall because he towered over his cousin. "It was taken just before they decided to help Candace with the laundry. They took all the clean towels out of her laundry basket and put them into the bathtub, which is where she used to sort her laundry." She started laughing. "Then they turned on the water and dumped soap into the bathtub. The whole thing was a mess. What could Candace say? He was trying to be helpful." She sighed. "Ah, he was always such a good boy, with a good heart. Tammy knows." She reached over and patted Tammy on the knee. "He is a good father too."

She smiled and squeezed her great-grandmother around the shoulders. "You're right, he is the best dad."

Grandmother Helen turned her attention back to the photo album, and she pointed and laughed again. "Michael was a good negotiator too." She indicated to a small picture taken of the two of them. "He was about 7 years old, and we took the train down to San Diego to visit his mother who was taking special courses in Spanish for her teaching. Michael stopped at some vending machines and wanted some peppermints. I told him no, not today. And he looked up at me with his big blue eyes and said, tomorrow okay?" She laughed and shook her head. "He could get anything from me, just with his blue eyes."

As we continued to look through the album, he grew up in front of my eyes. He went from a lanky pre-teenager to a tall, muscular young man. He had been involved in all the major sports in high school, basketball, baseball, and football. Michael was the type of handsome in high school that probably made him one of the most popular boys in school.

"Well, I'm getting a little tired," Grandmother Helen said.

"Oh, I'm sorry. We've tired you out today," I exclaimed.

"No, no." Grandmother Helen put her hands up. "I'm just tired of looking at old pictures. Elizabeth, would you mind reading your book to me? Tammy, it's on my bed table."

We put away the photo albums while Tammy retrieved the book. After making ourselves comfortable, I began with the first page, "It was a dark and stormy night." I smiled. I started all my books with this sentence. I read aloud for thirty minutes, and looked up, Grandmother Helen was snoring softly.

I stopped reading and silently pointed to the blanket at the end of the couch. Tammy covered her great-grandmother, and we quietly moved around the room tidying up. While we were in the kitchen doing the coffee dishes, the front door opened and Candace walked in. Tammy greeted her grandmother silently. She nodded and walked with Tammy into the kitchen.

"Hello Elizabeth, it's nice to see you again. I wondered who belonged to the Range Rover outside."

"Tammy and I took Grandmother Helen out to lunch, and then she shared old photo albums with us."

"Hope she told you all the stories about Michael. He was such a character growing up. You two are staying for dinner, right?"

I looked at Tammy before I responded. "Oh, no we can't, thank you though. We've got four hungry dogs at home."

"Those dogs won't starve to death. You're staying for dinner." Candace made it sound like an order.

"No, sorry." I shook my head. "We really can't. I have an old boy, my Topper, and he isn't in great shape. I need to feed him on schedule."

Tammy blurted in, "Yeah Grandma, he's an old one. Sorry, we've got to go."

Candace frowned. "The next time you and Michael come out, I will expect you to stay."

I nodded. We said our goodbyes to Grandmother Helen. She was sorry to see us go but winked at me. When we arrived home, Tammy took the dogs for a walk, and I started packing for my trip. She offered to drive me to the airport and bring my Range Rover back to my cabin. When I returned, I would be driving my little sports car up from Southern California.

It was past ten o'clock, and I had not heard from Michael. He had mentioned that he would be working at night because the alligators were more active then. My flight was early in the morning, and I couldn't stay up much later.

I crawled into bed, shut the light out, and the phone rang. His name flashing on the screen of my cell phone immediately made me smile.

"Hi," I said with my face still in a grin.

"Hey Babe, sorry I'm calling so late. I just returned to my room." His deep voice shot a thrill through me.

"That's okay, I just got into bed."

"Mmmmm…" he moaned over the phone. "That sounds good. Are you naked?"

I giggled. "No, I have my nightgown on."

"Well, I'll just pretend you're naked," he cooed softly.

I cuddled further down into the pillows wishing he was here next to me. "You do that."

"So, I heard you're in big trouble."

"Oh great, now what did I do?" I asked, and then thought of his mother. "Oh yeah, did Tammy tell you? Your mother wanted us to stay for dinner, and I told her no."

Michael chuckled. "Well yeah, she told me, but more importantly, my grandmother called me to tell me."

"Uh oh, I am in big trouble now. What did your grandmother say?"

Great, involved in family politics already. How did I manage to do this to myself? Kevin's parents never liked me, probably due to some inadvertent slip of the tongue early in our relationship.

"My grandmother loves you already and thinks you're perfect for me. She said she was glad you stuck to your guns and stood up to my mother. Mom tends to be a bossy boot," he joked. "Then she told me that I better not mess this up and hold onto you. So, do I get to hold onto you?"

"That depends on how tight you want to hold onto me," I teased.

"Right now, since you're naked, I want to hold really tight!" He chuckled again. "Grandma said that you liked her stories about me too."

"Yes, I have the impression that you were sweet in your youth.

He laughed heartily. "That was not an impression I hoped you had about me."

He continued to tease me for a bit longer, and then both of us yawned at the same time. We both laughed and agreed to was time to end the call.

I had that warm, satisfied feeling come over me again. The sensations I had for Michael were weird and wonderful. Kevin certainly never made me feel this way.

CHAPTER TWENTY-ONE

I was not looking forward to the book tour. I never did, but I did look forward to seeing my family and friends. Nancy honked and pulled up in her bright red Mercedes convertible outside the terminal at the Los Angeles airport. She helped me put my two suitcases on the small back seat, next to the surfboards. The surfboards made me grin.

She kissed and hugged me. A dark-haired beauty, her hair length alternated between shoulder length and a pixie cut. Today her hair was short. Her fair complexion was not the usual olive skin from her Italian heritage, but she did have the classic Roman nose. The Mediterranean descent gave her curves and a medium height. She had enough energy for the both of us, and it always seemed to be bubbling over the top as if she could not contain it. A natural byproduct of this oomph was her vivacious personality, and as a result, she was like a flame to moths. I had never met anyone with the ability to attract more men.

"I stopped at your house and picked up your board and suit. I figured with all the writing you've been doing you needed some downtime," Nancy said as she hopped into the car.

I frowned. "I haven't been doing that much writing.

"Ssshhh," she cautioned. "Don't tell that to Robin. We're having dinner with her tomorrow night. I hope you have something to show her. You know how she gets if she thinks you're taking too long to write."

This made me laugh. Robin was my editor and Nancy had described her perfectly. Robin sent me one-word emails that simply read *MORE*. "I think she will like this new one. It's going in a different direction this time, there's more intrigue."

"Elizabeth, you don't need more intrigue, you need more sex. I'm telling you that's what sells now." She winked and headed toward the freeway.

"Michael has read the latest one, and he was just fine about the sex in the book." I grinned at Nancy like the Cheshire cat.

"Oh yes, Mr. Michael. Now I want to hear everything you've been up to." She winked again while laughing. "And don't leave out anything!"

I filled her in on the last few days, including telling her again about the episode with Kevin. She had heard most of the story before, but we rehashed the details as only friends can do. She was properly horrified by the Kevin situation and peppered her words with a few expletives. Nancy was another friend who had never liked him. Every time he saw her, he made sexual overtures, and it became so bad that she would not come to the house. Early on in my marriage, his ill-behavior toward my friends had embarrassed me, and then, later on, it had disgusted me. His behavior toward my friends only made the divorce easier. When I accused him, he repeatedly denied the accusations, but all my women friends had been through his abuse.

We ended up at our favorite beach, which was only five minutes away from my house. After surfing through the morning, we stopped at our favorite sandwich shop, bought sandwiches to go, and drove to my house.

Because Kevin kept the house that we had shared as part of his settlement, I purchased the small bungalow after our divorce. Both my dad and sister's homes were in the same neighborhood. It was a cute tiny California style cottage house. Only two bedrooms and one bathroom. I considered myself lucky I was able to purchase it on my own.

My father had offered a bedroom in his house after my divorce, but I managed to scrape enough money together. The court rewarded Kevin richly in our divorce settlement since he had worked sporadically after I started writing and did not show much income. My alimony payments would finally finish in November, and I counted the days. His meal ticket was evaporating, and I wondered if that was the real reason for his recent visit to me.

The house was stuffy when we entered. It was a hot September afternoon, but after we opened all the windows, the ocean breezes quickly cooled the interior. Nancy and I sat at the minuscule dining room table to eat our sandwiches.

"So," she said waving her arms around, "you've decided to give up all this and permanently move to the cabin?"

I looked around and nodded. After my encounter with Kevin last weekend, I had decided to rent out the house. I realized that this house never held any part of me. It had become a place for me to rest my head and work on my books. The location had become too convenient for my ex-husband to drop by for a visit, which he had done frequently. Living in Mintock made it more difficult for a drop by to see how I was doing. Dating Michael allowed me to begin to understand what happiness was and my need to gravitate to that feeling was compelling. I would miss seeing my dad and sister, but it would give them an excuse to get away from their everyday lives to visit me.

"I'm not giving all this up. There will be people living in the house. I'm just going to use it as an investment now."

Nancy looked pointedly at me. "This Michael person really has thrown you for a loop. I have to meet this man."

I frowned back at her. "No, he has not thrown me for a loop. Yes, I do enjoy his company. He is fun to be with, but I love living in Mintock. The dogs love running with me in the morning. Down here, the beach doesn't allow dogs. I love going out on the lake. The lifestyle is slower paced, and you know I never liked the fast lane."

She looked at me with doubt on her face and shook her head. "No, I don't think so. This is so definitely about Michael." Nancy looked at me closer and then laughed. "Oh my god!" She exclaimed, "You are in love!"

I blushed from the roots of my hair all the way down to my toes and looked away.

"No, I'm not," I said with as much indignation as I could muster.

"The '*I am never going to fall in love girl*' is in love. I don't believe it. How long have you known him? Four weeks? And you just slept with him last weekend for the first time?" Nancy looked at me closely again, this time without the laughter. "You are head over heels in love."

I bit my lip and could feel my impatience rise. "Nancy, I am not in love with Michael. Now knock it off."

Nancy let the laughter go again and held up her hands. "Okay, girlfriend. I won't tease you anymore." She giggled and under her breath said, "Head over heels."

"Nancy I'm going to smack you." I frowned.

"If it makes you feel any better, I'm jealous."

I was surprised. "Jealous? Why would you ever be jealous with all the men that flock around you?"

"That's just it, you know, there is no one special in my life."

"Do you want there to be?" I asked.

She sighed. "Isn't that what we're all looking for?"

I squeezed her hand. "You should have been a romance writer."

Nancy laughed again, and I could feel the energy in her bubble over. "No, I just represent them and make sure they get a lot of money!"

We finished our lunch, and she left me to complete the chapter I was writing. I wanted Robin to have the first part of the book before we met for dinner so she could give me feedback during our meeting.

The afternoon grew increasingly warmer as it progressed. By five o'clock, I had all the fans on in the house, and I was still hot. My sister invited me over for dinner. I quickly sent off my email to Robin, and I decided to arrive at my sister's house early. Lisa's pool would cool me off, and it allowed me to spend time with my niece and nephew. My sister had let it slip several weeks ago that she and Bill were pregnant again. I was delighted with the news but had to admit I was envious too.

I walked the three short blocks to her house and rang the doorbell. The house was similar to mine, California ranch style, but with one extra bedroom and bathroom, and of course the cool pool in the backyard. The homes in the area were built right after World War II when all aerospace companies in the area were beginning to thrive.

Five-year-old Marybeth was at the door in a second and jumping into my arms.

"Mommy, Mommy, Aunty Bess is here," Marybeth called to her mother.

I carried Marybeth into the house and heard Lisa calling from the backyard. "Bess, back here. I'm in the pool with Jonathan." My family always had called me Bess. It went back to Lisa. As a child, she could not pronounce my full name, and it had stuck. As we grew up, it became Queen Bess as in Elizabeth the First, Queen of England.

I put Marybeth down, and she pulled me through the living room into the backyard. Lisa was sitting on the first step of the pool with her arm around three-year-old Jonathan who was kicking his legs in the water and giggling up a storm. Jon saw me, and immediately he put his arms in the air and yelled, "Uppy, uppy." That was my cue to pick him up and twirl him in the air.

Lisa stood. She wore a two-piece bathing suit, and her pregnancy had not started to show yet. Her features matched my father. Her hair was darker than mine, which she wore shoulder length and tucked behind her ears. She usually had it dyed blond, but with the pregnancy, she would let it go dark again. We hugged and kissed as she threw on her cover-up.

"Thanks for coming early. I appreciate it, now I can get dinner going. Bill should be home soon. Do you want to come in or stay out here?"

I grinned and handed Jon back to her. I pulled my long cover-up off. "Let me jump into the pool and cool down. I am hot! I'll be right with you."

The pool felt wonderfully cool, and I swam a few laps. When I got out, Lisa handed me a towel. As soon as my cover-up was back on Jon was back in my arms.

"What's for dinner?" I asked following Lisa into the house.

Marybeth ran to get her Barbie dolls so we could play before we ate.

"As soon as Bill gets home, he'll get the barbeque going. I made Mom's potato salad, corn on the cob, hamburgers for the kids and steaks for us," she replied, pulling the food out of the refrigerator.

Her husband Bill walked through the front door. The kids screamed and ran to him. He picked them both up and spun them around. Then he wrapped his arms around Lisa and squeezed her. "Hello, my love." His

English accent was smooth to my ears. "Good Queen Bess, it is good to see you." He gave me a hug and a quick peck on the mouth. Bill was my height, dark-haired and lanky. No matter what Lisa cooked, he never gained weight.

"How's the law firm?" I asked.

"Splendid!" He grinned. "Lots of people for us to sue. Let me change my clothes, my love." He looked at Lisa. "And I'll start the grill, shall I?"

A sharp knock on the front door twenty minutes later announced the arrival of our father. The kids beat me to the door, and both of them greeted him with shrieks of delight. Dad hugged everyone and left me for last.

He gave me a hard hug. "How is my Sweet Pea?"

I smiled at his very special nickname for me. "I'm doing good Dad. You look great."

"I feel good." He picked up Jon and put him up on his shoulders. "What do you say we go outside and give your mother some room to maneuver in her kitchen? Bess, would you grab a couple of beers. I'm sure Bill can use one."

I nodded and went to the refrigerator. "Why don't you go out and join them, Bess, I don't need your help in here," Lisa said.

"Are you sure I can't be of some assistance?" I asked.

"Oh, god no!" She laughed. "You know you're worthless in the kitchen."

I took three beers from the refrigerator and headed for the back patio.

"Good news about Lisa and Bill, isn't it?" I said.

Dad smiled. "Excellent news. I'm glad you're not stopping at two."

Bill laughed. "It was a surprise to me too. We had been talking about only having two children, but I guess she beat me to the gate."

I raised my eyebrow. "Bill you know where babies come from, it wasn't all Lisa."

Bill took a drink of beer. "Sometimes when you are in the midst of the conversation, you don't expect any surprises."

Okay, I was not going to touch any more of this topic. Something was going on between my sister and her husband and I did not want to know more information.

My brain told me to change the subject. "Dad, are you still riding your bike? You look great."

"Yeah." He stretched. "I beat Bill last weekend in a race."

Bill laughed. "Bob, I didn't know we were racing, or I would have participated."

Dad chuckled. "Didn't I tell you I do undercover racing?" They both guffawed. "Bess, what is this I hear about you renting out your house? When did this happen?"

"You know I've been thinking about it. I really love Aunt Ruth's cabin, and now since I finished remodeling it, I decided that I would make the Torrance house an investment," I explained.

Bill turned from the barbeque to look at me. "That and I heard that you have a new boyfriend, who lives next door to you up there." He winked at me.

I blushed.

Dad looked at me. "That would explain the strange conversation I had with the idiot boy Kevin yesterday."

I wrinkled my brow. "You talked to Kevin?"

"While I was on my bike, I literally ran into him on my way down to the beach. He told me that he stayed with you last weekend. At first, he made it sound like you were getting back together. I knew that wasn't true, so I pressed him a little further. Then he asked me if I knew about your new boyfriend. Lisa told me that you have a new friend living next door to you. He sounds normal. That's good." He shook his head. "Kevin is very disturbing. I don't feel right about him visiting you like that. You should see what he did to the house you two lived in. There must be 15 people living with him, and the back yard is trashed."

"Dad, it's his house. He can do anything he wants to it," I commented.

"It just isn't right. You paid for the house with the money from your books. It just isn't right," he repeated.

I did not want to get into this discussion with my father. Bill came happily to my rescue. "Bess, have you considered getting a restraining order against Kevin? I could help you with it."

I did not need this type of rescue. My father did not know about Kevin's penchant for violence toward me. We were all afraid Dad would do something drastic. He caught on too quickly.

He looked directly at me. "Elizabeth," my dad used my real name, which meant I was in trouble, "did Kevin abuse you?" He said it very simply. He was always straightforward and matter of fact.

I let out a big sigh. "Dad, it doesn't make any difference now. We're divorced, and he's part of my past. He can't do anything to me anymore."

My father's voice became very measured, and I could feel his anger grow. "So, was this physical or mental abuse?"

I did not want to discuss this in front of Bill. I actually did not want to talk about this in front of anyone. "Bill, would you excuse us for a minute?"

He scooped up the kids and went into the house.

I continued, "Dad, what Kevin did to me is over. Rehashing it now will not change it."

Now I was glad that I had not told Lisa about Kevin's brutality on Sunday. I could pretend that it was all in the past.

"Elizabeth, I want to know. Did he hit you?" My father was known for being very even-tempered, but on occasion could lose his hard-fought control.

"Yes Dad, he did. All through our marriage, he would abuse me mentally and then when he didn't receive the reaction from me that he wanted he would hit me," I explained. "That's why I finally filed for divorce."

He raked his hands through his hair and gave me an anguished look. "Why, Elizabeth, why didn't you tell me?"

"Exactly because of this reaction. Now that you know, you feel like you have to do something about it. I'm afraid that would land you in jail or worse. Please don't confront him, and let it rest." My eyes pleaded with him.

He squeezed my hand then put his arms around me. Holding me close he murmured, "Sweet Pea, I'm so sorry this happened to you. I wish I would have known."

I could feel the tears running down my face, and buried my face into his shoulder. "Please let it go. Let me get on with my life."

"Hey Bess," he tilted my face to look at me, "where's my fighter? Don't worry. I won't do anything to Kevin."

I sniffed back my tears wishing as always that I had a tissue in my pocket. I stepped back to look at him. "Okay," I said hesitantly.

He laughed his deep throaty father laugh. "But I may call a few buddies to check the zoning laws for his house, I think he has too many people living there. I'm also wondering about the registration of his vehicles."

"Dad," I cautioned him. "no interfering."

He looked surprised. "What? I'm just doing my civic duty. You know I'm a retired cop." He chuckled and called to my brother-in-law, "Bill, you better get your butt out here, I think something is burning."

We enjoyed a good dinner. My sister was a good cook, and I was a good dishwasher. The partnership still worked between us. Somewhere inside of me, I was glad that my father finally knew about Kevin. It was as if a secret burden had lifted from my shoulders.

While Dad walked me home, my cell phone started ringing. The display came up with Michael's name.

"Can I call you back in fifteen minutes? I'm walking home with my dad," I said while his voice told me that he was looking forward to speaking with me.

Dad and I continued walking. "Was that your new boyfriend?" he asked.

"Yeah. He's calling me every night so we can talk."

"Lisa told me about him. He sounds like a nice person. When do I get to meet him? I guess I could come up and visit you. Would that be okay?"

"Yeah, I'd like that. I miss you when I'm up there."

My father slipped his arm around my shoulder and squeezed me.

"Let's plan on it then. I want to meet this man and make sure his intentions are honorable."

"Oh, Dad." I giggled. "I'm thirty-eight years old. I think I can take care of myself."

He hugged me again. "Sweet Pea, you will always be my baby girl."

Dad and I said our goodnights. We set up a Dodger game at the end of my book tour when I swung back into town for the last stop. As I walked into the house, I pulled out my cell phone and plopped myself on the couch.

"Hey, Babe." Michael's voice came over the phone.

"Are you home?" I asked.

"Yeah, I got in late this afternoon, and before you ask, your children are doing just fine."

I laughed. "Thanks, for letting me know."

"How was dinner with your family?'

"Oh, the usual, you know nothing really changes. I did talk to my dad about Kevin."

I heard the relief in his voice. "Elizabeth, I'm glad. You needed to let him know."

There was a sound of him shifting around. "Are you in bed?"

He laughed. "Yeah, and I'm naked too. No, I'm teasing you. I am working on the photographs. My deadline is quickly approaching."

I whispered, "I would much rather hear about you being naked."

He chuckled. "I was wondering when my Hellcat was going to come out."

"You're never going to let me live down those few marks on your shoulders, are you?"

"I thought it was so funny you thought at first an animal had gotten to me. No, the nickname sticks, you are definitely my Hellcat."

I whispered, "Then I'm going to have to sharpen my nails and make sure I mark you again, so I earn my nickname."

"Promises, promises."

I whispered again, "I wish you were here with me tonight."

His voice became low and throaty. "Babe, you don't know how much I want to be with you tonight. You have no idea what you do to me. I want you naked and in my bed."

My stomach started to do turns, and my body reacted to his words. "Stop it, Michael, you're going to drive me crazy." My voice had turned low too, and it betrayed that I did not want him to stop.

He continued on the path down to ruin. "Then I want your long legs wrapped around my hips, so your luscious body is open to me. I want to feel your hands caressing my body, and feel your body moving against me." He paused. I closed my eyes, and I was lost in my thoughts of him.

"Are you still there?" he asked.

"Yes," my voice responded quietly. I was not thinking. Clearly, my entire body felt the heat he was sending through the phone.

He groaned. "Damn, Elizabeth it's going to be two weeks of phone sex isn't it?"

I exhaled, and my voice was breathy. "Yes," I replied.

"I'm going to be stuck retaking cold showers, aren't I?"

"Yes," I replied again barely able to catch my breath.

"Are you able to say anything except yes?" He chuckled.

"No." I giggled. "I'm sorry, guess I got caught up in the moment. We are so bad, and you know I want you too."

Michael sighed. "It's going to be a long two weeks for me."

"For me too," I acknowledged. "You're still going to call me every night, aren't you?" I asked, afraid that he would want to back away from me. The emotional pull we had on the phone was a heavy one.

"I will because it's the only thing that will get me through."

I understood the need in his voice because I felt it too.

CHAPTER TWENTY-TWO

On Friday morning after meeting with the rental agent at the house, I started boxing up the few personal items that were not going to be trusted to the moving company. They would pack everything else for the move up to my cabin. I felt more energized about the decision to permanently move after speaking with the agent. She expected the house to rent quickly and already had a few clients who might have an interest.

I pulled out a few items of special clothing that I would take back to Mintock with me. I had the perfect dress for Michael and his special evening at the aquarium. We had spoken about the evening a couple of times, and I could hear the excitement in his voice. He tried to downplay the honor in a show of humility, but I knew he was looking forward to the event.

It took me three years to get to this point. I was finally ready for this next phase. This house had been my refuge at first, but I could move on now. My dad told me he would keep my old bedroom open for me in case I changed my mind. It was time though to stop running back to my family and stand on my own.

I kept myself busy throughout the day organizing and packing. Nancy and Robin were meeting at my house, and we would go together to the restaurant for dinner. After I dressed, I called Michael.

He answered on the first ring. "Babe, are you okay?"

"Yes, everything is okay. I'm going out tonight and don't know when I'll be home. I didn't want to miss your call," I explained.

"Going out with the girls?" he asked. "Sounds like trouble to me."

"We usually don't get into too much trouble. Robin is married."

"There's always you and Nancy. From what you've told me about the two of you together, I think real trouble can happen."

"You sound jealous. Are you?" I asked, silently hoping the answer was yes.

"You know I am. I want you to call me when you get home. I don't care what time it is," he said.

"Are you sure?"

"Yes, I'll worry about you."

"You're so sweet."

"No, I'm looking out for my own self-interest."

Michael asked me about my day. He was surprised to hear that I had put the house up for rent. I could not tell by his voice whether he considered it good or bad news. He managed to keep the inflection in his voice very even. I was dying to ask him what he thought about it, but I could not push myself over that edge. His opinion was uppermost on my mind, but since I did not dare to ask, he did not tell either.

He had spent his day with our eagle couple who he had named Ethel and Fred. He had also taken the opportunity to read the notes I had written about my impressions of the eagles last weekend. He wanted to talk to me about it further, but the knocking on my front door interrupted us.

Nancy opened the front door. "Hello, hello!" She saw me wave the cell phone at her and she immediately closed her mouth.

"I have to go," I said to him. "Nancy and Robin are here."

"You girls have fun. I'll be waiting for your call tonight."

"You're just trying to check up on me," I joked.

"No, I want to have phone sex." He laughed.

I murmured into the phone, "We are not having phone sex."

"We'll see."

Both Nancy and Robin looked at me with raised eyebrows.

Nancy was the first to speak. "Phone sex? Oh my! How wonderful, I can't wait to meet Michael."

My blush broke out on my face. "We are not having phone sex."

Nancy looked at her nails and buffed them on her pants. "Oh, I don't know. Don't knock it unless you've tried it." She smiled a wicked grin at Robin and me.

"This is going to be quite the two weeks isn't it?" I asked Nancy.

"Yup, yup, yup." Nancy grinned at us again. "And, it starts tonight! Let's go, I'm starving, and I want to start drinking. I've had a difficult week."

I hugged Robin hello. We shook our heads at Nancy.

"Okay, let me put my shoes on," I said.

"Hey, not the three-inch ones, they make me look short," Nancy said pointing to my shoes.

"How can my shoes make you look short?" I asked Nancy while I continued to put on the shoes.

Robin laughed. "It's because you're all legs, look at you, especially with the short skirt. You make us look short."

"Robin, you're petite. You're not short," I said. Both girls frowned at me. "Oh, alright." I slipped on a pair of flats. "Better?"

A chorus of "*Yes*" answered me.

"So whose car are we driving?" I asked.

Nancy opened the front door. "How about the big black one?" She pointed to the large black limousine parked in the driveway. "This is a business meeting, after all. You're my client, and Robin, you're Elizabeth's editor. It's tax deductible!"

The three of us made quite the trio. Robin had soft brown hair and eyes that complimented her heart-shaped face and petite frame. Only a couple of years older than me, she had more wisdom than Nancy and I together. Her adorable bear of a husband gave in to her whims easily. What other man with such a cute wife would let her go out and party with the girls? Theirs was a special trusting relationship I often envied.

We climbed into the limousine, and Nancy gave instructions to the driver.

I looked at Robin expectantly. "Well?"

Robin glanced at Nancy. "Business first?"

Nancy nodded. "Absolutely, let's get it out of the way!" Nancy opened a bottle of champagne and poured it into small paper cups. She handed a cup to each of us. "You get nothing but class from me!"

We touched our cups together. In unison, we chimed, "To the book!" before drinking down the champagne in one gulp. Robin looked at me with a huge grin on her face, and I wanted to close my eyes, afraid of what she was going to say.

Her lips formed the words, and she finally spoke. "MORE!" Robin yelled. "Oh my goodness, this one is the best!"

The three of us started giggling in a fit of drama.

I threw myself prostrate across the seat. I pumped my arms in the air. "Yes! She likes it!"

Of anyone, Robin's opinion of my books was one of the most important to me. She, like Nancy, had been with me from the beginning of my book-writing career. They were the ones that guided me, cajoled me, and listened to my tearful pleas of writer's block. Robin was a merciless editor, helping me with the timing and flow of each book. At the same time, her praise was hard won and valuable.

"Where did you come up with Craig?" Robin asked about the male main character. "He's wonderful. I can really see Jessica ending up with him."

Nancy, while pouring us more champagne interrupted, "I think he's based on a real-life person. What do you think Elizabeth?"

I blushed. "No, not really," I answered.

"You are such a liar! A marine biologist? Robin, who do you think it is?" Nancy said giggling.

Robin looked at me with surprise on her face. "Are you basing Craig on your new hot man?"

I finally admitted that I did model the new character a little bit after Michael. I knew I was going to be in trouble when he read it. If he liked page seventy-five in the last book, he would really like the new one.

We arrived at our favorite restaurant in the marina. It was a noisy, large cavernous place with a bar in the center surrounded by all the tables on the outside in a circle. Nancy knew the owner, so we always had what we considered our table. One time she actually convinced other diners to move from our table. As I said before, she was very vivacious and could persuade just about anyone to see things her way, including me. The waiter brought our drinks as we sat down at the table. We were predictable if nothing else.

Nancy was hiding some information, and I could see she was bursting at the seams to tell us. Robin and I settled back into our chairs with our drinks and looked expectantly at her.

"I do have some exciting news for you Elizabeth. I was contacted last week by Triad Television," she said with a flourish.

"Aren't they the company that does the women's movies on the Lifetime cable channel?" Robin asked.

I did not want to appear too anxious because we had gone down this road a couple of years before with a company interested in making my first book into a T.V. movie. After a considerable amount of negotiation, the deal had eventually fallen through. The production company did not want to stay true to the flavor of the books, and I felt that I had a duty to my reader's expectations.

"Yes." Nancy took a big drink of her martini. "However, the part of the company that contacted me is a new offshoot of Triad, this is the theatrical arm. They're new, very independent, and apparently, the mother ship funds them well. They are interested in making your first book into a movie."

I sat in my chair looking stunned.

"Now mind you," Nancy continued, "we are still only in the talking phase. I did tell them however you would not be interested in anything unless they planned to follow the book, but we would be interested in seeing a script treatment. They sound honestly interested in doing this right."

"I don't know what to say." My mind was spinning in different directions, and I had difficulty focusing on any one area.

Robin put her arm around my shoulders. "Wow. This is awesome."

"So, let's not get too excited for right now, I've chased Bill's firm after them for the discovery documents. We'll see what happens," Nancy said.

A tall, dark-haired man I recognized as the restaurant owner walked up behind Nancy and interrupted her by giving her a kiss on the mouth. The kiss was sexually charged, and it was evident neither of them considered the spectacle they were making.

Both Robin and I looked at each other and shook our heads. "Enough already, you guys need to get a room. People are beginning to stare." Robin grimaced.

They broke their kiss and smiled at us. "Sorry," Nancy said dreamily, looking at him.

He straightened. "Ladies, have a nice evening, glad you're here." He winked at Nancy before walking away from our table. "I'll see you later," he mouthed in her direction.

Nancy kept smiling and almost laid her head on the table. "I'm quite a puddle now. He is so yummy. I love it when he does that!"

I pulled Nancy back up. "You told me you didn't have anyone special in your life. That guy looked pretty special to me."

Nancy kept the silly smile on her face. "That was his way of telling me that he missed me, I mean us. We haven't been here in a while you know."

I shook my head and picked up the menu to look at the appetizers. Mumbling mainly to myself, "He isn't kissing anyone else like that. We're talking about this one later."

We ordered our appetizers, and I dropped further discussions of Nancy's romantic intentions for now. I wanted to run into the women's restroom to call Michael and share the good news about the possible movie connection. Typically I would have called Debi, but the urge to talk with him now was stronger. I had never felt an urge like that before. With Kevin, I had to plan my words carefully since he would react unenthusiastically or at the worst violently.

At the end of the evening, none of us was in any condition to drive. I offered my spare bedroom and couch to the girls, but since we had the limousine, we did not have to worry about driving home. I wasn't drunk, but was not sober either, just that mood in between. Since it was almost two in the morning, I debated whether to call Michael. I knew I would not be able to sleep without hearing his voice one more time.

The phone rang three times before he picked it up. I had awakened him, but at least he did not wait up for me to call.

His voice sounded groggy. "Hello?"

"I'm so sorry for waking you up. I shouldn't have called you so late," I whispered into the phone.

"Elizabeth," he said when he figured out who was calling. It was obvious that he had been in a deep sleep. He made a noise to clear his throat. "No, Babe, I wanted you to call me." I could hear him jostling around in his bed. "Sorry, let me turn a light on."

I jumped in. "Michael, just go back to sleep. I'm sorry for waking you. We'll talk tomorrow, I mean in the morning, I mean later," I stuttered the words out.

"Babe, I'm fine." He cleared his throat again. "I'm awake now. Did you have a nice time with Nancy and Robin?"

"Yes, we had a great time. We always do. Nancy had some great news too." I could hear the anticipation building in my voice. I lay back on my bed and hugged my pillow to my chest. "She was approached by a movie company who is interested in making my first book into a movie."

"Sensational, that's impressive. So I'm going to be able to introduce you as my movie mogul girlfriend?"

I giggled, and we continued to talk. He was sincerely happy with the news. It felt good to relax and share my success with him.

His voice grew lower as he spoke to me. My body immediately began to react to that special tone. I sighed when my stomach started the flip-flops.

"I heard that sigh," he said. "So, are you naked?"

"Michael, we are not having phone sex," I countered but noticed my own voice was growing softer and less resolute.

"There is nothing wrong with a little phone sex my little Hellcat," he growled over the phone.

He had used the *H* nickname, and the whole bottom half of my body responded to his proposition by turning the heat on.

"You know if I were laying there next to you, I'd be running my hands down your body right now. Your body is pressing tightly against me, and you feel me nestled between your legs."

I let out a soft moan. "Oh, Michael."

He did what he set out to do. He seduced me over the phone.

CHAPTER TWENTY-THREE

On Saturday, I spent the day with my niece and nephew at the aquarium in Long Beach. Bill and Lisa were grateful for the time together, and I enjoyed the time alone with the kids. This was my one regret about deciding to rent out my house. I would be down for visits whenever I could, but it was not like seeing them almost every day.

Until I finished the current book, those visits would be impossible though. This book was to be the last of this series. Jessica's time was over, and it was time to move on. She had been with me since the beginning, and the newest character introduced into the book would be her forever love.

I pulled Lisa's Volvo station wagon into their driveway. My little Saturn Sky, a two-seater, would never have fit the kids, the car seats, the stroller, and all the other items that were necessary for a day's outing. The kids were fast asleep, and I was exhausted too. I dreaded the thought of packing for my trip.

Bill came out and carried Marybeth into the house. She was a little rag doll in his arms, still fast asleep and clutching her new stuffed sea otter. Jon woke up briefly as Lisa picked him up, but he just cuddled closer to her and fell back asleep. I followed with the rest of their belongings.

Lisa turned and whispered to me, "Let me get them into bed. I need to talk with you."

I nodded silently and went into the kitchen to wait for my sister. When they joined me in the kitchen, I scanned their faces, and they both looked serious.

Lisa sat next to me and took my hand in hers. "Bill and I want you to stay here with us tonight."

I am sure I looked as confused as I felt. "Why?" I asked.

Bill spoke up this time. "Kevin stopped here about an hour ago. He was drunk. He said he knew you were down in Southern California and he was looking for you. He saw your car parked in front of our house. It did not look like he was up to any good either."

I rubbed my forehead. I did not need this tonight. I was already tired. Trying to reassure their anxious faces, I calmly said. "Guys, I'm really sorry that Kevin is bugging you. I'll talk to him and make sure he understands that you are off limits as far as he is concerned. I'm not sure why he needs to talk with me, but I'll give him a call when I get home. I've got to pack for my trip tonight."

Lisa frowned. "We think it's a better idea if you stay here tonight. I'll go home with you now and help you pack."

I patted her hand in my big sister way. "I appreciate your concern, but it's not necessary." I rose up from the breakfast table.

Bill took my other hand. "While you are on the book tour, I will prepare a restraining order against him. Lisa and the kids will be included too. He is a nut case, and he should not be around us."

"I appreciate that, especially since he lives so close to you." I bent over and gave both of them a hug. "Don't worry about me tonight. Kevin is all bark."

Arriving home, I locked all the doors securely. This was the time to have the dogs around. They were always sure to bark and cause a commotion if anyone approached the house. After I switched on the television to give me a little noise and company in the house, I started packing. I kept hearing sounds in the house, and to tell the truth, it did give me the creeps. It would be like Kevin to sneak around. Just as I had the thought, my doorbell rang, making me almost jump out of my skin.

Moving the curtain aside, I peeked through the small window on the front door. Sure enough, it was him. Why couldn't he leave me alone? I left the chain in place and slowly opened the door only a crack. I asked him, "What do you want Kevin?"

"Let me in Liz, I want to talk to you," he demanded. Even behind the door, the smell of alcohol on him was evident.

"No. I don't want you in my house. Whatever you have to say you can say it to me through the door."

He tried to peer in through the crack in the door. "Come on Liz. Let me in. I need to talk with you."

"I said no. You hurt me the last time. I'm not going to be stupid twice," I said adamantly and began to close the door.

He shoved his foot in between the door and the frame. "I need to talk with you." He breathed heavily and gave the door a hard push.

I pressed my body against the door, but he had more pounds and muscles on me. I cried out in surprise as his force on the door broke the chain, and the crashing door propelled me out of the way.

"Stop being such a bitch," Kevin spit out. "I just want to talk to you."

I backed away. "Okay, what do you want?"

His breathing came in big gulps from the exertion. "My lawyer told me that my alimony check is stopping in two months. Why have you stopped the checks? You owe me."

I stood there in disbelief. "I owe you?" I sputtered out. "How do you figure that? I gave you a huge settlement. I've paid you every month for the last three years. It's over. You don't get any more money. That was our divorce agreement. The money stops."

"I don't care about our agreement," he argued. "You still owe me. Without me, you would have never started your stupid books. I taught you how to write. It was all my idea."

I concluded he was delusional. "You are not going to get any more money. Period. You need to leave me alone." I pulled my cell phone out of my jeans pocket. "If you don't leave now I'm calling the police."

He was surprised to see me holding the phone. "What about your new rich boyfriend?"

I looked at him incredulously. "Michael has nothing to do with this, and I don't want you talking with him again."

Kevin made a move to step forward, and I lifted the phone in my hand. He looked me in the eyes and reconsidered. "I will do whatever I want to do Elizabeth. Don't forget that. You can't stop me," Kevin said flatly, as he backed toward the door. His eyes showed no emotion, only cold darkness.

He rarely called me by my full name. That did scare me. Kevin glared at me for a moment. I stood there motionless with my hand wrapped tightly around the phone. He turned on his heel and walked out of the house not bothering to close the door. I watched him walk down the driveway and for once, he did not turn around. I did not move until he reached the curb.

At least he had not damaged the door, and I could still close it. I threw the deadbolt with a satisfying snap. Sitting down on the tile floor in front of the closed door, I wrapped my arms around my knees and pulled them up tightly against me. I did not cry. I silently rocked myself back and forth. In the heat of the summer's night, I was ice-cold.

Finally, when I rose from the floor, it felt like I had been there for hours. I was stiff and still frozen. My resolve to rent the house was even stronger now. I had to remove myself as far as possible from him. He would not be able to touch me as easily up in Mintock. Bill was right. I did need a restraining order against Kevin.

I finished my packing and tried to sleep. Michael had left a voicemail earlier in the day letting me know that he was going to be with the eagles tonight. He had wished me a safe trip and looked forward to talking with me when I reached Miami. There I was in bed, and I could not sleep. I had no dogs or Michael cuddled up next to me. Drowning in my own self-pity, finally, the tears did come. I missed my dogs, my home, and I missed

Michael most of all.

CHAPTER TWENTY-FOUR

I eventually drifted off to sleep very early in the morning. The doorbell ringing startled me out of my sleep. The clock showed that I had overslept. How had that happened?

Nancy barreled through after I unlocked the door. She looked at me with surprise. "You're not dressed yet? Girlfriend, get a move on we are going to be late with a capital L."

"I'm sorry. I overslept." I stumbled back into my bedroom. "I'm all packed. Let me take a quick shower."

"No can do, Elizabeth. Put some clothes on and get your butt into the limo. Thank goodness, we don't have to park. We cannot be late for this flight. You can take a shower when we get to the hotel in Miami. You'll have time to change before dinner," she said adamantly. She picked up my luggage sitting in the corner. "I'll get these out to the car."

I was dressed, had the house locked, and was in the limousine in less than 5 minutes. She helped me braid my hair while we sat in the back seat.

"I don't understand what the rush is about. We have plenty of time before the flight leaves."

"No we don't," she said holding my braid clip between her teeth. "We're catching the earlier flight to Miami. I left you a message on your cell phone yesterday."

I half turned to look at her, and she batted me back so she could continue to braid my hair. "You did? Oh, I turned my cell phone off. Where is my cell phone?" I started to look through my purse. "Oh damn, I left my cell phone on the kitchen table. We have to go back and get it."

"No," she said as she put the finishing touches on my braid. "We're late. It's going to be a rush to catch the flight anyway."

Curious, I asked, "Why are we leaving early?"

"We have a dinner planned tonight."

"With who?" I asked.

"The publishing company bigwigs," she said with a flourish. Her eyes were sparkling, and she was grinning like a mad person. When I didn't make a fuss over her announcement, she rolled her eyes. "You don't get it, do you? Number one, look at the New York Times Sunday edition. Your new book is on the top ten list at Amazon for the most pre-ordered book ever." She reached into her briefcase, pulled out the book review section of the newspaper, and handed it to me, pointing to the headline.

"Ever?" I said in a small voice. "Wow."

"Yes, wow!" Nancy grinned at me. "This is big stuff, and don't think they haven't heard about Triad being interested in your books. That just sells more books."

"It's a silly romance novel."

"Silly or not. It's serious. Your books always have done well and have had a strong following. You've seen the sales figures. I think it is because your characters are a little older than the normal romance characters. People like associating themselves into a book. America is getting older. It makes sense. But, whatever, you are on the big guys' radar. I spoke to Carol at Berkside Publishing yesterday, and they are increasing the security at the bookstores during your signings. They don't want anything to go wrong."

I sat back in the seat. My head was spinning. "All this and no coffee?"

Nancy laughed. "I will get you a Starbucks at the gate, okay?"

"Give me your cell phone." I held out my hand.

She hesitated. "You're giving it back aren't you?"

I rolled my eyes. "Yes, I'm just going to call my family to let them know I don't have my cell phone with me."

She handed it to me, and I called Michael, Lisa, and my Dad. I left each one the same message about my cell phone. I felt naked without it.

We made the flight in plenty of time and Nancy bought me the coffee she promised. Since it was Sunday, first class was almost empty. We practically had the cabin to ourselves. Both of us pulled out our laptops and headsets to start working.

The knowledge about the sales of the book was exciting. I was always amazed that people bought my books. This type of news made me feel more valued and talented. It was funny how a few dismal words from Kevin could bring me down and make me feel worthless.

I shook my head at myself and sighed. Nancy looked over at me and raised her eyebrows. "Are you okay?" she mouthed in my direction.

I nodded and turned my attention back to my laptop. The direct flight landed us into Miami in the late afternoon. Berkside had a limousine waiting for us, and we were quickly at the hotel in South Beach. The bellman showed us to my suite first. What a set of rooms! It overlooked the ocean and was bigger than my first apartment. The white on white décor in the place was stunning. I was almost afraid to touch anything for fear of getting it dirty. A vase with eleven long stem pink roses and one long stem red rose sat in the middle of the table giving the room a splash of color.

"How nice," I said, "they sent me flowers."

Nancy plucked the small envelope from the holder in the vase. "There's a card. The flowers are from somebody, these aren't from the hotel." She handed the card to me.

I slid the small card out of the envelope and read the card aloud. "*I've got you under my skin. I miss you. M.*"

"Hmmm, a red rose in the middle of the pink ones. Not too difficult to read into that imagery." She looked at the bellman. "You might as well show me my room. Elizabeth, dinner is at eight. I'll be here at seven. We don't want to be late."

I nodded, not really acknowledging her. The door to my suite closed gently. I stood there in the middle of the room holding the card and rereading the words. Even though I was standing still, my mind was jumping around singing, and a broad smile broke out on my face.

"My teddy bear misses me." I murmured to myself. The grin that had formed on my face wouldn't leave me.

Sitting on the white couch carefully, I picked up the phone and dialed Michael's number.

He answered up his cell phone right away. "Hi, Babe."

"How did you know it was me?" I asked surprised.

"Caller ID. You're the only one I know with a Miami area code."

"Oh, that makes sense. Thank you for the flowers, they are beautiful."

"I wanted to make sure you were still thinking about me Miss World Traveler."

"I think of you all the time. It's hard not to."

He laughed his deep throaty laugh. "Good. That's what I love about you Elizabeth. Your honesty is so refreshing. No games from you. How is your room?"

I giggled. "It's all white."

"What do you mean all white?"

"I mean it is all white, carpet, chairs, bedspread, everything." I laughed. "I'm afraid to touch anything."

He chuckled with me. "I think I'd be afraid too."

"The bathroom is beautiful too, not white though. Everything is marble, including the enormous tub. I'm going to treat myself to a bubble bath."

Groaning over the phone, he said, "I wish I were there with you. I love bubble baths."

I giggled. "Do you really? I wondered about your big bathtub in your bathroom." I smiled to myself. Another Michael layer peeled away.

"What are you doing tonight?"

"Tonight is a dinner with my publishers. That was a last minute surprise." I told him about the New York Times book review article.

"Very impressive. You know I've been meeting quite a few people who know your books."

"Have you been talking about me to other people?" My heart leaped to think that maybe I was on his mind as much as he was on mine.

"You know it. I've been bragging. That's the perk of being your boyfriend isn't it?"

His voice had a magical effect on me, and when he said *boyfriend,* he caught me up in the thrill of the word again. Every time I spoke with him, my heart beat faster, my skin flushed, and my stomach, oh yes; my poor stomach did those now familiar flip-flops, and everything tightened south of the equator.

After we hung up, I did as I promised. I took a long bubble bath. Without any windows, the bathroom was naturally dark. The hotel had placed candles around the tub area, and even though it was still daylight, they created a soft glow when I lit them.

The bath took away the tension of traveling. I was nervous about the dinner this evening, and if I had a choice, I would have preferred to stay in the room. Social occasions always made me nervous, especially if I did not know anyone. I knew Nancy. She was good at being the social butterfly, so I was glad she would be there.

Nancy, aside from being my agent, was one of my dearest friends. It was not only business with us. Yes, she had my back on all the business dealings, but she was more than that to me. During the worst time, when I was divorcing Kevin, she had been there for me. We spent countless nights together on the phone when all the issues with him had given me writer's block. She encouraged me to go up to my cabin to get away from him. She realized before me that I was the happiest there.

I slipped into a black sleeveless cocktail dress with a twisted ruching V-neck in the front and a plain V-back. The summer had tanned my legs enough so I could go without hose. The dress, longer than my usual dresses, came to the top of my knees and had a playful back slit. Even though we were on the ocean, it had been a hot and humid day. I was used to the drier California climate. I put my hair up, and I slipped on my three-inch black strap sandals, tall would be the word for the evening.

We met the group in the lobby of the hotel. I was well acquainted with both Samuel Wells, the president of the division, and Martha Cooper, the editor-in-chief. They had both been with the division for many years, and they would be attending Rom Con with us the following week in Las Vegas. Nancy and I would stop for two days at the yearly convention for book signings and panel discussions on our final leg of the book tour.

Sam looked like he could have been at home on a horse, roping cattle.

I always expected him to show up in a cowboy hat and boots. It wasn't only the Texan accent that made me think that way. He was big, the type of big that blotted out the sun when he stood next to you. He made me feel small.

Where Sam was large, Martha was tiny. She barely cracked five feet and was as round as she was tall. However, what she did not have in stature she more than made up in wit and wisdom. Martha was legendary in the publishing field for being able to discern a great book from a good book.

The new division vice president, Luc Thierry, transferred from their international offices in Paris. He appeared to be in his early forties and was the type of handsome that made women turn their heads with his dark hair that had barely begun to gray. His height had surprised me. When he stood to greet us, he was several inches taller than me, which put him at about Michael's height.

When he shook my hand, his face wore an expression of intrigue. He held my hand a bit longer than necessary. When I pulled back, his fingers traced along my palm as if he did not want to let go.

"I have heard so much about you Miss Sommars, and I can say that I am delighted to meet you finally." His French accent was soft, and there was almost a British ring to his words. It sounded like he had been educated in England.

"Please call me Elizabeth." I looked up at him and smiled.

"And you must call me Luc," he said looking straight into my eyes while he gently took me by the elbow. "I believe the car is waiting for us in the front?" Luc asked as he turned to look at Sam, Martha, and Nancy. "Shall we?" He led me outside with the rest trailing after us.

We drove to a private club and restaurant a short distance away. It was crowded when we walked in, but the restaurant portion was quiet. We sat at a large round table in the center of the room with Luc on my left side and Sam on my right. I guessed it was my turn to be the belle of the ball.

I had made it a rule never to drink during business occasions. I plainly did not trust myself. Luc called for champagne, and before I could protest, the entire table was toasting the new book and me. The champagne was good, and it made me feel very warm. Where one glass of champagne went, others followed along with the appropriate wine for each course we ordered.

By the middle of the meal, Luc and Sam had me giggling with their stories of publishing nightmares. Nancy kept flashing me looks of warning across the table, but I paid her and the looks no heed.

After dinner, our party went into the nightclub. It was crowded, and the music was loud. We had a special table close to the dance floor reserved for us. It was not evident to me at the time, but both Sam and Martha allowed Luc to monopolize me. I danced with him three times, with the last time being a slow song. He was not shy to hold me close either.

While we danced, I was not sure if what I felt was from him holding me so close or the alcohol in my system. My head started to swim, and I definitely needed some air. We finished the dance, and I was glad to be able to go back to the table. This time when we sat, however, he did not release my hand.

I tried to pull my hand back discreetly, but he did not take the hint and held on. The spinning in my head did not clear, and I started to feel ill. I was definitely going to need some air.

I leaned over to Luc and whispered, "Luc, I need some air. I'm not feeling well."

He looked at me intently and nodded. He stood up finally releasing my hand and announced to our little group, "Elizabeth is not feeling well. I will escort her back to the hotel and send the limousine back to the club."

"Elizabeth, why don't you let me take you back to the hotel?" Nancy flashed a look at me.

"Nonsense," Luc answered immediately. "She wouldn't want to ruin your fun. It is no problem for me to take her."

"No, I don't mind at all." Nancy moved to get up. He put his hand on her shoulder and pressed her back into her chair.

I didn't care who was going to take me back to the hotel. "Nancy, I'll be okay once I get some fresh air. I'm going right to my room. I probably just need some sleep. You enjoy yourself."

Martha patted me on the shoulder. "I'm sure you're tired from the traveling today. I hope you feel better."

Sam reached over and squeezed my hand. "Get some sleep Elizabeth. We have a big night tomorrow night. Have a massage tomorrow or spend some time on the beach, it will make you feel better. We'll make sure Nancy gets back to the hotel safely." Sam looked at Luc. "Take care of our little lady here."

While we waited outside for the limousine, I started to feel better. The fresh air, even though it was still warm and humid, was welcome.

I smiled at Luc. "Thank you. I'm sorry to end your evening so early."

"It is my pleasure to have even spent part of the evening with you." He smiled a smile that I am sure would have knocked many women off their feet.

Luc was definitely flirting with me. I am sure that three months ago his smiled would have thrilled me, and I would be drooling over him. Now I just wondered if he was married, which he probably was because most executives didn't get to their positions without a dutiful wife at home.

When we arrived at the hotel, he suggested a drink in the lounge. I shook my head and replied that I was tired and needed to rest. He insisted on taking me to my room. I let him, not sure on how to stop him anyway. As we reached the door to my room. I turned around to thank him for his kindness one more time. Luc leaned down and kissed me before my brain had a chance to process his movements. I pulled back as soon as I registered what had happened. I could see in his eyes that he expected me to let him into my room. I put my hand on his chest to put some space between us.

"Luc, that shouldn't have happened," I said with finality.

He replied in his charming French accent, "I can feel the connection between us."

I smiled thinking of Michael. "I have someone in my life." What a wonderful sentence. It made my heart sing.

Luc smiled lazily. "I understand, Elizabeth. I am married. However, it should not be so complicated."

Bingo! I thought to myself. I was tired of trying to be nice. "Your kiss did not arouse anything in me. Nothing. No flip-flops."

"What are these flip-flops?" he asked.

I laughed. "It doesn't matter. Thank you for bringing me back to my room. Goodnight, it was interesting meeting you." I opened the door and closed it behind me.

Michael's flowers were the first thing I saw after walking into the room. All I wanted was to hear his voice. His cell phone went to voice mail, and I asked him to call me no matter how late he received the message.

I changed into my nightgown and sat out on the terrace watching the ocean. The temperature was still very mild, and it was so peaceful I almost didn't hear the phone ringing.

I leaped out of the chair and ran to answer it breathlessly. "Hello?"

"Hey, Babe." Even though he was three hours behind me, and it was only nine o'clock in California, Michael's voice sounded tired. "How was your dinner?"

"Oh, as dinners go I guess it was the norm for me. I drank too much, became too silly, then I got sick." I laughed.

"Are you feeling okay now?" he asked, the concern sounding in his voice.

"Yeah, I didn't lose anything this time." I giggled. "Then, the new vice-president of the division made a pass at me."

He paused and then asked, "Should I be worried?"

"Don't be a silly boy. It was really quite funny. I think I may have insulted him."

"Better him than you," he said dryly. "Do I have to fly there and defend your virtue?"

"You know my virtue only needs defending against you."

This time it was his turn to laugh. "Or mine against you."

"Oh, you stop it." I giggled. "So, not to change the subject, but you sound exhausted."

Michael let out a long sigh. I could hear him rustling around and wondered where he was. "I just got home. I've been at the eagle stand all afternoon and tonight. We found more shotgun shells and the eagles have been acting very agitated."

"I don't understand, why would someone shoot at an eagle?"

"It's a challenge to a hunter, or they're just ignorant. Death by gunshot is one of the top reasons for an eagle's premature death. There is also a black market for eagle feathers," he explained.

"What are you going to do?"

He sighed once more. "I don't know Babe, but we've got an idiot out there trying to shoot the eagles. The park rangers don't have enough staff to keep guards out there all the time, so some of us are taking turns. The climate here is steady, so this pair probably won't migrate. I'm just hoping that we catch them soon."

"I can help when I get home. I'll stay at the eagle stand. I can work on my book anywhere you know," I offered.

"Over my dead body Elizabeth," Michael almost growled. "This guy is armed."

"You forget my dad was a cop. He taught both Lisa and me how to shoot," I said.

"You don't have a gun now do you?" he asked.

"Well, no."

"And, it is going to stay that way," he said firmly. "Guns are dangerous."

"Now you just sound like my dad," I protested.

Michael was very chauvinistic, and though I would not argue with him now about the subject, it was far from over. He remained quiet on the other end of the phone.

After a few seconds ticked by the silence got to me. "What? So are we fighting now?"

He said quietly, "Elizabeth, I'm tired. I'm not going to quarrel with you. You need to go to bed and so do I. You have to be exhausted too."

I rolled my eyes mainly because he was right. I was tired too. I had not slept well the night before because of the altercation with Kevin.

"You're right. I am tired."

"Call me tomorrow after the party okay? I look forward to talking with you about it."

"Okay. You go take your bubble bath." I chuckled.

"I will, and I'll be thinking of you."

"I hope so."

CHAPTER TWENTY-FIVE

I woke late the next morning, and the sun was streaming through the window. I had forgotten to close the drapes, and with all the white in the bedroom, it was startlingly bright. Still on California time meant it was really 5:30. I moaned, rolled out of bed, and shut the drapes. Flopping myself back into the bed I wondered if I would be able to go back to sleep. Just the barest of efforts brought the headache I was trying to ignore to the forefront.

My head started pounding. I should have known better. I hated champagne hangovers. I stumbled into the bathroom to find aspirin and swallowed them quickly, and then collapsed back onto the bed. No drinking for me tonight I promised myself.

Waiting for the pain to subside, I began to think about breakfast. Yes, only I could have a headache one moment and then think of breakfast in the next. My very favorite thing to do when traveling was to order room service. I always ate breakfast, and as far I was concerned, it was the height of decadence to have someone bring it to me.

The clock finally read nine, and I could call Nancy. It was one of her weird rules. She answered the phone in her bright and chipper nine o'clock voice. I invited her to join me on the terrace for breakfast. She thought it was a grand idea and let me know she would be right over.

While we ate, I shared my Luc experience with her. She made the appropriate disgusted noises, and then we both laughed about it.

"Should I mention it to Sam? Sam would fry his butt."

I grimaced. "While I think he probably deserves it, I'm sure he does it all the time. I think the insult I paid him was punishment enough."

Nancy waved her coffee cup at me. "What?"

"I told him I felt nothing from his kiss."

"Really? He was damn attractive."

"I thought about Michael when Luc kissed me and how much better I liked Michael's kisses."

"Girlfriend, you are so gone. It is too funny. The two of you are in love even though neither of you said the words yet." She took the last gulp from her cup. "You know I have never seen you like this. When we met, you were a torn-up woman. Michael has thrown you for a loop. You didn't expect it, but it happened anyway. He has swept you off your feet, and I'm sure by the look of the flowers he's feeling the same way."

I leaned over for the coffee pot and refilled both of our cups. "Oh, stop it."

"Just because I stop talking about it doesn't make it go away."

"Enough," I said.

"Okay, okay." She giggled with her hands up in surrender. "I set up massages and facials for us today. They come up here. I thought it would be fun to do it together. We can have them set up out here in the shade."

That is why I loved Nancy so much. Her teasing was gentle, and when I wanted her to stop, she did. Our friendship had come along when I needed her most. The fact that she was also a fantastic agent was secondary because she would always be my friend first.

We thoroughly pampered ourselves all day; it was pure self-indulgence. From the terrace, we watched workers setting up for my book party on the sand. They brought in an entire dance floor and laid it directly on the beach. Meanwhile, in another corner, another group built a catering tent with barbeques placed outside. The workers laid a new floor where tables and chairs were set up. When they started putting up the lighting and the stage, I gasped.

"Oh my Nancy, you've got to see this." I pointed to the thirty-foot signs they were constructing. The billboards were photos of the book cover and me. "Don't tell me I look like that." I never thought I'd see myself blown up to thirty feet.

She looked over the terrace railing. "Wow, that's cool. I've got to get a picture of this." She took her cell phone out of her pocket and snapped a picture. "They're doing a nice job with this."

I just stood at the railing not uttering a word. I could not believe the size of the pictures.

"Come on now, you've had other book parties. You can't stand there gawking like a tourist." She laughed.

I said dryly, "I am a tourist. I'd like to see your face plastered up there. I can imagine what my face must look like close up." I shuddered.

She laughed. "Elizabeth," she patted me on the shoulder, "enjoy it, it means your novel is hot. That's a good thing in my book." She turned and picked up her room key and her bathing suit cover-up. "It's time for me to get ready for the party. I suggest you do the same. Are you wearing your hair down?"

I nodded. "I hope it's not too windy."

Nancy smiled. "That's what the tents are for. I'll come and get you at seven. We're meeting Sam and Martha in the lobby."

"Luc isn't coming?" I asked, hoping the answer would be no. I felt stupid after what happened last night.

"No," Nancy answered slowly with a sly grin crossing her face. "It seems that he was called back to New York suddenly."

My hand went to my mouth. "Nancy, you didn't say anything did you?"

"No, I was a good girl."

"I don't believe you."

"It seems that you're not the only one he tried to get friendly with." She walked out toward the door. "Be ready okay?"

She left me on the terrace as I watched the party preparations with interest. It was exciting that all of this was for me. My family would have never believed it. Before turning my laptop off, I checked my email. Both Dad and Lisa had sent congratulatory emails. Tammy had also sent an email with a picture attachment. The picture was of her and the four dogs. I laughed because it appeared as if it took a lot to get all the dogs to sit still. The email read,

Dear Elizabeth,

We all send many congratulations on your new book release. Everyone is going to love it! I know I did. Your babies are doing great, but they miss you. They're keeping active, and all four of them are running with Dad. Since Topper has a hard time climbing the stairs up to my room he has been sleeping with Dad. Dad even built him special steps so he can get up on the bed. They are old guys together.

Love and kisses to you from us all (even Dad, he's with the eagles today.)

The email made me laugh envisioning Michael and Topper cuddled together.

Finally, I went inside to prepare for the evening. My outfit hanging in the closet was a retro-inspired strapless dress, with a fitted bodice, which had boning and smocked back. The sweeping skirt was full and had slouchy, oversized patch pockets. Large brightly colored flowers decorated the fabric in magenta, blues, and greens and matched the beach theme of the party perfectly.

We met Sam and Martha in the lobby, and all walked out to the party entrance together. Since both the print and television media were covering the event, it would be a busy evening for me. Nancy squeezed my hand as we entered, and I put on a bright smile. A steel band played in one corner near the dance floor, and the champagne cocktails were already flowing.

Sam signaled the band to stop playing. He stood on the stage to give a short introductory speech.

"It is my pleasure to introduce this little lady to you. A smart editor who saw the potential in Elizabeth introduced her to us six years ago. Trouble Comes Deep is Elizabeth's tenth book with us and her sixth Jessica book. Believe me when I say she does not disappoint with this outing. Jessica is as feisty as ever and the way Elizabeth describes her, I wouldn't mind meeting her myself. Ladies and gentlemen, it is my pleasure to present our New York Times bestselling author, Elizabeth Sommars. And I might add her book will be debuting in the number one spot!"

Of course, I was beet red walking onto the stage. Sam gave me a big hug while we waited for the applause to die down. "Thank you all for coming tonight, though I'm not sure what all the fuss is about."

Someone in the audience yelled out to me, "There's page seventy-five!"

I laughed. "Well, yeah, there is always page seventy-five. Get a little further in the book, it gets better!" Everyone laughed with me. "So, enjoy all the good food, this fantastic band, and of course enjoy Trouble Comes Deep." I turned to get off the stage and then turned back around. "Oh yeah, you better give me a good review too! I know who you are!"

The evening went smoothly. I gave the interviews everyone wanted, had my picture taken repeatedly, and signed copies of the book. Actually eating was rare for me during these events, but Nancy was able to sneak a few bites to me to stave off the hunger pangs because the smell of the barbeque was driving me nuts.

My favorite part was talking to the bookstore owners. More than one regaled me with stories of anxious fans waiting for the book to come out. Fans knew that most stores had their copies early although the stores had to abide by the release date. The bribery stories were the best. More than one fan had offered to duplicate page seventy-five to get an advance copy. I would seriously have to rethink the erotic angle in my books.

By the end of the evening, exhaustion had overtaken me. Nancy managed to have the caterers prepare a box of food for us and have it delivered to my room. When we arrived back upstairs, even though it was late, we laid our little picnic out on the terrace table. She opened the bottle of champagne and poured two glasses.

"Here's to our Jessica." She lifted her glass and we both toasted each other.

Ignoring my champagne headache from the morning, I took a sip. "Oh, that's yummy. Thanks." I tasted a bite of the chicken. "This is tasty too. I am starving."

"I always tell you to eat before the party. You know how it is. Everyone else gets to eat except you," she said.

We ate, talked, and giggled as we emptied the bottle of champagne. We had an early day ahead of us with the book signing which would take all afternoon, and then afterward we'd be on a flight to New York.

I checked the clock after Nancy left. Two in the morning, not too late to call Michael. I was hoping he was home. He answered the phone right away.

"Babe, what are you doing up so late?"

I giggled. "It's not so late where you are."

"Yeah, but it's late where you are."

I could hear an engine running in the background. "Are you in the jeep?"

"I'm on my way home from the eagles," he said.

"Tammy sent me an email and told me you were at the stand this afternoon, she didn't say you were going to stay all night."

"It's not all night. I'm just pulling onto our road. Did you like the picture?" Michael asked.

"You took the picture? I wondered how she was able to keep the dogs still and take the picture. Yeah, it was cute. Thank you."

"We figured you were missing us."

"It would have been better if you were in the picture too," I whispered.

He grew silent on the phone too and then finally spoke. "Are you missing me too?"

"Yeah," I replied. Both of us were quiet. "Are you still there?"

He chuckled lightly. "Yeah, sorry. It's been a while since someone has missed me." He cleared his throat. I heard the car door slam. "Well, someone else has been missing me too."

I heard the dogs barking in the background. It sounded like a zoo. I could imagine the four dogs crowding around him, jumping up for attention.

"Who else has been missing you?" I asked.

"Topper!" he exclaimed. "He and I are best buds now. He gets a cookie just before bed, and then he snuggles between my legs and goes to sleep. Of course, I can't move the rest of the night for fear of disturbing him."

I laughed. "Oh, Michael! You don't let him eat in bed and get crumbs all over do you?"

He laughed with me. "Absolutely, he gets anything he wants."

"Great, you're spoiling him. You know, if you move your legs he'll move to the bottom of the bed."

"Now you tell me. With me, he's like dead weight. I don't want to cut this short, but you need to go to bed, and I need to eat. I'm starving. We'll talk tomorrow okay?"

I almost nodded but realized he couldn't see me. "Yeah, sure, I'll talk to you tomorrow."

We disconnected, and sadness swept me immediately. I wanted to be at home. I took a deep breath and told myself to snap out of it. He had been right. The morning would come early for me. Packing was on the agenda before the book signing since we were leaving for the airport immediately after the event. A combination of the day's events and the champagne brought sleep quickly to me.

When the wakeup call came at eight, I growled over the phone because the voice on the other side announcing the time was far too pleasant for such an early hour. I showered, dressed, and called for room service breakfast.

While waiting, I dried my hair. I would wear it down because everyone was used to my hair down and curly. When the packing was almost finished, there was a knock on the door. I expected room service, but Nancy stood there also. The waiter set up our breakfast outside on the terrace while I finished in the bedroom.

She had already dug into the croissants and coffee by the time I joined her. "All done?" she asked waving a croissant at me.

I nodded, sitting down opposite her and poured my coffee. I took long drinks of coffee and then water. "Yeah, all ready to go."

Nancy handed me a small box wrapped in colorful paper and a big bow. I figured it was the final copy Trouble Comes Deep. Traditionally she always presented me with a copy of the book on the release date.

"I wonder what this is," I said tearing off the wrapping paper.

"I guess you'll just have to open it to see," she said with a mischievous glint in her eye.

Inside the box was indeed my book and a small tissue-wrapped item was tucked underneath. Quickly opening the package, I pulled out a small cell phone.

"Oh, Nancy!"

"You can't go through another two weeks without a cell phone. It's just one of those disposable ones, I think I put enough minutes on it unless you and Michael have phone sex again," she said while rolling her eyes and laughing.

I turned it on and saw his picture on the screen. "How did you do this?"

"You should know that I'm quite clever with computers and people's websites."

"You also programmed his number in too? I can't believe it."

"Lisa and your dad's are in there too. Maybe now you won't need to borrow mine anymore." She grinned like the Cheshire cat.

I hugged her. "Thank you for taking such good care of me."

She kept on grinning. "Let's eat! Even after last night's feast, I'm starving!"

We finished breakfast and had our luggage loaded into the limousine. I couldn't say that I was sorry to be leaving my white room behind. Too much white, I was constantly afraid of getting something dirty. A line was already forming when we arrived at the bookstore. Stepping out of the limo, I waved to the fans waiting in line. Their cheers greeted me.

The store was ready for us. After the introductions, they put me behind the table and placed a large nonfat latte next to me. Yes! They were going to take excellent care of me.

At eleven, the doors opened, and everyone came streaming in. I never had trouble connecting with my fans. We spoke the same language. There were shy admirers and bold ones who wanted kisses and hugs. The store had an unobtrusive security guard nearby, so I did not mind. I chuckled when more than one person asked me to sign page seventy-five. I certainly started something on that page. My reader's comments always interested me too.

My hosts brought me a soda and a sandwich at three o'clock, but I was so busy with the signing, I didn't want to stop to eat. They wrapped up the sandwich for me so I could have it on the way to the airport after the signing. At four, the line showed no signs of slowing down. I began to work faster. Our flight to New York was at seven. Speeding up the autographs, we began to limit the pictures. Nancy finally threw me into the limousine at five, and it was a mad dash to the airport.

"Elizabeth, I never thought you would stop yakking!" she said as she gave me half of the sandwich she unwrapped.

I took a bite out of my half and a gulp of soda. "Sorry. You know how I am. People wait in the line for so long. I hate to let somebody down."

She nodded and munched on her sandwich, "That's why you're so good at what you do. By the way, what's with page seventy-five? I'm going to have to reread that section."

"I think it's because it takes place underwater."

Even she colored at the thought. "Well. Yes, I do remember now."

That was a surprise to have been able to embarrass her.

The three-hour flight was uneventful. A waiting limousine took us from JFK to Manhattan. We checked into the hotel at midnight. The room, while nice, could not compare to my white suite in Miami. This suite had two adjoining bedrooms, and we were sharing, which actually delighted us.

As we rode up in the elevator, Nancy confirmed with the bellman that room service was still available. "That's why I like New York," she said. "You know the city that never sleeps. I'm starving!"

"Me too. The sandwich we had on the way to the airport just didn't do it."

"I couldn't believe it, only snacks on the plane tonight, and we were in first class too."

I could tell the bellman was biting his tongue, two silly women talking about food. He opened the doors into the suite and Nancy spotted them first, the roses on the table.

"I bet I know who these are for," she said. "And who they are from." Snapping up the card, she confirmed the envelope had my name written on it.

I read the card. "*I've got a crush, my baby, on you. Michael.*"

It made me smile. Michael was extra cute, and it finally occurred to me, he was using Frank Sinatra songs on the cards. The roses were beautiful, and this time nine pink roses surrounded the three red ones.

Nancy rolled her eyes. "I'll call room service while you go into your room and call him."

I almost skipped into the room and had the phone out before the door shut.

Michael answered the phone. "Hello?" His deep masculine voice gave me a thrill.

"Hi! It's me," I said gleefully. I sat in the chair by the window and turned the light on.

"Babe?" he asked.

"Oh, this is a temporary cell phone number," I explained, and then continued, "Thank you for the beautiful roses. You are spoiling me."

He chuckled. "I can't spoil you enough. I'm glad you like them."

"Like them? I love them, and I love the card too," I said softly. "And, I'm not doing anything for you."

"You are by calling me. Did you just get to New York?"

"Yeah, we landed about two hours ago." I opened the curtain to look out the window. "You should see all the traffic, and you can hear the noise all the way up here. I love it," I said excitedly.

"How did the book signing go?" he asked.

Our conversation continued until Nancy knocked softly on the door. "Elizabeth, room service is here."

"My food is here. We're both starving," I told him.

"That's a new one for you. I've never heard you talking about so much food," he laughed.

"It's what Nancy and I do when we travel. We eat."

"You go and eat. Thanks for letting me know you arrived safely."

I sighed. "I miss you." My heart was heavy, and I didn't want to end the call.

Michael's voice became soft and wistful. "Babe, I miss you too. I feel like we haven't had any time together at all. When I think back on our time together up with the eagles, it really wasn't that long ago, but it seems like forever…"

"I know." My voice matched his, and I leaned against the window. "I want you to hold me and make love with me."

"Damn it, Babe, next book tour I go with you," he growled over the phone.

I laughed softly. "Only if you take me on your photo shoots."

"I'm teaching you how to use a camera when you get home." He laughed with me. "Okay, go eat. Call me tomorrow night."

We ended our call, and I joined Nancy in the living room.

"You two have it bad," she said with a smirk.

"I know." I took a forkful of salad and munched on it thoughtfully. "I don't know if it's because we were interrupted with all our traveling as things were beginning, or if there really is something between us."

She gestured at the roses on the table. "Elizabeth, a man does not spend a small fortune on flowers, not to mention coming up with cryptic sayings on cards, because there is nothing between you. I think it's obvious that he is courting you."

I looked at her in surprise. "You're serious, aren't you? Where did you come up with *courting*?"

"By what you've described of Michael, he sounds fairly conservative, at least when it comes to women." She stopped to pop a small piece of bread into her mouth. "The flowers definitely point to wooing. He's cute with the cards too. Most men wouldn't even bother."

I smiled and sat back in the chair. "I like the sound of that. I'm being wooed."

"Yes, I think you are. Enjoy it. Men like him don't come around very often."

CHAPTER TWENTY-SIX

Insert whatever city you would like. We were getting to the grind of the tour. The signing in New York started at noon and was supposed to end at six. It didn't. Nancy and I stayed until eight, and we were almost late for dinner.

Sam and Martha met us at the restaurant. I was thankful Luc was absent again. I concluded that I most likely would never see him again. What had happened between the two of us was more than a little embarrassing. There were a few other people from the east coast publishing office also joining us. Overall, it was a pleasant dinner, but I was tired. Since we did not have the opportunity to go back to the hotel to change clothes, I felt grungy and dirty from the day. The dress I had worn at the book signing translated well for dinner, so at least I had chosen my wardrobe correctly.

I fell into bed exhausted. Michael and I spoke only briefly on the phone. He still watched the eagles and was under the opinion, that the threat, in all probability, were local hunters, single or plural. I asked him to be especially careful, and he told me he was always careful. I added him and the eagles to my list of worries.

An early flight to Chicago the next morning precluded the opportunity to sleep late. I had to forego my usual bliss of room service breakfast, but we managed to grab a coffee at the Starbucks next to the hotel before we left. The airline did serve us breakfast in first class, but it was not room service breakfast. I did not grumble too much because the next few days would be very tiring for both of us. A book signing felt like being on stage for six hours straight, smiling, laughing, being pleasant, with everyone focused on you.

A corporate representative from the chain of bookstores met us at O'Hare airport with a limousine. She was a pleasant and efficient woman. When I was tired, I appreciated efficiency. She took us directly to the bookstore for my television interview. The hotel was located conveniently across the street so we could check in quickly.

The reporter and camera crew were there when we arrived. Sandy had warned me in the limousine that they wanted to film me arriving at the store because the fans had already begun lining up.

In the face of cheers from the waiting fans, I waved and walked over. "Hey, how long have you been here?"

"We've been waiting since early this morning," a young woman at the front of the line said. "We heard about Miami and that you had to turn people away."

"Thanks for coming. We'll let you in a soon as we can," I said.

A young man further back in the line said, "We'll wait."

Another person yelled from the crowd, "We love Jessica, and we love you!"

I turned and waved again.

After we made the introductions inside, my makeup was touched up for the interview. The camera crew and reporter waited for me in a small lounge area of the bookstore set up with couches and chairs. The reporter and I chatted for a few minutes before we started to film. Since there was only one camera, we sat together. The couch was comfortable, but it was difficult with my long legs to find a position in which I did not slouch and one that would keep my legs together.

Melissa, the stereotypical blond reporter, leaned over to me and whispered, "I won't ask you on camera about page seventy-five, but why do you think it's getting so much attention?"

I laughed. "Honestly, I'm not sure why it's getting so much attention. Other parts of the book were racier. If I had to guess, it must be because it's underwater."

We started the interview, and she asked me how long I had been writing, where my ideas came from, and all the standard Jessica questions. When it came to Jessica's future, I still had not told anyone about ending the current saga, so I certainly did not want to discuss it during the interview.

"Elizabeth, there have been rumors flying around the past few days that there might be a movie deal in the works for the Jessica series. Can you lend any credibility to this story?" Melissa asked as she moved closer to me because she wanted to appear conspiratorially friendly.

I flashed a glance at Nancy who was standing behind her just off camera. She rolled her eyes and gave a barely perceptible shrug of her shoulders. I looked back at Melissa and shook my head. "No, nothing like that to report, although given the right circumstances the story would make a terrific movie."

She nodded and accepted my answer at face value. She looked directly at the camera and signed off. Melissa turned back to me and offered her hand as she stood. "Elizabeth, thank you for the interview, I'm looking forward to reading the book, especially page seventy-five."

I laughed and stood with her. "Hope you're not disappointed. There are other good parts of the book."

We said our goodbyes and Nancy pulled me over to her. "Good interview. Those S.O.B.'s at Triad have leaked it to the press. I'm going to kill them."

"Do you think it was them? Maybe Sam's people have leaked it. You know to generate more publicity in this book."

She looked at me considering the possibility. "Well, someone has leaked it. I'm going to call Bill's office and see if they have heard anything."

"Let me know." I turned to go, and Nancy grabbed me.

"Where are you going?" she asked.

I looked at my watch. "I have an hour before the book signing. I'm just going to run over to the hotel for a minute."

She grinned. "You can't wait, can you? You've got to go over to see if there are flowers in the room, don't you?"

I looked chagrined and nodded.

She rolled her eyes. "Go. But hurry back. We're supposed to have Chicago deep dish pizza delivered in a few minutes for lunch."

I nodded again and turned to the door. Nancy yelled out after me as she took her phone out of her pocket. "Take security!"

The rep, who had heard us, joined us quickly. "I'll go with you Elizabeth."

"That's sweet of you, but you don't have to. The hotel is only across the street."

"I don't mind. There is a big crowd gathering out there. John will walk with us."

She beckoned to the burly security guard standing by the door. We crossed the street without incident, probably because I stopped to talk to the fans again. Sandy rode up in the elevator with me.

"Elizabeth, if I could be so bold, why is it that you needed to come over to the hotel?"

I smiled. "It's really silly. My boyfriend…" I loved to linger on that word. The word alone could send little shivers down my spine and started my stomach flipping. "He has been sending me roses to each one of my book signing stops."

She nodded in understanding. "So you want to see if there are flowers here in Chicago. Will you be disappointed if they are not there?"

I thought about it for a moment before answering. "I guess so, but no really, I won't be. He's been very generous. There were flowers in Miami and New York. I'm only going to be here one night so it would be very wasteful since I can't take them with me."

We walked down the hushed hallway, and I slid the card key into the slot when we reached my room. The door snapped quietly open. The room again was a suite, and we had to step fully into the room.

Both of us gasped at the same time and then said "Aww" in unison. The pink and red roses were on the table by the window. I crossed the room to them and bent over to inhale their fragrance. Reading the card silently, "*We'll be together again soon. Hurry home. M.*" I tucked it into my jacket pocket. The rep had returned to the doorway to give me privacy. Had I been alone, the crying would have started. The roses and the sentiment on the card, made my heart sing. However, it laid heaviness on my heart too. I missed Michael more than ever now.

I joined the rep in the hallway and closed the door behind us.

"The roses are beautiful," she commented. "May I ask if there is significance between the pink and red?"

I smiled. "He seems to be adding a red rose every day and subtracting a pink one."

She nodded appreciatively. "Wow, he's very romantic and very visual too."

"Yeah, that must be the photographer in him."

We were finished by nine-thirty and made our way over to the hotel. I was tired and begged off dinner. We would be leaving early the next morning for a flight to St. Louis, and by the end of the day, we would be in New Orleans for the next stop.

When I reached my room, I was disappointed to have to leave a message for Michael after reaching his voicemail. I thanked him for the flowers and told him he was far too extravagant. I hoped he didn't listen to me. I loved getting flowers.

Tammy emailed more pictures of the dogs and herself. I laughed at the antics in the photographs since they were a little slice of home for me. I hoped there would be one of Michael among the pictures, but there wasn't. He had definitely taken the shots, and I began to recognize his style. I replied to Tammy's email thanking her for the pictures and told her I wanted one of her dad. I was curious as to how far that would get me, but I seriously doubted that I would see anything at all. I shut my laptop down and fell into an exhausted sleep.

CHAPTER TWENTY-SEVEN

The next morning we were up early again, and time enough for room service breakfast. We talked over coffee and eggs benedict. It was a busy day ahead, the book signing in St. Louis in the afternoon and then a flight to New Orleans. By this point, I had forgotten what day it was, and Nancy had to remind me it was Friday. It would be one more week on tour. I should have been enjoying the trip more and usually did. This time it was different though. I had someone waiting for me at home. Somebody wonderful who was sending me flowers.

We arrived in New Orleans late in the evening. Our hotel was in the French Quarter, and as expected, it was crowded even for a Friday night. I was thankful that my bedroom faced the courtyard, which meant it would be quiet. The book signing was the next afternoon, and then we would have the whole evening and Sunday free. We would fly to Phoenix on Monday morning.

Nancy came with me to my rooms first. She was as curious as I was to see if there would be flowers, and she spotted them first. They were sitting on the table in the front room. Six pink and six red roses were in the vase. My heart almost leaped out of my body.

She said merely one word. "Wow."

If I could have hugged them, I would have. I hadn't spoken with Michael since Chicago. I would track him down somehow.

"This one is a keeper," she whispered. "He's for real."

I only nodded. I hadn't looked at the card. I didn't want to with Nancy in the room. I wanted to cry by myself, and I was holding it together just enough to say goodnight to her. She understood without me having to tell her and quickly left me alone.

Opening the French windows to look out over the Quarter, I sat in the heavily brocaded chair by the window. Slipping the card slowly out of the envelope I read it aloud. "*Elizabeth, you brought a new kind of love to me. Michael.*" I gasped, and the tears slowly trailed down my face. "Oh Michael." I wiped the tears away and dialed his cell phone number.

He answered the phone with the first ring. My heart wanted to sing when I heard his voice. "Elizabeth, how is my woman?"

I said softly, "Hi, you're some kind of incredible."

"I am? Why do you say that?" The delight was evident in his voice.

"I love the flowers. You are so sweet."

He laughed. "I want to be something more than sweet. I want to be your sexy hunk of a man."

I giggled. "Oh, you're more than that. You know you are spoiling me. You shouldn't be spending all your money. You have daughters in college."

"You deserve to be spoiled. Indulge me," he said very softly. "Have you had a chance to look at your email?"

"No, I just got into the room. Did you send more pictures of the dogs?"

I pulled out my computer from my laptop bag and turned it on. He stayed on the phone with me as I opened the browser. There was an email from Tammy and, right below, there was one from him. The subject line on his email read "Private." I opened his message and found a photo attachment.

"Did you send me a picture?" I asked.

"Open it and see," he teased.

The photo took a moment to download. As it opened, I struggled for my breath. "Michael, you didn't?"

"If I see it spread on the internet, I'll know who did it." He chuckled.

"I could make a lot of money with this one." I sighed.

The picture was of him in his bathtub. The bubbles covered the important parts, but I could clearly see his chest, and he had his legs propped up together on the edge of the tub. Completing the effect were the burning candles surrounding the tub. The picture was deliciously sexy. His eyes looked at the camera, and I felt he was looking directly at me.

It made me shiver, in a very good way. "How did you take this picture?"

"Don't worry, I was alone." He laughed. "You know I am a talented photographer and know how to take pictures on timed release."

"Well," I cleared my throat, "this is ..." I paused for a moment while trying to gather my thoughts. He was chuckling in the background. "Hmmm, this is definitely yummy. You are my sexy hunk of a man." I wondered how this picture could be uploaded on my tablet.

"I'm glad you like it. We're going to have to take a picture of you for me, and I know just how I want you posed."

I giggled. "Oh, I don't think that is ever going to happen."

By the end of our conversation, Michael had me more than giggling. Our banter had refreshed me, and my bones did not feel as tired as before.

The laughter from the street below strangely comforted me also. The breeze carried into my room the smells of rain on the Mississippi. I always loved New Orleans simply for this reason. The city did not have the hustle of New York or the sassiness of Miami. It had its own personality, one of southern charm that captured long gone days. Nights spent on a verandah, sipping a mint julep, and listening to a Cajun beat. The first ideas of centering a new book in this city arrived that night.

Before our conversation ended, he reminded me that the wife of his colleague would be coming to the book signing. He described her and asked me to be on the lookout for her since she was shy.

I crawled beneath the feather comforter and cuddled up against the feather pillows, everything felt almost like home. The courtyard that the bedroom faced was quiet. The trees were rustling as the breeze increased. The lace curtains fluttered, and I heard the first drops of rain. The sound of the rain lulled me softly to sleep.

The next morning Nancy and I agreed to meet in the lobby. We walked to Café Du Monde for their chicory coffee and donuts. It had rained hard during the night, and the streets were still wet. The humidity and heat had not set in yet, but the threat was there. The outdoor café was located on the river. We ordered our *café au lait* and *beignets* and sat outside under the covered patio.

I had found the secret to eating the powdered sugar *beignets* was not to breathe while taking a bite. If you inhaled, your lungs filled with the powdered sugar and you had a coughing fit. Exhaling was almost worse. That created a chest and lap full of powdered sugar. Yes, it was better not to breathe at all until your mouth had the morsel safely tucked away. Even with this in mind, we still ended up blowing powdered sugar at each other while we were laughing.

The small shops in the French Quarter were opening as we strolled back to the hotel. We window-shopped, sipping the last of our to-go coffees. The limousine was waiting for us when we arrived back at the hotel.

Posters of my book and balloons decorated the outside of the store. A Zydeco band was playing. The line of fans had already formed. This was a party atmosphere, and I almost hated going inside the store. If I expected the interior of the store to be quiet, I was mistaken. This store had the music that was playing outside piped inside. The store employees happily greeted me. There were tables piled with food. The manager explained that they liked to have a party when they had book signings. Everyone volunteered to bring in food and the cousin of one of the workers provided the music.

It was delightful, not only the welcome we received but also all the special touches they made. Even though Nancy and I had just eaten breakfast, we sampled the food laid out on the tables. We both found the food was spicy hot and delicious.

I happily signed books, posed for pictures, and spoke with fans. In the late afternoon, one of the store employees brought a woman my age up to the table. She introduced herself as the wife of Michael's colleague. She was excited to meet me, and I wasn't sure where he had gotten the idea that she was shy.

Marie was a tall, beautiful, redheaded, and stacked woman. For a moment, I wondered if they were hers, but it was confirmed when she hugged me that her bosoms were natural.

"Oh *chère*, I've been looking forward to your visit to our city." She had a slight Cajun accent, and even though Michael described her as a schoolteacher, she did not look like any teacher I ever had.

I grinned. I liked her immediately. She spoke with us for a few minutes, and in that short time, I felt like I'd known her for years.

"I know you have to go back to your signing," Marie drawled. "But Tommy and I want you to come out to the house tonight for dinner. We're having some family over, and we wouldn't forgive ourselves if we didn't show you two some Louisiana hospitability."

I looked at Nancy, and she did not give me a look either way. "That is very nice of you, but we don't want to impose on you."

"Don't talk baloney *chère.* I've been planning this since Michael's visit. Everyone's excited about meeting you. Tommy is even planning to take you to see the gators. You will love it." Marie hugged us both, together. Nancy and I nodded while caught up in her arms. "Good," Marie said after releasing us. "My daughter Evelyne will come and pick you up at seven. You're staying at Maison? Wear something comfortable," She said as she turned, waved goodbye to us, and left.

Nancy and I stared at each other. "Well, this should be interesting," she said dryly.

I smiled and nodded my head in agreement.

We finished with the event, thanked all the employees for the great experience, and we were back in the limousine by quarter after six. I spotted Evelyne in the lobby as soon as we walked through the doors. She was hard to miss because she was almost an identical twin to her mother, but twenty years younger. She wore shorts and a tank top and did not look comfortable in the fancy lobby. We told her we would quickly change and be back downstairs in a flash. She looked relieved that she would not have to wait until seven.

The old gunmetal gray pickup truck Evelyne led us to had seen better days, but she was obviously proud of it. The three of us all squeezed into the front bench style seats, and when she turned on the engine, the radio turned on to a Zydeco music station that almost blasted us out of the windows. Evelyne looked sheepish and turned the music down promptly.

She mumbled a "sorry" under her breath.

When she pulled onto the highway, she appeared to relax. "I do not like to drive in New Orleans." She pronounced it Nawlins. "Momma wanted to make sure everything was ready for your visit."

I sat in the middle and Nancy clung to the door as if it were her very lifeline. Evelyne drove very fast, but she seemed sure of her direction.

"It's very nice of your family to have us out to your house," I squeaked out.

"Are you kidding? It's all Momma has talked about for the past week. She's so excited. All her lady friends were together reading your books aloud," she said looking over at me. I secretly wished she would keep her eyes on the road.

"Have you read my books?" I asked.

"Not yet. Momma said when I graduate high school next year I can read them. She said they are too adult."

"That makes sense." I couldn't believe that she wasn't over eighteen, because she looked like she could be twenty-five. "How long will it take to get out to your house?"

"Oh, we're about thirty minutes away from the city." She stole another look at me. "So Daddy says you're Uncle Michael's new girlfriend."

I coughed and sputtered, "Uncle Michael?"

Nancy gave me a wild look.

"Yeah," she nodded, "he's not really my uncle, but Daddy has known him ever since their college days."

I tried to contain my astonishment. "So your father and Michael went to Santa Cruz together?"

She nodded again. My thoughts were swirling. I would have a few choice words with Michael tonight if possible. At the very least, he could have prepared me for the meeting of what sounded like a close friend of his. Evelyne went on to a different subject and kept us entertained until we reached the house.

We drove down a long tree lined driveway and pulled up in front of a white two-storied plantation style house. There were small twinkle lights everywhere in the trees and wrapped around the large columns on the portico. The balcony on the second floor appeared to encircle the entire house. At least twenty parked cars were scattered in front and on the sides of the yard. Groups of people gathered near the front steps. The sun began to set over the bayou making the scene a postcard impression. We heard excited voices rumbling through the crowd as we stepped out of the truck.

Nancy pulled me aside and whispered, "I hear the banjo music from the movie "Deliverance."

"Oh stop it!" I looked at her shaking my head.

"No, I really hear the music," she muttered.

She was right, the music started up louder. It was not the music from the movie, but a small band on the corner of the porch started playing Cajun/Zydeco music.

Marie was instantly in front of us giving both of us hugs and dragging us along to everyone who had gathered at the bottom of the porch. Marie introduced us to her husband and then proceeded to make introductions to the entire crowd. There was no way that I would remember everyone, but I tried my best. Most of Marie's friends had my books, and they kept me busy for the first half hour signing them all. Nancy caught the eye of the attractive and single New Orleans district attorney, and as the music started in earnest, they started dancing.

Tommy came over to the crowd of women sitting with me. He looked at his wife. "Now y'all, are we going to keep Elizabeth all tied up with you gaggling hens?" All the women tittered. Tommy was a good-looking dark-haired man with a soft southern drawl and a sweet smile, which he turned on for all the women. "You know it's my job to make sure she has a good time. I'm going to take her out and dance for a while. I'll bring her back, and she can regale you with more stories from her books." He bent down and kissed Marie. He took my hand and lifted me to my feet. "Com'on *chère,* let's dance."

I tried to protest and said, "Really I'm not a very good dancer."

"Oh, go on Elizabeth, my husband is a great dancer," Marie said. "We'll join you out on the floor in a bit. Oh, and Tommy don't forget you need to take Elizabeth out to see the alligators tonight. Michael wanted you to show her."

He had my hand in his, and he looked over his shoulder at his wife. "Don't worry *chère*, we'll do that right after dinner."

All the songs were sung in French and in a dialect that I had a hard time following. The first song was a fast one, and as promised, Tommy was an accomplished dancer, so I was able to fall into step with him quickly. The second song was a slow song and danced as a waltz. It allowed us to spend some time talking.

"We sure were surprised when Michael told us about you during his visit," Tommy said in his southern drawl. He did not have as heavy a Cajun accent as Marie did, but it was still there. "You look a lot like the picture he showed us."

While we danced, I was able to take a better look at him. He was a tad taller than I was, probably putting him at six feet. His hair was dark, almost black, and wavy, with a sprinkling of gray on the sides. Since he and Michael had been college friends, I guessed he was the same age. Tommy was bulkier than Michael was, and a little heavier, due most likely to the fantastic food in Louisiana.

"Which picture did he show you?" I asked thinking it was the one on the back of my book cover.

"It was a cute little number with you in a bikini taken with Katy and Tammy." He smiled and winked.

I started blushing remembering the photo Michael had taken of us clowning around on the dock.

"Oh, that one." I looked down willing the blush not to creep up any further on my face.

He laughed heartily. "Michael was right, you are beautiful when you blush." He paused for a moment and when I didn't answer, "I'm sorry *chère*, I shouldn't have embarrassed you. Blame the Californian," he said referring to Michael.

The dinner bell interrupted our dancing. There were long tables set up on the porch. I sat with my hosts on either side of me, and Nancy sat next to her new best friend, Marcus, the cute district attorney. They seemed to have hit it off and appeared to be enamored with each other.

The women I had signed books for earlier started to bring out food, and it was a constant progression. Some of the dishes I recognized, like jambalaya, barbecued shrimp, and red beans and rice, but there was also fried catfish, crawfish etouffee, deep fried okra, Cajun white beans, Creole lima beans, and a fantastic cabbage concoction. They passed around huge baguettes to soak up the wonderful sauces that went with each dish. The bread also helped temper the spiciness of the food too. They expected me to try everything and piled my plate high.

The sounds surrounding us were delightful too. Aside from the continuous clinking of glasses for each new toast, music from a compact disc player played in the background, which went perfectly with the croaking of the swamp frogs. The fireflies twinkling in the darkness and the chirping of the crickets made it almost feel like a Disney Pirates of the Caribbean moment, except that this was the real thing.

The women surrounding me told me the recipes for each dish.

Marie laughed. "Don't worry Elizabeth. I'll email you some of Michael's favorites."

I didn't bother telling her that I didn't cook and that he would probably end up doing the honors.

"Michael doesn't eat everything since he's a vegetarian." Marie made the word sound as if it was dirt in her mouth. "But he does love my vegetable jambalaya."

A woman carried out a large platter, and everyone clapped.

"You'll like these." Marie put one down on my plate.

It looked like a deep-fried lump. As she passed some sauce to me, I poked it with my fork hoping that it wasn't somebody's road kill. I popped it into my mouth, and it tasted like chicken. Everyone looked at me for my reaction. I so loved to be the center of attention when I ate.

"It's delicious." I swallowed it almost whole. Actually, it tasted good, although I couldn't get the picture of a raccoon out of my mind. Not that I really thought it was one, but some confirmation would have been nice.

Tommy laughed loudly. "I think she likes gator."

Everyone clapped.

I merely smiled and silently thought, "*Oh my god, I just ate alligator.*"

Marie put her arm around me and hugged me. "We certainly don't make this for Michael!"

I kept smiling. "Yeah, I bet you don't."

Even though I was completely stuffed and thought I could not eat another bite, dessert came out of the house next. Placed in front of me was bread pudding with the most marvelous bourbon sauce I had ever tasted. I could have sat in the corner with a big bowl and a spoon and eaten it the rest of the evening. The sauce had to be one hundred proof, even though I assumed the alcohol content evaporated during the cooking process.

I was wrong. The alcohol was added to the sauce after cooking, so it was completely full strength. I sat at the table like a happy clam eating big spoonful's of bread pudding and sauce while the grin on my face got wider and wider.

The band started the music again, and Tommy called out to them, "Play something in English for our guests."

One of the guys yelled out, "How about *My Toot Toot*?"

My ears perked up. "Hey, I know that one!" I waved my arms around like the crazy drunk woman I was.

Tommy pulled me to my feet. "Well, get on up there girl, show us what you've got!"

Before I could say no and declare that I had consumed too much bourbon sauce, I was up in front of everyone singing along with the band.

Even Nancy had a surprised look on her face when I finished.

Tommy called out again, "Looks like we have our very own Queen Ida right here!"

Everyone tried to have me sing another song, but I firmly refused. Instead, one of the guests whisked me off to the dance floor. From that point on, I had a steady stream of partners. Several times, I looked over, and Nancy was dancing with Marcus and only with him. She seemed to have eyes for only him this evening.

Finally, after the ninth or tenth song, I held my hands up in surrender. I couldn't dance anymore. My feet hurt, and I was getting dizzy from twirling around. I joined the ladies up on the porch to cool off. There were huge fans scattered in the ceiling of the porch. The fans moved the air effectively, but it was still humid and hot. I did not think I would be able to adapt to weather like this quickly.

I discovered that the ladies on the porch were all relatives of some sort.

Marie and Tommy's mothers, grandmothers, and a few assorted aunts, and they all knew Michael. All of them were very interested in the new woman in his life, namely me.

"So *chère*, are you ready to go and meet some alligators?" Tommy asked.

I quickly nodded. "Oh yes!"

Marie asked the ladies if they'd like to join us, but none of them decided to be adventurous. Nancy was not interested in checking out the alligators either. She pulled me aside as we were walking away from the house.

"Elizabeth, Marcus and I are going to leave now. Is that okay with you? He lives in New Orleans, in the garden district, and has invited me to see his house," she whispered.

I raised my eyebrows and said dryly, "Oh really Nancy, is he going to show you his etchings?"

Nancy actually blushed, which she did not often do.

I laughed and hugged her. "Go have a good time."

"We're probably going to spend the day together tomorrow, so I'll call you tomorrow night when I get back to the hotel," she said quietly.

"As long as you make the flight Monday morning. Try not to miss the plane, okay?" I joked.

She nodded and went off to find Marcus. I caught up with Marie and Tommy, and we walked down the dock to the boat.

"Are Marcus and Nancy going back to New Orleans?" Marie asked as we walked out and passed through a large gate. The entire dock was protected by fencing.

I nodded. "He has invited Nancy to see his house."

Marie smirked. "He has a very nice house. It's a big old restored mansion. We were glad that Katrina didn't damage it too badly." She chuckled softly. "That Marcus. He knew he wasn't allowed to get to you."

"Now Marie, don't you go telling stories. You know he is a gentleman," Tommy added.

"Nancy is a big city girl. I'm sure Marcus will have his hands full with her."

"Yes, I'm sure he will," she said, and the double meaning of my sentence went over my head.

They helped me step onto the smallest of the three boats. Tommy locked the little gate behind us.

"Why do you have the gate and the dock fenced in?" I asked.

He moved his large flashlight over the shoreline, and I saw quick movement in the water. I gasped a squeaky, "Oh!"

He laughed. "The gators will pull you right off the dock, and you'd make a tasty little evening snack for one of them."

"Are we safe in the boat then?" I stood very still in the middle of the boat.

Tommy chuckled. "Oh sure *chère*, as long as you don't drag your feet or arms in the water."

"Alrighty then, I'll be sitting in the middle of the boat," I said.

After securing me in a life vest, he started the engine. As we moved from the dock, they explained their alligator management program. Tommy, who was a professor of conservation biology at the University of New Orleans, was in charge of the doctorate program. He also worked with the state of Louisiana on their alligator preservation plan.

My vision adjusted to the blackness surrounding us. Even with the light from the boat, I could barely see the low hanging moss from the trees. Tommy warned me not to panic if a snake dropped into the boat. Panic? I almost panicked at the mere mention of a snake. Snakes and spiders were not on this girl's most favorite things list. You bet I would panic!

He explained there were an estimated one million alligators in Louisiana. They were taken off the endangered species list in the late seventies but were still on the protected species list in all eight states where they lived. The alligator was considered a natural renewable resource, and the conservation effort encouraged the private landowners to maintain the alligator's habitat in a productive and natural environment.

The boat slowed down to a crawl and then he cut the engines. At first, there was complete silence, and then the first cricket chirp echoed. All of a sudden, a calliope of sound surrounded us. Tommy turned the boat's lights to the shoreline. Marie tapped me on the shoulder and pointed. There was barely a ripple as several alligators slipped quietly into the water. I gasped. He moved the light again, and I could see several pairs of eyes peering out.

"Alligators normally hunt at night, that's when they are the most dangerous. During the daytime, they like to lie out and sun themselves. It helps them digest their dinner from the night before," he explained.

Marie added, "We'll take you out again tomorrow. It's lovely during the day with the moss, and we even have a couple of eagles. Michael is very interested in those."

I nodded. "It sure is spooky at night."

Sure enough, just as I spoke, there was a *plop* noise on the floor of the boat right next to me. Tommy flashed his light in my direction.

"Sit still Elizabeth," he commanded.

From the urgent sound of his voice, I knew not to move. Marie was next to me in a flash with a long metal pole that had a hook at the end. She quickly scooped up the dark brown, almost blackish snake with the pole and threw it overboard.

I must have turned pale. "Was that a …" I didn't finish the sentence.

Marie sat next to me. "Yep, a little old water moccasin, or cottonmouth, as we like to call them." She slipped her arm around me. "You okay? Tommy let's start up the boat. We're lingering too long in one place."

I had a difficult time relaxing for the rest of the trip. My legs were tightly jammed together, and I didn't want to set my feet on the bottom of the boat. Every sound made me jump nervously. I had my doubts when Marie had mentioned going out again tomorrow, especially now.

We made our way back up to the house. Once there, Tommy told everyone the story of our adventure. Everyone extolled my braveness. I didn't feel courageous. I was only too glad to be out of the boat. Both Tommy and Marie suggested that I spend the night. Not wanting to intrude on their hospitality, I declined, but they insisted again. They finally wore me down with the argument that someone would just have to pick me up again in the morning to bring me back out to the house.

She showed me to my room upstairs, and a nightgown already lay on the bed for me, along with fresh towels in the adjoining bathroom. It seemed my staying was a foregone conclusion.

"Now when you're tired, you make yourself at home and go upstairs to sleep. I sure wish you were staying longer," she added wistfully. "But, we'll have tomorrow."

I liked her, she was fresh, and not the least bit pretentious. What you saw with Marie was what you got.

"I'll be down in a moment." Pulling out the little cell phone. "I want to call Michael before it gets too late."

Marie's eyes twinkled. "I would imagine you do. He is such a dear. Here, I'll give you some privacy. Come down when you're ready." Marie shut the door behind her as she left the room.

I surveyed the surroundings. The corner room had hardwood floors that were polished until they shined. The bright yellow wallpaper design and the curtains matched. White paint covered the pair of French doors leading out to the upstairs balcony as well as all the trim and the window. The room was comfortably furnished with a queen-sized bed covered in a white lace crocheted bedspread, a yellow upholstered club chair, and a cherry wood dresser by the window on the opposite end of the room.

I sat down on the bed and imagined what it would be like to have Michael here with me in this room, with his friends downstairs. I smiled to myself. Yes, he would like it very much, and so would I. I dialed his number quickly.

"Hi, what are you doing?" I said.

"Hey, Elizabeth." He sounded surprised but happy to hear from me. "It is too noisy at my house, so I'm watching the start of the baseball game on your big screen television."

"You are?"

"Yup. I could really get used to this."

I laughed. "Well, make yourself at home."

"I am," he said, crunching on what sounded like potato chips. "So, what do you think about New Orleans? Did you meet Marie?"

"Oh, I more than met her." I reviewed the day's happenings with him. "I'm now up in the bedroom ready to go back downstairs and rejoin the party. I held the phone away from my ear and pointed it toward the open French windows. "Hear the music?"

"Yeah. They throw a great party. Are you in the yellow room?" he asked.

"How did you know?"

"It was one of the first rooms that they restored after Katrina. I always stay in that room. I love it because of the French doors."

I didn't realize that Katrina had touched this magnificent house. "Did they have a lot of damage from the hurricane?"

Michael heaved a heavy sigh. "The main structure of the house was undamaged, but the roof, all the windows, and the outside of the house took a beating. They had tried to protect what they could of the windows and doors, but the force ripped them out. The whole first floor was completely flooded. Even though the house is up higher, the floodwaters rose almost to the second floor. The house is 150 years old, and part of the national registry, so they wanted to repair everything instead of tearing it down and rebuilding."

"No basements here, right?" I said.

"Right, no basements. You don't have to dig down very far before you hit the water in that area."

"No wonder everything looked so new downstairs. Marie has it beautifully decorated. The house has a real antebellum flavor to it," I said.

"They are both very proud that they were able to restore it. Oh yeah, and the room that you're in is haunted." He chuckled.

"Oh, stop teasing me." I looked around, but everything was perfectly normal. What did I expect, a ghost lurking about maybe?

Michael laughed again. "Don't say I didn't warn you. You should have me there, I would protect you."

"I don't know who I'm more afraid of, you or the ghost."

"True." He added, "Your virtue wouldn't be in jeopardy with the ghost."

"You can bet on that," I retorted. "Then again, I haven't had to worry about my virtue in a long time." I giggled.

"Really? So then, I'm not to blame for tainting your good name? That's a relief!" he said joking.

"What else are you up to this nice Saturday evening?"

"I just dropped off my date." He laughed.

I almost froze at first and then was nearly afraid to ask. "What?"

Michael chuckled. "Tammy and I went out to eat."

My voice sounded relieved. "Oh."

"Come on Babe, you don't think I could handle more than one of you, do you?"

The relief washed over me again, and then I felt stupid and lamely said, "Tommy and Marie seem to think you're quite the party animal."

"Great, now I have to live down that reputation too. Believe me, only in New Orleans, it is the party town."

I snickered. "If that's the case, you are definitely not going to New Orleans alone again."

His voice became quiet. "Is that a promise? You know how much I miss you." He whispered the last sentence.

"Only another week," I sighed. "I'll be returning home next Friday night. I miss you too."

"Good, let's have phone sex right now," he suggested while laughing.

I giggled. "We are not having phone sex. That is all I need. The windows are open. I could just see that and then walking downstairs afterward. I'd never hear the end of that one. And since the conversation has turned into the gutter, I better let you get back to your game."

It took me a long time to get to sleep after the party wound down and everyone trooped off to their own beds or homes. I was bothered Michael had again not given me the full story about his relationship with Tommy and Marie. After the experience with his relatives, it had appeared that we were on solid footing. To find out tonight that he had not given me the complete details and allowed me to walk into a surprise situation disturbed me. I could not understand what his motivation for the secrecy was, but our relationship did not stand a chance at survival if it continued. After spending years distrusting Kevin's every move, I refused to run down the same path with Michael. The more I thought about the situation, the more determined I became to discuss it with him.

CHAPTER TWENTY-EIGHT

I awoke the next morning to the delicious smell of baking croissants, coffee, and frying bacon. After quickly dressing and braiding my hair, I made my way down to the kitchen. The kitchen was full of people from the party last night. I wasn't sure if they lived here, just spent the night, or came over for breakfast.

Tommy greeted me with a glass of orange juice. "Good morning glory."

Marie, who stood at the stove was preparing massive quantities of bacon and stirring grits. "Hey *chère*, how did you sleep last night?"

"Okay I guess, I had some crazy dreams though."

Everyone looked at me.

"Not nightmares I hope?" she asked.

I shook my head and took a sip of the orange juice. "No, the strangest dream, over and over again. I dreamt civil war soldiers were walking through the room, and there was a little door in the corner of the room that led to a stairway leading up to the next floor. It was interesting, the bedroom didn't have any furniture in it, it was empty."

She smiled and turned the stove off. "So, what color were the soldier's uniforms?"

I considered her odd question. "The uniforms were gray, and so I guess they were southern soldiers."

Everyone in the room smiled, and Marie laughed. "Elizabeth, I dare say you must have some paranormal abilities. Our ghosts manifest themselves in the yellow room to people with the gift. During the civil war, our southern soldiers utilized the top floor as a lookout point. There would have been a steady stream of men tromping through the room to the small stairwell leading up to the attic. After Katrina, we closed off the door and steps to that part of the attic, so it's interesting that even though you didn't know it was there, you dreamt about it."

I shook my head in disbelief, while everyone else was nodding theirs.

Tommy took me by the elbow to lead me into the dining room. "Now, don't you listen to Marie's ghost stories."

I could not agree more, I certainly did not want to be a person with a gift, especially that sort of skill. People who lived alone as I did, needed no such talent. Talk about giving me the *heebie-jeebies.*

As we sat down at the long dining room table, one of the great-grandmothers took my arm and looked at it. She pointed out the many mosquito bites I had on my arms. I had not noticed them, and of course, now that I saw them, they began to itch. Great-grandmother said something in French and pointed to Marie.

Marie picked up my arm. "Elizabeth, you've been eaten alive by our mosquitoes. I've got Great-Me-maw's old herbal remedy for that, and it will help the itching and prevent infections." She grinned, "And if you're nauseous you can drink it, and it will fix your tummy right up. Great-Me-maw has been brewing it for years."

She came back from the kitchen with a jar of liquid that looked like tea.

"Brewing it?" I asked, taking the jar from her and looking doubtful, envisioning someone hunched over a bubbling cauldron.

"Yes, brewing it. Like tea," Marie answered. "Just rub it on your arms. Don't rinse it off. It will help. If you don't believe me, ask Michael, he uses it all the time. I sent the dried leaves home with him the last time he was here. He swore by it when the girls had upset stomachs."

I remembered the tea he gave me when I was sick the first time we met. I wondered if this was the same tea. I flashed again how he had not told me about this family, and it made me angry to think of his lack of trust in me. He did not trust me enough to confide in me.

After breakfast, back in the yellow bedroom, I practically bathed in the tea. Marie had been correct. The tea soothed the itching immediately. It was a relief not to be scratching myself raw.

Tommy met me down by the smaller airboat, which had a canopy. No snakes would be dropping in for a visit today. It would just be the two of us taking the tour. He had a bag of goodies for the alligators, and he assured me that they would come running when they heard the boat.

He took me further out than the previous night. The boat traveled fast, and we covered more distance. Stopping the engines, he showed me how to feed the alligators. I was surprised when they fought over the tidbits.

"Here *chère*, try this." He threw a chunk out. One alligator quickly swam to the shore and seized the piece of meat.

I watched the birds flying from the trees, and he pointed out an eagles nest to me. "I didn't know you had eagles in Louisiana."

He grinned. "I think that's why Michael comes to visit us so often because it can't be Marie's vegetarian gumbo or jambalaya."

"You and he are so different. I'm surprised you became friends. I mean you hunt and fish. He definitely doesn't do that."

He looked at me with a lazy smile. "Don't let him fool you. He hunts with his camera, and he gets the same adrenaline rush as regular hunters. We're both from large families, we're beer drinkers and love sports. What more do two college guys need in common? He has mellowed some in his old age, but he can still be very wild. Has he shown you the Mustang yet?"

"Yeah, he took me out in it on our first date."

Tommy whistled, "*Chère*, I think he likes you." He chuckled and turned to me. "Okay, how fast did he drive, were you scared?"

"No." I looked puzzled. "He drove very responsibly."

"Elizabeth, he is trying to impress you. He likes fast cars, fast boats, and..."

"...and fast women?" I asked finishing his sentence.

He shook his head and looked at me seriously. "No *chère*, he does not like fast women. He's conservative when it comes to his women. He didn't date for a long time while he was raising his daughters because he didn't like the influence the women were having on his girls. He is devoted to his kids. Believe me, if they didn't like a woman he brought home she wouldn't last long."

"Why are you telling me all this about Michael?"

"First, I like you. You're sweet, charming and like a cool drink on a long, hot summer's day. You're a damn sight better than that shrew he married. Second, I don't like the fact he didn't tell you about us. That isn't right. He's a good man, and he needs someone like you in his life, and I'm just giving you some ammunition."

"I'm surprised you don't tell me not to hurt him," I said.

Tommy dug in the food bag for the last bite, he threw it overboard, and an alligator snapped it up immediately. He stood up to turn the engine back on.

"Michael is a big boy *chère*. He can take care of himself. Don't forget that. He's not looking for a mother, he's looking for a lover, someone to share his life with."

I turned back around to face forward. I was blushing and knew I would not be able to turn it off no matter how much I wished it to be gone.

When we arrived back at the house, Marie was busy brewing tea for me. She gave me instructions to bathe in the stuff for the next couple of days. She had also packed a care package for me, which included extra dried tea leaves and a huge container of leftover bread pudding with extra bourbon sauce. I doubted the bread pudding would make it through the evening. She laughed heartily when she heard that.

They drove me back to my hotel in New Orleans. I was sad to be leaving them. Showing me more than hospitality, they made me feel like I was at home and part of the family. I left several signed copies of the new book with Marie. She was thrilled. I made Tommy promise me that he would try to read the book too. He winked at me when he hugged me goodbye and told me to take good care of Michael. I just blushed.

The blast of air conditioning hit me when I entered the hotel room. I lived the past twenty-four hours without air conditioning and did not seem to mind it at all. I flipped off the air conditioner and opened the windows to the street. The sound of the people from Bourbon Street rose up to the room and drifted in through the windows. I liked the sounds, and I loved the city and its people.

After leaving a message for Nancy, I stripped my clothes off and bathed in the tea. Next, I ordered a big glass of milk and a spoon from room service. When it arrived, I heated the bread pudding up in the room's microwave oven and ate the entire portion Marie had packed for me.

The sun was starting to set when I finished the dessert. I redressed, put on my walking shoes, and headed on out to do some exploring in the French Quarter. Since it was Sunday evening and most of the shops had already closed, I wouldn't get to do much shopping, but I was sure I would be able to find a few touristy places still open.

I found a few shops and selected some t-shirts and little souvenirs for Tammy and Betsy. I also bought two stuffed alligators for Marybeth and Jon. Finally, I picked up several boxes of beignet mix and cans of chicory coffee from Café du Monde for everyone else.

When I returned to the hotel, I met Nancy in the hotel lobby. She grinned at me. Sitting next to her was her suitcase.

"Are you going somewhere?" I asked when I sat down next to her.

She nodded her head. "Don't hate me Elizabeth, but things are kind of clicking between Marcus and me. I've checked out of the hotel, and I'm going to stay the night with him tonight. I'll meet you at the airport tomorrow morning." She stood up as Marcus walked into the lobby and over toward us. "The limousine will be picking you up at nine tomorrow morning. Okay?"

I gave her a hug while laughing, "You two have fun. I know it wouldn't mean anything if I said to behave yourself. Don't be late."

Marcus reached us and took her suitcase. "The car is parked outside. Hi Elizabeth, thanks for letting me borrow Nancy for a little while longer."

I took a longer look at him. Marcus did have dreamy brown eyes and a melt in your mouth southern accent. I could see what she saw in him. She was almost giddy. I'd never seen her so excited about a date. She certainly deserved her share of happiness too. She took his hand and followed him out of the lobby.

Michael and I did not connect, which made me miss him even more. While I was out on my walk, he had left a message indicating he would be out for the evening visiting his parents. Tammy emailed another picture of the dogs, which had me rolling with laughter and missing them fiercely.

CHAPTER TWENTY-NINE

Nancy came rushing up as the plane was boarding. She hugged me from behind. "See I made it!"

I turned. "Only by the skin of your teeth. I was sure you were going to have to take the later flight."

As we waited in line to board the plane, I stole a glance at her. There was something different about her. She looked brighter and more animated than ever.

After settling into our seats, I said, "Okay, what gives? Something is going on with you."

She giggled. "Does it show?" Her eyes lit up like a Christmas tree, and her grin was almost goofy.

"Does what show? I want to know why you're all happy and bubbly. Is Marcus having this effect on you?" I asked.

She sat back in her seat and closed her eyes. She still had a silly smile. "Oh yes, Marcus. He's so very nice." She appeared to be bursting with something. "Don't think this is stupid, but we're engaged!" she said with a flourish.

I managed to sputter out with shock on my face, "You are what? Nancy, what is happening?"

"I know we haven't known each other long."

"Long?" I interrupted, "How about one day?"

"It was really two nights," she answered. "Come on Elizabeth, haven't you ever felt right about something? We stayed up all night on Saturday night."

"I bet you did." I rolled my eyes.

"No." Her eyes pleaded with me. "It's not about the sex, well, maybe a little, I mean he is fantastic. Oh, man, does he rock my boat!"

I covered my ears with my hands. "No, too much information. I don't want to hear this."

She pulled my hands down and held them. "I want you to hear this. We talked and talked on Saturday night. There is so much we have in common. Our life view is the same. The things we value are the same. I didn't think I would ever find someone like him."

"You are nuts and are being swept away by the romance that is New Orleans. Both of you have real lives. You live in Los Angeles, he lives in New Orleans, and there is too much distance between the two of you."

"I can do my job anywhere. I don't need to live in Los Angeles. We're not worried about that," she countered.

I shook my head in disbelief and pursed my lips while sitting back in my seat. "Don't do something foolish, or something you're going to regret."

Nancy lost the smile on her face. "Of all the people I know, I thought you would be the most understanding. You know people's dreams do come true. Look at you and Michael. You have dreamt about someone like him for as long as I've known you!" She sat back in her seat and folded her arms.

I almost commented that we were not a dream comes true yet, but this was not about us, so I held my tongue. I remembered Tommy's comment about Michael being able to take care of himself. Nancy was an adult, she could make her own decisions, and if that included making the biggest mistake of her life, then she had to live with the consequences.

She touched my hand halfway through the flight. I took off my headset and looked at her. "Are you okay with me?"

I squeezed her hand. "Of course I am. If you're hell-bent on taking this course, I'll be there for you when you come to your senses and help you pick up the pieces."

She giggled. "There won't be any pieces to pick up. I want you in the wedding. Will you be my maid of honor?"

Before I nodded, I rolled my eyes upward. "Yes, of course."

Nancy pointed to her laptop screen. "See."

I leaned over and shook my head with skepticism. She had already started planning for her wedding.

"Are you planning a big wedding?" I asked humoring her.

Nancy nodded earnestly. "Oh yes, Marcus has a large family too."

"Great." I nodded my head and went back to my laptop.

Shortly after we landed in Phoenix Nancy had her ear glued to her cell phone. "No, I miss you more my cuddly-wuddly."

I grabbed my laptop bag and made my way off the plane. I hoped she was not planning to continue this nauseating speech for much longer. No such luck though, the limousine took us straight to the bookstore, and the phone was stuck to her ear the entire way.

It would be another late night for us since the line was around the block.

When we arrived at the hotel, I was tired and wanted to go to bed. My mosquito bites were itching, and my mood was not a happy one. Thankfully, Nancy finally surgically removed the phone from her ear and actually spoke to me on the ride over to the hotel. Of course, her entire conversation revolved around Marcus. I sat next to her repeatedly rolling my eyes.

"Do you think Michael sent flowers again?" she asked as we were walking down the hall toward our rooms.

I stopped short in front of the door behind the bellman. How could I have forgotten about the flowers? I turned around and grinned at her.

"I hope he remembered."

The bellman opened the door to my suite. Nancy quickly gave him his tip and shushed him away. A big smile broke out on my face, and suddenly everything was okay in my world again. On the table sat the vase of red and pink roses. This time the red roses outnumbered the pink ones by three.

Nancy nodded her head. "Oh, he's good. I told Marcus about the roses, and he told me that it sounded like something Michael would do."

"Does he know Michael?"

"Oh yeah, he, Tommy, and Marcus are all buddies."

Nancy closed the door behind her as she left. I plucked the card from the holder and smiled as I read it. "*Elizabeth, the best is yet to come. Michael.*" I smiled and held the card to my chest. He was right. Everything was going to be okay.

My fingers pushed the buttons on the phone quickly. As if Michael was waiting for my call, he answered immediately.

"Hi, Babe." His voice was smooth and silky, and it made my body shiver.

"Is the best really yet to come?" I asked.

"And it will be very soon Elizabeth."

"Thank you for the flowers. I love them."

"They express how I feel about you."

I almost asked if eventually, they would be all red, but I was not bold enough. I tried to push myself over that edge but could not.

"Did you enjoy New Orleans?" he asked.

My voice took a slightly hard edge. "Yes, I did Uncle Michael. You know we're going to have to talk about this."

He sighed. "Yes, I know, I did it again. I'm sorry. Do we have to talk about it tonight?"

"Not tonight. But we will talk about it. I need to understand why."

He heaved a heavy sigh again. "I know."

"But on to better subjects. Nancy is engaged to Marcus," I told him.

"What? Did I hear you right? How can they be engaged?" Michael's voice sounded incredulous. "What did you guys do in New Orleans?"

"We didn't do anything, but they hooked up right away. She seems to think that they are fated for each other. How well do you know Marcus?"

"I've known him as long as I've known Tommy. We all went to UC Santa Cruz together. Marcus is a cousin to Tommy on his father's side."

"So is he an ax murderer? Do I have anything to worry about?"

He laughed. "No, he is safe. He's a very bright guy and richer than you can imagine. His mother, the other side of the family, comes from old money. And, he was a confirmed bachelor up to about 24 hours ago. I wonder if Tommy knows."

"I'm sure everyone is going to know pretty soon. Nancy was making extensive plans on her laptop. I don't think he knows what he's getting himself into."

Michael chuckled. "And the same goes for her. Marcus is a character. He's very southern, aristocratic, and chauvinistic. It should be interesting to watch."

He told me that he would be out of town for the rest of the week following a whale migration on a ship. I told him that as long as he was home by Saturday night, he could follow any migrating thing he wanted. He laughed and promised he would be home in time. We talked a while longer, and while he was reluctant to end the call, I finally begged off. I needed to bathe my bites. Michael laughed heartily when he heard I was using the tea on my mosquito bites.

CHAPTER THIRTY

The flight to Las Vegas was quick. How Nancy managed to stay off the phone during the trip amazed me. As soon as we landed, she was back on the phone. Fortunately, she was using her earpiece, but I never knew whether she was talking to Marcus or to me. And, didn't he have to work? I guessed not, because he was spending every waking moment on the phone with her. She had even admitted to me that they fell asleep last night on the phone. I just rolled my eyes, something that I was doing a lot of lately.

By this point, when we checked into our rooms at the hotel, I knew there would be roses waiting for me. The question was how many red ones would there be? Half of me wished I had not come to expect the roses to be there. Michael had set up my expectations, and usually, when that happened to me, there would always be a disappointment.

Sure enough, when I walked into the room the vase with the roses was sitting on the table. My heart gave its little flutter, and it was easy to count how many red ones there were because this time only one pink rose remained. The attached card was intriguing this time too, no title of a Frank Sinatra song, only the words "*enough said.*"

I was not sure exactly what he meant. His phone went to voice mail, and I left him a message anyway on the off chance that he might be able to retrieve it. I missed not being able to talk with him and realized that it would be a long three days with no Michael communication.

Interviews, meet and greets with fans, and panel discussions filled the next three days. I didn't see much of Nancy since she was busy courting potential new clients at this convention. Not only was it a big romance reader conference, but it also drew many authors like me. The little cell phone she provided gave up on the first day in Las Vegas, so I was stuck with using the phone in my room.

By Thursday night, my frustration level was high. It was close to midnight when I entered my room after the convention closing ceremonies. Michael's cell phone went straight to voice mail, and I left him an inane, not very intelligent message.

I fell into bed. Our flight to Los Angeles was early the next morning, and we had the last book tour stop in Westwood at noon. It would give me enough time to stop off to see my sister and Dad. I wasn't in bed for more than fifteen minutes, and the bedside phone rang jarring me awake. If it was Nancy, I was going to kill her.

I answered the phone gruffly. "What do you want? I'm trying to go to sleep!"

"Oh sorry Babe, is now not a good time?" It was Michael's voice coming over the phone.

I sat up in bed. "Oh, is it really you? Where are you?"

"I'm at the San Francisco airport. I just got in from the Aleutian Islands up in Alaska."

"Wow, you went up there to do your whale thing?"

He laughed. "Yeah, I'm part of a marine biology project that is studying the effects of global warming on the gray humpback whale. The whales will start their migration late next month."

"Are you there in a photographer capacity or as a marine biologist?"

"No, strictly a photographer, my biology days are way behind me. Hey, I'm sorry for waking you up. You sound really tired."

I sighed. "I am tired. I can't wait to go home."

"Well, you'll be home tomorrow."

"I'll be in Los Angeles, I won't be home. Los Angeles isn't home anymore." Both of us were quiet on the phone. I wasn't used to long pauses and wondered if the call disconnected. "Michael, are you still there?"

"Yeah, sorry. I guess I'm tired too. I'm going to let you go. Get some sleep, Babe. I'll see you on Saturday. Call me when you leave Los Angeles. Do you think you'll make it up here in one day?"

I giggled. "You bet on it. I drive really fast!"

Dawn woke me with a sense of anticipation. Wanting to get this trip over, I was anxious to go home. Dad picked me up at the airport, and we had a teary reunion. We stopped off at my sister's house first so I could deliver the gifts I had collected on my trip.

The kids were excited to see me. They loved the stuffed alligators I brought them. Lisa brought me to date on the renting of the house, which was going very well as there were already a few people interested. She had also arranged for the movers to move the stuff I would be keeping. Since I didn't have room in the cabin, donating most of the furniture made sense. She excelled at this type of organization, and I was happy to have her help.

Dad then drove me over to my house. The four of us were planning to attend the Dodger game after I finished the book signing. He had owned season tickets for years. After my mom passed away, the fifth ticket went unused. At first, it didn't seem right to have someone else sit in her seat, but eventually, we always found someone to invite. They were playing the Giants, and I wondered if Michael would watch the game on television.

Thankfully, Lisa had stopped by the house and opened the windows for me. I carried my luggage into the house. The first thing to find was my cell phone. Not having it felt like I was missing my right arm. I spotted it immediately sitting on the dining room table, right next to the large vase filled with long stem red roses. My heart stopped when I saw them. He didn't, did he?

There were no pink roses. None. Just eleven red roses. I counted them twice. The florist must have made a mistake with the count. It didn't matter to me. I looked for a card. There didn't seem to be a card. Maybe it dropped. I checked around the table. No, I hadn't missed it.

I turned my phone on, it still had a charge. I dialed Michael, and the phone went straight to voice mail. I disconnected and called Lisa to ask her how the flowers arrived.

"They were by the door when I got there this morning," she said.

"No card?" I asked.

"I didn't see one," she answered. "I've got to go. Both kids are driving each other crazy right now."

The flowers had to be from Michael even if there wasn't a card. I smiled. I had received dozens of flowers in the past two weeks, and these thrilled me just as must as the first ones did. I loved it!

I put on my jeans and tucked a white cotton short-sleeved blouse into my pants. It was difficult living out of two different houses. I rummaged through my closet and was happy to find my old Dodger sweatshirt, which would come in handy at the game. Even though it was still very much summer in Los Angeles, the nights could get breezy at the stadium. For the drive to Westwood, the convertible top on my little Saturn Sky would be up, so I left my hair down too. My hair was curling down closer to my waist and knew it was time to cut it again.

I left myself enough time to get to the bookstore with time to spare, but as usual, the Friday Los Angeles traffic started early and didn't let up. I found myself using side streets and rushing to get to the bookstore.

The valet parked my car, and Nancy handed me a latte as I rushed through the door.

"Moments to spare," she said. "You look good."

"Thanks," I said taking a gulp of coffee. "How's Marcus?"

Her eyes took on a faraway look. "Oh, he's dreamy. He's coming for a visit next week. You know there is so much to do for the wedding."

I laughed and shook my head in disbelief. "Have you set a date yet?"

"Yes, next spring."

"Why are you waiting so long?"

"It's going to be a big wedding. There's a lot to do!" she said as if I should have already understood this.

Nancy led me in and introduced me to everyone. A small table and a couple of chairs were set up in front of the large posters of my book.

The fans were friendly, and again I received requests to sign page seventy-five. What was it with that page? I had reread it several times, and it didn't seem that unusual to me. At four, I checked my watch. I had to leave no later than five to make it to the game in time.

As I was looking at my watch, the next fan opened the book to page seventy-five, and he laid a red rose down over the page.

"I think this one was missing this morning."

CHAPTER THIRTY-ONE

My ears heard the words, but my brain had a difficult time processing them. I was confused until I looked up. Michael stood in front of me. My incredibly gorgeous, hunky man was there, not on the phone, but in person. I leaped up almost knocking the little table over and threw my arms around his neck. He wrapped me in his arms and pulled me close. Our lips found each other's, and we kissed deeply for what seemed like hours.

I heard someone in the distance saying, "Will she kiss all of us like that?" Then I felt Nancy tugging on my jeans. I wanted to swing my arm down to knock her hand away because nothing was going to interrupt my kiss. Well, until the hooting, whistling, and catcalls started.

We broke apart and immediately the blush formed on my face. Michael touched my lips with his fingertip. Nancy was still tugging at me. I leaned over. "What is it?" I asked her.

She pointed to the waiting fans. "Ahh…you're in public, and there's a line."

I giggled. "Oh yeah. I guess I should get back to work." I introduced the two.

He winked at her. "Thanks for all your help."

She laughed. "Think nothing of it. I was glad to help."

I looked back and forth at each of them. "How did you?" I paused and then it clicked. I looked at her. "You knew about the roses all along didn't you?"

She nodded.

Michael laughed. "Babe, I'm not that clever." He squeezed me. "Nancy let me know which hotels you were staying at and when."

I looked again at both of them. "Great. Keep everything from Elizabeth. Thanks, Nancy."

She hit me playfully on the shoulder. "You loved every minute of it!"

He pulled up an empty chair next to me and moved as close as possible to me without sitting on my chair. I glanced over at him. He looked delicious in his jeans, which were so faded they were almost white. The rip at the knee was especially sexy, not to mention his plain black polo shirt, which fit him tightly enough to show off his muscles. How could I have forgotten how beautiful his sky-blue eyes were? I wanted to fly in them.

The next girl in line pointed to him. "Is he your inspiration for Jessica's love interest?"

I laughed and blushed, of course. "No, not in this book. The next one."

He spoke up, "But we're seriously going to try page seventy-five."

"Michael!" I blushed again.

Everyone standing within earshot laughed.

As I signed books, he interacted with my fans. He was casual and easy going. He seemed especially shy around the women, who made suggestive comments, which I thought made him look even more adorable.

He obliged the fans who wanted pictures with me, and he played photographer with their small digital cameras. If they only knew an award-winning professional photographer had taken their picture.

When we were almost finished for the day, Michael leaned over and whispered in my ear, "What time do we get to leave so that I can have my way with you?"

I grinned and kissed him. My eyes grew wide when I remembered my evening plans. "Oh, I forgot, I agreed to go to a Dodger game with my family."

He groaned. "Oh no, can you cancel it?"

I shook my head looking at Michael. "I'm sorry, I can't do that. Wait. Let me check, my dad has an extra ticket. Do you want to go with us?" I asked.

"I'm not letting you out of my sight. If that means sitting through a painful Dodger game, then so be it."

"Hey, you!" I exclaimed. "Watch it." Then I remembered. "They are playing the Giants."

Dad still had the extra ticket, and I let him know that Michael would be coming with me. I finished up with the fans by five as planned. Michael had the valet get the car for us as I said quick goodbyes to everyone.

I hugged Nancy last. "Call me. I'll be home tomorrow night."

"I will. Have fun with your honey tonight." She winked. "If you know what I mean."

I giggled. "I'm planning on it." Waving goodbye to everyone, I made my way outside.

My car and Michael were waiting. I slid into the driver's side and pulled into the traffic.

Michael turned to me. "I'm a little surprised you drive a sports car."

"Why?"

"I don't know. It just doesn't seem like you."

"You know, I'm full of surprises. Don't think you'll ever be able to categorize me."

Michael laughed. "No, you're right. You continually surprise me."

He held my hand in his and kissed my palm. His tongue traced light circles on my wrist. Fire heated through me and I found it challenging to focus on the road ahead. I wanted to feel the lips that were caressing my hand on other parts of my body.

I cleared my throat and swallowed. "Stop it," I said, barely whispering the words. "I can't concentrate."

He laid my hand on his thigh with his hand over mine. This position was a little better, but not by much. Leaning over, he pulled my collar away from my neck. His lips first grazed my neck and then his tongue lightly licked my ear lobe.

"Is this less of a disruption?" he murmured in my ear.

"I'm driving in heavy, Friday night, Los Angeles traffic, and your kisses are a distraction. I don't want to explain to a cop and my dad why we were in an accident."

Michael straightened up and moved back into his own seat. "Okay." He grinned. "As long as I know you want me as much as I want you. I can't believe you are dragging me to a baseball game."

I laughed. "I thought you liked baseball."

His grin was wicked. "I like you a whole lot more. Besides, I haven't been away from baseball for three weeks." He moved his hand to the top of my right thigh and squeezed my leg. Before I had a chance to say anything he added, "Let me just rest it here. Okay?"

I put my hand on top of his hand resting on my thigh. "Okay, but you've got to be a good boy." I turned the car to enter the freeway. "I need to pay attention to what I'm doing. Tell me about the whales." I thought that maybe he would stop if I changed the subject.

He turned again in his seat and looked directly at me. "No, I'd rather talk about what we're going to do when we get back to your house tonight, after the longest game in my life." His hand started massaging my thigh. "Where I'm going to lick you and kiss you and…" he trailed off.

"Michael," I whispered. I wanted to close my eyes and let him take me in his arms.

He chuckled. "Okay. I'm sorry. I'm supposed to be a good boy."

He managed to maintain his good boy status for the rest of the drive to Dodger Stadium. I had no idea what would happen after the game. There was no way we were going to make it to my house in one piece.

We met my family at the entrance to the stadium. Michael was very polite and called Dad "*Sir.*" That alone earned him extra points with my father right off the bat, which he lost right away when he announced that he was a huge Giants fan.

Lisa mouthed, "He's cute."

We were off to a good start. Then the nicknames started and I had to explain the various nicknames my family had for me. I was glad that Michael did not add in his *"Hellcat"* nickname for me. I wasn't prepared to explain that one to them. Why could no one simply call me Elizabeth? Plain, simple, and straightforward.

My sister and I made our way to the seats while the boys stopped for hot dogs, peanuts, beer for themselves, and soft drinks for us since we were the designated drivers. Dad sat in the middle with Lisa and me on either side of him. Michael and Bill flanked the outside of our group.

We settled down to watch the game. The first five innings were a pitcher's game, and neither team was hitting. At the bottom of the sixth inning, the Dodgers finally hit a double with no outs. We were hooting and screaming. I had not noticed that Michael slipped his arm around my shoulders and his other hand was again on the top of my thigh. My father certainly saw, giving us both a wagging look. Michael tried to remove his hand, but I clamped mine over his. I stared back at Dad. He pulled back and smiled.

I leaned over to him and whispered, "You don't need to take your hand away. I'm a grown woman."

He whispered back, "I will have my hands all over you later tonight. I'll let your dad win this battle, but I will win the prize."

I grinned. "Smart."

"Hey, I'm familiar with dads." His eyes were sparkling, and I knew it was not just the stadium lights that produced the special glint.

The Dodgers scored two runs, and the Giants quickly tied up the game during the next inning. At the bottom of the ninth inning, the score was still a tie. The first Dodger up connected with the ball so hard the bat broke, and that ball sailed out of the park. Everyone was on their feet cheering, including Michael.

"What are you so happy about?" I asked him as we were applauding the team.

Michael hugged me. "I never wanted the Giants to lose as badly as I wanted them to lose tonight. I wanted this game over."

We said our goodbyes to my family and hurried out to my car. The drive back to Torrance was quick in just under an hour. We barely had the front door closed, and Michael had my blouse pulled out of my jeans. Standing in the entryway, his hands were working on the buttons to my top while I tried to pull his shirt over his head.

I giggled. "Wait."

I pulled the blouse off over my head, and he did the same with his shirt.

His fingers immediately unhooked my bra and pulled it off. It fell on the pile with our shirts. His lips and hands reached my breasts simultaneously. As he caressed them, my eyes closed, and I leaned back against the wall. My fingers stroked through his hair and down to his shoulders as I pressed him closer to me.

"Oh Michael, I want you." My whisper was barely audible, but he responded by moving his lips up to mine.

His kisses were deep, and when our tongues met, it was like setting a fire. His hand lifted my leg, and it easily curled around him. I could feel the heat from his body through our jeans and my hips pressed against him seeking the warmth.

"Bedroom?" he rasped out.

I pointed over his shoulder past the living room. "Shower first?" I suggested weakly.

Michael shook his head. "No." His hand moved to the button on my jeans, and his lips went back to my breasts. "First you." He said in between brushing my nipples with his tongue. "Bedroom. Now."

With each rough sweep of his tongue against my nipples, a small, "*Oh*" escaped from my lips. My legs were not going to hold me up much longer. I pushed him back, and he grinned as I took his hand and quickly led him the short walk to the bedroom.

Kicking off my shoes, I sat on the bed as he knelt down in front of me. The button to my jeans was undone, and he quickly unzipped them. I was not wasting any time getting out of them either. I lifted my hips and helped him slide the jeans down my legs.

His eyes sparkled as he looked at me. "Anxious?" he whispered.

His hands spread my legs apart as he bent to kiss my inner thighs. I laid back and ran my fingers through his hair urging him closer. I was not wearing my sexiest panties, but it did not seem to make any difference to him as his lips traveled further up my thighs to nuzzle me. Nothing was moving fast enough for me. I hooked my fingers through the top of my underwear and started to pull them down.

Michael straightened and chuckled. "I like this eagerness." He pulled my bikinis the rest of the way off.

I reached for his belt. "Your turn," I said as he stood to accommodate my undressing him.

His erection was already straining against the material, and I groaned in frustration when I saw he wore button fly jeans. My fingers fluttered over his pants not able to undo the buttons fast enough.

"Here let me help," Michael said as he effortlessly unbuttoned his jeans and removed his shoes and socks.

I reached over and tugged him closer to me. Kissing his stomach, my tongue followed the light trail of hair leading from his chest, past his waist, and disappearing into his briefs. As my tongue and lips continued down the path, I pulled both his jeans and briefs down in one motion, and he stepped out of his clothes.

Michael was definitely ready for me. I held his hard length in my hands and looked up at him. My tongue just barely touching his glistening tip.

I felt him shudder and his eyes closed as a groan passed through his lips. "Oh, Babe."

Quickly scooting back on the bed, I turned toward him on my hands and knees, beckoning to him with my finger.

"Come and get it," I teased.

His grin was wide as he came toward me. "You are my Hellcat."

His hands felt electrical against my skin as we embraced. His lips drank from mine, and I gasped for air when he broke the kiss. My leg wrapped around him and I pressed myself fully against him. The urgency in him was evident. His hand traveled in between my leg, and I moved so he could fully explore me. The need to have him touch me was too great, and I moved my hips up to meet his fingers. Shockwaves coursed through me when I felt his fingers inside of me.

Michael growled in my ear as he explored me, "Babe, you are so wet."

"Oh, no more foreplay, I've been ready for you all night." I buried my head in his neck and pleaded, "I want you inside of me now."

Immediately when we joined, I lost all sense of time and place. The desire grew in me with each thrust, and I could feel the pending eruption coming quickly. With our labored breathing, the wave was on the horizon, just out of reach. I whispered his name.

He had other ideas though as he steadied his pace hitting the exact spot I needed. "Scream for me Elizabeth."

I did what he asked. The impact of the orgasm hit me harder than ever before, and his name was on my lips again, along with a healthy scream and a few other choice words. At this inducement, his thrusts became more and more rapid. His powerful release followed mine quickly.

Michael collapsed on me, and I did not mind his weight because at that moment all I wanted was his closeness. He rolled off gently pulling me against him. Our bodies were slick with perspiration while we were still trying to catch our breaths.

His hand tilted my face up, and he kissed me softly. "Wow," he said. His eyes met mine. "I want you to scream for me like that every time."

I giggled almost shyly. "I've never done that before," I admitted to him.

"Losing control the way you do is a huge turn on for me." He kissed me again.

Even though we had just made love, I could feel the blush rising in my face.

He chuckled. "As is your blushing," he said sweetly.

"I've never felt anything like that either. I mean, I didn't think it was possible. I've written about it, kind of tongue in cheek, but…" I trailed off. "Sorry, I guess that sounded stupid."

Michael laughed. "Nothing you say sounds stupid, although you do sound a little like my eighteen-year-old daughter. No wait, that's too weird. Just ignore that."

I laughed. "I missed you."

He sighed. "It was a long three weeks. I don't think I could live through that again."

"Good," I said wrapping my arms around his neck, snuggling closer, if that was even possible. "We'll have to make sure it doesn't."

We kissed and cuddled together for a while. Finally, I moved to get up. "I need to take a quick shower."

"Can I come with you?"

"No. And don't get your feelings hurt, but you'll wet my hair, and I don't want to sleep with it wet tonight."

"You don't trust me?" he said batting his eyelashes.

I laughed and patted him. "That's right."

"Go have your shower. I can't move my legs yet. I'll take one after you."

I got out of bed and looked around for my robe.

Michael called to me, "Babe, turn around." I turned to face him expecting him to ask me something. "You're beautiful," he complimented. "You don't have to cover yourself."

I blushed and waved him off. Once in the bathroom, I took a deep breath looking at myself in the mirror, enjoying a moment of quiet. My face appeared happy, if not a little out of focus. After my shower, I wrapped a big towel around myself. Back in the bedroom, Michael had straightened out the bed and was lying there munching on a bag of cookies. I pulled a negligée out of my closet.

He shook his head. "No, you don't."

I looked at him puzzled. "What?"

"You're not wearing that with me."

"What do you mean? It's cute." I held it up to show him.

He got out of bed, took it from me, and hung it up back into the closet. "When you're sleeping with me, I want to feel you, not some nightgown." Michael wrapped his arms around me and whipped my towel off.

"Hey!" I exclaimed.

He pulled me tighter against him and kissed me. "Now doesn't this feel better?"

Well, I did admit that it did. I loved the feeling of his body against mine. I laughed. "Go take your shower." I reached down and squeezed his butt.

"There's my Hellcat." He kissed me again.

I called to him as he left the room, "Hey Hoffman, you have an adorable butt."

He laughed and waggled it at me before disappearing into the bathroom.

While Michael was in the shower, I clicked off the lights in the bedroom and snuggled down into the pillows to wait for him. Promptly falling asleep, I did not feel him crawl in next to me. When I woke up a couple of hours later it took me a moment to figure out where I was, then I felt his arms around me as he spooned alongside me. Sighing contentedly, I cuddled up closer against him.

CHAPTER THIRTY-TWO

At dawn, I slipped out of bed and quietly dressed in the living room. I wrote a note to Michael and left it on my pillow. I didn't want him to get up while I was out getting breakfast for us. My favorite bakery, known for their fresh croissants, was located a couple of miles down the road. They opened early and sold out quickly.

When I returned from the bakery, the house was quiet, which meant he was still asleep. I prepared the coffee maker so that we could flip the switch on. Back in the bedroom, he must have woken and read the note because it was sitting on the nightstand. Sleeping again, he was on his back with his arm raised above his head. He had pushed the comforter down to his hips, and one leg was sticking out of the covers, but the rest of him was primly covered. While I stood over the bed, I admired him. He had an incredible body. A shiver went through me remembering how he used his body with mine.

I pulled my sweatshirt over my head. No bra. Then I unzipped my jeans and stepped out of them, putting them on the chair behind me. I kneeled quietly on the bed. I heard Michael clear his throat and looked up at him.

"You forgot to take off your panties." He grinned, still covering his eyes with his forearm.

"You're awake!" I exclaimed and smacked him with a pillow.

He reached out for me, but I backed away. "Un uh," I said wagging my finger at him.

He leaned up on his elbows and looked at me with his eyebrows raised. I slowly peeled off my panties and tossed them aside. I looked at him for a moment, then pounced on him and merrily had my way with him.

We lay together afterward and cuddled. With my head on his shoulder, he leaned down to kiss me with sweet and tender brushes of his lips.

"I could get very used to this," I said, stroking his chest.

His laughter sounded like a growl. "I already am." He squeezed me.

A car pulled up in the driveway, the doors opened, and we heard kids yelling.

"Oh, I completely forgot, Lisa was coming this morning. She's here with the kids!" I said.

I moved to get up, and Michael was right with me. He had his pants on and his shirt over his head before I even got out of bed.

"I'll keep your sister company while you get dressed," he said, walking out of the bedroom.

I nodded, and he closed the bedroom door. As I dressed, I heard their voices in the living room, with both kids making most of the noise. After running a brush through my hair, I joined Lisa in the kitchen. She had already turned the coffee maker on and popped the croissants into the oven.

"Where's Michael?" I asked.

Lisa waved to the back yard. "The kids seemed to be enamored with him, which is unusual for them. He sure is handsome. What kind of work does he do again?"

I peeked out the curtain and saw him swinging them around and playing monster with them. Both kids were hurling themselves at him, and he was catching them and swinging them up in the air. They were screaming with glee.

Turning back to Lisa, I answered, "He's a wildlife photographer."

"God, does he make any money doing that?" she asked with an eyebrow raised.

I poured myself a cup of coffee. "I don't know how much money he makes, but he seems to be doing okay. He's won a lot of awards, and he works for National Geographic all the time," I said with a proud tone in my voice. "And, he's putting both of his daughters through college."

She leaned back against the counter. "Yeah, you mentioned he has kids. They're grown so you won't have to take responsibility for them, will you?"

"The three of them manage just fine." This line of questioning was beginning to irk me. That was like Lisa though.

"Well, let's hope he makes more money than Kevin did, he absolutely bled you dry."

"Not for much longer," I added. "We are officially done at the end of this month."

"Wow, three years went by fast. I didn't think he deserved a dime from you, especially the way he treated you." Lisa crossed the kitchen to the window and peeked out. Michael was still twirling the kids around. "I hope he doesn't make them sick."

I rolled my eyes and took a big gulp of coffee. I had to get Lisa out of here because when she was in one of her critical moods, I normally wanted to kill her.

Sitting at the kitchen table, I changed the subject. "Let's go over what needs to get done with the rental of the house. I really appreciate your helping me with this Lisa. You're so much better at this than I am."

At this, she smiled and looked interested in the information she needed to relay to me. We were able to firm up all the plans within fifteen minutes. After offering everyone croissants, which Lisa turned down, I ushered my little sister and her kids out the door.

Michael took a big bite out of his chocolate croissant. "That was fast," he said leaning up against the kitchen door that led into the entry hallway.

The chocolate from the croissant was decorating the corners of his mouth. I reached over and licked the chocolate off one corner.

"Yum," I said licking my lips. "She was driving me crazy and either my little sister had to leave, or I was going to bump her off."

He laughed. "Oh, sisterly love, I love it! She did have a lot of questions for me."

I took a bite of his croissant. "Really? Like what? She's always been a nosey girl."

"Well, she wanted to know if I spent the night. She didn't ask though what room I slept in, I had an answer all ready for that."

I grinned and put my arms around his waist. "I bet you did."

He took another bite of the croissant, and when he kissed me, I could taste the chocolate. "Yep, and I would have told her what you did to me this morning too."

"Michael!" I exclaimed, "You wouldn't!"

"Oh, wouldn't I? I did it to my sister one time, and she never asked something like that again."

I leaned in for another kiss. "You are terrible."

He kissed me and finished off his croissant. "I know how to stop nosey questions."

He cleaned the kitchen, and I washed the sheets and towels. While they were drying, the final boxes shipping to my cabin were packed. My family's church would be receiving most of the household items for their thrift store. The trunk of my car was tiny. With Michael's bag, I had limited room, so I was choosing carefully what I could not live without for a few weeks.

Since Michael's aquarium event was only a couple of weeks away, the dress I would wear was making the trip with us. Zipping up the garment bag, I handed it to him when he came into the bedroom to pick up the last of the stuff to put into the car.

"Here, put this on the top of everything," I instructed. "Gently," I added.

He held the garment bag up. "What's in here?"

"That's the dress I'm wearing to the aquarium party."

"Oh! Can I see it?" He reached for the zipper.

"No!" I grabbed his hand. "It's a surprise for you. It's vintage and one-of-a-kind."

"Oh." He nodded his head and grinned. "You know as long as you're in the dress, I'm going to love it." Michael bent down wrapping his free arm around my waist and kissed me.

I pushed him toward the door. "Go take care of my dress."

After locking up everything tight, he held his hand out for the keys.

"I figured you wanted to drive," I said.

He chuckled. "Babe, you do not want me grabbing you for the next ten hours, because if you drive that's what I'll do."

I giggled and handed him the keys. The top was down, my hair was braided, and we were good to go. We took the coast highway, which would be a slightly longer trip, but it was cooler with more to see. We stopped every hour so he could stretch his legs. My little Saturn did not have a long drive train, and while it was okay for me, the car designers did not take into account Michael's five extra inches.

While we were sitting in a restaurant booth having lunch, he called Tammy. "Honey, it is Dad. Yeah, we're okay. Listen sweetheart, Elizabeth and I are going to be really late tonight, why don't you go ahead and stay with Debi and Don again tonight." He paused. "Okay. I'll see you in the morning." He disconnected the call.

I looked at him puzzled. "We're making great time. Why did you say we're going to be late?"

Grinning, he put his arm around my shoulder, and leaned over to whisper in my ear, "Because, tonight I'm going to make you scream in my bed."

I blushed and giggled. "Oh. Okay for tonight. You're right, I can't sleep at your house with Tammy there."

It was his turn to look puzzled. "Why can't you sleep with me while Tammy's there?"

I blushed again. "You know," I stammered, "she might hear us."

"Well, we're not sleeping at your house. I don't want to leave Tammy alone in the house, it's not safe. Besides your bed is too small." He said it as if he had settled the matter.

"Michael, I can't sleep with you while Tammy is upstairs. I just can't."

We had reached an impasse. He looked at me, I was glad he did not remove his arm from around my shoulders. Were we having an argument? It was hard to tell.

Our food reached the table, and he stole one of my French fries.

"Hey, those are mine!" I yelped.

"Come and get it," he said, hanging the fry loosely from his mouth.

I leaned over and bit off the dangling fry. I giggled and chewed it.

He kissed me. "We will figure out the sleeping arrangements. But, for tonight you're in my bed."

"Screaming," I replied, forever blushing.

It was late afternoon by the time we hit Big Sur, and I made Michael pull over to put the top up on the car. The fog was rolling in, and it was cold. When we were barely past San Francisco and heading inland with another two hours to go, he asked me if I wanted to stop for dinner. If he could last, then I could last until we got home. He agreed and continued on the road. Up to that point, I had been a good passenger. I kept him entertained through the entire trip. My battery was running on low though, and I was getting tired. Laying my head on his shoulder, I fell fast asleep.

The next thing I knew he was kissing me gently. "Babe, we're home."

I opened my eyes and stretched. "Oh, already?" I put my arms around his neck and kissed him back. "You are so yummy. Did you know that?" I blinked up at him.

He chuckled. "And you're still half asleep."

Michael helped me carry my stuff into my cabin. "I'm going to order pizza and salad. Come on over when you are ready."

I nodded. "I'll be right there. Open up the wine."

He grinned and leaned down to kiss me. "I don't know if I want to do that because wine may make you sleepy."

I encircled his hips with my arms and kissed him back. "Don't worry about me. I had a nice nap." I ran my hands down his backside and squeezed his butt.

"Oh, so I'm merely a sexual object to you." He teased me with a mock frown.

"Not only that, you're entertaining too." I pulled one hand back to his front and pressed the obvious bulge in his jeans. "We're going to have to do something about this too." I squeezed him gently.

He groaned heavily into my lips. "Oh Babe, you're going to be the death of me."

I stepped back, and he almost fell toward me. "Go get pizza, because I need to be fed first."

He laughed and saluted me. "Yes!"

As he left the cabin, he turned and told me to hurry. I smiled and nodded. None of the stuff had to be unpacked, but I did throw a load of laundry into the washing machine. I quickly leafed through my mail and found nothing remarkable. The cabin was quiet without the dogs, and it was almost spooky.

Walking into Michael's house, I heard him in the living room on the phone with Tammy. I was glad he let her know we were home. I giggled to myself when I heard him say that she was not to come back tonight and no, he was not going to explain why.

The backdoor bell rang, and Michael pointed to his wallet on the dining room table. I nodded and took it to the back door to pay for the food. As I pulled out the money, I noticed photos of the girls. Then I found my section. He had five pictures of me in his wallet, including the bikini one. The discovery made me grin. I paid the pizza person and brought the food into the kitchen.

After loading pizza slices and salad on plates for both of us, I poured the wine that he had already opened. We carried everything into the living room, and he switched on the television to watch the end of the Dodger and Giants game while we ate our food.

We finished off the last of the pizza, and I carried the dishes back into the kitchen. Taking the remote control from his hand, I turned off the television. He sat on the couch looking up at me. I had gotten his attention. Next, I pulled my sweatshirt over my head.

He audibly sucked his breath in. I smiled, fully aware of the effect I was having on him. The material on the beige bra I was wearing was transparent, and it was almost as if I had no bra on at all. I knelt down in between his legs and ran my hands up his thighs. The swell in his jeans became evident as I ran my fingers lightly over his zipper. I gazed up, and his eyes were intent on me. He was silent as I moved my hands up under his t-shirt. His t-shirt was off in a flash.

Sitting next to him on the couch, I bent over and kissed his stomach. My lips trailed up to his chest, and I lightly flicked his nipples with my tongue. As they hardened for me, I nipped them with my teeth. This elicited an "*Oh god*" from Michael.

I straddled his lap and put my arms around his shoulders. In this position, my breasts angled directly within reach of his mouth. He put his hands on my back to bring me closer, and his mouth connected with my breasts. He sucked and teased my nipples with his mouth through the material of my bra. It was my turn to gasp.

I whispered, "If you go run a bath for us, I will take off the bra and show you what I'm wearing under my jeans." I brought myself down into his lap and wriggled my hips against him.

He pressed me firmly to him and whispered in between kissing me, "Elizabeth, you are my Hellcat."

Giggling, I sat back down on the couch and pointed to his bedroom. "Go, and let me know when it's ready." I poured myself another glass of wine while he drew our bath.

Michael called me about five minutes later. I walked through his bedroom and stood at the bathroom door. He had done well. Candles completely lit up the bathroom. He was already in the tub surrounded with bubbles.

"Now it's your turn," he called to me.

I grinned at him and very slowly unbuttoned my jeans. His eyes were watching my every move. Drawing the zipper down slowly, I paused, to unbraid my hair. Everything was unhurried and languorous. After my hair was undone, I pulled it forward to cover my breasts. I reached around and undid my bra. My breasts fell forward, and I covered them with my forearm while pulling off my bra. I dropped it to the tile floor.

Michael swallowed hard when I placed a hand on each breast and leisurely ran my hands over them and down my stomach. When I arched my back and sighed he looked like he was going to faint, but still, he did not move. My hands inched my jeans over my hips. The pants finally dropped down to my ankles, and I stepped out of them. I stood there in a beige colored thong.

Shifting forward, he leaned up against the edge of the tub. I turned around and pulled off the thong, bending over to make sure I completed the view for him.

He uttered a low growl. "Oh Elizabeth, I want you."

I turned around. "So do you like what you see?" I purred.

He stood up in the tub, and it was plain that he liked what he saw very much. He helped me step into the tub and then pulled me down into the water. Between the bathtub and his bed that night, Michael made good of his promise to make me scream several times.

CHAPTER THIRTY-THREE

As the days progressed, we all fell into a routine. I did give in, well, sort of. I slept with Michael every night, curled up next to him in his bed and usually awoke sprawled out on top of him. The timing of our nightly activities was limited to more quiet behavior when Tammy was home. During the days when she was at school, we simply ran amok.

Our dogs now ran together in a pack with us in the mornings when we jogged. Michael was faster than I was, and he usually would take the lead. Topper and I, being the slowpokes often lagged behind.

While working on my book, the dogs liked to lie around my feet because I would drop little snacks for them on the floor. I typically wrote in my cabin, but he set up a small desk for me in his bedroom too. I was often there while he was working in his office.

We regularly visited the eagles too but did not spend the night. I knew all along that the overnight trip we had spent together was an excuse he had used to get me alone. A very clever man. He shared his newest project, the eagle book, with me and suggested we partner on the effort. He wanted me to write a story about the eagles on our mountain. I spent a little time every day developing the story with him.

Working together was heavenly. I had never had the kind of working relationship with Kevin that I was sharing with Michael. As it turned out, we were excellent collaborators too. He was open with his praise and accepting of my ideas.

I still had not approached him on a discussion about him not being entirely truthful about his friendship with Tommy and Marie. At the moment, I wanted to stay blissfully ignorant, but I knew that it would eventually bug me enough to mention it.

Our trip to Monterey came up quickly, and I looked forward to another road trip with him. He had been away several days to do the additional shooting on the whale migration project. I had offered to drive him to San Francisco, but he turned me down and told me to spend the time on my book.

Tammy and I put the evenings to good use. I helped her with an English paper that was due. She was agreeable to having me around and happy she would not have to stay with Debi and Don. I slept in Michael's room and joked with him when he called that he needed more pillows on his bed. He made me promise that I would not get any more. He complained that it was crowded enough with the dogs. I teased that I could always go home to give him more room. This elicited a negative response, which thrilled me.

By Friday morning, I woke thinking about both his homecoming and the Monterey trip the following day. By the time I returned from my jog, Tammy had already left for school. I fed all the dogs and made my coffee and breakfast. There were always such different ingredients packed in their refrigerator. Many things that I would never consider buying. He was insistent about buying free-range organic eggs, and if we were going to eat meat that had to be free range too. Far from being a vitamin nut, he preferred to get most of his vitamins from the vegetables and fruit he ate. It made me dizzy trying to keep track of the massive quantities of food he ate, but he never seemed to gain weight.

Michael called me as I ate the last of my toast. "Babe, I'm glad I caught you."

"Hi honey," I said swallowing my toast. "Where are you?"

"I just arrived in San Francisco, and I'm waiting for my luggage. Can you do me a favor?"

"Sure."

"Give Annie a call and confirm that I'll be at her house this afternoon at three. I need to finish up the pictures of her baskets," he said over the drone of the airport announcements.

"Of course. Can I come with you?" I asked.

"I'd love that. I'll see you in a little bit."

I sat down to write in the little corner of Michael's bedroom that he had arranged for me. With new music queued up and my headphones on, I was set to go into the zone. Lately, I was less likely to feel blocked, which made the entire writing experience easier. The story was flowing from me quickly, and I felt more relaxed as my deadline was approaching. Before I knew it, a couple of hours had passed.

Suddenly, my heart leaped into my throat. I felt arms around my shoulders, and I let out a loud piercing scream. It took me several moments to realize that the hands touching me were not Kevin's but Michael's. The hands that I thought were wrapping around my neck were really stroking my face. My entire body shook, and the tears quickly started to flow.

"Oh God," I said crying and holding my hands to my chest trying to steady my breathing, "I thought you were Kevin."

He pulled me up into his arms and enveloped me. "Babe," he said trying to soothe me as I stood tightly embracing him, "I'm so sorry. Come on, come sit down." He led me over to the bed and pulled me into his lap. He slipped his hand under my chin lifting my head up. "I'm here, and you're safe."

I nodded. He placed a soft kiss on my lips. "I'm sorry. It's just that Kevin used to…" I trailed off.

"Sshh. You don't have to explain. I know," he murmured into my hair as he pulled my head against his shoulder holding me securely against him.

Michael patiently sat on the bed holding me while I attempted to recover myself. My tears stopped, and I snuffled into his shirt. He smelled good, and he was wearing what had become my favorite cologne. I lifted my head slightly and kissed him below his ear along his jaw.

"Feeling better?" he asked tenderly.

He wiped away the teardrops still on my face gently with his fingers. He put a light kiss on my forehead, and then his lips moved down to mine where he put a much stronger kiss. I scooted off his lap and lay back on the bed pulling him with me while he continued to kiss me.

We both broke the kiss simultaneously when we heard Tammy's voice. "Oh, are you two at it again?" She had a grin on her face when we looked at her.

Michael spoke first, "School?"

She answered rapidly, "Friday, short day. I thought Elizabeth would like to have lunch with me, but I can see she's otherwise occupied."

"You know, lunch does sound good," I said.

He raised an eyebrow. "Better than this?"

"I'm hungry. It's been a long morning," I said.

He rolled his eyes and rolled off me. "Fine. Go have lunch."

I got up, and he called to me, "Next time, I need to shut the door."

Both Tammy and I giggled. "Do you want to come?" I asked.

"Yeah, might as well." He lumbered off the bed.

After Michael took us to lunch, we dropped Tammy back home and drove out to Annie and Frank's house. They lived outside of Mintock on several acres of land, which was part of the Pomo reservation. Their property butted up against the mountain on the other side of the lake. Annie spent most of her days in the summer in her little shop in town where she sold her baskets to the tourists.

She had been my aunt's best friend. My aunt was a little scatterbrained, so when I would stay with her during the summer, Annie always kept her eye out for me. She also managed to keep Don, and I separated long enough so no romance could bud between the two of us. Now I was glad because I saw Don as a brother. At sixteen, I thought she was meddlesome.

During my mother's illness, and then subsequently my aunt's, I was happy to have her in my life. Their passing happened very quickly, and my dad and sister were no help to me since they were grieving too. At the time, it had never occurred to me that Annie was also grieving at the loss of her best friend. Now she was my mom here on earth.

We pulled up in front of the modern ranch style house. Dogs ran around to greet us as we exited Michael's jeep. Frank came out of his four-car garage, which was full of antique cars, and it was easy to see where Don had developed his love of cars. He wiped his hands on a towel, gave me a big hug, and shook Michael's hand.

"Annie," he bellowed. "They're here!"

She came running out of the house, wearing her usual outfit of blue jeans, boots, and a colorful denim blouse. She had braided her long hair and wrapped it as a bun on the back of her head.

"Oh Mija, I'm so glad to see you." Annie hugged me almost as hard as Frank had and then she turned to Michael. "Hello, handsome man." She wrapped her arms around his waist, and she barely came up to his chest. She hugged him with enthusiasm. Then she winked at her husband. "Look at the handsome man I found. Are you jealous?"

He laughed and looked at Michael. "You can have her. She has been hell on wheels today."

Michael laughed and wrapped his arm around my waist. "I think one Hellcat is enough for any man."

Frank laughed again. "See, what did I tell you? The leaf didn't fall from the tree."

"Hey, we're standing right here you know," I protested.

Frank put his hand on top of my head and stood on his toes. "Michael, do you hear something?" He looked around and past me.

"I don't think the boys want any lemonade, do they?" Annie grinned and took my hand. We went into the house and left their laughter behind.

Her bright and sunny kitchen was in the back of the house overlooking the lake. She poured four glasses of lemonade and placed two on a tray. I took them out to the men and found they were already sitting in the chairs on the front porch. Annie carried out the other two glasses for us.

"Debi and Don are coming for a barbeque tonight with Betsy. I told them to pick Tammy up on their way out. Jason should be home for the weekend, and that will give Tammy some incentive to come." Annie explained. "Don't worry Michael. I have some meatless burgers for you."

He grinned. "Thank you, Annie. I better get started before I lose the light."

Michael had decided after seeing the antique cars to use one of the convertibles and put the baskets in the back seat. Frank trailed after Michael to help. I sat with Annie on the front porch. She handed me a half-finished basket and supplies, and I started weaving as we talked.

"So, I heard that you're pretty much living with Michael and Tammy now," Annie said.

Her hands moved swiftly over the basket she was weaving, adding different colors as she went along.

"Debi has a big mouth. We're not living together," I countered.

"You wake up together in the same bed, don't you?" She looked at me over her glasses.

I merely nodded sheepishly. Why did I feel like I was sixteen with her? I was a grown woman, wasn't I?

"Don't get me wrong, Mija. I like Michael. He's a good man. And, he's good for you."

I smiled and nodded. "Yes, I like him too."

"Oh, I think it's a little more than like."

I blushed and studied my basket.

"He's powerful Mija, and he's a very sexual man."

My blush deepened, and I studied my basket even closer. "Yes, he is."

She snapped at me, "Elizabeth, the size of a man's penis does not define the sexuality of a man. A man's sexuality is defined by many different things, and most of them are not physical. It is the essence and emotional makeup of the man. How he treats others, his own self-confidence, and his love and respect for women. Do others judge him as an honorable man who stands by his convictions? Does he have compassion for others in need? Many criteria judge a real man." She leaned forward. "Elizabeth, not many women are fortunate to experience a good man. My Frank is a good man, Don is a good man, and Michael is the same."

"You make him sound perfect. You know he does have flaws." Of course, at the moment his shortcomings escaped me.

"And you do too Mija. No one is perfect." She continued weaving.

I picked up my basket again. "I'm glad you like him. It is important to me that you do."

She nodded, and we worked with the tranquility surrounding us.

"Annie, why did you discourage Don and me from dating?" I asked, breaking our silence.

She laughed and picked up a different color to blend into the basket. "I knew the two of you were not right for each other. Do not get me wrong, Mija, you are good as friends. But as husband and wife, no." Annie shook her head. "No, it would not have worked. Don needed a different kind of woman." She put the basket down and looked over at me again. "You, Elizabeth, are like the eagle. You soar above the trees. When you want something, you zero in on the target and pick it up easily. You find comfort and safety in building your nest and in one man. You need someone as quick and sharp as you are. Don would have bored you after a while. He is a big lumbering bear, and he needed another bear to keep him in line, to keep him straight so to speak. Debi is that bear. They are good together."

"So, is Michael also an eagle?"

Annie smiled. "I'm not sure yet, what animal he is. I need to know him better before that can be decided."

"Do we have to be the same animal to be good together?"

"Oh no, usually it is better to be different animals," she said.

"What animals are you and Frank?"

Annie laughed. "Oh, I am the mountain lion. I care for all my cubs. Frank is the salmon. He will always provide, and he is persistent. When he and I met, he chased after me for two years. He has provided well for me."

She looked young, and her eyes sparkled when she talked about Frank. I could imagine them as a new couple making a home for themselves.

She leaned over and smacked me on the thigh. "Hey! Earth to Elizabeth. Come into the house with me. Help me wrap the potatoes and make the salad."

Shortly after we started in the kitchen, the front screen door slammed shut. "Hey Mom, we're here!" Don's voice called out.

Suddenly the house was full. Debi and Betsy came into the kitchen to help with dinner. I told Debi that I was going to kill her for telling Annie about Michael and me sleeping together. She made her impression of a Cheshire cat grin.

"Where are Tammy and Jason?" Annie asked.

Debi laughed. "Oh, you mean my joined at the hip pair? They are out helping Michael finish with the photographs. I don't think we have a chance of separating them this weekend."

Don, after saying hello, went out to the back yard to light the barbeque. Frank soon joined him with a couple of beers, and I figured we would be lucky if the back yard did not go up in smoke.

After dinner, we sat by the fire pit. The sun set quickly over the lake. Autumn had definitely arrived.

Frank handed Michael another beer and looked at me. "Are you driving tonight?" he asked.

I nodded. "I think he's is a little too tired to drive too."

Michael nodded too. "Yeah, I was up in Alaska early this morning. It's hard to believe."

I shivered and leaned back into him. He put his arms around me.

"Cold?" he asked.

"No, I'm okay now. Guess I'm tired too. I didn't really do anything today though," I said.

He whispered into my ear, "Let me finish this beer and we'll go."

"No, that's okay. You enjoy yourself," I whispered back.

We ended up staying quite late. Since we were leaving for Monterey in the morning, Tammy had decided to stay the night at Don and Debi's house. Don quietly assured Michael that he would keep an eye on both Tammy and Jason. Michael was already very suspicious that Jason would come home for a visit when he was going to be out of town. Later in the car, I told him to relax, and he had better realize that Tammy and Jason were adults.

"I don't have to like it," he replied.

I smiled. "Your baby girl is growing up."

"I still don't have to like it." He frowned.

"Remember my dad at the baseball game?"

"Am I that bad?" he asked.

I took his hand and kissed it. "Not quite as bad as my dad, but you could give him a run for his money."

Michael sighed and stretched. "I guess all dads are alike."

I laughed. "Yes, especially when it comes to their baby girls and other men."

"Speaking of girls and men, Katy called this afternoon, and she's coming out with Paul next weekend. She has a week free from school, and Paul was able to arrange vacation time."

"That's wonderful. I'm looking forward to meeting him."

He frowned. "I'm not."

"Oh, lighten up. Don't you remember what it's like to be young?"

He kept the frown on his face. "That is exactly what I'm worried about."

When we arrived home, we carried the camera equipment into the house. I put out fresh water for the dogs while he took his shower. By the time I appeared in the bedroom, he was already in bed and fast asleep.

I shook my head and mumbled to myself, "Wouldn't you know it, the first night we are completely alone, and he falls asleep. Men."

Michael heard me and roused himself. "Sorry babe. I must have fallen asleep."

"Go back to sleep. I haven't had my shower yet. Get some rest," I told him.

He nodded, and he was back to sleep before his head hit his pillow. I took my shower and finally climbed into bed. Over the past several weeks, I was used to going to bed naked. It was actually liberating and made things much more comfortable when we became amorous. He was on his back, and I got into my favorite position by turning on my side, lying up against him with my head on his chest. I threw my right leg over his so that it was nestled in between his legs. After I settled down, Michael wrapped his arms around me. This was heaven for me.

CHAPTER THIRTY-FOUR

The next morning, Michael was still asleep when I awoke. While I was in the kitchen making coffee, Tammy walked in from the back door.

"You're home early," I said.

"Jason likes to sleep in, and I had restless energy. I decided to work on my paper while he slept. He'll call me when he gets up. Is Dad still asleep?" she asked.

"Yeah, he was exhausted when we got here last night." I took a sip of coffee.

She started to feed the dogs their breakfast.

"I'll feed the dogs. You go work on your paper," I said.

"That's okay. Like I said I have nervous energy."

"Okay," I said. "If you see your dad let him know I'm over at my place packing."

She nodded.

Topper and Samantha did not know whether to follow me or stay for the food. "You guys stay with Tammy."

It was beginning to get difficult for me to have two separate places. I didn't leave clothes at Michael's, and I felt silly every morning marching over to my house in my robe. The reason I hadn't moved anything over was that he hadn't invited me to move in. It definitely was a little confusing for me. I wasn't sure about his expectations of me, well, not all the expectations. The nighttime expectation was clear, his bed, naked.

Since he'd been away for several days, we had not made love, and I for one was definitely missing that. Did he notice it too? There were all my insecurities again. Just when I thought I had buried them good and deep, they always came up bubbling to the surface.

One thing for sure, I would have Michael all to myself for the entire weekend. The thought alone made me giddy with anticipation. I held up my black taffeta dress against me while looking in the full-length mirror by the bathroom door. I nodded my head with approval. He will like this dress. It was conservative, but the bodice showed off my cleavage enough to make it interesting. After zipping the garment bag closed, I started looking for my shoes and the new underwear I recently purchased.

A loud knock sounded on my back door, and Michael called as he opened it, "Elizabeth, it's me. Okay if I come in?"

"I'm in my bedroom," I shouted back.

I was digging through shoeboxes in my closet when I felt his hands on my hips.

"You have plenty of shoes," he commented, laughing. "I thought my ex-wife had a lot of shoes, but you have her beat."

I pulled out a box and straightened up. "What?" I said turning around.

"Shoes," he pointed, "you have a lot of them."

"If you think this is a ton, you should see Lisa's closet. She has taken over her spare bedroom's closet solely for her shoes." I put the box on the dresser, opened the lid, and pulled out black sandals. "What do you think?" I held up the shoe to him.

"Gorgeous, but can you dance in them? What are they, four inches?"

I put my arms around his neck and leaned into him.

"I can do quite a bit in these shoes," I purred into his ear.

"Mmmm..." he whispered back while he opened my robe and wrapped his arms tightly around me. "Then I definitely like those shoes." His mouth lingered on mine kissing me and taking my breath away. "Now I need you to get dressed and ready to go or else I'm going to attack you, and we'll never get to Monterey. Then, I'll have to call everyone and let them know that it was all your fault."

I let my lips trail down his chin to his neck. "That would be okay with me, but, it wouldn't be very nice to deprive them of their guest of honor, would it?" Lowering my arms, I squeezed his butt through his jeans.

He laughed and stepped away. "Get away from me you temptress." He held my robe open for a moment to take a long look at me. "You're driving me crazy!"

I playfully pushed Michael away. "Go on. Get thee away! Let me finish packing!"

It did not take me long to assemble the rest of my clothes. The weather was still warm for the beginning of October, and I put on a red gingham checked sundress. The spaghetti straps tied up on my shoulders, and the bodice was tight enough that I did not have to wear a bra underneath. The red sash underneath the bodice gave me an hourglass figure, and the full skirt completed the look. Since we were driving the Mustang with the top down, I braided my hair and put on a small white cotton sweater jacket.

Michael gave me a wolf whistle as I carried my small suitcase outside.

He placed it and my garment bag in the trunk. If I could have, I would have whistled back to him. He was dressed in black dress slacks, and dress shirt with the sleeves rolled up his forearms. Looking sexy and inviting in his clothing, if the opportunity had risen, I would have dragged him back into the house.

Opening the car door for me, he leaned over as I situated myself into the seat. "Did I tell you how beautiful you are today?" He beamed at me.

I grinned and batted my eyelashes at him. "No, I don't think you commented on my beautifulness yet."

He kissed me. "You are the most incredibly gorgeous woman I've ever seen."

I giggled. "Oh, that will do me for today, and may I say, you are some kind of sexy today." I put my hands around the back of his head to bring him closer to me and kissed him.

We finally managed to tear ourselves apart and set off on our trip. We stopped at a small restaurant in San Francisco for lunch. I loved it when he received a big eye from our waitress. He would be friendly to her but would continue to look at me. He held my hand as we snuggled together in the booth. Before dating Michael, this type of behavior would have embarrassed me. Now I reveled in everything he did for me.

Back in the car, we headed toward Monterey for the last part of the trip.

I leaned over to him and whispered in a sultry voice, "I have a surprise for you."

He raised his eyebrows. "You do?"

I nodded, took his free hand, and pulled it over to me. I shifted in the seat, so I sat on my side and leaned toward him. He grinned while I took his hand and placed it under my skirt on my thigh.

Stealing a glance at me, he said, "What are you up to?"

I smiled a devilish grin and leaned toward him further. My hand grasped his forearm and led it further up my thigh. My whisper into his ear was light and breathy, "I'm not wearing anything underneath my dress.

Michael threw his head back and gasped while his hand traveled under my dress as if to prove my words. "Damn Babe." He laughed. "It's a good thing you didn't tell me in the restaurant because we would not be headed toward Monterey right now."

I sat back in my seat giggling because it made me happy to have such an effect on him. The remainder of the trip to Monterey he kept his hand under my dress tracing circles on my thigh. I had to admit those circles had quite an effect on me too. He had me squirming in my seat, and it served me right.

We parked in the underground parking structure at the hotel. When he helped me out of the car, he pressed me back against the closed door. Michael's arms were around me, and I felt him pick up the back of my dress and cup my naked butt with his hands. I was glad we were alone in the garage because it was becoming hot between us. I had played with the swelling in his pants in the car, teasing him even more while we were driving, and now, that bulge insistently pressed against me.

His kisses were intense, and when our tongues met, I felt little explosions between my legs. I threw my head back as he lifted my leg to wrap it around him. I pressed my hips closer to him.

"Oh babe, I can't wait," he murmured into my neck. "Let's get checked in so that I can really be inside of you."

"No, now." I held him tightly, grinding my hips against him.

Michael grinned. "I wish I had my camera to capture your face. I've never seen you so wild before." He let my leg down and straightened out my dress. "If someone caught us though you would lose that wild look quickly, and you would be mortified, especially if it was someone I knew."

I giggled. "You're right, besides this isn't very comfortable."

Cooler heads prevailed, and we unloaded the luggage from the trunk. Sure enough, as we did, several people that he knew exited from the elevator. The aquarium was only a block away from the hotel, and everyone who was coming in from out-of-town for the special event was staying at the hotel.

The hotel was small, and it seemed as if Michael knew everyone working there on a first name basis. It made me realize that there was a lot of his history I did not know. The suite he had arranged for us was beautiful. The balcony connected to both the living room and bedroom and it overlooked the ocean. The two bathrooms would typically have been overkill, but it was welcome if we were both getting ready at the same time.

We barely had the door shut before we embraced. Our lips found each other as he picked me up while I wrapped my legs around his waist. He made his way into the bedroom, and we both tumbled on the bed without separating.

I straddled his hips and sat up. "Help me with my dress," I said, barely able to get the words out of my mouth because I was breathing so hard.

Michael sat up on the edge of the bed with me still in his lap and reached behind me to unzip my dress. He couldn't find the zipper. I lifted my arm and pointed to my side. He shook his head in disbelief, but the zipper came down quickly, and he had my dress pulled over my head with one movement. He marveled over the fact that I really was completely naked under the dress. Pulling me close, he kissed my neck and worked his way down to my breasts, leaving a snail trail of soft kisses.

"Now you," I whispered. He pulled his shirttails out of his pants and started working on the buttons. I sighed in frustration.

"Let me," he said in a voice just as breathless. He pulled his shirt off over his head. He turned his attention back to my breasts, and he teased each nipple to a firm peak. My arms wrapped around his neck, and I threw my head back.

"Michael, I want you now," I whispered. I stood and reached for his belt.

We pulled back the covers and blankets. He kicked off his shoes, and after I removed the rest of his clothes, he scooted back on the bed against the headrest. He crooked his finger and beckoned toward me. I had a lazy grin on my face. Crawling over to him, I straddled his lap.

I was more than ready for him, and as our bodies connected, both of us groaned a low growl of each other's names. He let me set the pace as we moved together. He knew I was close when my rhythm quickened, and he held my hips to keep us connected.

He whispered in my ear, "Let go, my little Hellcat, let go."

With those words, everything came crashing around us. Time stopped with my scream of his name. At that moment, there was only him and I in the world, and nothing else existed. Holding each other tightly, we remained together, caught in those hungered for waves of pleasure.

When we broke apart, it was if he was taking part of me and I part of him. We lay on our sides gently touching each other. Michael touched my face softly and kissed my lips. I traced my fingers along his shoulder and down his chest. Leaning over I kissed his chest.

He spoke first. "Wow."

I whispered, "Double that wow."

"I think I have just enough energy, would you like me to open the balcony window and get a little air?"

"Yes, it's a little stuffy in here."

Michael got out of bed and opened the sliding door. His movements gave me a full view of his body. I sighed.

"What's wrong?" he asked as he crawled back into bed with me.

"Your body is beautiful," I said simply.

He grinned as he lay next to me and wrapped his arms around me. Cuddling up to him, I got into my favorite position with our legs intertwined.

"We have time," he spoke softly. "Why don't you sleep for a little while?"

"Are you sure?" I murmured with my head on his chest.

He answered, "Absolutely, I know how you love your naps."

A soft ocean breeze was blowing into the room from the balcony. It cooled down our warm bodies and dried the perspiration quickly. I shivered, and he pulled the sheet up over us. We slept.

Michael gently nudged me awake as the sun was setting and the light in the room was now faint. "Hey sleepy head," he whispered. "It's time to get up."

Rolling off him, I stretched out my arms and legs. He turned to bend down and kiss me while I put my arms around his shoulders. "That was a nice rest."

"You were out like a light." He kissed me again. "I'm going to get dressed in the other bathroom, and you can have this one all to yourself to get ready."

I nodded and stretched again while he got out of bed. I watched him walk around the room naked and realized how comfortable he was with his body. It would have been far more difficult for me to walk around like that.

He turned quickly toward me. "Caught you looking!" he kidded.

I laughed and pulled the sheet over my head. "You better put some clothes on, or I'm going to ravage you all over again," I called from under the sheet.

"Promise?" he answered and then gathered his stuff, closing the door to the bedroom as he left.

I heard the shower in the other bathroom and groaned when I threw back the covers. It had gotten cold in the room with the sun setting, and I closed the balcony door. The shower was steamy and hot and felt good. While I was showering, Michael had switched on the Giants baseball game on the television in the bedroom. His yelling at the tv in the other room made me smile.

Blow-drying my hair took ages, but eventually, it was dry, and I loosely braided it. Next, I pinned it up in a chignon at the nape of my neck. I added a little more makeup than I usually wore because I thought the lights would probably be set lower.

The sexy lingerie was next. Even though the dress had boning in it, and I would not need a bra, undressing with the bra was far more exciting. I was looking ahead to later on tonight, although after this afternoon's romp I didn't know what to expect. Since the dress was strapless, the bra needed to be also. The sexy sheer bra didn't offer any support, but that wasn't the point, was it? The best was the garter belt, and I figured with a vintage dress what could be more appropriate? I put the garters and stockings on first and then the panties. I know, everyone else reverses it, but it was far more practical when I had to use the bathroom. Besides, I intended leaving on the stockings later tonight.

My dress was a vintage 1950s floating black chiffon Ceil Chapman dress that was gathered and draped to perfection. I found it in a small Hollywood consignment shop after I had sold my first book and never had an occasion to wear it. The strapless, fitted bodice led to a fitted draped skirt with a floating partial overskirt. From the back or sides, it appeared as if I had a full twirling skirt on, and from the front, I had a sexy, tight figure. The bottom of the dress hit just below my knees. The black sandals made my legs look long and shapely. A small diamond necklace and a matching pair of earrings finished the ensemble.

I gave myself one final look in the full-length mirror then walked into the other room. Michael stood by the television and turned. My breath caught in my throat. I had never imagined him in a tuxedo. My rugged, outdoorsman looked amazingly suave, and James Bond-like. He didn't say anything either.

It felt likes minutes had passed, and then I finally broke the silence. "Is this okay?" I gestured to my dress.

He still did not speak. Taking both of my hands, he brought them up to his lips. "Elizabeth, you look…you did this for me?" He bowed his head over my hands and gently kissed them. "I can't believe you are mine."

I touched his face tenderly, and he caught my fingers again kissing them.

"Do you really like it?" I asked.

"I didn't think you could get more beautiful, but I was wrong."

A blush crept onto my face. "You cut quite a figure in your tux."

He kissed my lips. "I am looking forward to showing you off tonight." Then he laughed. "Do you have underwear on?"

I pursed my lips. "Of course I do."

"Show me."

"What? You don't believe me?" I teased with disbelief. "Oh, I get it. You just want to look at my underwear." He kneeled down in front of me and placed his hands on the bottom of my dress. "Michael, get up. Don't ruin your pants. I'll show you."

He didn't stand up but continued to kneel on one knee as I inched the dress up. When I got to the top of the stockings and the garter belt, he gasped. "Babe, I'm going to be hard all night." He leaned in and kissed the top of my thigh.

I closed my eyes and swayed, not sure my feet would hold me upright. I continued to inch the dress up until just the bottom of my panties were visible. I felt his lips trail up to the elastic bottom of the bikini and his mouth pushed the edge higher as he planted another kiss.

Somehow, I found my voice. "Are you satisfied now?"

He grinned and as he pulled my dress down, he planted another kiss on my knee.

Michael stood up and said roughly, "No, that did not satisfy me." He pulled me close. "So tonight, every time I kiss your hand," he said fixing a kiss on my palm, "think that I'm really kissing you in between your legs and tasting you."

I closed my eyes and swayed in his arms. "Now, I'm going to be wet all night long," I whispered in his ear.

He grinned. "Good. Both of us are in the same state. We're starting the evening out right."

We managed to make it to the lobby to meet the two other couples who were taking the limousine with us. On the short ride over to the aquarium, I became acquainted with the two other honorees for tonight's festivities.

Starting with cocktails, we mingled around the softly lit tanks with their diverse fish in them. Many of Michael's former colleagues approached us. Admittedly, I was nervous. I wanted to make a good impression with his former working associates. He didn't seem the least bit uncomfortable, but then, he wasn't trying to remember everyone's name. He introduced me to the chairman of the board and his wife.

As I shook their hands, the wife immediately put me at ease by commenting on my dress. "Elizabeth, your dress is almost too delicious for words! I think I had one like that way back when. Is it a Ceil Chapman?"

I nodded my head in amazement. She linked her arm with mine and pulled me away from Michael. "Come with me darling, I have to introduce you to Betty. You know she was madly in love with Michael, but oh my, she's what, thirty years older than he is. She is going to love your dress. Why is it that women don't dress like that anymore?" She clucked her tongue and continued with what had become a one-sided conversation.

I threw a wild look at Michael, and he just winked at me. "Mrs. Chapman," he called, "I want Elizabeth back for dinner."

She just waved at him and continued to pull me through the crowd, which magically parted, for her. I was introduced to all of the other board members, and they all told me how much they valued Michael. Finally, we wended our way back to him. He wrapped his arm securely around me when I returned.

"Sorry," he whispered in my ear. "I couldn't prevent that one. There's only one more person I'd like you to meet. She's the executive director of the aquarium. Jennifer and her family are responsible for starting the aquarium."

We turned to a woman in her early fifties standing next to him, and he introduced her as Jennifer Page. She had a firm handshake and a warm welcome for me. "Thank you for coming, Elizabeth. This is an honor way overdue for Michael."

I smiled. "This is a treat for me. I've never been here. It's beautiful."

"You've never been here?" She glanced up at Michael. "You're neglecting your duties. You need to bring her here tomorrow afternoon for the grand tour."

He nodded. "It's already on the agenda, after the Chapman's brunch."

Jennifer grinned mischievously. "Yes, well we can't forget the brunch, can we? Welcome Elizabeth, please excuse me, I have to get to my MC duties." She left us while we found our seats at the head table.

"Brunch?" I murmured as we sat down.

Michael grimaced and quietly said, "Yeah, I just found out about it. We're expected tomorrow at eleven at their home."

"Where do they live?"

"Carmel. I've been there a couple of times. It's very nice. You'll enjoy it."

We settled into our chairs, and the program began. Honored first for some discovery that I could never pronounce, let alone spell, were the two marine biologists who accompanied us in the limo. Then a slide presentation started as Jennifer spoke.

"I first met Michael Hoffman when he was a young man studying marine biology at UC Santa Cruz. I should have known something was unusual about him at that time because every time I saw him, he had a camera around his neck. After we opened the aquarium, we offered a position to the newly graduated marine biologist. Little did we know that we were receiving a two for one package. Michael started honing his photographic abilities in his spare time, and I saw photographs pop up on the staff's walls. She paused and up on the large screen next to her appeared one of Michael's otter photographs. Jennifer waited for the applause to die down. "When he finally found the nerve to show me a photograph, I was completely blown away. At that moment, I knew we had found our photographer. Michael became our go-to person for all of our photography. We called him the eyes of the aquarium. We were not the only people to notice his photography either, and he began to make a name for himself in animal conservancy photography. Now he is the man to contact if you want to call attention to your project, from polar bears to penguins. Currently, Michael is working on the whale migration project, which, when completed, we expect will greatly add to our knowledge of migrating Orcas. Please join me in congratulating Michael on being this year's recipient of the John F. Page Monterey Bay Aquarium Excellence in Conservancy award."

The applause was deafening with a standing ovation, and I realized how little I knew about Michael. These were his friends. It was evident that he was the reason they had all attended. As he made his way to the podium the pride that I felt almost made my heart burst open. I couldn't believe that he wanted me here with him. I felt like the most special woman in the room.

Michael gave a hug to Jennifer as he stepped up to the podium. The crowd settled back in their seats as he began speaking.

"I want to thank you all for coming tonight. I can't tell you how much this award means to me. The Monterey Bay Aquarium is doing such important work in marine conservancy, and as I travel, I always hear about the aquarium breakthroughs. '*Saving the planet and the animals*' is not just a catchphrase for me. It is about respecting all life whether it walks on two legs, or four, flies in the air or swims in our seas. We were made the stewards of all life on Earth, and it is our responsibility to ensure the well-being of this planet, not only for us but for future generations as well. My only desire through my photography is that it provides the catalyst for making a change in our thinking. Okay," he laughed, "I know I'm preaching to the choir. So, I'll just end with a big thank you for this incredible honor."

Michael received another standing ovation, and I waited for him to give him a big hug when he reached the table. Sure enough, he lifted my hand to his lips and kissed it. He looked at me, and I raised my eyebrows, which is when I felt the tip of his tongue lightly touch my knuckles. At that point, my knees almost buckled as a flame of desire shot through my body. He chuckled, and I vowed under my breath to get him back later tonight.

"Promise?" he asked.

We were beginning to attract attention. "Sit down, and behave yourself," I whispered.

We sat, and he took on a devilish grin showing his deep dimples. "I am not going to behave. Not tonight, I feel too good."

Our dinner arrived, and as we ate, our dinner companions kept Michael's attention in conversation. I did not participate much in the discussions since it was mainly surrounding his days at the aquarium. I was also a little intimidated, and I felt out of my league with a table of mostly scientists. When he was not eating, his hand kept drifting to the back of my neck, and he gently caressed my shoulders. He was able to concentrate quite well on the dialog around the table, and I was becoming a little puddle in my chair with his ministrations. His eyes kept glancing over to me, and his smile was soft and warm.

The small band started playing dance music, and couples began to rise from the tables to dance by the large windows overlooking the bay.

Michael looked over at me. "Would you like to dance?"

I nodded, and he took my hand to lead me to the dance floor. Before we started dancing, he kissed my palm, and again, I felt his tongue against my hand. I blushed.

He put his arms around me, and I whispered, "Stop that."

He smiled the same devilish grin. "Stop what?"

He held me tight as we slowly danced to "Put Your Head On My Shoulder." If there was a heaven, then this was what it was like. He moved me effortlessly around the floor. If nothing ever happened between the two of us again, I would be content forever with this memory. Our dance was as if we were the only two people in the world. The outside world had vanished entirely. When the song ended, we stood perfectly still holding each other. He placed the tenderest of kisses on my lips.

The bolero-mambo "Sway" started next. Michael began dancing with me again.

I shook my head. "I don't know how to do this."

"It's like a cha-cha, just follow my lead, and shake your hips in time to the music. You'll be fine," he said as he twirled me around and then pulled me close. We moved together in time to the music. He was powerful and easy to follow. As he spun me around, I noticed not many other couples were dancing, and it was then I realized that we were probably making a spectacle of ourselves.

I thought, what the heck? I'm having fun. I'm with the man of the hour, and luck held, he'd be making love to me later tonight. I started to move to the music, and Michael let me loose. I danced around him with my arms in the air and shaking my hips. The beautiful dress, with its half skirt, was perfect for the dance. I felt gorgeous in his arms. He caught me again, and we both laughed. We continued dancing together until the end of the song when he dipped me down deeply. His strong arms held me steady; he kissed me and then brought me back up.

The crowd had been watching us and applauded when we finished. I turned to everyone, and instead of blushing I curtsied, and then we both laughed. He pointed to the door, and we slipped outside to the back patio overlooking the ocean. The ocean air felt good, it was cool and smelled of salt.

"Is it too cold out here for you?" he asked.

I shook my head. "Not at the moment. Maybe later, but I need to chill a bit."

We stood at the railing looking at the waves crashing against the rocks below us. I leaned back into him as he wrapped his arms around me from behind.

Michael rubbed my forearms. "Let me know if you get cold."

"Right now, I'm very toasty."

He kissed my neck and whispered, "I'm delighted you were here to share this with me tonight."

"I have a new understanding of you."

"You do?"

I nodded and turned into his arms. Looking up at him, I could see the moon's reflection in his eyes.

"I understood that you are a passionate photographer, but I never realized where the dedication came from. I didn't understand how important your work is to you and how valuable you are to the whole movement."

He chuckled, and he pulled his jacket off wrapping it around my shoulders. "Elizabeth, while my ego would like to believe that I'm worthy. If I dropped off the face of the earth, someone else would fill my shoes quickly."

"I really don't know that much about you."

"We're getting to know each other by spending time together aren't we?" He lifted my chin up. "I'm nothing special. I'm just a man."

My arms wrapped around his waist, and I pressed my head to his chest. "You are special, and you are very yummy."

We stood there quietly in each other's embrace listening to the swirling water below.

Even with his jacket on, it became too cold to stand outside on the patio. We danced more but did not repeat the exhibition we had earlier. Several men wanted to cut in to dance with me, and he reluctantly let me go. It became my turn to share him, and he danced with many of the older ladies. He had a way with them as they batted their eyelashes at him, and he flirted with them. His behavior didn't bother me though, as it would have with Kevin. There was nothing sleazy about Michael's actions, and he was simply very gracious and good-natured.

Later that night, after we finally made it back to the hotel room, we made love at a slow and languorous pace. We took our time exploring the other's body, as we tasted, tested, teased, tempted, and yes, we even tortured each other. At the end when we reached the culmination together, it caught us in a moment when our hearts beat as one, and our bodies fused together as a single entity with only one mind and one thought.

Neither of us spoke afterward as we lay together, our bodies' slick with the perspiration of our efforts and the brisk ocean air cooling us down and clearing our thoughts. Eventually, Michael reached up and traced my face with his fingers while I lazily drew circles with my hands on his back feeling his hard muscles.

His look was hopeful as he broke the silence with the first words. "I'm in love with you Elizabeth."

My hands stopped their motions. My eyes grew wide, and I stopped breathing. He had said words that I had only dreamt of hearing. He loves me. It was a statement, not a question. My mind was spinning, and I wasn't breathing.

Michael chuckled warmly and kissed me. "Breathe. I don't want you to pass out."

"You said you love me?" I said, and the tears started to form in the corner of my eyes. I tried to blink them back, but they insisted on coming out.

"Yes, Babe, I love you," he whispered, kissing me again tenderly. "Why are you crying, is my telling you that I love you a bad thing?"

"No," I shook my head, "not a bad thing. Oh, Michael, I'm just so happy."

These were feelings I had not dared to admit to myself. My tears started to come faster, and I covered his face in wet tear-stained kisses.

I softly declared aloud what had been brewing inside of me for weeks, "I've fallen in love with you too."

When my voice spoke the words, my heart burst open, and there was no one else in the world except my Michael.

CHAPTER THIRTY-FIVE

I awoke happy and with a smile on my face. Neither of us had moved much during the night. I was in one of my regular positions, which meant I was sprawled all over Michael with my head on his chest and our legs intertwined like a pretzel. He was still sound asleep. Well, most of him was, because when I lifted up the sheet and looked down, there was part of him eager to go. He did not get to sleep long.

We enjoyed our day together. The home we were visiting was on the famed Seventeen-Mile Drive outside of Carmel. Dr. Chapman wanted to hear all about Michael's current whale migration project, and as it turned out, he had recommended him for the job as well as donating most of the research funds. Both of the Chapmans were intrigued by my romance novels, and she copied down the titles of the books promising to read them immediately. I could only imagine what she would think when she read page seventy-five in the latest novel.

The staff at the aquarium treated us like VIPs. Michael's status with the aquarium gave us entrance into areas not accessible to regular visitors. During our visit to the otter area, we stuffed food into their toys and hid the toys around their enclosure. I watched with glee when they scampered around discovering their treats. The idea behind this was to give the otters stimulating opportunities that mimic a part of their life in the wild. The time at the aquarium had been such fun, that at the end of the day I did not want to leave. The experience gave me another glimpse into his past.

Michael's cell phone woke us up early the next morning. He looked at the phone's screen. "Why is Tammy calling? Tapping the front of the phone, he said, "Tammy, honey what's wrong." His voice immediately took on one of concern, and he sounded like my father. "Honey, slow down, I can't understand you. What do you mean your mother has come for a visit?"

He rose from the bed. "No, do not put her on the phone." He walked into the other room, but I could still hear the muffled conversation. "How long are you staying?" There was a break in the discussion, and Michael raised his voice slightly. "No, you are not staying in my bedroom." Another pause and it was obvious he was speaking with his ex-wife who apparently was visiting Tammy.

"Put Tammy back on the phone. Tammy, your mother is not to stay in my bedroom. She can stay in the guest room. Who is Paul? … Oh him. No, he is not sleeping in Katy's room. You and Katy will have to bunk together. No, I am not mean. I do not want your mother in my bedroom. Is that clear? ... No, it is none of your mother's business where I am or what I am doing." His tone became exasperated. "I will be home in a few hours. Do not do anything until I get there." He tapped his cell phone off as he walked back in the bedroom. Sitting on the edge of the bed, he sighed heavily.

I sat up next to him. "Crisis at home?"

He put his arm around me. "Nothing I can't handle. But we do need to go."

I leaned over and kissed him lightly on the corner of his mouth.

Michael turned and gently pushed me back on the bed. "But, I do need my morning fix though."

Leaning over me kissing my lips, he ran his hand from my waist down to my hips, onto my thigh, and other places that made me squirm with delight and press against him. He reached for a condom packet on the nightstand and before he tore it open, I stopped his hand.

"I don't think we need to..." I paused. "We both know I'm not able to get pregnant and I think we're both safe as far as other stuff…" I trailed off again.

He looked at me with a bemused smirk on his face. "If you're sure."

Tossing the small package to the side, his kisses covered my face before the condom hit the floor.

I smiled broadly meeting his kisses with my own passion. "Alrighty then," I murmured, and we gave in once again with reckless abandon.

When we checked out of the hotel, the weather was overcast and looked ominous. It was almost as if the weather began to reflect the mood we faced at home. I didn't want to lose the happiness we experienced here. The time spent with him, and our visit to the aquarium had been delightful. I wanted to revisit the aquarium and watch the otters and penguins for hours. The smell of fish lasted on my hands, and I was sure cats were beginning to follow me, but Michael said I only smelled like the salt air. I suggested taking another mini-vacation to Monterey and volunteering at the aquarium. He told me he had seen the excitement in my eyes yesterday and was sure the conservation bug had bitten me.

We were both quiet during the long ride home. The rain started just outside of San Francisco. Large drops hit the windshield. As we drove, Michael appeared to be lost in thought, and I didn't want to disturb him. Occasionally, he would pick up and kiss the back of my hand. After his kiss, my hand always lingered on his face. He had not bothered shaving, and his stubble became more pronounced as the morning moved into the afternoon. It made him look more delectable and sexier.

The rain pounded off and on all the way home. The Mustang was drafty, and the heater did not work well. I should have worn warmer clothes, but we had been so out of touch for the weekend, and it had suddenly turned into autumn.

The first thing I noticed when we drove up behind our houses was the small champagne colored Mercedes parked by his back door. This had to be the dreaded ex-wife's car, and I thought, no wonder she needed money. I shook my head to vanquish the petty thoughts from my mind. I wanted to give the woman the benefit of the doubt. Tammy called us three times on our way home. She was almost reminiscent of the child in the back seat asking, "Are we there yet?"

Michael parked the Mustang behind my cabin but left the engine running. This was not a good sign. He helped me carry my things inside and then stood on my back porch running his hands through his hair.

He blew out a big breath. "Let me survey the situation, and I'll give you a call."

I nodded. Leaning down, he gave me a dry kiss on my cheek. Oh, not a good sign at all.

While I stood on the porch, I watched him pull the Mustang into his garage. Tammy opened up the back door, and my dogs came running out. They looked at me from a distance and bounded down the porch, running toward me. She waved at me with a bright smile. I waved back at her. She looked pleased as she hugged her dad. He did not look back at me but instead went inside the house with her. A terrible sign indeed.

At least the dogs were excited to see me as I wiped their feet off with a towel that I kept by the back door. I gave them both treats and put fresh water in their bowls. I wanted to kill some time. I hoped that Michael would call me at any moment but knew it would be awhile. I took a shower and put on my jeans and the aquarium sweatshirt Michael purchased for me. Settling into the couch, I watched a movie.

Topper woke me for dinner. A glance at the clock told me I had slept for two hours. I fed the dogs. The waiting was driving me crazy. Boldness took me over, and I decided to go over to Michael's house.

Knocking lightly on the back door and then testing the doorknob, I opened the door and called out, "Hello?"

He, Tammy, and his ex-wife were in the kitchen making dinner. Well,

Michael was making dinner, and the two women stood watching.

He called to me, "Elizabeth, there you are." He looked genuinely glad to see me. He put his arms around me and kissed me. "I tried reaching you, but you didn't answer. I figured you probably took a nap."

"Oh." I looked surprised and stared at the black screen on my cell phone. "I must have let it run out of power." I felt foolish after waiting for his call and taking a nap on top of it.

"No matter, you're here." He took a drink from the glass of red wine he held and slipped his free arm around my waist. "Let me introduce you. Elizabeth, this is Margaret, she is Tammy and Katy's mother." Michael did not bother telling her who I was as if it was implied.

Margaret was beautiful. She was everything that I had always longed to be. Her shoulder length hair was blond and framed around her face. I could see some resemblance to Katy, but Michael's influence in the girl's features was stronger. Her figure was very trim and petite, and I estimated that she was no taller than 5' 4". Also, to top it off she had huge breasts and a tiny waist. I felt like an awkward monster towering over her with my gangly arms and legs.

She looked at me with sharp eyes, almost the same as when a hawk eyes its prey. "Elizabeth, how nice to meet you." She cracked a smirk, which made her face look pinched. "So you're my competition?"

I just stared at her blankly not sure how to respond to her comment. Michael handed me his unfinished wine, and in a quick tip of the glass, I drank down the rest. His reaction somehow comforted me.

"Come over and taste the sauce Elizabeth, let me know what you think. Tammy, could you get Elizabeth some wine?"

He dipped a spoon into the creamy red sauce and held it out for me to try. I held his hand steady and blew on the sauce while looking up at Michael through my lashes. He winked at me and smiled.

"Mmm...," I said after tasting the sauce. It was a chunky intensely flavored sauce with mushrooms, roasted zucchini and peppers, and garlic. "This is really good. I'm starved."

"Good, it's ready to go." He turned to Tammy and Margaret. "I'll leave you two to do the garlic bread and pasta while Elizabeth and I enjoy the sunset on the front porch. Give us a shout when everything is ready." Michael picked up the two wine glasses and the bottle of wine and motioned to me to follow him.

I didn't look back but could feel Margaret's eyes piercing my back. I'm sure I had a self-satisfied grin on my face because he managed her without me getting my hands dirty.

Wrapping his arms around me from behind, we stood on the porch. The sun was making a beautiful display over the lake. I had always loved autumn at the lake when the leaves on the trees started to change and the evenings cooled down quickly.

"So, what is the state of affairs at the Hoffman house?" I asked settling back against him.

He took a moment to reply, and the sigh in his voice was evident. "She'll be here a couple of weeks. I told Tammy no more than that. Right now, she's up in the spare room, but Katy and Paul will be here next Friday. So, I don't know what's going to happen on Friday. Maggie has gotten it into her head that she wants to stay in my room."

I stiffened and was sure he could feel my physical reaction because he tightened his arms around me. "Why would she ever get an idea like that? It doesn't make sense."

"To her warped mind, it does. She reasoned that we had been married at one point and we slept together all those years. I don't know Elizabeth, she's nuts. Katy and Tammy will have to stay together in a room. The problem is those rooms are so small they only have one twin bed each." Michael sighed again.

"I have an idea," I turned to face him, which wasn't easy to do since he was holding me so closely. "Paul can stay in my guest room."

"Well, that is one possibility," he answered.

"You know I'm not going to be able to stay in your house with her here."

He closed his eyes and bent his head leaning it against my forehead. He whispered, "I was afraid you were going to say that."

I tipped his chin up with my hand and looked him directly in the eyes. "Michael, I just can't."

"I know." He turned me around again. "You're missing the sunset."

I rested back against him.

"That's not the worst of it either," he murmured into my hair.

"What else?" I groaned.

"I have to leave for several days. The whales have started their migration. I'm flying up to Alaska on Wednesday to catch up with the ship."

"Maybe that's a good thing. Then the girls can enjoy their mother all to themselves, and you won't have to be disturbed about it."

"I'm not disturbed."

"Yes, you are. I can feel it in you. Every time you mention her you stiffen up."

Michael laughed low in my ear. "You want to talk stiffening up?" He growled and nibbled on my earlobe.

I pressed myself into him and wriggled my hips against him. "Behave," I said laughing low. "And stop changing the subject."

"Can you hold the fort down while I'm gone? You know with Katy, Paul, and Tammy. I'm installing a lock on my bedroom door tomorrow before I leave. I'll give you a key."

"Yes, I can watch things for you. I can't imagine what type of trouble your ex-wife can get into alone, in your house, with Tammy in school."

"Don't laugh. You don't know her," Michael said. "By the way, I have your Monterey dress with my tux, and Tammy will drop it off at the cleaners for us."

Dinner was ready, and we sat around the table, one large happy family. Tammy appeared to be enthralled with her mother being there. I tried to be friendly, but Margaret kept throwing barely veiled insults my way any time she could.

First, she discounted romance novels as trash reading and was surprised at the taste of the American public. Then she asked me if I had any children. When I said no she launched into her next discussion about how important children were to her and Michael's life. Moreover, she couldn't really see him with anyone who didn't want children.

Even though he was trying to avert her barbs, they just kept coming. When she finally told me that my dogs were fat, well that did it. I scooted my chair away from the table.

"I'm sorry. I need to get back home," I said standing.

"Oh, Elizabeth, yes, that's probably a good idea." She smirked at me.

I almost told her that when she did that with her mouth, she didn't look sexy at all if that was what she was going for; instead, it caused wrinkles around her lips. I bit my tongue since she probably would not take my constructive criticism very well.

Michael sprang to his feet. "Elizabeth, wait. I'll walk you back to your house."

Margaret looked peeved. "Are you coming back?"

He looked at Tammy. "Don't wait up for me, and help your mother with the dishes, okay?"

I felt bad after we left the house because Tammy had looked so disappointed.

He chuckled. "Damn that woman is a piece of work. I'm sorry Elizabeth that you had to go through all of that."

I squeezed his hand before I put my arm around his waist as we walked toward my cabin. I hadn't left the lights on which was unusual for me and Michael insisted on going in first to make sure everything was okay.

I sighed when he came back and reported that all was in order. "Guess in my haste to get over to your house and protect you, I forgot."

He laughed as he wrapped me in his arms. "Protect me huh?" His lips brushed the tip of my nose before moving down to my lips.

"Are you going to stay the night?" My voice sounded hopeful.

He leaned back from me. "Babe, I can't."

I frowned. "I know. Will you wait until I fall asleep?"

Embracing me again, he rubbed my back, his hands moving underneath my sweatshirt.

He whispered in a rough tone, "No bra, I like that."

He grasped the bottom of my sweatshirt and pulled it over my head. I smiled, took his hand in mine, and led him to my bedroom.

When I awoke, it was dawn. I was alone, except for the dogs. It was too early to jog, and I lay in bed thinking of Michael. I knew where that path was going to lead. Knowing he was always happy to see me in the morning, I wondered if he'd like some early morning company. Especially since he was leaving for his trip soon. Besides, I needed to retrieve my laptop, which was still in his bedroom.

I crept into the house. It was quiet and dark, and no one was up yet. Waiting for my eyes to adjust to the darkness, I slowly made my way to Michael's bedroom without running into the furniture. I was surprised the dogs didn't hear me, but then they had grown accustomed to my presence in the house.

Opening his door slowly, I went into the room. My mouth gaped wide when I saw the display in front of me. Michael was lying nude on his side facing toward the opposite wall. Spooned up against him, equally naked, was his ex-wife. I couldn't believe my eyes and my brain was not processing the information fast enough for me. The scene in front of me burned into my conscious for a very long time.

In my haste to exit the room quickly, the door slammed shut in front of me. The noise woke both Michael and Margaret. I still faced the door and heard him.

"What the hell? Maggie, what the hell are you doing here, and why, for god's sake, are you naked, and…" he paused as he was trying to process the scene when he saw me. "Elizabeth?"

I turned around to look at both of them. His look was one of confusion, and she looked like a cat with a bowl of cream in front of her. She looked at both of us and stretched to make a show of it for him.

Touching his chest, she purred, "Well, I don't know why she's here, but you invited me. You were wonderful last night."

He actually flinched away from her with a stare of pure disgust. Grabbing the quilt at the bottom of the bed, he wrapped it around himself and stood up.

"Good lord Maggie, have some decency and cover yourself." He pulled the sheet over her.

I stood at the door fighting back the tears that were welling in my eyes. She looked at me and then at him. She kneeled up on the bed and reached for him.

"Michael honey, after what we shared last night, I wouldn't think you'd react like this. You told me you were ready to try again with me." She put on the same pouty lip face I had seen before, and then a thought struck me that made me laugh.

Both of them looked at me as I stood in the doorway. Laughing, I clapped my hands together in applause.

"Brava, Margaret. Well done, you almost had me going." I walked over to Michael and leaned up to kiss him. "Good morning my love, that's a nice quilt you've got there."

His face greeted me with a quizzical expression.

I turned back to Margaret who still had the pouty expression on her face. "Be careful, you wouldn't want your face to freeze that way, it's most unattractive."

"Babe, I didn't. I swear I didn't." He looked at me in earnest.

I smiled and patted his stomach. "I know you didn't, sweetheart." I turned to look at her. "Margaret you look confused that your little game didn't work on me. You see it has been a long time since you've actually been with him. I know certain things about him now that you don't, and you really overplayed your hand." I looked at Michael. "I'm sorry if this hurts your feelings hon." I stared back at her. "He made love to me last night, for a very long time. In fact, he made me scream at least three times if I recall correctly."

Michael smiled and nodded his head in affirmation.

"He was quite busy and thoroughly exhausted when we finished, thank you, babe." I reached up to kiss his cheek. "So, Margaret, physically," I shook my head, "it could not happen with you last night. It might have been even doubtful this early in the morning too."

The fiery look of anger on her face made her appear ready to explode, and I almost stepped backward.

Thankfully, Michael took over for me. "Maggie, I suggest that you retrieve whatever dignity you still have and leave my room. You are not welcome in here, and if it happens again, I will forcibly remove you from my house. That goes whether I am here or not. You may continue to stay here because of Tammy and Katy, but let me remind you, you are a guest in my house, and I would expect you to behave in that manner. Am I clear?"

She gathered the sheets around her and did indeed muster her decorum, moving past us in a huff. "Well, I never."

He called after her as she was leaving, "Yes, you have." He put his arms around me. "You are amazing."

I smiled. "Being in love will do that to a person. Now, we need to talk. But, it will not be in here, at least not until those sheets are run through the washer a couple of times with hot water." I shuddered with the remembrance of the sight of her body. If I had thought yesterday that she was beautiful, I was ready to revise that opinion.

Michael nodded. "Come with me to see the eagles today."

"Okay, let me know when you're ready." I walked over and picked up my laptop. "Oh yeah, that is after you've changed the lock on the bedroom door and taken a hot shower with a lot of soap."

I could hear him chuckle as I left the room.

CHAPTER THIRTY-SIX

On our drive up to the eagle's nest, I finally felt relaxed for the first time since we arrived home from Monterey.

"Tell me the boobs are not hers," I said, turning to Michael while he drove the jeep.

He laughed and nodded his head. "No, I think she bought and paid for them after we were divorced."

"And, she's not a natural blond, is she?"

"I think you saw that for yourself today."

I giggled. "Yeah, I saw far more than I would have liked to."

He turned the jeep off the highway. The barriers blocking access to the road were no longer there.

"What happened?" I looked around. "Did they remove the barricade?"

Nodding, he sighed. "There was an argument about whether it was necessary or not. We haven't found anything around the area for several weeks. The parks department is thinking it may have been a tourist shooting at the eagles."

I frowned. "I hope they're right."

We reached the end of the road and Michael loaded us both up. He carried his camera equipment, and I brought the water and snacks he had made for us. The walk to the tree stand was enjoyable while we hiked slowly and held hands.

"I have something for you," he said, reaching into his backpack. He pulled out a small black camera with a lens attached and handed it to me. "This is your first real camera. I want to teach you how to use it."

"Oh!" I clapped my hands together taking the camera from him. "This is so sweet."

He put the camera strap around my neck. "Turn it on this way. I set everything for automatic. Look through the viewfinder, and you won't see an image on the screen until after you've taken the picture. Press this button here." He moved my finger up to the button.

I stepped away and took a picture of him. "Oh wow, my first one." I showed him the photo when it popped up on the screen.

Michael laughed and could tell that I was pleased with his gift. "Later on, we'll work on changing the settings, but first I just want you to get used to the camera."

"Thank you." I reached up and kissed him softly.

We climbed up into the tree stand. It was beautiful and bright, the rain we had on the previous day had washed everything. The air was fresh, and a slight breeze blew. I enjoyed this type of autumn afternoon the most. The eagles were not in the area yet, so we sat in the stand and waited.

He sat with his back up against the tree trunk with one leg propped up so that I could snuggle up against him and lay my head against his chest. We were quiet for a long time listening to the blowing leaves at the bottom of the tree.

I finally broke the silence. "Has your ex-wife always been nuts?"

Michael looked at me realizing I was not joking. "I'm beginning to think maybe she does have some serious problems, especially after the stunt this morning."

"Well yes, that was just plain crazy. I don't know what she thought she'd accomplish."

Michael drew a deep breath. He laid his arms on my hip as he adjusted his position slightly. "I think she's out of money and she's desperate. She'd do anything besides getting a job. I'd help her if she wanted to go back to school, but that would mean she'd actually have to go to school and not fake it."

"How did the two of you ever get together?" I asked while I lifted his t-shirt up and started running my fingers along his flat stomach feeling his hard muscles.

He caught my hand. "If you want me to tell you the story you have to stop that."

I grinned and nodded. "For now."

His story started while he was in college. They met during his last year and her first year. He had a reputation of being a ladies' man by dating several girls in quick succession.

"I don't think I deserved that reputation at all," he said laughing.

"Tell me about it my stud muffin." I kissed him on the stomach.

Michael laughed in jest. "Now Elizabeth cut that out, or I won't tell you the rest of the story."

I pursed my lips together in a contrite manner. "I'm sorry, go ahead."

They dated for about six months, and he had already started working at the aquarium on the weekends, in addition to working as a lab assistant to

Jennifer at the university during the week. He was also trying to do as much photography as his school schedule would allow. Shortly before graduation, Michael had started to pull away from Margaret, ready to end their relationship. She recognized the warning signs and announced that she was pregnant.

They were married in a quick ceremony in Las Vegas, much to the disappointment of his mother. But once he let his parents know she was pregnant, they understood and were thrilled to be expecting their first grandchild.

I started to do the math in my head. "Wait a minute, that doesn't add up. Katy is only twenty, and you graduated three years earlier. Something happened, didn't it?"

"Yeah. She was about four and a half months pregnant and miscarried."

"Oh Michael, I'm sorry." I sat up and touched his face.

"Babe, it was a long time ago." He kissed my hand. "It wasn't meant to be."

I settled back down with my head in his lap.

He blew out a deep breath again and continued. Margaret had taken the miscarriage badly, so any thoughts of splitting up or leaving were out of the question. By this time at the aquarium, he had a permanent job, and they were living in a small apartment in Seaside. Two years later, she announced she was pregnant again in the spring, and Katy arrived the following January.

"She was the most beautiful baby I had ever seen. Long fingers and long toes with expressive eyes. I couldn't believe how alert she was when she was born." He stared off into space with a soft smile remembering Katy's birth. "She was all little girl when she was small too." He chuckled. "She hated for her hands to be dirty, and we never had any problem getting her to take a bath."

Then two years later Tammy was born. This was the point when Michael started to travel for photography jobs. Margaret was not happy with the traveling he did, but she enjoyed the extra money that it brought in, especially when they were able to buy a house and a new car.

When they weren't physically apart, they started drifting mentally apart. He was engrossed with growing his photography business and raising his daughters and did not pay much attention to Margaret.

He raked his hand through his hair. "I've replayed our whole relationship over and over the past several years. I know it was mostly my fault because I was not there emotionally for her. I didn't want to be." He sighed heavily. "We had nothing in common, no bonds, only the children. She was not happy about having to take care of them while I was traveling. She was under the impression that I was living the high life when I was away." He snorted. "She didn't realize or refused to recognize, that I lived out of tents and sleeping bags. It was definitely not glamorous, it still isn't. What got me, she was the one who wanted children right away, yet when she finally had them, she couldn't be bothered."

When Michael first found evidence of her infidelities, he ignored it. He refused to consider she was having an affair. True, they were intimate less and less. Even after she started taking birth control pills, he wanted to believe her excuses that she was tired or not feeling well.

"I was stupid," he exhaled. He ran his fingers through my hair while he spoke. "And, finally I didn't want to take it anymore. I've asked myself many times if I ever really loved her."

I opened my eyes wide and looked at him shocked he would have considered the possibility. "And, did you come up with an answer?" I hesitated to ask.

He nodded. "Yes. I have my answer now."

I grew quiet and sat up. "When I left Kevin, he told me he never loved me."

He pursed his lips together and raised my hands to his lips. "That hurt you, didn't it?"

I nodded. "At first I didn't believe him. However, I do now. I don't know why he married me though if he didn't love me. That's why people get married, isn't it?"

Slowly placing a soft kiss on my hands, he said, "Not always, Elizabeth."

He pulled me into his arms and held me against him. We stopped talking and looked for the eagles.

The eagles returned to their nest, and both of us took out our cameras. Michael took pictures of the eagles, and I took pictures of him. We were both happy to be working together.

He convinced me to stay with him that night. He would be gone on the whale migration expedition until Sunday. Tammy and her mother went out to dinner, so we had the house to ourselves. After making love, we lay intertwined and murmured sweet nothings.

We heard Tammy and Margaret come into the house.

Michael held my face between his hands. "I don't want you to let Margaret get to you while I'm gone, okay?" I nodded, and he brushed his lips against mine softly. "Remember I love you, and it's you I want to be with."

The following morning I woke while he was getting ready to leave. I padded out to the kitchen and found Tammy already with the coffee on. I poured Michael and myself cups. She handed me the front-page section of the newspaper while she ate her toast.

"Your mom not up yet?" I asked.

"No, she usually likes to sleep late."

I nodded adding extra cream to my coffee because Tammy had made it strong. "I was thinking about driving down to see your great-grandmother on Friday afternoon before Katy arrives. Would you like to go with me?"

Tammy looked up from her paper. "Yeah, that would be good. I talked to Great-grandma yesterday, and she was complaining no one was visiting her. It would give her something to look forward to."

"Would your mom like to come along with us?" This was my attempt to reach out to Margaret one more time.

"I don't know. I'll ask her."

Michael came into the kitchen, and I handed him his cup of coffee.

"Thanks, Babe." He sat down between us, and she handed him the sports section.

She rose and grabbed her book bag. Bending over she kissed him on the cheek. "Be careful Dad. Have a good trip."

He smiled and hugged her around the waist. "Will do honey. See you on Sunday."

Tammy touched me on the shoulder. "I already fed the dogs."

I smiled. "Thanks. I'll run them this morning."

She nodded and with a quick "Bye" she left for school.

"She was a little frosty to you this morning," Michael commented.

"Actually, she's warmed up a little. I know it's hard for her to be caught between her mother and me," I said.

"Margaret can be very persuasive, but Tammy is a bright girl." He drank down the last of his coffee. "I'm loading the jeep. I'll be right back, meet me in the bedroom."

He met me there a few minutes later. He slipped my robe off and let it drop to the floor before wrapping his arms around me. "I wanted to feel you naked before I left."

I laughed. "Hey, no fair. What about me?"

He leaned in for a kiss. "If I only had time."

His kiss was deep and lingering. I wanted to drag him over to the bed but knew that wouldn't happen, so instead, I was content to rub myself against him. His hands cupped my butt and lifted me up. We both groaned into each other's mouths and then laughed, parting reluctantly.

CHAPTER THIRTY-SEVEN

After Michael left, I took all four dogs for a run. When we returned to the house, Margaret was in the kitchen drinking coffee and reading the newspaper. I considered making a fresh pot of coffee, but when I saw her, the thought left my mind. She turned to look at me when I walked in with the dogs.

"Good morning," I said without warmth or sincerity in my voice.

"Well, good morning. I suppose we're alone in the house. Isn't this cozy?" she said, barely containing the malice in her voice.

"No, actually I find it quite awkward."

"I wonder why that is? Could it be that you don't belong here?" she said slyly. "I mean, this really isn't your house, is it? You and Michael have just started dating, haven't you? Yet you walk around here as if you are his wife."

I simply looked at her not believing my ears. This woman definitely had the audacity.

Margaret continued, "You know Elizabeth, you are not marriage material for Michael, so don't think you're ever going to go down that aisle." She laughed at her own pun. "I've heard that you can't have children."

She was good. Somehow, she knew which words would hurt me the most. She plunged her words into my heart and twisted them like a sharpened knife. She peered carefully at my face. She was judging my reaction to her words. I tried to mask my expression, my eyes but wasn't able to master that even after all these years. I could not speak to defend myself.

"Our babies created a bond between us. That bond is deep, and no one can ever sever it. This is something that you'll never have with Michael. If you knew anything at all about him, you would know it is his love for his children that drives him."

Her murder of me was nearing completion. Of course, she did not stop there, because her delivery of the *coup de grâce* was still to come.

"Oh Elizabeth, I'm so glad that we're able to talk. Please don't be upset by what I'm telling you, it's only the truth, and I'm trying to save you from being hurt down the line."

"So you're saying all this for my benefit?" How should I respond to this woman?

She smiled, her eyes gleaming with insincerity. "Yes, Elizabeth because you deserve to be warned. Michael will use you for a little while and then when he gets tired of you, and he always does, well, then you'll be left with nothing because you can't give him what he truly wants."

I could feel my breath catching in my throat. I had a horrible flight impulse to escape her devastating words. I looked toward the back door. I had to escape, or I would break down and cry. I did not want to cry in front of her.

"You'll have to excuse me, but I need to get to work. I will take the dogs with me so they won't be in your way." I stumbled over the words as I made my way to the door.

Again, her smile reminded me of a cat in front of a bowl of cream.

"You do that," she said with a satisfying smirk.

I took a deep breath as I stepped outside hoping that it would help clear my head. It did not. Somehow, I managed to get back to my cabin as the tears had already begun to spill down my cheeks. Once inside the house, I made my way to my bedroom and collapsed on the bed with my box of tissues and four dogs. Blowing my nose, I looked around the bed. There really was not enough room on my bed for four dogs and me. I rolled my eyes at the situation. At least the dogs wanted to be with me. Yes, I know they really loved me for the snacks I always dropped for them, but they were here.

Pulling myself together, I managed to write most of the day. I even worked a bit on the eagle book too, knowing that Michael would be pleased with my progress when he arrived home. This is not to say that I completely forgot what Margaret had said to me in the kitchen. No, the words still stung because I was afraid she spoke the truth.

Tammy came by around dinnertime to collect the dogs. She invited me to join her and her mother for dinner. I politely declined and let her know I wanted to finish the chapter I was working on. Tammy nodded at me and then said that her mother would be joining us on our trip to see Great-grandmother Helen. I nodded back hoping she didn't see me grimace because the last thing I now wanted was to be on a car trip with Margaret. Yippee.

Instead of finishing the chapter, I went for a long run. The run helped me think. All day, Margaret and her hateful words had been stewing in the back of my head. Running as a replacement for punching her was a good option.

After showering and putting on a nightgown, I looked at my bed. It did not look inviting. I thought of Michael's bedroom and his bed. His bed sounded like a better choice. Besides, I reasoned with myself, I didn't have my dogs here. I slipped into my robe and slippers.

The house was quiet when I entered. Margaret's car was gone. It appeared that she and Tammy must still be at dinner. I remembered Michael telling me that she did not cook and ate out often. The dogs greeted me at the door. I hurriedly went to his room and unlocked the door. The dogs followed me and bounded on the bed. Yes, I had made the correct choice.

I crawled into the bed and curled up to his pillows. Something was not right, the bed felt wrong. I lay there a few minutes and then grinned. I pulled back the covers and took off my nightgown. Yes, that was better after cuddling back up to the pillows. My hands felt something under the pillow.

"What is this?" I said aloud while sitting up. Turning the light on, I pulled out a sealed envelope. I recognized his handwriting with my name scrawled across the front.

Inside was a handwritten note from him, which read, "*Babe, if you're reading this note then I know you're sleeping in my bed. I love you for being a strong woman. I'll see you on Sunday, and I will miss you every moment I'm away. Love, Michael. P.S. I have left a few other notes for you in the bedroom. I hope you find them.*"

Sitting on the edge of the bed, I reread the note several times. The tears fell freely because there was no reason to hold them back. He always knew how to do just the right thing for me. I dried my eyes and put my robe on. Where would he hide notes for me? How many were there?

There was a knock on the bedroom door, the dogs ran over and snuffled at the bottom of the door.

"Come in," I called.

Tammy poked her head in. "I saw a light. I hope I'm not bothering you, but I wanted to check on the dogs."

"Come on in."

She entered the room and saw the envelope and note I held in my hand. "Did Dad leave you some notes to find?"

I nodded with a question on my face. "How did you know?"

She smiled. "Oh, he used to do that with us whenever he left on a trip. It was always great fun for us. He'd leave trinkets or money in the envelopes too, and we'd tear the house apart looking for them. He hasn't done that in a while for us, at least not at this house. He'd always leave clues for us. It was like a mini-treasure hunt. Would you like some help finding them? I'm good at deciphering his clues."

"Okay, thanks," I said nodding enthusiastically.

"Good. Let me see the first note if that's okay. Was it hiding under your pillow?"

I nodded again and handed her the note. She read it and said, "Okay, this is the first one, and it's not numbered so it won't be part of the note total."

"The note total?" I questioned.

"You'll see. The notes are all located in the bedroom because that's the room he is mentioning in the first note, which can include his office, bathroom, and closet since he considers all this his bedroom." Tammy smiled as she explained the clues. I could tell she was enjoying herself. "Then he mentions the bed, so most likely there's a note by the bed. Dad usually won't leave them out in plain sight, he liked us to hunt for them, but he also wouldn't put them in inaccessible places either."

Both of us looked under the bed. No note. We checked on the windowsill and no luck there either. I opened the top drawer of the nightstand, and there was the note. Actually, there were two envelopes, one with my name written across it and another with Tammy's name. I handed it to her, and she took it with glee on her face.

"Oh goodie, a note for me too!" She tore the envelope open, pulled out the small piece of paper, and read it aloud, "*No hunt for you today my sweetest baby girl. Know that I love you more than you will ever understand, and I am so very proud that you are my daughter. Love, Dad. P.S. Thank you for helping Elizabeth with her first hunt! P.P.S. Here's something a little extra, maybe a new outfit?*"

She pulled a fifty-dollar bill out of the envelope. "Yes!" she said excitedly. "Okay, what does yours say? Oh, see there are numbers on the front." She pointed to the numbers written under my name.

"One dash four. What do they mean?" I asked.

She answered while I opened the envelope. "There will be four notes, and this is the first one."

I opened my envelope. "*My fair lady, if I were there right now, I would be your shining knight and bestow a fluttering of kisses on your hand as I did in Monterey.*" I blushed because I knew what the referenced hand kisses really meant and was very glad that she did not.

"Wow, there's not much to go on there in the note, but if I were to guess…" She trailed off and opened the closet door.

I had never been through Michael's things and didn't feel right about it now. Tammy seemed to be quite at home though. I wasn't surprised. His closet, like the rest of him, was neat and tidy. His clothes all arranged by type and color made it easy to find anything. All I could think was that he would have fun organizing e. The flannel shirts were the most interesting hanging on the side. I couldn't imagine him wearing them.

Tammy opened up the middle drawer of a file cabinet tucked away in the corner and pulled out a large black notebook full of DVDs. She opened to the page that contained the *My Fair Lady* DVD, and there was the envelope marked two dash four.

"I can't believe it, how did you know?" I laughed taking the envelope.

Tammy grinned. "Oh, I've been doing this for quite a while now. I just seem to know Dad's clues."

"I would say so." I tore into the envelope. "*Elizabeth, my love, I love to watch pearly drops of water running down your back when you step in the shower.*" I stopped reading aloud. "I don't think you need to hear any more of this."

She giggled. "Oh, it's just Dad being romantic, it's kind of gross, but it's cute too. I would have never thought he could be that way. Definitely, the clue leads to the bathroom though."

I read the rest of the note silently. He wrote, "*Running my mouth over your bottom, I catch the drops with my tongue as I get closer to your heat.*" The room felt considerably warmer even with the window open and the cool evening breeze coming in. I was going to need a cold shower after this one.

We both went into the bathroom where there weren't many places to hide a note. There were no notes in the medicine cabinet or the drawers. The closets that held the towels did not reveal anything either.

"Wait," I said. "If I were taking a shower, I'd need a towel." I lifted up the top towel in the cabinet, and there was the envelope underneath.

"Awesome Elizabeth, you're getting good."

I opened this envelope carefully not sure what would be inside. I read the note silently, "*My lover, it makes me so happy that you share my passions with me. Not only the desire we share in the bedroom, but also the commitment we have for making the world around us better. I love you for sharing my eagles and the love you show for them.*" I folded the note over, smiled and said, "I'm not sharing this one either. Office. It has to be something to do with the eagle pictures."

She giggled again. "It's okay Elizabeth. I understand. It's still gross though, I mean, that's my dad, yuck."

I laughed with her. "You'll feel the same way about Jason."

"Yeah," she answered and pointed to the note. "But that's my dad, double yuck."

We looked around his office and did not have any success. "Maybe it's something else?" she suggested.

Then I spotted my new camera case on the floor pushed under the desk.

"That's strange. How did that get there?" I picked up the case and peered inside. The envelope was lying right on top.

Tammy clapped her hands. "There you go!"

I gave her a hug and held the envelope to my chest. I wanted to open this one slowly and savor it.

Tammy smiled. "Okay, I guess I'll leave." She smiled and waved the fifty-dollar bill at me. "I get to go shopping! Good night!"

When she left, I opened the final envelope and read, *"My little Hellcat, I hope you miss me as much as I miss you."* I nodded to myself and silently mouthed, "More than you know my love."

"Look at the last picture on your camera. I took it last night while you were sleeping. I'm the devil, aren't I? You looked so peaceful, and I couldn't resist. Know that I love you. M."

I turned the camera on and stared at the small LCD screen. I don't know how he managed, but there was a picture of Michael and me in bed. We were lying together naked with him spooning against me. I had to see more.

I loaded the compact flash card from my camera into my laptop and waited for the picture to download into my computer. When the photo came up on the screen, I gasped at the scene that he had captured. He had been right. My expression was one of extreme peace. My hair covered his face. However, the position of his hands was poetic. They lay against my breasts splayed wide, and they showed incredible strength and tenderness in the way he held me. I had always admired his hands, but until now, I never knew their true beauty. Even though we were spooned together with our legs intertwined, it appeared that I was leaning back against him, which is why there was such a clear view of my face. The moon shining through the window lit the darkened room. Since we had entangled our legs, the musculature in his legs was evident. His right leg covered my hip, and my right arm and hand covered his thigh. I was breathless looking at the picture, and even though it was not explicit in its nudity, it still was very erotic. This was better than the famous bathtub scene, which I loved.

I set my laptop on the nightstand so I could fall asleep looking at the photo. I slipped out of my robe and lay in Michael's bed feeling very contented. I stuffed the extra pillows I had brought from my bed behind me, while I wrapped my arms around his. Sticking my nose into them, I inhaled deeply, enjoying the memory of his scent. And, while he wasn't there with me at that moment, I could sleep knowing that he did love me.

The next day I avoided everyone. After my run, I worked continuously at my house. The book was picking up steam and moving along. When Tammy retrieved the dogs for dinner, I let her know I would be working late into the evening. I finally walked across to Michael's house around midnight and fell tiredly into his bed.

In the morning, Tammy already had the coffee made when I stumbled into the kitchen.

"You were late last night," she said as she poured me a cup of coffee.

"Yeah, I was in a good part of my book, and I felt like writing," I said, taking the mug from her and sitting down at the table.

"And here I thought you were trying to avoid my mother." She smirked at me.

I frowned. "You know it isn't like that." I felt guilty because that was precisely the way it was.

"Then I suppose you'll be disappointed to know that Mom won't be going with us this afternoon on our visit," she said, looking at me carefully for my reaction.

I tried to keep the smile off my face, but it was hard, and I was failing miserably. "Really? I hope nothing is wrong."

"No, nothing is wrong. Mom remembered that she and Great-grandmother don't get along very well."

"Oh?" I asked, curious for more information, although I knew I should have left it alone.

Tammy giggled and lowered her voice to a whisper, "Yeah, she called Great-grandmother a witch and then Great-grandmother called her a bitch. It wasn't a pretty fight."

My hand went to my mouth, and my eyes grew large. "What was going on?"

She looked at me conspiratorially. "Well, you know how Great-grandmother Helen sees the future?" I nodded while she continued, "She didn't see a good future for Mom, and then she said she saw a brighter future for Dad."

I laughed and then covered my mouth. "I can certainly understand why your mom would be upset. Well, we'll have a nice time. When you get back from school, come on over to my place, and we can leave straight away."

She agreed and told me that Katy had called and was looking forward to her visit. That reminded me that I needed to get my guest room ready for Paul. Tammy also asked if we could go out on my boat, and I quickly nodded since the weather had improved after the rain.

The drive down to Calistoga was fast, and since I had made it several times on my own, I no longer needed directions. Grandmother Helen was pleased to see us. She liked the chicory coffee and beignet mix I brought her from New Orleans, along with a package of tea from Marie. Michael's parents were coming over for dinner, and since we had fed the dogs before we left Mintock, we stayed to spend time with them too.

Candace managed to get me alone in the kitchen after dinner while we were doing the dishes.

"So, Michael has allowed Margaret to stay in the house." She shook her head and rubbed the plate she was washing so hard I thought it might break. "I can't believe it after all that woman has done to him. He keeps letting her come back into their lives."

"She is the mother of his daughters Candace, and I can understand why he does it," I replied, not wanting to get into this conversation with her.

"Every time she flies into Tammy's life it takes her weeks to get over it.

She actually does damage to Tammy by filling her head with stupid ideas and promises. Margaret never follows through with anything. One time she had the wild idea to move to Hawaii and take the girls with her. Michael had to give her extra money to get her to drop the idea. She's evil, and if the opportunity arose, she would probably try to destroy his life. She hated all of his friends and his family as well. I never could understand why she even bothered with him."

"Michael is phenomenal." I smiled.

Candace put down the pot she was cleaning and put her arm around my waist.

"He is a great boy." she corrected herself, "man, isn't he? And I know he thinks you're special too, as do the rest of us. Take care of him for me."

Wow! I believe I may have passed the mother test. A feeling of warmth went through me as she hugged me close.

Michael's father came into the kitchen looking for dessert. "Hey you girls, Helen said she made a pineapple upside down cake."

Candace laughed. "Steve, your timing is impeccable."

I went to the refrigerator to pull out the cake while he wrapped his arms around his wife and kissed her on the neck. "Mmmm…my sweet sugar candy."

She blushed. "Steve, now come on, I'm washing the dishes."

Smiling to myself, I realized that the leaf hadn't fallen far from the tree and was happy to see their affectionate nature. They reminded me of my own parents.

Tammy and I left late. She was quiet in the car for the first part of the trip, and I chalked it up to being tired. I was the chatterbox for a change.

Then she hit me with the bombshell. "Elizabeth, what would you say if I decided to go off the pill?"

I looked over at her in the dark car, and she looked serious enough. "Why? Did you and Jason break up?"

"No. But Mom and I were talking, and she said that if I feel like I found the right guy, it might be time to start our life together. A baby would certainly keep us together."

My head started spinning. Why wasn't Michael here when she made these announcements? What was her mother thinking? The woman really was nuts, suggesting that Tammy go off the pill and have a baby.

I began slowly searching for the right words. "Jason has just started school. It is going to be at least eight long years before he becomes a doctor. And, what about you? Don't you think veterinarian school is going to be hard with a baby?"

"I've been thinking about that too. I really want to be with Jason." She sighed.

My only thoughts were that Candace had been correct. Margaret tried destroying anything she met.

"Tammy, I know this is a difficult time for you, especially since you've spent the whole summer together with Jason. However, all relationships go through a time of being apart even if you are living together. Look at your Dad and how much he travels, and how much I travel too."

"Elizabeth, what if Jason meets someone new? What if he decides that he really doesn't love me?"

Ah, there was the crux of the problem, and it was easy to see where she had gotten the idea. That sounded like her mother.

"Tammy, that can happen whether you have a baby or not. Nothing can force him to stay with you if he doesn't want to."

"Yeah, like Dad left Mom," she retorted.

"I can't comment on what happened to their relationship. All I know, babies don't guarantee any relationship is permanent. I think you need to talk to your dad about this before you make any decision, and, it would be a good idea to talk to Jason too. It wouldn't be fair to spring something like this on him, would it?"

She would be a fool, but I knew to tell her that, it would shut her down completely. I hated Margaret for this. I couldn't believe she would set out to destroy her own daughter.

She sat back in her seat, and we were quiet the rest of the way home. I was thankful Katy and Paul would arrive the next afternoon and relieved Michael would be home on Sunday.

The kids arrived shortly before dinnertime Saturday night. Paul was delightful, and as it turned out, he was not a New Yorker, but a transplant from Atlanta. I could easily see how Katy had fallen for him because I too was falling prey to his southern charm, especially when he started calling me Miss Elizabeth.

We took Paul's suitcase over to my cabin and got him settled into my guest room.

"This is very kind of you Miss Elizabeth," he said as we put the suitcase into the room.

"Think nothing of it. The two houses are becoming one quickly. Just think of mine as an extension of the other one," I said showing him the bathroom.

Katy smiled shyly. "So, do you think it would be a problem if Paul had company in the middle of the night?"

I grinned at them both. "I don't know how anyone would know if he had company in the middle of the night, and since this is my house, I don't mind what goes on in the privacy of the guest room."

She hugged me around the waist. "Thank you."

Paul didn't look up but appeared to be very interested in the patterned bedspread.

We went to the Spanish restaurant, and coincidentally, met Debi and Don there. Margaret was uncharacteristically quiet during dinner, which made me thankful. I looked around the table and was surprised to find myself in this situation. If someone had told me that I would be sitting with Michael's family, including his ex-wife, three months ago, I would never have believed them. It also made me miss him even more.

He called me from the San Francisco airport the following day. He sounded exhausted on the phone. I didn't talk to him about the week's happenings because it would be better to tell him face to face.

After we disconnected, I busily set about straightening up his bedroom. I changed the sheets and set out candles in the bedroom and bathroom. Even if he were too tired to do anything, I would at least pamper him tonight. Giddy with excitement, I could hardly contain myself.

Katy, Paul, and I were in the living room drinking wine when Michael walked into the house through the back door. He greeted us, and the exhaustion was evident on his face. Nonetheless, he looked happy to see us. He hadn't shaved since he had left, and his day's old beard made him look all the more masculine and sexier. I wanted to jump into his arms but managed to hold back, and I could see in his eyes that he wanted to do the same with me.

Paul, true to his southern style, called Michael, "Sir." Paul was definitely a smart kid. I knew at thirty, he was no longer a kid, but fortunately, he was smart enough to show him respect, just as Michael had shown deference to my father.

We sat together in the living room drinking wine and talking when Margaret and Tammy came into the living room. Tammy had our dry-cleaning in her arms, and she hung up the tuxedo and my Monterey dress in the doorway of his bedroom. I saw immediately that there was a problem with my dress.

I bolted up from the couch and ran over to the dry cleaning. "What the hell?" I said as I ripped off the plastic wrapper.

He could hear the distress in my voice, "What's the matter, Babe?"

I whispered, "Oh my god, Michael, my dress."

Margaret looked directly at me with hate in her eyes. "Isn't that a wonderful dress Elizabeth? Katy left this dress for me, and you know she's taller than me, so I had to have it altered to fit me. It's wonderful. It fits like a glove now. The dress looks perfect on me."

"Mom that isn't the dress I left for you." Katy stood too.

I burst into tears fingering the dress that would no longer fit me.

Tammy looked from me to her mother, and then to her father.

"I," she stammered. "I let Mom take the dry-cleaning in. Oh Elizabeth, oh my god."

As I slowly crumpled to the floor, Michael caught me in his arms. "Oh

Babe, I'm so sorry honey." I could feel the rage building in his body as he stiffened. He stared at Margaret. "Get out. I want you out of my house, and I don't want you ever to step foot in here again," he said resolutely.

"Daddy!" Tammy cried out, her tears falling fast. "Don't Daddy, she didn't mean it."

He focused on her. "You can go with your mother, and you're a fool if you think she didn't do this on purpose." Michael led me over to the couch and sat me down. "And you're a bigger fool if you think getting pregnant is going to get Jason to marry you. I will lose all respect for you if you do that. That is not how I raised you. I raised you to be an honest woman. How could you do that to Jason?"

Tammy looked at me, and I shook my head. He continued, "No, Elizabeth didn't tell me. Katy called me on my way home. Why would you want to trap Jason?"

"So I trapped you?" Margaret yelled viciously. "That's a great thing for you to tell your daughters. Guess what girls, your father felt trapped by you."

Everyone looked over at her with surprise.

Michael said with a cold voice, "Margaret, what are you still doing here? I thought I made myself clear. Get out."

Tammy came over to me, knelt down in front of me, and put her hands on my knees. "Elizabeth, I'm so sorry about your dress. I'm sorry about everything." Her tears had turned to sobs.

I touched the top of her head. "I know honey."

Tammy twisted around to look over at her mother. "Mom, you better leave."

Margaret didn't say a word. She turned on her heel and left the room.

Michael concentrated his attention on us. "I'm sorry for this. Paul, I'm sorry. We're not normally so explosive a family. Tammy, why don't you take the dress and put it somewhere, so it's out of our sight."

She looked at me, and I nodded to her. She rose, picked up the dress, and left the room.

Michael sat next to me and held me. "Babe, I will replace your dress. Honey, we'll find one just like it."

The four of us sat quietly in the room until we heard Tammy and her mother come downstairs with Margaret's suitcases. The backdoor slammed shut, and there was an audible sigh from everyone in the room. Tammy came back inside a few minutes later, and she looked at us with despair and tears on her face. Michael patted the place on the couch next to him and reached out his arm to her.

"Come here baby girl," he beckoned to her.

Tammy quickly sat next to him, and he kissed her hair while wrapping his arm around her shoulder.

"I'm sorry Daddy." She buried her head in his neck.

CHAPTER THIRTY-EIGHT

We managed to salvage the evening by ordering pizza and indoctrinating Paul into the Hoffman's style of Monopoly. No surprise when Michael won, although it was possible that Paul let him win, which was smart on his part.

Even though the guest room upstairs was now free, Paul chose to continue to stay at my cabin. Michael did not say a word when Katy and Paul departed together for the night. While he and Tammy did the dishes, I prepared our bedroom by lighting the candles and running the bath water. I also wanted to give them a little alone time too. They had to do some rebuilding of their relationship. It was surprising to me how accurate Candace had been about Margaret. It was time though to forget about her. She was part of the past, and there was definitely no room for her in our future.

I slipped into a very sheer white nightgown and sat on the bed to wait. All the lights were off, and only candles lit up the room. With Barry White playing over the speaker, everything was perfect.

Michael's knock on the door was soft, and I could hear the wine glasses clinking in his hands. "Babe, it's me."

"I'm ready for you," I said, trying for a sultry voice. Yes, I was ready for him. I wanted to jump into his arms when he walked into the room.

"Oh, wow," he said as he walked into the room.

I stood up from the bed. We just looked at each for a few moments.

"The bath is all ready for us."

Michael smiled, and he put the wine glasses and wine on the dresser opposite the door. He walked toward me, and the anticipation of feeling his arms around me was slowly driving me mad. Finally, he wound his arms around my shoulders and pulled me close. I sighed as I felt his hands moving down my body coming to rest on my bottom. His lips found mine, and his kiss answered any of my worries or insecurities.

I brought my arms up around his neck as my hands stroked his hair and the side of his face. Michael's hands cupped my bottom and pulled me up tight against him. I could feel his hard length pressing against me. The intense feeling my lower body was producing made slow moans escape from my throat. My hips moved against the soft material of his jeans, and I wanted to be closer to him, but tonight was not for rushing anything.

He continued to knead my butt with his hands in a circular motion, which more than provoked a response from me. His lips traveled down my chin to my neck. His head lowered to my breasts and he slowly took a nipple into his mouth through the sheer fabric of my nightgown. His teeth grazed it, and it sent shivers through me. A moan escaped from his lips. His beard brushed against my skin, and it felt rough and soft at the same time.

"Do you want me to shave babe?" he whispered as he paid the same attention to my other nipple.

I only shook my head and arched my back to bring his mouth closer. "Oh, Michael. That feels so good."

He chuckled deeply. "I can't believe what I get to come home to. You are amazing."

He stepped back from me while I pulled the straps on my nightgown down over my shoulders. The gown slipped to the floor in one fluid movement, and I stood naked in front of him.

He breathed in sharply. "I cannot get used to seeing you. You are so beautiful."

I took his hand. "Come with me. Your bath is all ready for you."

I led him into the bathroom. He had a wonderful grin on his face, and he was waiting for my lead, which is precisely what I wanted from him. I pulled his sweater over his head and dropped it on the floor. My hands splayed over his chest feeling the rippling of his muscles. His nipples reacted, as mine had when I laid kisses on them. The groans from deep in his chest told me he enjoyed the attention his body was receiving from me.

Kneeling in front of him, I unbuckled his belt and unbuttoned the top button on his jeans. He stood very quietly watching my every move. I grinned up at him, as it was evident his erection was straining against his pants. I laid kisses below his belly button and ran my tongue to where the zipper on his jeans began.

Michael rocked back on his heels and hissed through his teeth, "My little Hellcat, you're going to drive me wild tonight aren't you?"

I looked up at him almost shyly. "Payback."

Slowly pulling his jeans down over his hips so that he could step out of them, he stood in front of me only in his briefs. I had to get him naked. I slid his briefs down, and there he was front and center. Grinning, I took him in my hands and tasted him. By his murmurs and sighs, I knew my action hit the mark.

Michael reached down and pulled me up. His eyelids were almost closed. "Bath time." He barely breathed the words.

"You get in. I'm going to bathe you," I whispered.

He settled into the water, watching my every move as I knelt down on the tub steps. I soaped a washcloth and ran it over his chest and shoulders. He closed his eyes while I leaned over and kissed his face softly. The washcloth floated away as I ran my hand down his chest to his belly. He leaned back in the tub, and my hand went lower to his thighs. I swirled the water around lightly touching his taut skin. His erection pressed up against his abdomen, and I ran my hand up its full length feeling its thickness and weight.

Michael watched my face carefully. I was in awe of this man. It was still difficult for me to believe that he was here for me.

"Come here baby," he whispered as he pulled me into the water.

He pulled me into his lap and wrapped my legs around him. His mouth once again surrounded my nipples, and the feeling of his tongue against them shot straight down to the area between my legs. My lower body rocked against him trying to get closer somehow. I could feel him in between my legs and with each rocking motion, the feelings intensified.

"Oh baby," I whispered. "I want you so bad."

My voice seemed to wake him. He stood and gently pulled me up. His kisses rained down on my face finally kissing me deeply as he held me against him. Our breathing was heavy and labored. He gently toweled me dry. The glint in his eyes told me bath time was finished. Michael stepped out of the tub and picked me up in his arms. His strength surprised me. He walked to the bed and laid me down gently.

His kisses started at the top of my head and trailed down across my eyes, to my mouth, where he lingered again kissing me deeply. His hands caressed my breasts and then slowly trailed down my belly. Parting my legs for him, I hoped he would continue his journey downward. I lifted my hips as soon as he touched the heat between my legs. His mouth accepted my kisses, and the thrusts of his tongue matched those of his fingers. It didn't take my body long to shudder against his fingers as my release came hard.

"Oh god, Michael," I cried into his ear. "Oh my god!"

His fingers didn't leave me but continued to caress me softly as my hips moved to their rhythm.

"You let me know when you're ready," he whispered to me.

"I'm ready," I said in a deep purring voice.

He slid inside of me slowly, and I gasped at the powerful feeling the motion created. As our bodies intimately connected, we moved together in a shared tempo. The incredible friction built up an intense desire of need between us. Again, the movement brought me to a crescendo exploding into a cascade of stars around me.

All I heard was his voice urging me on. "Come for me Babe, come for me."

He sat up and wrapped my legs around him, kissing me deeply. As my breathing slowed, he moved me on my back and caressed me with his mouth. He entered me, and again I could feel his need. My movements urged him on, and the rise and fall of his body against mine were ecstasy.

I whispered, "Baby, don't hold back, I want all of you."

He smiled and kissed me. His movements varied, and the sensations were filling me again. As he increased his speed, I felt the ascending need in me. In the blink of an eye, he was pushing me over the edge for the third time. As I fell into that endless world of pure sensation, and as my body trembled against his, his release came. His body quaked, and then he fell against me, holding me to him tightly. We lay together for a long time trying to control our breathing, not speaking, softly touching each other in wonderment.

Michael chuckled deeply. "We didn't have any wine."

I giggled. "I don't think my legs can move enough to get up. Besides, I definitely don‘t need any now." I stretched out fully against him and sighed.

"What did you think of the picture I left for you?" he asked.

"I love it." I smiled touching his chest softly. "You know what I'd like?"

He shifted as he stroked my shoulders. "What would you like?"

"Okay." I giggled. "I want you to frame the picture and put it up in here."

"You do?"

"Yes." I nodded. "And, I want you to take down Margaret's picture."

Michael laughed. "If you're going to be a photographer, you're going to have to notice when things change. It's been gone. I took it down weeks ago."

I whipped around and looked at the wall. He had taken it down and replaced it with a different baby picture of the girls. My heart felt like it was going to burst with happiness, and I covered his face with kisses.

"I love you," I whispered.

CHAPTER THIRTY-NINE

Our days fell into a wonderful pattern. We enjoyed the week with Katy and Paul. The autumn weather was still warm enough to take the boat out on the lake. The men took turns driving the boat, and while I watched them, it occurred to me Katy had found someone much like her father. I wondered if women tended to do that or just the opposite, choosing men who were nothing like our fathers.

We said goodbye to them at the end of the week. Michael appeared to be satisfied with Paul. Although I was sure, a father is never delighted with the man his daughter chooses.

The leaves were quickly changing and falling on the ground. Halloween time was rapidly approaching, and I looked forward to decorating the house for the holiday. I was down to the last few chapters and needed to be alone when I wrote the climax of the book. Michael was too distracting. If he worked in his office, one of us would be checking on the other, nibbling on each other, kissing, and dragging the other off to bed, and I was the offender more often than not. Therefore, I exiled myself to my cabin.

About a week before Halloween, Debi was due to drop by in the afternoon. We planned a trip to the local nursery for pumpkins. I worked at my desk while I waited for her to arrive. I had the stereo blaring loudly with operatic music. I found it best fit the bill when writing drama. The music reminded me of my mother too, and lately, I had been missing her. She had introduced me to music when I was young, and I would never forget our first trip to the Los Angeles Opera when I was sixteen.

I often wondered what she would have thought about Michael. I laughed at myself, and I knew she would have loved him. What was there not to love?

A knock on the front door jolted me out of my daydreams. I looked out the window and waved to Michael. He was always cautious about surprising me now, especially in my cabin. I opened the door.

"Is it loud enough in here?" he shouted as he walked into the room.

"Sorry. You know me, I get carried away." I turned the music down.

"Isn't that Turandot?" he commented.

I looked at him with surprise. "You know opera too?"

"I come from a German and Greek family, what do you think? Lunch is ready next door if you're interested."

"Oh," I covered my mouth with my hand, "I'm sorry I didn't tell you. I'm going with Debi this afternoon to the nursery, and we were going to get some lunch on the way. Can it keep?"

"No worries Babe. You and Tammy can have it for dinner tonight?"

"Where will you be?" I asked.

"Frank said they found a disturbance again up near the eagle's nest, and I'm going to go by and check on it."

"Please be careful. It doesn't sound like tourists anymore."

"I know Babe." He nodded in agreement. He wrapped his arms around me. "I'll probably be late because I'm meeting with the park rangers too."

I laughed. "Oh, so it's going to be a gabfest too."

He kissed me. "You know us guys, and once we start, we can't stop."

I threw my arms around his neck and kissed him back. "Don't I know it!"

Debi walked into the cabin while we embraced. "Well, well, well, I see you two are at it again. Don't you guys ever come up for air?"

I broke our kiss to look at her over Michael's shoulder. "Would you?"

She laughed. "Never!" She hugged him and, still joking, she said, "Okay, I want the same sugar."

He bent her over on her back, planted a big wet kiss on her lips, and then brought her upright again.

"Oh baby, I like it!" She laughed again swatting at his chest. "You know, all I get are promises from him."

"You know, I always say promises are better than denials." I laughed.

"You got that right. So, I'm starved are you ready to go?"

"Let me turn off my computer."

The three of us walked out to the back. Michael waved goodbye and blew kisses at both of us.

"Oh momma," Debi exclaimed. "He is one fine specimen of a man. How do you not attack him every minute of the day?"

"I had to banish myself to my cabin to write because I kept jumping his bones." I giggled.

"So are you living with him now?" she asked, as she started up the truck and pulled out to the main highway to town.

"If you call sleeping with him every night, then yeah, I guess I'm living with him. He made it easy, especially with me living next door."

"It's moving fast." She looked over at me with concern on her face.

"I don't know Debi." I shook my head and then paused a moment. "It doesn't feel fast to me. It feels like it is supposed to." I paused again and sighed. "It feels right. When I'm with him, everything seems complete. I don't know how to explain it. It was very different with Kevin."

She frowned. "I know, that's what is worrying me. It went very fast with Kevin. First, you met him at your job, then you were dating, and then it seemed like you were married, with no thinking time in between."

I nodded in agreement. "Yeah, that was a whirlwind. Kevin didn't give me time to think. With him, it was either say yes now, or I'm leaving your life. Michael isn't like that. His style is more relaxed and easier. Except for his work. He is intense about his work. He doesn't do anything halfway. He refuses to cut any corners, and it's amazing to watch him work. He is not lazy and does not shrug work off on someone else. I love working with him too. He's so generous."

Debi laughed. "Wow girlfriend, take a breath. I get it, he's Mr. Wonderful."

I puckered my brow with concern. "I thought you liked him?"

"I love Michael, as a neighbor and a friend, but now he is treading on dangerous best friend territory. I want to make sure that it's not moving too fast between the two of you."

"Don't worry. I've got it handled."

We stopped at the café before heading over to the nursery. My mood brightened as we lingered over lunch. Debi did not mention my relationship with Michael again, but he did come up in the conversation, plenty. It was late afternoon by the time we arrived at the nursery.

We were directed to the small utility road that led to the pumpkin patch. I always tried to be in Mintock for Halloween, one, because I loved to carve pumpkins and decorate the house, and two, there was a big Halloween costume party every year in the barn adjoining the nursery.

It took us a while to choose our pumpkins because we were looking for the perfect ones. I saw a big fat pumpkin and pointed to it.

The nursery owner smiled and shook his head. "That one is for Annie."

Debi laughed. "How does my mother-in-law rate the largest pumpkin in the entire place?"

He whispered, "It's not just for Annie. It will be the centerpiece of our Halloween decorations in the barn this year. Annie will be carving it, and she is making special baskets for all the decorations this year. It will be our finest Halloween yet."

"Leave it to her to make a big production out of Halloween." She turned to me. "Speaking of which, do you know what costume you're wearing this year?"

I grinned wickedly. "Well, yes, I do. I'm going as La Diabla."

"I am looking forward to you as the female devil. I'm sure your dress is short and red."

I leaned over and whispered, "And, very tight too."

"Poor Michael, he doesn't know what he is getting himself into, does he?"

We drove home and enlisted Don's help unloading my pumpkins. For dinner, Tammy and I shared the quiche and fruit bowl, which originated as lunch. She had a study group, so I ended up with the dogs waiting for Michael to come home. Since there was no cell phone reception on the mountain, I couldn't even call him to ensure everything was all right.

At eleven o'clock, I closed down my computer and closed the windows in Michael's bedroom. The nights were definitely chillier, and his big bedroom was drafty. I heard Tammy come home an hour earlier, and she checked in with me. She was surprised that her dad was not there, but she shrugged it off, knowing that he could take care of himself.

I turned out the lights in the bedroom and left the small nightlight on in the bathroom. He installed it in his bathroom when we began to stay together, mainly because I kept tripping over everything in the middle of the night.

I woke up at one and reached out across the bed. No Michael. I checked my cell phone and no voice mail messages either. I was beginning to worry about him. This was not like him. At two in the morning, I heard the bedroom door open. I switched the light on, and he was creeping in. He was trying to be quiet, but I was a light sleeper, especially when alone.

"Michael, it's so late."

"Sorry baby, I didn't mean to wake you up." He had a silly grin on his face.

I got out of bed and put my robe on because it was cold in the room. Wrapping my arms around him, I kissed him while he was trying to take his shoes off and almost knocked him over.

"Careful Babe," he said.

The look on my face must have said it all, "Have you been drinking?"

"The guys and I stopped tonight and grabbed a few beers," he said lightly.

"It smells like more than a few beers. Did you drive like this?"

He shook his head no. "Frank drove me home."

I stepped back from him and knew my face showed disapproval. "Michael, you're drunk. Why didn't you call me?"

He looked at me, and his anger was rising, "Now you sound just like Margaret. I don't need that tonight."

My voice rose. "You don't need to bring her into the conversation. I only said you could have called me. Didn't you think that I'd be waiting for you?"

"Look Elizabeth, you don't need to be so loud," he said with a bite in his voice. "You'll wake up Tammy."

"You might have thought about that before you came home at two."

"I would like to go to bed, I'm tired."

"Fine. You go to bed, but we need to talk tomorrow." I made a move toward the door to leave.

He grabbed my arm to stop me. "Where are you going?"

"I'm going to my house. You don't expect me to sleep with you, not in the condition you're in, do you? Let go of me." I wriggled free of his grip. My mouth was like cotton. I certainly didn't envision this night ending with an argument with Michael, not after all the thoughts I had about him before falling asleep.

"Is that your solution to everything? Running away Elizabeth? You really need to start confronting issues instead of running away from them," he scowled at me.

I turned around to face him. "Oh really? You're the one who said you wanted to sleep. Well buddy, since you're so wide-awake, then I will confront you. You better sit down for this one." I was surprised when he actually did as I said. I stood over him and looked down. I crossed my arms over my chest. "I don't think that I can believe anything you say to me. I never really get the whole story from you. It's always in little pieces, never a complete story."

He raised his eyebrows and looked back at me, "Really, like when?"

"Oh, you want examples? You know exactly what you do. When we drove to Calistoga, you forgot to mention we were actually visiting your grandmother. You gave me no opportunity to say no. Perhaps I didn't want to visit someone I didn't know!"

"That's just another example of you running away and not wanting to get involved with people. I knew if I told you, you wouldn't want to go." He frowned.

"So you gave me no chance of maybe saying yes. You just decided to spring it on me like your relationship with Tommy and Marie. Did you forget to mention this was your best friend? No, I think you knew exactly what you were doing. It's like you're parsing your life out to me in what you think are palatable amounts. I hate it!"

Michael stood up and towered over me. "And what about you? You're hiding the Kevin abuse from everyone, aren't you? You came back up here because you wanted to run away from the situation instead of confronting him and telling him to leave you the hell alone!" He said it with so much force I actually took a step back. He saw me flinch, and his expression on his face changed to a pained one.

Sitting on the edge of the bed, he buried his head in his hands. "Margaret hated my family and friends. She actually called my grandmother a witch. Well, that was the last time she was welcome in my grandmother's house. And, she hated Marie. She tried to seduce Tommy one time. Tommy! Can you believe it? He didn't tell me until years later because he didn't want it to ruin our friendship. He thought I would have never believed him. Yes, I used to hold back information from Margaret since she would normally blow a gasket if I ever planned something." He looked up at me openly and whispered, "I didn't want to make another mistake with you."

I kneeled down in front of him. "I'm not Margaret," I whispered back.

He blew out a long breath and ran his hand through his hair. "I know it Elizabeth. You've never made me feel like she did."

I answered him sincerely, "Then Michael, you can trust me. Tell me the whole story, and trust me with the facts. Trust me to make the right decision."

"I'm sorry I didn't call you tonight. I should have. I have to learn too that you're not going to react the way Margaret used to."

"I will try not to overreact either. I have to remember that you're not Kevin too."

"I guess we've just had our first fight. Is it over now?" he asked.

"Not yet. We still have to deal with me 'running away" from my issues." I used my fingers as quote marks.

He blew a deep breath. "Do we have to do that tonight?"

I closed my eyes and shook my head. "No. We don't have to talk about it tonight but soon."

"Can we go to bed?"

I turned the lights off and then lay next to him. At first, he reached out to me, and I wrapped my arms around him. We slept like this, he fully dressed and me in my robe until dawn.

CHAPTER FORTY

When I awoke, he was gone from the bed. The quilt covered me, and my robe was still belted tightly around me. Stiff from sleeping in one position all night, I rose slowly from the bed and looked out the window. Michael sat at the edge of the dock.

He stared into space when I approached him. The ducks had already flown south for the winter. He squinted up at me and patted the spot next to him. I sat down next to him with foreboding. This was not the way he normally greeted me in the morning. This reflective man was alarming.

"Elizabeth, after our talk last night I stayed awake thinking about everything that was said." Michael held my hand in both of his.

I closed my eyes because I didn't want to cry, but I could feel the tears brimming up. I did not want to hear what he had to say. I wanted to run away. He had been right.

He continued, "Things between the two of us has been moving fast, it might be time for a cooling off period."

Inside my entire being was screaming, NO! Oh, please no. My voice shook when I spoke. "What do you mean by cooling off period? Do you not want to see me anymore?" The tears were so close to coming. I inhaled, and it hurt to breathe. Was something crushing my chest? No, it was probably just my heart-shattering. The tears, one by one, started to fall down my face,

"You said you loved me," I whispered the words, and they were almost inaudible.

"Babe, I do love you, and that is why I think it might be a good idea if we take it slow for a while. We need to learn more about each other. I don't want to take you for granted, and I think that's what I did last night. I'm making you do a lot of the care for Tammy and I shouldn't."

"But I like to take care of Tammy," I protested, the tears falling harder.

He cupped my face in his hands. I moved away from him, which took him by surprise.

"I don't understand your rules, Michael. Tell me what to do, and I'll do it."

"That's exactly the problem Elizabeth, I feel like you are forming yourself to what I want. I want you to be who you are and to not get dragged down with my problems." His voice laced with an edge of regret. "Babe, I want you to be true to yourself. I don't want to smother you."

"So are we not to see each other?"

He reached for me again, and I let him. "Let's date again."

I scowled. "I thought that's what we were doing."

"Elizabeth, we are essentially living together, which is my fault."

"So you don't want to live with me?"

Michael shook his head and stared up as if he was searching for the words. "No, I do want to live with you, and I do want you in my bed every night, but I think we both need more time."

I stood up abruptly. "Okay. We'll give it more time." He didn't try to stop me as I started to walk away. I turned around, and he looked at me. "Let me know when you're ready Michael."

He didn't answer.

I walked back to his house. I dressed and gathered my belongings from his bedroom. I took the framed picture of us that he had taken the previous week. He had given it to me, it was mine, and it was coming with me.

Tammy saw me carrying my possessions. "You and Dad had a big argument last night." She said it as a statement and not a question.

I nodded again trying to hold back tears.

"So will you still be around?"

I smiled and nodded. "Of course, Tammy. I'm just next door. This does not affect you and me at all. You are always welcome to come over anytime, and you know you never have to knock. Your dad and I need a little breathing space. Whenever your dad isn't home, make sure you bring the dogs over to me for the day."

She smiled encouragingly. "I will."

"When you get home from school this afternoon, come over, and we'll carve the pumpkins, okay?"

"It's a date."

I left Michael's house and, of course, the tears came streaming down my face once again. What did he mean by cooling off? Did he even want to see me anymore? Entering my house, I went straight into my bedroom. As I passed the front window, I could see him still sitting on the edge of the dock with his back turned to the houses. I closed the drapes in my living room and closed the blinds in my bedroom. I knew the dogs were anticipating their run, but I didn't want even the slightest chance of encountering him, not this morning. Crawling into bed and pulling the covers over my head, I fell into my thoughts. Samantha and Topper were happy cuddling up next to me while I put my head back on my pillows. Realizing I forgot to bring my pillows, which remained on Michael's bed, I frowned. I needed to retrieve them later, much later.

Surprisingly, I fell asleep and woke two hours later feeling groggy. I looked at myself in the bathroom mirror. I was a sight with swollen eyes from crying, and there were dark circles under them from not sleeping the previous night. A long groan came from deep inside, but I resolved not to cry.

The shower made me feel better, somehow it always did. I braided my hair and put on shorts and a t-shirt. The day was warming up and appeared as if we were in for a warming trend even though the nights would probably stay cool. In the shower, I had considered my options. I wanted to fly down to Los Angeles, but with the house rented now, that was not a practical idea. I definitely did not want to stay with my sister or my father because I did not want to explain my visit. Nancy wasn't an option either because she was off visiting Marcus in New Orleans and expected to be there through Halloween. Besides, a trip to Los Angeles would be running away as Michael so adroitly observed.

My book deadline was quickly approaching, but after the emotional upheaval, there wasn't much romance left in my heart to write. Since that had never stopped me before, I fired up my laptop and sat at my desk hoping inspiration would strike me. Unfortunately, the only thing that did strike me was my continuous thoughts about Michael. That would teach me to base one of my characters on a real person.

Inspiration finally hit me, and I was lost in the world of my romance novel so deeply that I didn't hear Tammy come into the room.

"Elizabeth, it's me, Tammy," she called walking in from the back door. "Elizabeth?"

I heard her and held my hand up not turning around. She knew this was a signal to wait for a moment while I finished the paragraph. I turned in my chair after a few minutes, and she was already sitting at my dining room table with a small pumpkin in front of her.

"Hey, how was school today?" I asked, walking over to look at the pumpkin she chose.

"Good," she said.

I handed her a tarp to put on the table along with some newspapers, then opened the refrigerator.

"I don't think I've eaten today."

My refrigerator was empty. I'd forgotten Michael had all the food at his house. I made a mental note to make a trip to the grocery store soon.

She turned to me. "You haven't eaten today?" A worried look crossed her face.

"No, I wasn't hungry until now."

I opened the freezer and only found the chicken for the dogs and an old box of frozen pizza appetizers.

Tammy finished laying out the newspapers on the table. "I can't believe you don't have any food. Dad didn't bring over some lunch?"

"Don't worry about me. I'm not going to starve. I just need to go shopping."

I pulled out the pumpkin carving knife sets from the drawer and handed them to her. She laid out the tools while I picked up the phone and called Debi.

"Hey," I said when she answered. "We're ready for you and Betsy. Oh, can you bring me a sandwich please?"

They arrived about thirty minutes later bearing a platter of sandwiches, brownies, and sodas. Debi looked a little dubious at me, and I flashed a look, which meant an explanation would come later. I quickly ate half a sandwich, and we began the pumpkin carving process.

This was an art I practiced every year. Both my mother and my aunt loved Halloween, so Lisa and I learned early to join in the festivities. Aunt Ruth started the annual party over twenty years ago, and it instantly became a perennial favorite of the town. With the cabin being the last house on the lane, we never received many trick-or-treaters. Instead, we substituted this huge bash.

During the day, the kids participated in pumpkin carving and costume contests. Our baseball club always made enough money selling waffle ice cream cones at our booth to purchase new baseball equipment for the following year. In the evening, there was a big costume dance for the adults and onsite daycare for the kids to enjoy their own nighttime spooky activities. The pumpkin-carving contest was one of my favorites, and I had won my share of blue ribbons.

Annie helped me make my costume this year, and I had hoped to overwhelm Michael with it. Now, I didn't know what would happen. Though I certainly would not pass up Halloween.

We sat together around my table carving pumpkins, eating sandwiches and brownies, and laughing. It felt good to laugh after the day I experienced. Debi and I stepped outside to breathe the fresh, crisp air leaving Tammy and Betsy to work on their pumpkins.

"So what happened darling?" she asked as she settled down in the front porch chair.

Sitting opposite her, I nibbled on the edges of the brownie in my hand and sighed. "Michael and I had a fight last night."

"Yeah, he was really drunk. Frank dropped off Don last night too. The boys had too much beer. Thank goodness, they had the sense to let Frank drive them home. What did you argue about?"

"It wasn't the argument, it was afterward," I said gloomily.

"What happened?"

"This morning," I said while I fought back the tears, "Michael said we needed to cool things down between the two of us, and that things were moving a little too fast."

"And what do you think?" Debi leaned forward in the chair putting her hand on my knee.

"His response to our argument was confusing and hurtful to me, and I don't know what to think or where we stand." I sighed again looking out at the lake.

We would have a full moon for Halloween this year. I placed my hand on top of hers and directed my gaze back at her.

Her lips pressed together, and she squeezed my hand. "Want to know what I think?"

I nodded.

Debi smiled kindly. "I think you have scared Michael to death. I don't believe he has ever met anyone like you. You are an amazing woman." She chuckled. "Not only are you beautiful, but you are talented, strong, and have made your own way in the world."

"Oh, stop it. I'm not any of those things," I disputed.

She looked back at me in amazement. "Girl, you are all those things and more. I know more than one man in this town, who is either scared or in awe of you. Yep! You have frightened our little boy who probably always had it easy with women. With his good looks, I wouldn't be surprised that all he would need to do is crook his little finger, and they would come running. With you, however, he has watched other men watch you, and probably has realized that if he isn't careful, he could lose you." She sat back in the chair satisfied with her answer.

We sat a while longer, and then the two girls came out looking for us to get our approval on their pumpkins. As we stepped back inside, there was a knock on the back door. Debi and I looked at each other, and I shrugged my shoulders.

"Come on in," I yelled from the dining room table.

It was Michael. He came into the room, and the whole place seemed to light up with his presence. He looked uncomfortable standing by the kitchen. "Hi Debi, girls. Elizabeth, can I talk to you for a moment?"

I nodded and walked up to him, ignoring my desire to throw my arms around him, and silently telling myself to show control.

"What's up?" I asked.

He paused, and everyone's eyes were on him. "Can we talk outside?"

"Sure." I walked out to the back porch with him behind me. He closed the back door as he stepped outside. The room we left was quiet, and I was sure three people were trying to listen in. We stood close together.

Michael stepped back to put more space between us. "I'm going down to San Diego, to the zoo, tomorrow."

He already told me about the beginning of the zoo project. We discussed me accompanying him, but now I guessed this was not why Michael wanted to speak to me. I also inferred I probably would not be traveling with him.

"Could you keep an eye on Tammy, you know, if she needs anything?" he asked.

"Of course, she's welcome to stay with me."

"Well," he paused, "you could stay at," he paused again, "um, next door."

I closed my eyes. I only wanted to put my arms around him and hold him close, but there was no invitation from him, so I had to protect my heart in the only way I knew.

"No, she should stay with me."

He nodded. "I'd appreciate it."

"So," I said trying to prevent my voice from trembling, "will you be back in time for the Halloween party?"

"Party?" He blinked at me not comprehending.

"Yes, the Halloween party. It's next Friday night."

"Oh yeah, yes, I'll be back in time. Maybe you and I could go together. You know on a date."

There was the stupid date word. I thought it was silly when he initially said it. We were way beyond normal dating.

"I'm working the fair during the day, at the baseball booth, and I'll be dressing for the party with the other girls. So, I'll probably see you there."

"Yeah, okay."

"Was there anything else?"

We had both moved close to each other again, and I felt like he wanted to put his arms around me.

"No," he said, "that's all I needed."

I turned the doorknob. "I hope you have a good trip."

"Elizabeth," Michael said softly.

As I turned around my heart leaped into my throat, and I could barely croak out, "Yes?"

He leaned down and kissed me on the forehead. His arms went around my waist as he pulled me tightly. I let go of the door and put my arms around his neck. Our lips met, and I knew he was holding back, but the kiss he gave me was soft and gentle. I melted in his arms, and when we pulled back from the kiss, I put my head on his shoulder, and we held each other.

Moments passed, and he whispered, "Give me a little time."

"Is it me Michael?" I searched his face for some indication.

He pulled away from me. "Babe, no, I've thought about this all day today. I need to understand why I doubt myself. I'm sorry Elizabeth. I shouldn't be putting you through this."

I pressed my lips together. "I'm not going anywhere."

"I'll see you at the end of the week. Thanks for being there for Tammy."

He walked off the porch and headed back over to his house. As I watched him go, I wondered if his pain was anywhere close to the agony I felt. How did we get to his point? What cues had I ignored? Everything had been going fantastic between the two of us, and suddenly it explodes. How did I fail to see us heading toward this crisis?

Before he went inside his house, he turned and waved at me. I didn't respond, only tried to blink back the tears once again. I stayed out on my back porch until I had myself under control and then went inside to join the girls.

After the girls left, I wrote at my desk. Before I knew it, the clock showed that it was after midnight. It felt odd to wear a nightgown after so many weeks of sleeping in the nude. Getting used to anything was possible I guessed. I snuck a peek out the window. Michael's bedroom light was still on, and I assumed he was preparing for his trip. He always repeated this scenario since he usually slept on the plane.

I lay in bed for almost an hour tossing and turning. Sleep was evading me thoroughly. Both dogs finally jumped off the bed since I moved around continuously. Looking out the window again, I noticed the light on, but this time it looked like only the glow from his laptop. I wondered how he would receive me if I showed up at his door.

Finally, I threw off the covers and put my robe and slippers on. If he rejected me, it would not be for the lack of me trying. I slipped in through his back door and knocked on his bedroom door.

"Come in," he called. "Tammy, you should be sleeping." Michael used his firm dad's voice, and it was reminiscent of my father's voice.

I poked my head into the room. "It's not Tammy. Can I come in?"

He sat on his bed leaning up against the headboard with his computer on his lap. "Of course, what's wrong?"

"I saw that you were still up. I couldn't sleep and thought you'd like some company," I said meekly, realizing my excuse to be there was weak at best.

I stood by the door rather awkwardly, but Michael smiled and patted the space on the bed next to him. I smiled back, climbed up on the bed, and sat with my legs folded next to him.

"So you couldn't sleep?" he questioned.

I shook my head. "No, I tried. Too keyed up I guess. What are you working on?" I peered at his computer but at the same time was eyeing him.

He wore only his jeans, and I had a difficult time stopping myself from undressing him in my mind.

"I'm getting ready for my meeting tomorrow."

"I'm sorry, am I interrupting you?" My voice sounded flustered, and I'm sure Michael could tell I was insecure about being there.

"No, you're not," he said quietly. "I'm done. I was only reviewing my notes."

"Will you tell me more about the project?" I grasped at straws to keep him talking.

He looked at me probably to determine my level of interest, and I tried to appear eager.

"Okay," he said as he launched into his polar bear conservation project with the San Diego Zoo.

I decided to be bold again and lay down next to him. I put my head on his stomach ostensibly to get a better look at the laptop screen. He put his arm around my shoulder, and this act of snuggling made me very sleepy. By the third picture, I fell asleep.

Realizing that I was asleep, he must have set aside the computer and inched his way down next to me. I had felt some jostling but not enough to stir me from my sleep.

I awoke just as he was leaving the room the next morning. I was lying on my side hugging his pillows to my chest. I looked up. "Michael?"

He turned. "Shhh, go back to sleep, it's still early. I'll see you on Friday." Leaning over, he kissed me softly.

I nodded and lay my head back down. As he left the room, I stretched out to get into a more comfortable position and felt the envelope hidden under the pillows. Sitting up immediately, I turned on the light. The note read, "*Good morning Babe,*" at least I was still his Babe, "*No treasure hunt today. Thank you for coming back last night. It was courageous of you. Love, Michael. P.S. I'll see you on Friday, and that's shaken and not stirred.*" I smiled and tucked the note back in the envelope. Perhaps there was something to look forward to after all.

The week went quickly. Tammy and I alternated between the two houses since she preferred my big screen television. I was close to finishing my book and tried to be diligent during the week. Tammy spoke with Michael every night, but he and I remained off the phone. Things were still not resolved between us, but I felt far more positive than I had at the beginning of the week.

CHAPTER FORTY-ONE

On Friday morning, Debi arrived at the house early after Tammy had left for school. Debi, Angel and I drove to Annie's house. We tried on our costumes, and of the three of us, my sultry devil outfit was definitely the most revealing. Debi's was a classic sexy witch, and Angel, of course, in daring angel attire.

Annie had done a fantastic job with the costume, albeit, I thought it was too short, as it barely covered my butt. The shirred red dress with elastic on the sides and the front gave it a very tight and figure enhancing fit. I actually had to pull the dress down over my body. The lacey halter barely covered my bust and left my back bare. The four-inch red heels showed my legs perfectly, and since the dress was so short, there was no way to wear hose. With a red satin thong underneath, I hoped the dress wouldn't inch up as I walked.

Annie made my little red horns out of the dress material and attached them to a thin headband. With teased hair, all that would be noticeable would be the horns peeking out. Frank, Don, and Lewis walked into the living room while we were strutting around with our costumes.

Don was the first to comment. "Man, Elizabeth, Michael doesn't stand a chance does he?"

We laughed and shooed the boys into the kitchen. After we changed back to our regular clothes, we drove over to the nursery to set up the fair booths. Since the kids only had a half-day of school, the fair began at one o'clock. I wasn't sure what time Michael would appear, but Tammy had told me he had an early afternoon flight back up to Northern California.

There was a lull in the early afternoon as the adults went home to dress for the evening. The adult party started at eight. As we put on our costumes inside the restrooms, I kept glancing at my watch.

"Nervous?" Debi asked while she teased my hair.

"A little," I answered. "You know nothing is really resolved between Michael and me."

"Honey, don't expect everything to be resolved tonight. In fact, it would probably be better if nothing was settled tonight. Just give him a preview of what he's missing." She grinned at me in the mirror as she placed the horns on my head and fixed my hair around them.

Angel had applied sparkling gold makeup around my eyes, and with my dark lashes, the look was smoldering. She clapped her hands. "Perfect. I can't wait to see his face."

"Speaking of Michael, has anyone heard from the boys? Is he there yet?" I worried that all this preparation might be wasted.

"Jason said when he picked up Tammy that Michael was home. Tammy invited him to come with them, but he said he'd see them at the party," Debi shared.

Annie squeezed my shoulder. "Don't worry Elizabeth. I don't think he will miss this. He's curious."

"You think he's really coming as James Bond?" Debi asked.

"His note said, '*Shaken not stirred.*' I can only guess that's what it means," I replied.

We arrived at the party shortly after eight with the party already in full swing. I looked around and did not see Michael. Don, dressed as a pirate, had saved us a few seats at the bar and the bartender made us drinks.

I was always surprised by how Annie could transform the barn. They constructed a large dance floor in the middle of the barn. Throughout the entire structure, there were strings of colorful lights and small tables and chairs surrounded the dance area. The band on a raised pedestal played requests.

Don ordered me another after I quickly downed the first one. "Slow down a bit Elizabeth, I don't want to pick you up from the floor."

"I'm nervous," I replied.

Debi bumped my shoulder. "No reason for you to be. You are beautiful and incredibly sexy tonight." She had turned to face the dance floor. "In fact, I would say there are a couple of men making some circles around you, but I think Don is scaring them off."

He laughed. "As it should be, Michael is my buddy."

The band started to play disco music, and the dance floor was crowded. I still sat with my back to the entrance nursing my second drink. Debi elbowed me in the side.

"Ow!" I said complaining.

"Oh my!" she exclaimed elbowing me again. "James Bond has just arrived."

"Really?" I said excitedly.

"No, don't turn around. He's looking for you. He's spotted me." She laughed. "But, I don't think he's recognized you yet. Oh man, he is sexy. He's wearing a tuxedo." Debi leaned over to get the bartenders attention and ordered a vodka martini. "Don't turn around, he is on his way over here. Michael has figured out who you are. Oh, the ladies in this place are on the prowl." She giggled. "Women's heads are turning like whiplash! Wait, he's being stopped by one. No," she paused. "Okay, it appears he's safe. Do not move, Elizabeth."

The bartender put the martini down in front of me. At first, I was going to say that I didn't want a martini, but then I understood why she ordered it.

I felt Michael's presence behind me. He didn't speak.

I could tell he nodded at Debi and she answered him, "Hi Michael."

I picked up the martini and swiveled my barstool around. He seemed to be trying to capture the entire picture in front of him, from my crossed legs to my short skirt, halter, and finally my eyes.

I handed the martini to him. "Hi, shaken not stirred, I think is how you ordered it."

He smiled but still didn't speak. I thought I heard a hitch in his breathing.

His voice growled low, "Elizabeth, you look, ah, you look." He stopped again and blinked. He looked around him as if he was searching for someone to help him.

Don laughed and took Debi's hand. "You are on your own. Come on baby let's dance." They left us alone.

His eyes went back to me. "Babe, you are so hot. Your eyes are like fire."

I stood up, and my shoes made us the same height. I was close enough to almost brush against him and was glad that I had the extra cocktail in me because my knees felt weak. Touching his hand, I felt a jolt run through him as if he were stunned.

"Dance with me," I whispered so quietly he had to lean over to hear me.

When he did, my breasts brushed lightly against him, and it was as if I had sucked the wind out of him. I didn't wait for his reply. While I took his hand, he drank the martini down in one gulp and followed me out to the dance floor. We started dancing, and I turned to rub my back against his front. His groan was quiet, but it was there. His hands pulled my hips against him, and we stood dancing while my hips gyrated against him.

He whispered in my ear, "I don't think I should be dancing with the devil. Oh Elizabeth, what are you doing to me?"

I laughed a deep throaty laugh while turning in his arms. My leg went up between his legs, and I shimmied down his body and then back up again.

"It's not what I'm doing to you now. It's what I'm going to do with you later," I growled softly in his ear.

He gave me a passionate look, which showed his interest had been piqued.

I grinned wickedly. "Be very afraid Michael."

He pulled me against him hard, and we slowly swayed to the beat of the music. One hand was cupping my bottom and the other pressed against my bare back. Tingles of excitement pulsed through me as we moved together. It felt wonderful to be in a room full of people yet have the sense we were alone. My hands rubbed his neck and shoulders, he felt so firm under my caresses. I also felt a hard part of his body pressing against me. I reveled in the fact I was responsible for his reaction to me. He made me feel powerful and free.

When the music stopped, he kissed me, the first of the evening. The kiss was a hot eager one that made my knees weak. Annie and Frank danced by us.

Frank looked over and smiled. "Am I going to have to pull the two of you apart?"

We both laughed together and separated.

She wrapped her arm around Michael's waist. "Thank you, my son, for the wonderful pictures you took. The Smithsonian loved them, and we're sending my baskets."

"That's great. I'm glad I could help." Michael beamed down at her.

"And what do you think of my dress creation? This is your thank you present. Although, I don't think the dress does justice to our beautiful model. Do you?" She smiled stealthily.

His eyes widened with amazement. "You made the dress Annie?"

She simply nodded.

Michael hugged her and almost lifted her off the floor. "Thank you!"

She giggled and grinned. "I'm sure you will be thanking me late into the night. Come sit with us when you're tired of dancing."

We continued to dance to the next song. It was a slow song, and we wrapped our arms around each other and slowly moved to the music.

"I love the fact you're as tall as me," he murmured in my ear. "It's much easier to talk to you."

"You want to talk?" I questioned with uncertainty in my voice.

"No, I want to dance, but I love to whisper sweet things in your ear."

"You do? Like what?"

"Like, do you forgive me for being the biggest jerk on this planet?" He whispered it so softly. I had to look at him to make sure I heard what he said. Michael nodded. "Babe, I'm so sorry I was blaming you for my insecurities. You are nothing like Margaret, and it's stupid of me to keep treating you that way. Instead, I was an incredible idiot and then missed taking you down to San Diego to meet the cutest polar bears you have ever seen."

We stopped dancing and stood to look at each other.

"You're going to make me cry and ruin my makeup," I said softly.

"Are they unhappy tears?"

I shook my head. "No, but Michael you almost broke my heart."

He frowned and kissed me softly. "I'm such an ass. Please forgive me."

"I won't be able to take it again." I knew my words sounded intense. "Do you understand?"

"I promise Elizabeth. I'm trying very hard."

"Don't leave me again like you did. We can work out anything, okay?"

Michael pressed his forehead against mine. "I'm sorry, Babe."

"I forgive you," I said it slowly with resolve in my voice.

"I love you."

"I love you too."

Debi glided by with Don. "Sounds like a couple has made up. You two may want to vacate the dance floor if you're just going to stand there."

All four of us laughed.

Michael took my hand and led me off the dance floor. "I need some air."

I nodded, and when we left the barn, he put his arms around me again.

"You know, we can sit in the hay and make out for a little while. Or we can go home and have makeup sex," he murmured in my ear.

I wrinkled my nose at him. "It's too early to go home, besides I have something else in mind for later."

"You do?" His voice sounded excited. "What is it?"

"It's a surprise for later."

We stood in the dark, away from the crowd gathered around the bonfire. I reached around, grabbed his butt, and squeezed it. I must have surprised him because he let out a yelp. I giggled.

"Hey, what is good for the goose." He paused to pull up my dress in the back and groaned. "Oh god," he growled as he touched my naked bottom. "Are you wearing?" Michael paused as he felt the top of my satin thong. "Oh man, I am going to love taking these off of you."

I giggled again. "Pull my dress down, there are people around."

He righted my dress. He kissed me, and by the action of his tongue, I knew he was gearing up for later tonight. I lifted my knee in between his legs and stroked his crotch.

He grunted. "You're trying to kill me."

I giggled. "I'm the devil aren't I?"

We finally rejoined the party inside. Annie and Frank were at their large round table with our usual gang. I caught Debi and Angel leaving the table to get food and joined them.

Debi immediately started the conversation as we headed toward the buffet. "So what happened?"

"He apologized," I said simply, not elaborating.

She did not press for more information. "He certainly appreciated your costume. I didn't expect Mr. Cool to react that way. I thought we were going to have to roll his tongue up and put it back into his mouth."

"Yeah, his response was gratifying, but he is always like that with me. He's sweet with his compliments."

Angel giggled. "From across the room, it looked like he was going to have his way with you right there at the bar."

Debi giggled too. "Yeah, I could see that, Michael running his arm over the bar to clear all the drinks off and throwing you on the bar..."

"Okay ladies, knock it off," I pleaded, stopping her from continuing the comments.

Debi rejoined, "What? You know we're just jealous."

The three of us carried plates full of food back to our table. I sat my plate in front of Michael.

"Sorry there wasn't much in the way of vegetarian selections, but I brought what I could find," I said.

"That's okay Babe," he said eyeing me hungrily. "I don't have much appetite for food right now. Maybe later after I burn off some of this excess energy I have."

"Oh, do you want to dance some more?" I solicited innocently.

He pulled me down into his lap and whispered, "Now you know that is not the physical activity I am referring to." He looked at me with intensity. "I'm thinking a bit more horizontal."

It wasn't his comment that made me blush as much as my thoughts. It was all I could do to wipe away the image of us making love, especially since I was sitting in his lap, and the evidence of his arousal for me was pressing against me. He loved it when I blushed, so for him, this was entertaining.

He reached over and picked up a bunch of grapes off the plate. "Want one?" He put it up to my lips, and when I nodded, he dropped it inside my mouth.

The grape was delicious, and I picked up some cheese from the plate and waved it at him. "Want some?"

We were lost in our own little world feeding each other the tidbits from the plate. No one was interrupting us, or for that matter, paying attention. The public display of affection was a little more difficult for me than Michael, who obviously had no problems with being demonstrative. I couldn't remember a time that I would have sat on a boyfriend's lap while we fed each other. With him, it was different, I wanted everyone to know how I felt about him, and certainly didn't want to hide it.

One of his hands was casually resting in my lap, but the other one was busy stroking my back and playing with my hair. He pulled me forward to whisper, "Let's go home."

I stared into his blue eyes, and the flood of desire was there, so I smiled wickedly. "So, Mr. Hoffman, you're ready for your night of pleasure to begin?"

He kissed me, probing my mouth with his tongue. I met his kiss head-on matching his exploration with my own. We both looked up suddenly when Frank taped him on the back.

He stood above us smiling, but he addressed Michael, "Get a room son."

I turned around. Everyone at the table peered at us grinning.

"That's what I was telling Elizabeth." He lifted me off his lap, and Michael stood next to me, buttoning his tuxedo jacket. "We're leaving now."

Everyone at the table applauded as we left. I blushed.

The drive home was quiet. I had my head on his shoulder, and he had his arm around me. He pulled up in behind his house.

"Drop me off at my house and come over after you've parked the car."

"Oh? Not my house?" he questioned with a spark in his eye and a grin on his face. He drove to the back of my house. "Elizabeth, what are you planning?"

I squeezed his erection through his slacks gently. "I have to audition a new scene for my new book. Hurry," I whispered in his ear.

He visibly shuddered in response.

I entered my house and turned off the lights. I lit the candles that were already set up in the bedroom and drew the shades. I pulled back the comforter and folded it at the bottom of the bed. The bedside drawer contained a box of chocolate covered cherries, which I unwrapped and left on the top of the table. Then I removed all the pillows from the bed, except a large one, which leaned up against the headboard.

The back door closed, and Michael locked the door.

"I'm in the bedroom," I called to him.

He leaned against the bedroom doorway, still in his tuxedo. His eyes were dreamy and hooded. "Wow, you're even more beautiful in candlelight."

I took both of his hands and pulled him into the room. Waiting a moment before I spoke. "Michael, this is your night, but my rules. So, your hands won't be necessary tonight."

"They won't?"

I shook my head. "Let me tonight, okay?"

"Are you going to torture me?"

"There might be a little of that," I giggled, hoping I would be able to pull this off. It was always easier to write about it in a book than actually performing the magic.

Michael closed his eyes and held out his arms. "Do with me what you will my queen. I'm your servant."

I giggled again. "That's good, and I'll use it in the book."

I removed his jacket from his shoulders and hung it on the chair. I untied his shoes, and he slipped out of them easily. Next, standing in front of him, I untied his tie, and let it drop on his jacket. He reached up for the buttons on his shirt, and I shook my head.

"No, let me." He nodded and lowered his arms. I kissed him on the jaw and trailed my lips over to his ear. "Thank you," I whispered softly.

Michael closed his eyes again as I slowly unbuttoned his shirt. When I got halfway down, I kissed the hollow of his throat, trailing my tongue down his chest to the next button. His breathing became more rapid, and he was straining not to help me finish. I pulled his shirt free from his pants and undid the remaining buttons. Smiling when I saw the cufflinks in his sleeves, it pleased me that he was old fashioned enough to wear them. I set them on my dresser then went back to remove his shirt.

I pulled his shirt down off his shoulders. When I exposed his back, I shuddered. His muscles were firm, and they flexed softly as I ran my hands over them. I used my nails at the top of his shoulders and gently raked them down. The muscles rippled as my nails moved downward.

Soft moans were coming from Michael. "Oh Babe, I want you."

I pressed myself against his back. "You'll have me. You have to be patient."

My hands ran down his chest, feeling his nipples, and the muscles in his abdomen. I flexed my fingers and slipped them under his waistband to touch the tip of his erection. He took a sharp breath and reached out to grip the dresser tightly.

"Elizabeth, you're torturing me for real." He groaned as his voice was barely above a sigh.

I moved to face him while my hands didn't leave his body. Unbuckling his belt and the button to his slacks, I grinned at him. "I think you need to sit down. You look like you're going to collapse."

I kneeled down to remove his socks. His hands shifted to his zipper, and I playfully swatted his hand away.

"No hands." I shook my head slowly. "Let me."

Still kneeling in front of him, I slowly pulled the zipper down. His pants fell quickly around his ankles, and he stepped out of them. I picked them up and put them with his jacket while he stood by the bed. Coming back to him, I knelt down. Everything was evident in his low-rise boxers. It thrilled me to see the outline of his excitement. Again, the effort not to touch me created tension in his body.

I kissed the area just underneath his navel while I slowly pulled his boxers down. I examined every detail of him, and he watched me closely.

Standing, I placed my hands on his shoulders.

"Lay down," I whispered hoarsely. This was getting to me too.

Obliging me by putting his head on the one pillow remaining on the bed, he stretched his body out. I pulled up the sheet to his waist and tucked it firmly around him. If this move surprised him, he didn't show it because he stretched out and folded his arms under his head. Michael's expression was one of bemusement.

I stepped away from the bed, pulled the headband out of my hair, and shook my hair loose. It fell around my shoulders and down my back. His eyes were twinkling, and I knew he was itching to touch my hair. I untied the halter straps behind my neck and slowly let them down revealing my breasts. Closing my eyes, I ran my hands across my breasts and cupping them with my hands testing their weight. My nipples already were firm and peeked out from between my fingers. Opening my eyes, I stared directly at Michael who now was thoroughly enjoying the show.

I pushed the dress the rest of the way down exposing my red satin thong, and he almost sat up when he saw it. Standing only in my heels and thong, my hands moved over the sheet covering him, up his legs and to the juncture where his legs joined his body. My fingers lingered on the sheet lightly massaging him. He moaned, and his back arched away from the mattress. Slipping off my shoes, I climbed onto the bed and straddled him around his waist.

He looked surprised when I reached for the chocolate box. "You're not planning on eating chocolates now are you?" He groaned as he started moving his hips underneath me.

I nodded and took a bite off the top of the chocolate. I chewed it purposefully, inching up a bit, so his hip movements were not touching me directly. I scooped the cherry out of the chocolate with my tongue and held it between my lips. I leaned over and pressed my mouth to his while he took the cherry from me.

Next, I leisurely poured the remaining syrup from the chocolate over his nipple and bent over to lick it off. His hands moved up from under his head to hold my hips. I stopped and looked at him raising an eyebrow. He removed his hands and laid them out away from his body. Smiling, I continued my clean up job gradually swirling my tongue around the firm little peak. After licking him clean, my teeth grazed his nipple, biting down softly. He let out another groan.

"Elizabeth, you're killing me."

Grinning ruthlessly while taking another chocolate out of the box, I repeated each step for his other nipple. This time, however, I put the cherry on my tongue and offered it to him. He sucked the cherry off my tongue as I twirled it around the inside of his mouth. I wasn't sure how much of this I could continue because at this point I wanted him as badly as he wanted me.

The third chocolate poured drop-by-drop down from his chest to his navel. I had to scoot down, and my body now was in direct connection with his hard length. As soon as he felt me, his hips immediately bucked up and began a rhythmic dance against me. Knowing I didn't have long before Michael's resistance would crumble, and he would start breaking my rules, I scooted further down on his legs. I lay down against him and licked the sticky syrup drops while I slowly moved my body against his heat to keep him contented. He twisted his body against me, and the sweat started to bead on his forehead.

When I finished licking his torso, I pulled down the cover to expose him fully. His erection sprang to life after the sheet had bound him. I grinned and reached for another chocolate.

Michael grabbed my hand in his and with a growl said, "Don't you dare."

I giggled. "Oh, okay."

He let go of my hands, and I wriggled off him.

"Where are you going?"

"I'm right here." I pointed to my thong, "I have to get this off first."

"I'll help." He grinned.

I had it pulled off in an instant without his help. He watched me with a gleam in his eyes and patted his thighs as a signal for me to come back to him. I moved over him knowing the fevered state we were both in that nothing was going to last for long. He pulled me down to him and started kissing me. Centering myself over him, I moved against his length, and the sensation made me breathless.

I lifted myself slowly above him, and he slid inside of me. We both let out deep sighs of pleasure. We moved together building a steady rhythm, our breathing coming quickly. The waves of sensation began to take me over as my cries brought him to the edge with me. My mind centered only on the core of pleasure he brought to me, and my ending movements placed him in the same space. The sound of his release rang in my ears as pure joy. He held me tightly against him, and the strength of his tremors made me shudder with gratification.

I moved to roll off him, but his arms held me where I lay. "No, stay. I want to feel your weight on me."

We kissed with love and contentment.

He gazed at me with devotion on his face. "I love you, my little Hellcat." Michael chuckled. "I will never look at chocolate covered cherries the same way again."

My eyes gleamed slyly. "Oh, would you like some more." I made a false reach for the box.

He laughed. "Elizabeth, no more. You have exhausted me, thoroughly and completely."

We fell into the deep sleep of lovers.

CHAPTER FORTY-TWO

We awoke early to Michael's cell phone ringing. By the time he was able to find his phone the call had gone to voice mail. He checked the caller ID.

"Who called?" I asked him.

He shook his head. "Park rangers. That's strange." He hit the send key to call them back. "Hey, it's Michael, what's up?" He paused to listen and then spoke again. "No problem, I'll check it out this morning. Yeah, I'll call you back." He looked grim when he turned to face me.

"What happened?" I got out of bed and put my robe and slippers on.

"The town's police arrested a drunk driver last night, a reservation teen."

"And?" I asked, wishing he would just tell me.

He took a long sigh. "He had a rifle and three eagle tail feathers on the back seat. They called in the park rangers. The rangers couldn't tell if the feathers were from one of our eagles. I'm going to go up to check them." Michael reached for his pants.

I opened my top dresser drawer and took out panties and a bra. "I'm going with you."

He turned. "Ah, Elizabeth, no you're not, it may be dangerous."

I already started for the bathroom to turn the shower on. "Yes, I am going with you. I'm not letting you go alone." I flashed him a defiant look. "Don't argue with me on this, you won't win."

He looked at the determination in my face and nodded. "Okay." He rubbed his hand across his stomach and grimaced. "Hell, Elizabeth. I'm all sticky."

I laughed while I stepped into the shower. "You weren't complaining last night!"

"Meet me outside in a half hour. If you're not there, I'll go without you," he called to me as he left my bedroom.

True to his word, he had his jeep running in front of my house thirty minutes later. I grabbed my jacket and ran out of the house to join him. Leaning over, I kissed him on the cheek as I fastened my seatbelt.

Michael turned to kiss me properly. "Good morning my lover."

How could he turn me into jelly in an instant with only a kiss and a few words? I did not know, but I loved it. We drove in silence through the town and took the highway up the mountain. The jeep turned onto the utility road and followed the path into the woods.

A blast of cold air hit me when I climbed out of the jeep. I was glad I had brought my jacket with the hood because my braided hair was still damp from my shower. Tugging it on, I pulled the hood over my head and zipped up the front. Michael opened up the jeep's back door and removed his handgun from the locked case. The gun fitted into the holster he wore inside his jacket. He extended his hand to me and comforted me while we walked to the eagle stand.

"Are you cold?" He asked, "Do you need my jacket, I have a sweatshirt on underneath."

"No, I'm okay; the walk is warming me up."

We trudged through the forest. So many of the leaves had already fallen off the trees. The forest floor was a mixture of red, orange, and yellow. The air smelled of fresh pine and the sun had started to peek through the trees. It would have been a beautiful walk for us, except we had a clear sense of impending doom. The feeling settled on us. It was a dark mood, and it stretched out to make itself at home.

"Annie called me before we left," he said.

"She knows it's a Pomo teen?" I asked already knowing the answer.

"Yeah, Frank finally told her. They are convening a tribal council at the reservation offices."

We stood in the clearing, and I held Michael's hand. Seeing the empty cartridge shells around the tree stand, he swore under his breath. I moved to walk forward, but he caught me to hold me back. He pointed to the sky. I looked up, and an eagle was flying in circles above us.

"Is that her?" I was sure it was the female eagle we had named Ethel.

He nodded silently. "She's agitated. You can tell by the way she's flying in circles."

He climbed up into the tree stand, and I followed him up.

Surveying the surrounding area with the binoculars, he scanned everything repeatedly, then suddenly swore loudly, his voice anguished, "Oh, god no, shit!"

Michel climbed quickly out of the tree. He ran toward the ravine where the eagle's nest was located. When I reached him, he had already sunk to his knees.

"Oh god no," he repeated with a tortured grimace.

I dropped to my knees next to him and looked over the ledge. About twenty feet down, the male eagle lay dead. The sight was as if someone had hit me in the chest hard, and all the air escaped from my lungs in one big whoosh. Michael's shoulders were shaking. He was down on all fours now, and I wrapped my arms around his side and back trying to hold him to give him some sort of comfort.

His sobs were gut-wrenching, and my own tears started to flow down my face. We held each other for a long time. The crying call from Ethel brought us back to reality, and we looked up at her. She landed in her nest all alone.

Michael spoke first. "Elizabeth, I need you to go back to the jeep. We won't get a cell phone signal here, and maybe you won't where the jeep is parked. You might have to drive the jeep back to the main road. I want you to call the ranger station. The number is on my cell." He handed his cell phone to me. "Let them know where I am. I'm going to stay here. The eagle is crime scene evidence, and I don't want an animal to get to it. Can you do that for me?"

I nodded. "Are you going to be alright, I mean, here by yourself?"

He kissed me. "Yes, Babe. Please, tell them to come quickly, and call Frank and Annie too."

I nodded again and wiped my eyes with the edge of my jacket. He grabbed my hand and squeezed it, the tears still in his eyes.

I leaned over and brushed my lips against his forehead. "I love you, Michael. I'll hurry."

I ran back to his jeep as fast as I could trying not to trip over the tree roots and limbs sticking out. Staying on the path this time, I reached the car in record time completely out of breath.

Neither of our cell phones worked on the utility road, and it wasn't until I reached the main road that I finally had a signal. I scrolled through the alpha listing on his phone until I found the correct number and pressed send.

"Mt. Mintock Ranger Station, Ranger Harry speaking."

I tried quickly to spit out the information, but my mouth was so dry it was difficult to be clear.

"Excuse me, lady, could you slow down, please. Now, what was that about an eagle?"

I rolled my eyes. Why did I manage to get the dim person answering the phone? "This is Elizabeth Sommars."

"Oh, hi Elizabeth, I know you, we met at one of the baseball games. You have a mean fastball," he said with a friendly voice.

I almost screamed. "Ranger Harry, please. I have information about the eagles up on Mt. Mintock. My boyfriend, Michael Hoffman received a call this morning about the eagle feathers the police picked up last night with the drunk driver. We, I mean Michael, just found one of the eagles dead. He's at the tree stand and needs someone to come up. Right now!" I shook my head in disbelief hoping the message was clear to Ranger Harry.

"Oh!" he exclaimed. "Okay, yes. Oh my gosh! Yes, we'll get up there right away. Where are you?"

"I'm on the main highway and the utility road junction," I answered, glad he finally recognized the urgency of the call.

"Can you wait right there until we arrive, just in case?"

I agreed, and we ended the call. I followed up with a call to Frank and Annie. Frank was still at home. Annie had already gone over to the tribe's offices. Frank told me he would be there shortly.

I hung up and waited in the jeep. Annie and Frank both arrived in separate cars at the same time. She hugged me tightly, and the tears I had been holding back came out. Always prepared, she had a pack of tissues in her sweater pocket. I wiped my nose and eyes while she held me around the waist.

"Frank, go with Elizabeth back to Michael. I'll wait here for the park rangers." She squeezed me and looked at me directly. "You go back to your man. You need to be there for him."

Frank followed me in his truck down to the end of the utility road. "How far down is the eagle?" Frank asked as he opened the back of his pickup pulling out rope and climbing apparatus.

"Not more than twenty feet," I answered.

Frank handed a camera to me. "Did Michael bring his camera?

I shook my head.

"Okay, you carry the camera and this." He handed me a black plastic trash bag.

Tears started streaming down my face again. Not a very glorious ending for a magnificent creature, stuffed inside a trash bag. Frank, already wearing his service revolver on his side, picked up his shotgun and slung it over his back. We walked quietly and quickly to the clearing.

Michael was still sitting at the edge of the ravine and stood when he saw us approaching. I immediately went to him and wrapped my arms around him. Burying my head into his neck, I sobbed. Frank patted Michael on the back. We stood there a while trying to give comfort to each other.

"Are you up to taking pictures?" Frank asked him.

He nodded and sighed. "Yeah, I never thought these were going to be the type of pictures I would take."

"Sorry the camera isn't a fancy one," Frank said under his breath.

He turned on the small digital camera. "It will do for our purpose. The rangers said you caught the guy who did this?"

"Yeah, one of my guys pulled him over last night. He was weaving all over the road and drunker than a skunk. We have him locked up for the drunk driving. The eagle, well, this is tribal land, so the tribe and the Feds have jurisdiction. The elders have already met this morning. They are waiting for you to let us know if it was our eagle. I guess we have the answer now."

Michael nodded and began taking pictures. Two rangers and Annie joined us a short time later.

Annie walked up, and when she looked over the edge, she spoke several sentences in her native Pomo tongue. Standing between Michael and me, she put her arms around both of us.

"I just said a short prayer for the eagle," she whispered. "It will speed his soul into the afterlife. The tribe must perform a cleansing ritual to erase the violence done here. This land is sacred for the eagle and us. The eagle is our brother, and we have shamed ourselves. I don't know why the young man did this. We Pomo have never collected eagle feathers. It is not part of our culture to do so. He has brought disgrace to the entire tribe."

One of the rangers, using the rope Frank carried, lowered himself into the ravine. He took a few more pictures and then put the eagle in the plastic trash bag. The men pulled the ranger back up again.

When the bag reached us, Michael pulled the eagle out to examine him. He drew a heavy sigh and nodded. "Yeah, he's missing his tail feathers. Frank, you have our culprit."

"There had to be more than one person involved. He could not have gotten out of the ravine by himself," I interjected.

"Maybe, if that is where the eagle fell once he was shot. It could be that he was shot and after his tail feathers were removed he was tossed into the ravine," Frank answered. "Don't worry Elizabeth, we'll get to the bottom of this."

"Do you need us any further?" Michael looked at Frank and the two rangers.

Frank shook his head slowly looking at the eagle lying on the plastic bag. "No. Thank you both for coming out here to help us with this today. We'll complete the investigation out here."

"Let me know what happens." Michael shook hands with Frank and the rangers.

"I'll walk out with you two." Annie looked at Frank. "You're going to be late aren't you?"

He nodded, and she gave him a hug. "I'll see you at home."

The three of us were quiet until we arrived at the utility road. Annie hugged Michael before he entered into the driver's side of the jeep. I walked with her to her car. Annie slipped her arms around my waist.

"Be patient with him, he is suffering like he lost a close friend."

"What should I do?"

"He is your lover Elizabeth, just follow your feelings, they will guide you." She hugged me tightly. "I'll call you later. Okay?"

I closed her car door and returned to the jeep. Michael started the ignition after I climbed in, and we drove slowly out following Annie's car. He was silent. I took his hand in mine and held it in my lap. We drove home, and he pulled in front of my place to drop me off first.

As I exited the jeep, I turned to him. "Are you hungry? Do you want me to make you something to eat?" I'll admit it was a stupid offer considering I could barely boil water.

"I'm not really hungry, but thanks."

"What are you going to do now?"

"I'm going to take a shower and lay down for a while. I'm tired."

I looked back at him hopefully. "Would you like some company?"

"I'm okay. You don't need to mother me." I know he tried to say it kindly to me, but it came out abruptly. "I'm sorry. I want to be alone for a while."

"Okay. Let me know when you want some company. I'm planning on writing today."

He grabbed my hand and squeezed it. "Thanks, Elizabeth."

Tammy's note left on the kitchen counter indicated she was at the park with Jason and all the dogs. My bedroom was still in disarray from the previous evening. I picked up the clothes we had tossed to the side and made the bed. Holding one of the pillows to my face, I breathed in deeply. I could smell Michael's cologne. Discovering a new resolve, I walked over to his house.

Letting myself into the back door, I heard water running. I found the same note from Tammy that she had left for me on the kitchen table. I dug around in the refrigerator for fruit and cheese. I cut up a few different varieties of cheese and fruit into edible chunks. I looked through the cupboards for crackers and could not find any, but I did find pumpkin muffins Tammy had made. I sliced up a few and added those to the plate. I heard the water stop while I put roasted almonds into a small bowl. Lastly, I took two bottles of water out of the refrigerator and put everything on a tray.

I carried the tray to Michael's bedroom. His door was closed, so I knocked briefly. He called from inside. "Tammy, I'm trying to get some sleep."

I put a smile on my face and went on in.

"I said I was sleeping," he called before he looked up from the bed. Oh, sorry. I thought you were Tammy."

"Nope." I put on my brave smiling face. I placed the tray on his bedside table.

"I'm not really hungry." He looked at the tray anyway and picked up a grape and a piece of cheese.

I smiled inwardly. "I know, but I was a little hungry and thought if I was going to make myself a snack I might as well share." Walking to the other side of the bed, I pulled my t-shirt over my head. I slipped off my jeans next.

When I reached behind to unhook my bra Michael finally spoke. "What are you doing?" He stuffed another piece of muffin in his mouth.

"I'm taking my clothes off," I said simply. "I know you don't like me to wear anything to bed, so I'm undressing."

He chewed thoughtfully. "But why are you taking your clothes off?"

I pulled off my panties and put them with the rest of my clothes on the chair. I slipped between the covers. Inching over to Michael, I leaned on him to pick up a piece of cheese. I lay back on my side with my head propped up on my arm. "I'm going to take a nap with you. Is that okay?" I chewed on the cheese. He handed me a slice of apple, and I ate that too.

He turned toward me and likewise propped himself up on his elbow. "Yeah, that's okay." He ran his hand down my shoulder. "I only want to sleep is that okay with you?"

I smiled and gave him a soft kiss. "Yes, that is all I want from you. Now put your arms around me so we can cuddle and take a nap."

"You are something else, you know that, don't you?" he said as he wrapped his arms around me.

I pressed myself next to him throwing one leg over his hip. We intimately connected, merely one-step from making love. "Yes, I know. Now get some rest."

I woke up about an hour later. Michael was on his back with his forearm over his eyes. I lay against him on my side with my head nestled on his shoulder, and one leg was thrown over on him. Opening my eyes and noticing the plate was empty, I smiled. I was glad that he ate. He felt me move and looked down at me.

"Are you okay?" I asked softly.

He blew out a breath. "Yeah, I'm sad though."

I snuggled up against him and ran my hand over his chest. "I know, so am I. I feel empty like something is missing."

He sighed. "We'll be missing something more too."

I propped myself up on my elbow and looked at him. "What do you mean?"

He removed his forearm from his eyes and turned on his side to look at me. "Ethel will look for another mate. She may have to travel some distance, and she may not come back here."

"Really?" My lower lip trembled, and my eyes filled with tears. "She won't come back?"

He reached behind my head and brought my face closer to him. Michael kissed my lips softly. "I love you so much Elizabeth. You're crying for a stupid eagle."

I wiped my eyes. "They are not stupid," I protested. "They are magnificent creatures, you taught me that."

There was a knock on the door, and a voice called from the other side. "Dad, I heard about the eagles. I wanted to let you know how sorry I was about the news."

Michael kissed my forehead and mouthed, "Later" to me. He called to Tammy while moving out of bed. "Honey, we'll be right out, have you had lunch yet?"

CHAPTER FORTY-THREE

As Michael predicted, Ethel left the nest and did not return. Recovering from the loss of both eagles was difficult. I knew that Michael felt it more deeply than I did since he had bonded with the two birds after spending countless hours watching them. He grieved for them almost like grieving for a friend. At times, he remained distant from me, and I would have to redouble my efforts to bring him around again.

The young man who had shot the eagle was under eighteen. He had done it on a dare, and there had been two other boys with him. The other boys didn't have the nerve to shoot at the eagle, this one unfortunately did. The tribal council decided not to turn the case over to the Feds. Michael was angry enough to approach the board to argue for appropriate punishment. The boy's punishment for the drunken driving offense was a state matter, but it appeared his punishment for the eagle would be community service.

We visited the nest often in hopes that Ethel would return. Annie announced the tribal council would do a cleansing ceremony in early December, and they invited both of us to attend.

As the weeks grew closer to Thanksgiving, Michael's spirits seemed to brighten more. We would be celebrating the holiday with his family at his grandmother's house. Katy and Paul surprised us by flying in to spend the long weekend with us. They were now living together in New York, and amazingly, Michael agreed to let them stay together in her room. Somehow, I convinced a reluctant Debi to let Jason come with us to Grandmother Helen's house for Thanksgiving. I suspected, however, that Jason and Tammy would be eating two meals that day.

During this time, I finished writing my book. I worked with Robin and planned to finish the edits by the end of the month. Michael bugged me about letting him read it, and I relented. He approved and laughed when he recognized himself as the main character. When I asked him if he minded, he grinned and inferred we could retest the chocolate covered cherries pages anytime I wanted. I replied that it would make him fat if we did. He lazily smiled again and said we would work off any extra calories.

Angel let us use their mini-van for the trip down to Calistoga so we could all go together in one car. There was much bustling in and out of the house loading the car before we left. Finally, Michael issued an ultimatum to everyone. The bus would leave in five minutes with or without you. We set off on our adventure, Michael and I in the front, Katy and Paul in the middle seats, and Tammy and Jason in the back row.

This felt like my family, my very own, something I thought I'd never have. I was always a sister, an aunt, a daughter, but never a mother. It shocked me when I realized I had maternal instincts. How could this have happened after only three months? I didn't know, but I reveled in my new role. It was evident that Michael enjoyed viewing me in the job also. His stepping back had been subtle, but he allowed me to direct more in his house. He left it to me to arrange Katy's visit and ensuring that Jason would be with us for Thanksgiving.

Us. Michael and I had become us. It was almost a transparent change in the dynamics of the relationship. It happened one afternoon, right after Halloween, while Michael arranged a football outing with his friends. He checked with me first, to make sure we did not have plans. It hadn't struck me at first but sitting in the van with the entire family made me smile because of the change, a family was forming.

When we arrived in Calistoga, the house was already full. Michael's parents, sister, aunts, uncles, and assorted cousins were milling around the front yard, inside the house, and in the back. I lost count at thirty, and still more were pouring into the house. Grandmother Helen, in the kitchen, was in the center of all the action.

The weather was beautiful, and it would be a perfect day to be outside enjoying the autumn sun. Tables and chairs were set up in the back yard so I guessed we'd be eating there. Greek music playing from loudspeakers filled the yard and filtered into the kitchen. And the food! Extra tables had been set up in the kitchen and dining area solely to hold the food.

Michael and I stood in the kitchen surveying all the activity. His arm wrapped around my waist and he held me, my back against his chest.

"That is a lot of food." I pointed to the counters.

He chuckled softly in my ear. "There are a lot of people."

"I know, I lost count." I noticed a tall woman making her way over to us. She had sandy blond hair and the same sky-blue eyes as Michael. I guessed it was Christina, his sister. I stepped aside as she approached us with arms wide.

Christina threw her arms around his neck and hugged him. "Hello, my big brother."

He squeezed her. "Hello, my baby sister."

Still keeping one arm wrapped around his shoulder, she turned to me. Her eyes sparkled, and a wide grin formed on her face. Her dimples were in the same place as Michael's dimples.

"This beautiful woman must be your Elizabeth."

Christina stuck her hand at me, and when I offered her my hand, she pulled on my arm and embraced me.

"It is a pleasure to finally meet you Elizabeth." She paused. "All of Michael's emails go on and on about you. I figured he had fabricated you. You sounded too perfect, but now I see he was right!" she exclaimed.

I blushed. "It's great to meet you too. I can't believe how much you resemble each other."

Christina laughed. "Hell, I hope I'm better looking than this guy."

He slipped his arms around both of our waists. "I think I'm surrounded by two of the most beautiful women in the world."

"What a silver-tongued devil my brother is," she said, shaking her head while she laughed.

Candace came up behind us and squeezed herself in between Christina and me. "Girls, you are needed in the kitchen. Michael, you go outside, and make yourself useful out there."

Christina pouted. "Why do I have to stay in the kitchen? I'd rather be useful outside."

Candace looked at Christina. "What are you, fifteen? Stop whining."

As Candace led us away, I shot a look at Michael. He mouthed the words, "*Have fun*" to me. I rolled my eyes in response.

While the men set up a large screen television outside so they could watch football, all the women started their tasks in the kitchen. Christina and I sat at a table cutting up vegetables and peeling potatoes.

"Do you do a lot of cooking?" I asked her.

Her face took on a bemused look, and she snorted. "Hardly. I never had much time for cooking. I always preferred to be with the boys. My kitchen in my home is untouched except to make coffee. I can't live without my coffee. Michael, on the other hand, is the kitchen's darling."

I eyed him working in the back yard, and a smile crept onto my face. "Yes, he is. His kitchen-produced masterpieces always amaze me. My mother and sister tried so hard to teach me, but I was their failure. I can follow box directions well though."

Christina chuckled in response. "Boy, do I understand that. Michael was born creative. I think I was a disappointment for my mother that I didn't enjoy the kitchen more. From what I hear, you're no slouch either in the artistic department. I checked out the bookstore when Katy first told me Michael was dating you. You take up two shelves at the bookstore, well, at least the one in Manhattan. Sorry I wasn't able to make your book signing. Katy told me it was a grand affair. I wanted to meet the gal who was knocking my brother off his feet."

I stopped peeling the potato I had in my hands. "Did he tell you that?" I was curious he would speak about me to his sister.

She laughed. "He didn't have to. First, you have to realize everything is broadcasted in this family quickly. Five minutes after you left this house the first time, email and text messages were sent around the world."

Wrinkling my brow. "Why? Was my visit so unusual?"

Christina threw her hands up in the air. "Oh my, yes. My brother never, and when I say never, I mean ever, brought anyone home to meet my grandmother after Maggie called her..." Pausing, she leaned over, and whispered, "A witch. Can you imagine that?"

I glanced over at Michael's grandmother, and she was directing the traffic in the kitchen from her chair. I remembered my first encounter with her and the comment she had made. I could imagine Margaret in her viciousness saying something back to Grandmother Helen just for spite.

She continued, "After his divorce… and boy, I wish he had gone first. You know, I was the first one in the family to get one. I'll never live that one down… Anyway, he wasn't going to take a chance and bring anyone home because none of us liked Margaret. Everyone was shocked when you showed up." She leaned in closer. "You should have heard my grandmother. 'Oh, she's so beautiful and such a lady.' And, my mother raved on and on about your intelligence and the fact you are a writer."

Michael's mother raved about me? I bet that was a first. I couldn't imagine having that much of an impact on Candace.

"You would have thought you were the second coming, and I was prepared not to like you. I mean, because my mother did. However, when I heard about the nice things you were doing for him and his kids," she sighed. "He needs someone to do nice things for him. He's always there for everyone in this family and his friends. Always doing and never expecting anything in return. He literally saved me during my divorce. I was very depressed, and he pulled me out of it."

"Michael told me that you did wonderful things for him when he was divorcing Margaret," I said.

She shrugged it off. "I was so happy to be able to finally do something for him. I love the girls, and Maggie was screwing them up. To see someone coming into their lives again, it makes me feel good. You're good for him."

I blushed. "Well, he's good for me too." I looked at her directly in the eyes. "I love him." I couldn't believe I was confessing this to someone I had just met.

Christina smiled and took my hand. "I'm so glad Elizabeth. He is a tremendous man, and I know you make him happy."

Michael caught my eye from outside the patio door. The slider opened, and he walked into the kitchen.

"You're not letting Christina fill your head with all the family gossip are you?" he asked with a wink.

Dinner was a feast. The menu included turkey and all the fixings, and also barbequed lamb and baked ham. There were dishes I didn't recognize too. Michael and Christina explained them to me as I took small tastes of each in the buffet line. We sat together with the girls and their boys as a family.

After dinner, everyone moved the chairs into a large circle in the backyard. Several instruments appeared, and one of Michael's cousins handed him a bouzouki. He strummed the strings.

I looked at him in amazement. "You play?"

He smiled at me and nodded, playing a few chords. He chuckled. "It was either learn how to play or dance." He pointed to a group of men standing in a circle.

"I thought you liked to dance."

"Not with other men."

I clapped my hands together. "Oh good! They're going to dance."

"Only you would be happy to see men dancing."

Leaning over I whispered in his ear, "Only you dancing, and that would have to be naked."

He laughed heartily, and as he got up out of the chair, he leaned over and kissed me. "We'll see what we can arrange."

As Michael joined the other musicians, I appreciated his backside view and looked forward to the possibility of naked dancing later on in the evening when we were alone. I settled back in my chair while Christina and the girls sat next to me.

As the day wore on, there was music, dancing, football, deserts and of course leftovers. The evening wound down, and the younger kids began to nod off. We said our goodbyes and loaded into the minivan.

The drive home was quiet. Everyone, full of turkey, was napping. When we hit the road behind our houses, we dropped Tammy and Jason off at Debi's house. I felt sorry for them knowing they probably faced another meal. Michael next stopped in front of his house to let Katy, Paul, and all the leftovers out. The next to last stop was my house.

I turned to him. "I'll be only a few hours Michael. I promise. Let me finish the edits that Robin sent to me and then you can have me the rest of the weekend."

Michael sighed and jokingly said, "Go, get thee away woman."

I laughed and winked. "Get that bouzouki ready for the naked dancing." I shut the door, and he drove off to return the van to Angel.

CHAPTER FORTY-FOUR

As I unlocked the door, it hit me that the lights were not on in the house. I thought I had turned them on in the morning, but in the rush to leave, I guessed I forgot. Closing the door, I fingered the wall for the kitchen light switch.

Before I knew it, two arms grabbed me from behind. I didn't have a chance to scream because a hand clamped tightly over my mouth. My arms were held down together against his body. I struggled, but he was strong, and he pushed me toward the living room. I could smell sweat and alcohol on him.

"Well Liz, how have you been?" The voice, it was Kevin. I continued to struggle. "I'm going to let my hand off your mouth, if you scream, I will kill you. Is that clear?"

He sounded deadly. I nodded my head. His hand moved from my mouth to around my neck, and he squeezed my throat hard.

I managed to squeak out, "Kevin I can't breathe." He loosened his hold around me ever so slightly so that at least he wasn't cutting off my air. "What are you doing here?" I rasped out.

His voice contained venom that oozed out. "Oh my dear Liz, this is just a friendly visit. Since you cut off my money, you've put me in a rather bad position. I'm afraid something needs to be done."

I struggled again to no avail, and he just laughed. "Please Kevin, let me go. You're hurting me."

"Oh baby, you're going to hurt a lot more than this by the time I'm finished with you tonight."

"Michael will be here any minute now," I tried pleading.

He squeezed my throat again, and I started seeing stars.

"Liz, you are such a bad liar." The words hissed through his teeth. "He's not coming over here, well at least not for…what did you tell him you needed? Oh yeah, a few hours. So we're going to have some fun first, and we'll see if there is anything left of you for him."

I fought back again, and this time was successful in breaking free from his grip. I ran toward the front door figuring it was a shorter distance than the back door. I slipped on the area rug, and he grabbed me by the hair. His arms came crashing down on me, pushing me to the floor. Screaming, I hit the hardwood floor roughly, and he was on top of me in an instant. The fall had knocked me breathless, but we continued to grapple. He was simply stronger than I was. He quickly flipped me on my back and straddled my hips. I continued to wrestle him with my arms.

"Get off of me Kevin, I mean it!"

He laughed and pulled a switchblade from his back pocket. It popped open. The blade was long and large.

"I would suggest you settle yourself down a little Liz."

I stopped moving when I saw the gleaming knife. "What are you going to do with that?"

He drew his face close to mine pinning my arms between us. I could smell the stench of the alcohol on his breath. It was obvious he had been drinking heavily which lead to this bravado.

"Let's say this is my persuader." He ran the knife's edge against my jawline. "You and I are going to have a little fun first. I would have preferred something more comfortable like your bed, but it looks like you chose the floor."

He moved his lips over mine and bit my lower lip hard. I screamed a muffled cry and ran my tongue over my lips to see if he had drawn blood. Unfortunately, he took the action as encouragement.

He smiled. "That's good Liz. All I want is a little cooperation from you." His voice and eyes filled with poison.

As he straightened, I could feel the tears welling in my eyes. They started to run out down to my ears.

"Please Kevin don't do this, please," I begged.

He laughed. "Oh, you still know how to turn me on. I always loved those tears. They make me hot," he hissed again. He moved against me making grinding motions with his hips.

"I'll give you money. Whatever you want. Just stop this!" I sputtered out in between sobs.

"Oh, I know you will. But first, let's work off some of this tension, shall we?"

He ran the knife up my blouse, and the buttons ripped away exposing my bra. Sliding the blade under the front of my bra, he lifted it up and cut it open. Then he ran his sweaty hand over my breasts and pinched them hard, his grimy nails digging into my skin.

"I know you like this, don't you? Tell me you like this!" he yelled.

Bile rose up in my throat and made me nauseous at his touch. I shook my head from side to side and cried, "No! You're hurting me, please stop."

My tears turned to sobs. I struggled under him, and as soon as I did, his fist came down onto my face. The hit was so hard I wouldn't have been surprised if he had broken my jaw.

"Stop fighting me you stupid bitch, or I'm going to make this even more painful!"

The pain on my face was unbelievable, but I froze under him. He pushed my skirt up to my waist, and he made fast work of my panties by cutting them off roughly. His knee forced my legs apart.

"Please Kevin, don't do this," I pleaded.

He laughed viciously. "Keep on begging. It gets me hotter."

I shrank down against the floor as he waved the knife around me. He ran the blade down my stomach to the area between my legs.

He laughed again. "Hell, maybe if I fuck you enough, I'll get you pregnant. Didn't you always want that? What would your boyfriend do if you were pregnant by me?"

Shock and confusion registered on my face, and when Kevin saw it, he sneered at me. "Yeah you stupid bitch, you were the gullible fool weren't you? You never knew I slipped the birth control pills in your coffee every morning. I paid that damn doctor to lie to you. I always controlled everything."

The tears ran down my face. My brain was not registering what he was saying. "Don't do this, you can leave, I won't tell anyone, please."

I heard his jeans unzip, and actually hoped he would be aroused enough because if he wasn't, I would pay for it with more beatings. When my body didn't excite him enough, hitting me usually did. I looked down at him, and he was still flaccid.

His punches began. First to my ribs, and I felt something give way deep inside of me. I screamed from the pain. My breaths came in short gulps because it hurt to breathe.

Following quickly, he delivered an open-handed blow to the other side of my face. Wetness started to trickle from my nose and mouth. Another raging blow to my face made my vision blurry. I closed my eyes. The fury and loathing on his face was startling. He wanted to kill me. I was not going to let this happen.

Struggling again, I yelled, "No!" and "Help me!" Someone had to hear me. I fought him with everything inside of me.

I did not see the knife go into my body. I did not even feel it at first. I became conscious that he had buried that large blade into my left shoulder when I turned to look at it. I don't think he realized that he had done it either. When he pulled the knife out, I heard it grind against my collarbone. That was when the sharp, searing pain started. The pain was hot and burning as it flashed through me. I screamed. It was as if I woke Kevin from a dream. His eyes stared as he held up the bloody knife, and my blood slowly dripped onto my bra.

I screamed again. Again, his fist connected with my face, pounding me on the side of my head. His fingers wrapped around my throat and squeezed to prevent my screams. In the distance, someone was calling my name. My real name. "Elizabeth!" It was Michael's voice. I was sure of it. I couldn't see anything except for black spots. I felt a heavy weight lifted off my body. I heard scuffling and the breaking glass. I wanted to scream, "*No he has a knife!*" but the world went all black.

CHAPTER FORTY-FIVE

I awoke to the incessant alarm clock. All I heard was beep, beep, beep.

"Will someone turn off that damn alarm clock? It's too early to get up," I said drowsily. I moved to reach over to shut it off, but someone held my hand. My body hurt. Why did my body hurt? "Oh, god." I moaned. I hurt badly.

"Dad, she's awake." It was Tammy's voice. What was she doing in our bedroom?

I looked over to the person holding my hand. It was Michael. Why was he sitting on a chair next to the bed with his head on the mattress? Why wasn't he cuddled up with me? I tried to move again, but something was sticking to my arm.

He raised his head to look at me. "Shhh … Babe … it is okay." He pulled my arm down. "No honey, don't pull those out." He motioned to the tubes.

I looked around and concluded we were not in our bedroom. This was a hospital. I was in a hospital bed. The persistent beeping was a machine next to me.

All the memories flooded back to me in a flash. "Oh god, Michael, Kevin."

"It's okay my love, it is okay." He held my hand against his lips.

I brushed my fingers along his cheek. He had a deep bruise under his eye.

"They're letting us take turns in here. Your dad and Lisa are waiting outside. Do you want me to get them?" He turned to Tammy. "Please let the nurses know that she's awake."

She nodded and left the room. He turned back to me. I continued to cling to his hand, and he brushed through my hair with his other hand.

"Tell me what happened. Why is your eye like that? I heard your voice calling to me."

The doctor and nurse bustled in. I could hear Tammy and my family talking before the door closed again. The doctor held my chart reading the pages.

He leaned over the bed. "Good morning Elizabeth, I'm Doctor Howard, how are you feeling?" He reached above me and flipped a switch that turned off the beeping. "Susan will you get another bag?" he instructed the nurse.

Michael started to back away, but I clung to his hand, so he remained seated.

"Elizabeth, let go of your husband's hand and let me examine you. He'll be right there," Doctor Howard said.

I flashed Michael a look, but he just smiled at me and winked.

The doctor started to probe my chest and rib area, and I cried out in pain. "Still a little tender there? We'll take care of that." He checked his watch and wrote on my chart. "Let's give her some more of the pain meds too."

He lifted up the bandage covering my shoulder, and I looked over to the area. There were neat stitches in a row where Kevin had stabbed me.

"This looks good." The doctor smiled at me. "The blade didn't go as deep as we first thought, so you should heal up very nicely. I'll stop back this afternoon, and we'll see how you're doing. If everything is going okay, we'll think about sending you home tomorrow."

The doctor closed the chart and handed it to the nurse. He left the room and Michael moved back over to the bed to take my hand.

As the nurse left, she said, "Your family is waiting to see you. You can have two visitors at a time. Would you like me to let one of them in?"

"Thanks," I said, "but, give me a few minutes, please. I'd like to talk to Michael for a moment."

She nodded and left.

I gripped his hand. "Husband?" I queried.

He looked chagrined and ran his free hand through his hair. "Yeah, it was easier. The paramedics wouldn't let me ride with you unless I was your husband. Then later here at the hospital, you seemed to calm down more when I was in the room with you. So we just continued with the charade."

"My dad and Lisa went with it?" I asked.

Michael smiled. "Yeah. You seemed pretty upset every time I left the room."

"Was I conscious?"

"In and out." He sighed squeezing my hand to his cheek. He appeared as if ready to cry. "You don't remember?"

I shook my head with a bewildered look.

"I guess it was the morphine they gave you. You were in a lot of pain," he said, bringing my hand to his lips.

"Why does my side hurt so much?" I felt around under the covers and found my torso covered with tape.

"You have two cracked ribs and bad bruising but thank God no internal injuries. God, Elizabeth it was so awful. That animal beat you with his bare hands."

He shook his head and rested his forehead on the mattress. When he lifted his head, tears ran down his cheeks. My heart felt like it was breaking when I saw his face. His eyes showed nothing but deep pain.

"There was so much blood everywhere. On your face, your body, the floor." His body shuddered. "I thought I had lost you. I wanted to kill him and to break him with my own hands. You were lying so still. Then I saw your shallow breathing. Oh god, I cried when I saw you breathing."

"You were there, I heard you, I couldn't see you, but I heard your voice. How did you know to come?"

He drew a long breath and wiped the tears from his face. "I was talking to Lewis after bringing back their van. All of a sudden, I remembered that the lights were not on at your house when I dropped you off. I recalled you turning them on before we left. If I hadn't seen the scene so clearly in my mind, I wouldn't have panicked. I took the keys, yelling at Lewis to call the police. It was dark in your house, but I heard you screaming, and I saw him on top of you hitting you. Oh god Elizabeth, the blood, it was all over his hands and the knife." His forehead rested again on the bed while he shook his head back and forth.

He took another deep breath and raised his head to look at me. "Oh, baby. I pulled him off you, and he had his pants open. I knew what he wanted to do to you. He went for me with the knife. I was able to get it away from him. I wanted to kill him."

My eyes widened. "Michael did you…?" I stopped before finishing the sentence.

He shook his head. "No, we fought, and he heard the police car siren and ran. I just wanted him out of my way so that I could get to you."

"Where is he?" I asked shifting uncomfortably in the bed.

"The police caught him just outside of town, he is in jail." The worry in his eyes was evident. As much as it appeared I was clinging to his hand, I knew he was holding on to me too.

I closed my eyes feeling dizzy. How did this all happen? "What day is it?"

"It's Sunday."

How could I have lost three days? All I remembered was the attack, and that was Thursday.

The door opened, and my father's head popped in. "Hey Sweet Pea, how are you doing?" Just like my father, never waiting for an invitation. He walked over to the bed.

"Hi Daddy, I bet I look like a mess," I said, trying to smile, but it hurt.

Michael stood to leave. "I'll give you guys some privacy."

I grabbed his arm and cried out, "No! I don't want you to go."

"Honey, he's been right by your bed for days. Why don't you let him go home so he can get some rest?" Dad suggested.

I looked at Michael and realized that I had not noticed his three-day beard. I looked ashamed. "I'm sorry. Yes, of course, you can go." I let go of his arm.

He leaned over and brushed my lips with his. It was the barest of touches, and I could feel that my lips were swollen. I remembered how hard Kevin had hit me to make my mouth bleed.

Michael straightened up and squeezed my free hand. "I'm not going anywhere, Babe. I'll be right outside."

I saw my father give him a hard glance, but he simply ignored it. I nodded. "Okay."

After Michael left, my father sat on the edge of the bed. "You're selfish Bess. He has been here for three days. The hospital finally let him use the shower in the doctor's lounge. He hasn't moved from your bedside, sleeping in that chair. Lisa and I are here, we can take care of you."

I didn't reply but just looked at him. My father made me feel bad, but I couldn't bear to have Michael leave me. Not right now. That thought made my chest hurt.

My father told me that Kevin had stolen the car he was driving. He had borrowed heavily on the house in Torrance, and it was in the foreclosure process. Kevin had a document in his possession that he was going to force me to sign to continue the alimony payments, plus a lump sum. My father had already spoken to the county district attorney. They were going to charge him with attempted rape and murder as well as extortion. Kevin would face a very long sentence.

When the nurse bustled into the room, she looked at me. "Just a few more minutes of visiting, and then you need your rest." She changed out the IV bag and then pressed the pain medication syringe into my IV. "We're going to start pulling you back from the heavy-duty pain meds. This should make you feel better. Your husband asked us to get you some gelatin and some broth because he was worried you'd be hungry. I'll get that for you right away." She left the room.

My father gritted his teeth and said under his breath, "Husband." He huffed.

"Daddy, what's going on between you and Michael?"

"Nothing for you to worry about Sweet Pea." He patted my hand protectively.

"Dad?" I said insistently pursing my lips together, which made them hurt and I winced.

"Honey, you know Lisa, and I can take care of you. You don't need to have him around."

I looked at my father squarely. "Dad, I'm in love with him."

His eyes showed shock. "When did this happen? Bess, you have only known him for a couple of months. Please don't go and make another Kevin mistake. Has he said he's in love with you?"

I nodded slowly. "Yes." The Kevin comment rubbed salt in my open wounds.

Dad raked his hand through his hair and sighed heavily. "Bess I want you to be careful."

I pursed my lips again, this time prepared for the pain, so I didn't wince. "I'm tired, Dad."

He sighed again and rose from the bed leaning over and kissing my forehead, which was probably the only place on my body not bruised. "I almost lost you my sweetest of peas."

Michael chose that moment to walk back in carrying gelatin and pudding cups. My father flashed him an even more hostile look and left the room.

He sat down again in the chair by the bed and put the food on the bed table. "The nurse is bringing you some broth." He stuck a spoon into the gelatin. "Will you take a bite for me?"

"Only if you promise me to go home and get some rest," I said taking the spoonful. I made a face as I put it in my mouth. "I hate gelatin. Let me have the pudding instead."

He scooped pudding onto the spoon and gave it to me. "I am not leaving the hospital until you are ready to go home."

I ate the pudding slowly, licking it from the spoon. "They are not going to release me today. So please, for me, go home. I'm sure other people can feed me pudding." I motioned to all the flowers in the room. I felt the pain medication beginning to take effect. "Please, go home. Take a bath. Get some rest. You can come back tonight. Otherwise, I'm just going to lay here and worry about you."

He rose from the chair and sat on the edge of the bed. Leaning over me he softly licked some pudding that had landed on my chin. His lips moved to my mouth, and they kissed me softly. I couldn't move my lips enough to respond to his kiss, so I brushed my hand against his face.

"I love you my beautiful, strong woman. I will never leave you, but I will go home for a while."

He continued to kiss me softly. His kisses touched my cheeks, eyelids, and all those places that surely showed terrible bruises. I wanted his arms around me, holding me close, but I knew that would be a fool's folly. I hurt barely breathing. I didn't want to imagine what actually moving was going to feel like.

Standing up from the bed, he resigned to leave. "I'll be back tonight."

"I'll be here waiting," I said, closing my eyes. As he left, my sister came into the room to take her turn.

True to the doctor's words, the hospital released me the following day in a flurry of activity. I was bound to a wheelchair in my house for a week. Even though my legs had no injury, the doctor did not want me falling with my cracked ribs. I was supposed to allow someone else to push me around in the chair. I would be a terrible patient at home.

Arriving home, I was afraid to see the condition of the house after the attack. Katy and Tammy had cleaned the mess after the police were finished. Two lamps and several nick-knacks were broken in the assault, but overall the damage was minimal.

My first act was to veto Michael's suggestion that I stay at his house. Lisa and my father were downright shocked at the proposal. I hadn't enlightened them that we were almost living together before the attack. He said it made sense because Lisa could sleep in my room and my dad could have my guest room.

The next step was to send my dad home. He had started to hover over me. Since Michael had already taken that position, my dad just rumbled around my house angrily slamming cupboards. My father didn't go easy, but Lisa helped him see reason.

The damage to me was quite a different matter. My first real look in the mirror at home took me by shock. Insisting that I needed a bath of some sort at home, Lisa helped me wrap my shoulder in plastic to protect my stitches. Then I threw her out of my bedroom. I wanted to be alone for the reveal. The bruising on my face was almost beyond recognition. It was still black and blue, and none had turned to the familiar yellow yet. My face was a puffy swollen mess. My neck showed Kevin's fingerprints, and there was more damage to my breasts and torso. Sitting in the wheelchair facing the mirror, I put my head in my hands and wept. I didn't know how anyone could stand to look at me. I was ugly.

Michael came into my bedroom and closed the door behind him. "Go away." I cried, looking up, and then put my head down again and continued to weep.

He put his hands on my shoulders gently from behind and looked at me in the mirror. "Babe, what's the matter? Let me help you."

"I look and feel awful." I cried, my head still in my hands.

"Elizabeth, it's all going to heal. You'll be back to normal soon." His voice was reassuring and soothing, but I was having none of it.

I looked up at our reflection. The sight made me want to retch up my lunch. "How can you say that? Look at me. I'm a monster! Just leave me alone. I can't stand to have you see me."

His eyes showed shock and then hurt. He rubbed my shoulders with a soft touch. "You have to give it some time."

I shook my head and wished I hadn't because it made me dizzy. "Just go, Michael. I want to be alone. Okay?" My voice was getting higher, and I was on the verge of being hysterical.

At the sound, Lisa poked her head into the room. "Is everything okay? Bess do you need some help?"

"No!" I shouted. "Would everyone please leave me alone?"

He backed away from me. "We're right outside the door if you need us."

"Go already!" I yelled.

When I was alone, I sat on the edge of the tub and slowly bathed myself while wiping tears from my face.

As the days progressed, I felt all the after-effects of the attack. The physical ones started to heal. The bruises went through their transition into the splotchy yellow color, and the swelling on my face and neck seemed less. The mental effects however began.

First, the nightmares came. Each time it was the same, a replay of the violence. With each one, I would awaken bathed in sweat, my hair, and nightgown clinging to me. Every time the dream occurred, I faced the same inability to scream or run away.

I began to pull further away from everyone. As my withdrawal went deeper, both Lisa and Michael hovered close to me as if they were trying to drag me back. I didn't want to come back.

CHAPTER FORTY-SIX

By the beginning of December, I barely came out of my bedroom.

The day for the eagle cleansing ceremony was soon upon us, and I did not want to go. I simply did not have the energy. Michael tried to explain my reluctance to Annie on the phone, but she showed up at my door not forty-five minutes later. I could hear both Lisa and Michael arguing with Annie in the living room. Pulling the covers over my head, I tried to ignore the noise.

My bedroom door opened, and I groaned underneath the covers. Annie's voice was first giving Lisa directions to pull clothes out of my closet for me. Next, she told Michael to put his cameras in the car, and we would be there shortly. She shushed the dogs off the bed, and I felt her sit next to me. I sighed knowing what was coming for me.

Slowly, I felt her pulling down the feather comforter, and I opened my eyes. I saw Annie's eyes showing kindness, but determination.

"Mija," she said. "It is time for you to get up and out of bed. Today is a good day to do this, we have someplace to go."

"Leave me alone. I just want to sleep." I tugged at the covers, but they didn't budge because she held them tightly in her hands.

My sister came out of the closet with a pair of jeans and a sweater. "Okay, these should be loose enough to go around the bandages."

She looked over her shoulder and nodded. "Just leave them there. Close the door on your way out, okay?"

I heard the door shut while I looked at Annie.

"I'm not going anywhere. I don't feel good, and I'm going to stay in bed."

She looked at me, and it was not merely a plain look. "Elizabeth, you are going to get out of bed. I am going to help you get dressed, and you will go with us to the ceremony." Her voice matched her look, firm, but gentle and quiet.

I felt like a petulant child whose mother was chastising her. "Why should I go? It's not that important."

She rose from the bed and picked up the jeans that Lisa had left lying on the dresser. She put the jeans on the edge of the bed.

"Michael needs you to go." She again said it simply and then remained quiet.

I bit my lip and stared at her. She knew exactly how to get to me.

"Annie," I said with exasperation in my voice. "Why is it so important I go?"

Sitting back down on the bed, she took my hands in hers. Her eyes were serious as she spoke. "Did you not consider that maybe he is suffering too?"

"What do you mean?" I knew her answer deep in my heart, but I had to ask anyway.

Annie smiled and gently brushed my hair back with one hand while she held my hands in her other. "I know what Kevin did to you makes you forget about Michael's heartache. He lost a dear friend up on that mountain and then almost lost you too. Don't you think it is time for you to stop and think about him?"

The look she had on her face made me feel uncomfortable, to say the least. I was squirming under her gaze. I sighed heavily because I was not winning this battle. I moved to sit, and she helped me dress.

"You know I can't walk very far," I said, again my voice sounded bad-tempered.

"We have already thought about that Mija. The boys have borrowed an electric cart from the nursery, and they cleared a path to the eagle stand. The ride might be a little bouncy, but you should be able to manage the short trip."

I frowned. It seemed there were several people behind this plan to drag me from my bed.

After dressing, Michael helped me into the jeep. He had to help me with my seat belt because the movement in my shoulder hurt. There was silence between the two of us, and then he finally spoke.

"I told Annie you didn't feel well enough to go," he said by way of an explanation.

I sighed, and he kissed me on the forehead. The trip up to the mountain was a quiet one. When we arrived at the utility road, a small group appeared to be waiting for us. There were more cars parked on the side. I was surprised that when we arrived in the clearing, a crowd was gathered. I knew all of the tribal elders through my association with Annie and her family. More than one hundred people were milling around a large bonfire. When we joined the group, a circle formed around the fire and we sat down on the ground. Both Michael and Don lowered me gently down, and Debi had been thoughtful to bring a pillow for me to sit on.

Annie stood outside the circle behind us. I was surprised to see the three boys who perpetrated the killing walk up and stand beside her. Michael's body stiffened when he saw them, but other than that, he sat there quietly. A tribe member who sat opposite to me started to thrum quietly on a small drum he was holding between his legs. A tribal elder walked in from the other direction and stood on the outside of the circle, but he did not stand with Annie and the boys.

She and the boys started walking around the outside of the circle slowly. She chanted a prayer in her native Pomo language and then repeated it in English. "Our eagle brother, it is to you we dedicate this home. You are our eyes in the heavens, and we are your feet on the earth. We are brothers by the fire, and together we hunt on this land. Your flight is sacred to us, and we bid you return to us, our brother. We purify this earth by burning that which was taken from you."

With that, Annie and the boys entered the circle. They stood close to the flames and each boy one after the other, dropped a tail feather into the fire. Sparks flew up, and the fire quickly consumed the feathers. The tribal elder chanted behind us, and when he finished, he joined the circle. Next, Annie joined the circle and sat between Frank and me. She squeezed my hand and then reached around me to take Michael's hand. They rested their clasped hands in my lap, and I laid mine over theirs. He did not smile when he looked at me. He had a far off look on his face, and there were tears, but they had failed to leave his eyes.

Lastly, the boys joined the circle with their families. No one spoke a word. We sat together watching the fire as the cold December air whipped around us. Together we all hoped the eagles would return.

CHAPTER FORTY-SEVEN

Michael and my sister were not getting along either. Both of them had different opinions on how to handle me, and I disagreed with both of them. He was not sleeping in my bed, and wouldn't go home, so he slept on the couch. The two of them argued frequently, and at first, I didn't have the energy to object, but finally, it grew even too much for me.

After almost two weeks, when their bickering was getting on my nerves, I hobbled out to the living room to put an end to the disagreements. I leaned against the doorway and said, "What are you two fighting about now?"

Both of them looked surprised to see me.

My sister spoke first. "Dinner. Michael is insisting that we make pasta without meat sauce for you. I think you need the meat to get your strength back."

He frowned. "That is absurd. Elizabeth does not need meat to keep her strength up. She needs protein. She can get protein from other sources."

I raised one hand. "Enough!"

She opened her mouth to say something, but I beat her to the punch. "Enough! Did either of you consider asking me what I wanted? I don't really want pasta tonight. Lisa, what are you doing here? I love you, and you are fantastic to be here taking care of me, but you have a husband and two babies to take care of. Besides, you are pregnant. Go home. If you leave now, you can be home by tonight."

She looked at me, and her bottom lip trembled. "Bess, I want to be here taking care of you." She put her arms around me.

I patted her back. "I'll be fine. You've taken such good care of me, and I feel so much better. Christmas will be here sooner than you know, and you have to get ready at home. Why don't you pack your stuff, call that handsome husband of yours, and let him know you are coming home.

Michael can drive you to the airport." I looked at him, and he nodded.

She turned to look at him. "Thank you, Michael. I'm sorry I've been such a pain in the butt. Bess is my big sister. I don't know what I'd do without her."

He put his hand on her shoulder, and she immediately turned in to hug him. "I understand. I have a little sister too," he said it gently.

She smiled. "Okay, I'll call the airlines and get a ticket." Lisa almost skipped off toward the guest room.

I looked at him squarely. "You need to leave too. I don't need you here taking care of me."

He stared at me, and said through his teeth, "I am not going anywhere."

I walked back into the bedroom. "Oh yes, you are. You need to get on with your life."

He followed me into the bedroom closing the door behind him. "You are my life Elizabeth."

Ignoring him, I walked over to the bed and straightened out the covers. I turned to look at him. He still stood by the door with a look of frustration on his face.

"Look Michael, when Kevin attacked me my life changed. I'm not the same person I was. I'm somehow darker. I don't know how to explain it. It's the nightmares. I just keep reliving it over and over. I need to get past this, and I think I have to do it alone."

"What are you going to do?" The angry expression grew on his face.

His face almost made me crumble. I couldn't handle any more irritated men. Angry at me for what? I could feel tears welling in my eyes.

"I think I need to go away for a while."

Michael's anger lashed out. "There you go Elizabeth, running away again."

I looked at him shocked. I wasn't running away. No, I was just going to leave for a bit to sort out things. That wasn't running away.

"Damn, Elizabeth, I am sorry I didn't get to you sooner. I'm sorry you had to go through the violence and the abuse. If I only would have realized that the lights were off. I could have gotten to you before the attack." He ran his hands through his hair pacing back and forth.

"The attack wasn't your fault. You didn't know. You did save me. I don't blame you for this," I said, sitting on the bed feeling horrid that he would blame himself.

He walked across the room and stood in front of me, his voice harsh. "Then why are you punishing me?"

I looked up at him, tears running down my face. "Michael…I'm not…" I paused as his words started to sink in. What was happening here? Did I blame him for what happened to me?

"That's what you need to figure out Elizabeth." He turned for the door.

"I'm going to help your sister. Let me know."

I collapsed back on the bed, and the tears ran down my cheeks. Lisa came in briefly about an hour later to say goodbye. She told me she left sandwiches in the refrigerator for lunch and was sure Michael would make a nice dinner for me. I wasn't too sure about her last statement. He didn't come into my room to say goodbye. I didn't know if he would even be back. We hugged and kissed and then she was gone.

Alone in my cabin for the first time since the assault, I felt strange. There were no voices, and it was completely quiet. I started a fire in the fireplace, and it began to rain. The weather turned stormy, and I regretted sending Michael out. I ate one of the sandwiches Lisa had made and drank a glass of milk.

After eating, I went back to bed. Everything was so quiet. Finally relaxed, I fell asleep. When I awoke, it was dark outside. Someone had turned on a small light in the corner of my room. I wondered who did. Walking into the living room answered my question. Michael was lying on the couch covered up with my quilt. His clothes were on the arm of the chair and he slept soundly. I knelt down in front of him and watched him sleep. His face was peaceful and beautiful. I was ashamed that it had never occurred to me what he had gone through when I was injured. My dad was right, I was selfish. Annie was right too, I had never considered Michael's feelings.

How could I consider leaving this man? What was the matter with me? I was nuts to throw everything away. At that moment, I knew I could never leave him. I loved him too deeply. To leave him would be a pain I would never be able to bear, far worse than the physical pain I felt. Moreover, his love for me knew no bounds. He put up with my family, and most of all, with me. He brought me back from the brink of hell.

I stroked his face tenderly.

His eyes fluttered open. "Elizabeth, are you okay?"

"Yes, my wonderful man. I am just fine." I kissed him, and his lips responded to me quickly.

He sat up and pulled me into his lap. We kissed for what seemed like ages. His hands roamed my body gently as I nestled into his neck.

"Michael," I whispered softly. "I need you to do something for me."

"Anything Babe, you know that."

I sat up and caught his face between my hands. I kissed him and ran my tongue across his lips gently, probing his warm mouth.

"I need to remove the remembrance of Kevin's hands on my body. I need you to do it…" I faltered a bit. "I need you to make love to me."

Michael didn't answer. He carried me into the bedroom and laid me gently on the bed. As he took me tenderly in his arms, he quietly took the pain in my soul away. Together we all hoped the eagles would return.

CHAPTER FORTY-EIGHT

Christmas came quickly. We had a quiet celebration. Tammy decorated the house and made it festive for us while I added the last changes on my book, finally sending it off to my publisher.

We spent New Year's Eve alone together since Tammy was down at Stanford with Jason. Friends sent us invitations to parties, but I preferred a brief toast alone with Michael at midnight. He already made plans for us to fly to New Orleans to celebrate Mardi Gras in February with Tommy and Marie. Of course, Nancy and Marcus would be there too. He surprised me with a vintage dress and the trip to New Orleans as a Christmas present.

We started to settle into the routine we had established before Thanksgiving. I reveled in the winter days with him, and although I wasn't yet up to jogging, we would take long walks together by the lake with the dogs. My strength was coming back slowly, though I still tired easily.

One activity we did not limit. We spent the long winter nights in bed. Tammy would just roll her eyes, as we would drift off into the bedroom early in the evening. She said we were boring like an old married couple. Her comment made the two of us laugh because it was anything but dull.

Michael still went regularly up to Mount Mintock looking for eagles. He postponed our book until I felt better. I knew we would start it up again soon, and I found him working on his eagle pictures often.

Several weeks after the New Year's holiday, we visited our favorite Italian restaurant in Ashley. I ate too much food, but Michael always enjoyed watching me eat. I knew I had overeaten because the next morning I had to run to the bathroom to vomit. The nausea was strange because once I emptied the contents of my stomach, I felt fine and was ready to eat breakfast.

The next morning when the nausea repeated, and the bout of vomiting followed, I was sure I had caught some stomach flu. The flu was going around, and it appeared to have latched itself onto me. The nausea made me tired, so I spent most of the day in bed.

By the third morning, I knew something was wrong. I had never been sick like this, and I knew a doctor's visit was in order. Fortunately, they had an opening, and I drove into Mintock that afternoon.

Doctor Helga came into the room. "So you've got the flu?"

"Yeah, past three mornings I've been nauseated and vomiting. But I feel better right afterward."

"Okay," she said, putting her stethoscope against my back. "Breathe in, and out."

I followed her instructions. She looked at the thermometer. "Are you able to eat afterward?"

I nodded again. "Oh yes, I'm usually starving."

"When was your last period?"

I thought back, I realized it had been some time. "The end of November."

"You haven't had a period since the end of November?" she asked.

"No. I figured with the attack it probably just skipped a month."

"Could you be pregnant?"

I looked at her with wide eyes. "No, of course not. You know I can't get pregnant."

"Elizabeth, you have always said that, I haven't," she replied coolly. "Are you having unprotected sex with Michael?"

"Well yes," I said slowly.

"Well then, I think you're pregnant."

"What? How?" I stuttered out. My mind started swimming. I didn't know what to think.

"I would hope you know the how Elizabeth," Dr. Helga replied. She had me lie back on the table, and she performed a quick exam. "We'll do a blood test to confirm. But, let's use this first." She pulled out a home pregnancy test from the drawer. "Go pee on the stick, and let's see what it says."

I took the test from her and went off to the bathroom. As I waited in the examining room for the results, I flashed back to Kevin's attack. He had told me that the doctor lied, and he had been giving me birth control pills. Could it be true?

Dr. Helga joined me back in the examination room. "Congratulations. I would say you are about six weeks pregnant, and what you are experiencing is morning sickness. It should pass as you hit three months, but some women are unfortunate and have it during their whole pregnancy."

I looked at her, and she had a bit of a smirk on her face. My mind was reeling. How could I be pregnant? What would I tell Michael? How would I tell Michael? He remarked only recently that he had his life back now since his last daughter was in college. He was not going to want to start all over again with a new family.

Doctor Helga sensed my confusion. "I know you didn't expect this honey." She patted my hand. "But I know you have always wanted to have a child. Everything will be fine. The nurse will contact you to set up your prenatal care routine."

I was glad that Michael was out when I arrived back home. I needed to think. I needed to make a plan. I didn't want to panic, but it was quickly taking me over. After dinner, I went to bed complaining I was tired and feeling ill. When he came to bed, I cuddled up in his arms, and felt safe and loved. As he lay next to me, spooning me and holding me against him, his hand lay over my womb as if he was cradling our baby. I knew all this would be ending soon. I spent the whole night knowing I had to tell him the news soon.

The next morning he was up early and in the kitchen eating breakfast when I came out to join him after my heaving session in the bathroom.

"Hey, sleepy head. Are you feeling any better this morning?"

I nodded. Actually, I was miserable. Sleep had avoided me most of the night, but I put on a happy face for him since he appeared to be in such a good mood.

"I have a surprise for you. We are going to take a little field trip today up to Mt. Mintock. The weather looks like it is going to be sunny for us. Do you feel up to it?" He had such a delighted smile on his face that I couldn't bear to disappoint him.

"Okay." I nodded. I would tell him right after we returned from the trip.

We dressed warmly. Although it was sunny, the air was cold and would be colder still on the mountain. We parked in the usual spot off the utility road.

"Are we going to the tree stand?" I asked as we headed through the forest in that direction.

Michael took my hand in his and nodded. "Yup. I've been waiting to show you this until you recovered. I made everyone promise not to say a word to you."

"What?" I asked, now my curiosity was peaked.

"You'll see." He had a big grin on his face and was almost beside himself in excitement.

When we arrived at the tree stand, I looked around and didn't see anything unusual. I looked up at the old eagles nest and took a deep breath when I saw a little white head pop up. "Oh Michael." I grabbed his arm. "Is she back? Is Ethel back?"

Michael smiled and hugged me tightly. "Do you think you can climb up the tree stand?"

I nodded. The strength had come back in my arms since my ribs and shoulder had healed. I went up first, and he followed me. He handed me the binoculars. There she was, sitting in the nest. "Michael, why is she sitting like that?"

Michael grinned at me again. "There's another surprise." He pointed to the sky, and I put the binoculars down. "Look there." He pointed to an eagle flying above the lake.

I looked at him in amazement. "She found another mate?"

He smiled and held me closely. "Yes," he whispered. "She is sitting in the nest because she is sitting on eggs. Her new mate is out hunting food for her."

I looked at him, and he had tears in his eyes.

"Eggs?" I asked.

He was beaming. "She came back to us," he whispered into my ear. While he held me, he reached into his pocket. I looked down, and he had a small black box in his hand. "Elizabeth, will you…"

I placed my hand over his mouth to stop him. "Michael, before you say it, please wait a moment. I need to tell you something, and you may regret your question."

He looked at me with puzzled eyes. They were so blue today, and I knew I wouldn't be seeing them much longer. I lowered my hand and took a deep breath. I didn't know how to say it, so I just blurted it out.

"Michael, I'm pregnant."

He closed his eyes and then he opened them slowly. He looked as if he saw me for the first time.

I continued to blurt out, "I know you're ready to start your new life with Tammy going off to school in a few weeks. You can be in the baby's life as much as you want. I hope you would want that, but I would understand if you don't. We'll live next door to you, and if you wanted to move away, I would understand that too," I stammered.

I didn't know what else to say. Michael was so quiet.

"You're having our baby?" he asked.

"Of course. I wouldn't…" I stopped and hung my head down. I ran my hand lightly over my abdomen feeling comforted knowing our baby was there. We would be all right, the baby and me together.

Michael lifted my head with his hands and held my face. "Why would you ever think I wouldn't be absolutely thrilled with this news? Elizabeth I love you madly. I cannot live without you every day. Besides giving me your love, you are giving me the greatest gift I could have ever asked. You are giving me our baby. I don't know how this miracle happened, but I am not going to question it."

"But," I could feel tears running down my cheeks, "you said you'd be happy to be starting your life."

He kissed the falling tears on my face. "I would be happy to be starting it with you my love. That is what I said. I am starting my life with you. Now let me get back to my question."

He carefully pulled the diamond ring out of the box and placed it on my left finger. It felt so right there as if it had always belonged.

"Elizabeth, will you make me the happiest man in this world and become my wife?" he asked, his eyes staring into mine.

"Yes, Michael." I gazed into his sky- blue eyes and knew they would always be mine, forever.

He was my dream come true …

CONTINUE THE STORY...

REVEALING DESTINY

secrets ... trust ... love ...

Michael placed a ring on Elizabeth's finger, and you would think that would be *The End.*

This sequel to the sizzling romance *Eagle's Destiny* continues in the vibrant city of New Orleans during the wild and colorful festival of Mardi Gras!

Secrets are revealed, and trust is put to the test. Sometimes the obstacles may be insurmountable when love is on the line ...

... will their love survive to happily ever after?

An excerpt from

Revealing Destiny

CHAPTER ONE

Fury filled his eyes. His face was red with anger as he shoved the knife into my shoulder. Anger? Hate. It was pure hate. What had I done to him to make him hate me? I couldn't think; I couldn't breathe. The pain sliced through me.

I woke with a scream, thrashing against the arms that held me.

"Let me go!" A sob choked my voice. "No!"

"Elizabeth, it's me! You're dreaming," a deep and comforting tone called out to me. It was Michael, my Michael. Thank God he was here.

"Baby?" His hand rubbed my back in soothing strokes. "You're okay. I'm here."

Cupping my chin with strong masculine fingers, he tilted my face up to look at him. Even in the dark, I could see concern in his sky-blue eyes. I pressed my damp forehead against the dusting of whiskers on his cheek.

"Michael," I gasped his name.

"Was it the same nightmare? Kevin stabbing you?" he asked gently. At the mention of my ex-husband's name, I shuddered in his arms.

"Yes," I whispered.

I'd been having the same nightmare for the past month, always ending the same way. The ugly red scar on my shoulder proved that, unfortunately, the hellish nightmare was reality.

He wrapped me tighter in his protective embrace. "I'm here, baby. He won't ever hurt you again. Do you think you can go back to sleep or do want some tea?"

Tea. Michael's answer to stress.

"No. I'll fall back asleep. I'm sorry I woke you."

"It's what I'm here for – we're in this together," he murmured and rolled onto his back, smoothly pulling me down with him.

I rested my head on his chest and reveled at his hard body. Idly stroking his chest, my hand roamed down to his defined abdomen, the only sound in the room the soft rain from outside. His fingers lightly brushed against my back, and moved lower, all the while making seductive circles. His touch sent serious sparks to my core, heating the flame of desire he could always elicit from me. My caresses moved south, too, to the soft trail of hair below his navel.

His arm moved as he placed his hand over mine, interlacing his fingers with mine. Softly he murmured, "Elizabeth, aren't you trying to sleep?"

I lifted my head to gaze at him and inched my way up his tall muscled frame until I could snuggle into his broad shoulder.

"It's raining," I whispered back as if that would be a suitable explanation.

He shifted to look at me. "So it is, and my question again is, why aren't you trying to sleep?"

He kissed my finger as I ran it against his soft, lush lips. "I'm listening to the rain."

Michael sighed and smiled. "What am I going to do with you, babe? You need to sleep."

"I need you more." I leaned over and softly kissed his mouth. My tongue traced a line down his square jaw and I nipped at his whiskers while they prickled my lips and nose. My hand found his happy trail once more, moving down to the tip of his quickly growing erection brushing against me.

He was my refuge after the nightmares. His hands and mouth on my body gave me comfort, made me feel secure.

Michael understood my intentions immediately. "Come here, my little Hellcat." His voice was seductive as he gently pushed me onto my back, returning my kisses and claiming my mouth with a silky touch of his tongue. "You are not going to let me get any sleep, are you?" he asked with mock resignation, his lips hovering close to mine.

I giggled wickedly, kneading the bunching muscles of his shoulders as his mouth began its intoxicating exploration of my body.

"You better get used to losing sleep at night," I teased, my breathing started to roughen. "Let's begin practicing now."

"Don't forget I've done this no sleeping thing twice before," he murmured as he slowly drove me out of my mind.

CHAPTER TWO

The next morning, I woke up with the spot beside me empty. Figuring that Michael was on his morning jog, I remained in bed, trying to bolster my courage. I knew when my feet hit the floor a wave of nausea would strike.

Placing a hand on my abdomen, my smile broadened - at six weeks it was too early for a baby bump, but the connection was there nonetheless. My little Muffin. Inhaling deeply, I swung my feet over to the floor. Sure enough, as soon as I stood, queasiness made me run for the bathroom. I barely had the toilet lid up before I heaved, retching miserably.

Sitting on the rim of the cold tub and wiping my mouth with a hand towel, I waited for the second round to come. I grasped the towel tightly, making my knuckles white. I now knew after the second purge, I would feel fine.

"Babe?" The question accompanied a small knock on the door.

"Don't come in, I'm getting sick," I called out as I leaned over the toilet once more.

I gripped the seat cover firmly and felt Michael's warm hands on my back. While I heaved, he wound a hand into my waist-length auburn hair, holding it out of the way. As quickly as it came, it finished. I straightened stiffly, and Michael pulled me into his arms.

My head fit easily on his shoulder as I pressed myself against his long muscular body. At six-foot-four, Michael had a way of making me feel petite, which was no small feat since I was just an inch shy of six foot myself. He was pleasantly shirtless, and I ran my fingers through the smattering of tawny-gold hair on his chest that matched the soft wavy hair on his head. He wore sweat pants slung low on his hips, the way I liked, which showed his happy trail extending from his belly button downward.

His hands caressed my back, eventually coming to rest on my naked bottom and he squeezed. "I'm sorry you have to go through this, baby."

I kissed his neck softly and looked him straight in his worried eyes. “It’s okay. It comes and goes quickly and so far hasn’t bothered me during the day.” Then I quipped, “And, I’m really hungry afterward, too!”

“I’m glad you're hungry, breakfast is ready. Do you want to eat it in bed or come into the kitchen?”

“Oh, you’ve already made breakfast? Didn’t you go jogging this morning?” I asked, slipping on my robe before I rinsed my mouth with cold water.

“I thought we could run together with the dogs after breakfast.” As Michael mentioned the dogs, Max’s nose appeared from around the door, followed by his big bushy tail, which was wagging furiously. We were a blended family, his and mine. My two cocker spaniels, Topper and Samantha, and his two dogs, Max and Molly, who were mixtures of terrier and German Shepherd, made up the four-legged types in charge of the house.

I laughed as I petted Max under the chin. “Come on then, lead the way to breakfast. I’m starved.”

As soon as we got into the kitchen, I wrinkled my nose with distaste when I saw the two bowls of oatmeal sitting on the table. Blech, I hated oatmeal - I was *not* going to eat oatmeal. I opened the refrigerator and rummaged around.

“What are you looking for?” Michael asked as he poured orange juice into two glasses.

"Isn’t there some leftover streusel coffee cake from Debi?”

“Babe, you don’t want to eat coffee cake for breakfast. Look, I put nuts and dried fruit in the oatmeal.”

I wrinkled my nose again. “I don’t like oatmeal. Besides, there is nothing wrong with coffee cake.”

Michael was a vegetarian and, although he didn’t insist his two daughters, or I follow his eating routine, he was still adamant about the type of food he wanted in the house. This meant we purchased our eggs from a local farmer who raised free-range chickens. We bought our cheese and meats from companies certified in the humane treatment of animals, and all our fruits and vegetables were organically grown. That suited me fine because he normally did all the cooking, anyway. I was cooking impaired.

“Just try it for me, please?” He looked at me with his blue puppy dog eyes, the very ones I could never say no to.

I frowned and grabbed the Greek yogurt and honey before closing the refrigerator. “Oh, alright. Don’t think pregnancy will make me eat healthy stuff, though.”

We sat down together at the table and he watched me sprinkle a healthy spoonful of brown sugar on top of the oatmeal. I did it not because I had a particular sweet tooth, but more to show him that I was going to be in charge of my own eating routine.

Despite my protests, the first bite of oatmeal was delicious. It was definitely *not* the same oatmeal my mother made, which always tasted like paste left in the sun to dry. Instead of being flat and mushy, this was nutty in flavor and chewy in texture.

"Okay, I suppose this is good," I reluctantly admitted as I took another spoonful.

Michael gave me a self-satisfied grin. "It's called steel-cut. I suppose I shouldn't tell you it's full of fiber, protein, and lots of good minerals to make you a healthy pregnant woman."

I laughed with him as my cell phone rang. "No, don't tell me it's healthy. Healthy tastes bad!" Glancing at the phone, Nancy's name flashed, and I quickly ran my finger over it to answer. "Hi!"

"Good morning! How is my favorite romance author, my best client, and my sweetest friend?" Nancy's cheery voice greeted me.

"Don't you sound chipper this morning?" I replied, taking another bite of oatmeal.

"As well I should. How are you feeling? Did the doctor confirm the flu?"

I couldn't help but giggle. "Turns out it is not quite the flu."

"Oh?" The alarm in my friend's voice was unmistakable.

"No, nothing is wrong," I assured her quickly. "Can I put you on speaker? Michael is here."

"Oh oh, what's up, Elizabeth? Are you okay? Yes, put me on speaker. I have news he'll want to hear, too."

"Really? What is it?" I asked as I pressed the speaker button and placed the phone on the kitchen table.

"No. You first," she said.

"You know how I went to the doctor because I was getting sick? I knew it had to be the flu, but it wasn't."

"Yes…and?" she interrupted, "Elizabeth, stop being dramatic. This isn't one of your novels."

I laughed. "I'm pregnant."

There was a long silence on the other end of the phone then I heard a little voice. "Oh My God! Elizabeth, are you serious?"

I smiled broadly and looked over at Michael who was grinning too. "Yep. Me, pregnant lady."

"When? How?"

Chuckling, Michael spoke up. "About six weeks ago, and, as to the how, ask Marcus. I'm sure he'll be happy to explain it to you."

"Oh you know what I mean. This is incredible news. Congratulations!"

"And it doesn't end there, Nancy," I revealed. "Michael asked me to marry him."

"I would hope so!"

"Just a minute," Michael interjected, leaning forward toward the phone. "I asked Elizabeth to marry me *before* she told me she was pregnant. That is an important order of sequence."

"Michael, that isn't important," Nancy replied. "I'm so happy for both of you!"

"What was your news? Is it something to do with your wedding?" Nancy was due to marry Michael's best friend Marcus in less than three months.

"Actually this has to do with you and I would have said to open a bottle of champagne, but, due to your condition, maybe some sparkling apple juice will have to do. Triad Productions has just given the green light for the making of *Trouble Always Happens*."

I dropped my spoon into the bowl of oatmeal. It made a loud clattering sound as it jumped out of the bowl and came to rest at the edge of the table. "You're kidding," I uttered, my voice barely above a whisper. A wide grin grew on my face as Nancy's words sank in. I jumped up from the table, pumping my fist in the air. "Yes!" I shouted with elation and threw my arms around Michael's shoulders.

He laughed and pulled me down into his lap. "Baby, this is great news!" He echoed my excitement

Trouble Always Happens was my first book and part of a suspenseful romance series I'd been writing for the past five years. The production company, after indicating their interest in turning the book into a movie, had first contacted us at the end of last summer. Having already been through the mill once before, I didn't put much hope into the project. Nonetheless, I had spoken with the screenwriter several times to review parts of the book.

Nancy joined us in our reverie. "This is the real deal, Elizabeth. They have a script they would like you to read. We made sure in the letter of intent you'd have full approval. You should have it today. If there are parts you don't like, they want you to work with the screenwriter. Triad is anxious to get this kicked off. They've already chosen the director, Raven Jay Taylor."

"Taylor wants to direct the movie? Wow!" He beamed. His big grin and the pride showing on his face made my heart clench, happiness filling me from the inside out. Being able to share my success with him was something I was unable to do with my ex-husband, but it was so easy with Michael.

Nancy continued, "I know, can you believe it? It looks like we're going to have a lot to celebrate when you come down next month for Mardi Gras."

"Are you officially in New Orleans now?" I asked. After Nancy's engagement, she began to move her base of operations from Los Angeles to Marcus' home.

"Yep, all moved in. It's a big change, but we're having fun trying to clear closet space for my clothes. He actually suggested I take over one of the guest bedrooms for my clothes."

I laughed at the vision of them trying to move Nancy's belongings into his house. Even though the house was a mansion, Michael had told me Marcus was quite the clotheshorse himself.

"We're looking forward to seeing you both," I said excitedly. "I'll start reading the script as soon as it arrives today. I can't wait to see it!"

After we said our goodbyes and disconnected, Michael wrapped his arms around me, hugging me from behind. "I'm so proud of you babe," he whispered, his lips close to my ear.

I grinned. "Can you believe this?"

"You're going to be a busy girl today. Let's see, you have to call your sister, and then there is Debi and Annie. Do you want to tear yourself away for a jog first?"

"Of course, I'll run with you, but first," I handed him my empty oatmeal bowl. "Can you make me some more oatmeal?"

CHAPTER THREE

My hands shook with anticipation as I opened the FedEx package, which arrived that afternoon. Even though we tried to relax, waiting all day for the package had keyed me up. We lived at the furthest point from the center of town and, as a result, we were always at the end of delivery schedules.

Michael and I met last summer when he moved into his newly renovated house and became my new next-door neighbor. Our homes, located on the shore of Lake Mintock, were the last houses on our side of the lake. His was far larger than my little two-bedroom cabin, and, as our relationship heated up over the autumn, it was natural for me to move my things to his house. My cabin became our offices.

While I wrote my romance novels, he edited his wildlife photography, and, together, we worked on an eagle storybook for children. The mountain connected to our town and the lake had two nesting eagles; I was convinced that our love of these eagles had brought us together. When we teamed up to work on the book, it became a magical time for both of us. I had to admit, writing a children's book was new for me, but his praise and encouragement pushed me to stretch myself as a writer.

"Michael! It's here!" I exclaimed as I walked into the kitchen from the back porch.

He handed me a champagne flute filled with sparkling apple juice. "Congratulations, my love. Open it- let's see!"

My stomach started the flip-flops, but it was definitely *not* morning sickness. Sitting down at the small kitchen table, I read the title page aloud, "*Trouble Always Happens,* based on the novel by Elizabeth Sommars." I turned the page and continued, "Opening Scene: Focus in on our heroine - Wendy Bolton is tied to an office chair inside an empty cavernous warehouse…"

Looking up at him, I clinked my champagne glass with his. "They have the beginning correct, now let's see what they did with the rest." I took a sip, "Mmmm… this is good. I suppose you just *happened* to have this in the pantry?"

Michael bent over and kissed me. "Of course, babe," he laughed, "And I had to scour three markets to find it today."

A knock at the back door interrupted our revelry. "Who could that be?"

Grinning, he went to open the back door. "Just a little surprise for you."

"Hey darling, whatcha doing?" The voices of my girlfriend Debi and her husband Don greeted me as they walked into the kitchen.

Michael came up behind them. "I invited Debi and Don for dinner tonight to celebrate with us. Annie and Frank are coming over too."

"Oh!" I exclaimed, hugging both of my closest friends. Debi's hug took my breath away, it always did. The top of her dark blond head barely reaching my shoulders.

Don not much taller than Debi held my arms out from my sides and perused me up and down. "Yeah. Definitely pregnant," he proclaimed.

I pushed his shoulder, "You can't tell like that." I giggled.

"I'm right, aren't I?" He chuckled.

I shook my head and rolled my eyes. "Debi, I don't know how you put up with your silly man."

Debi winked at me, "He has his good ass...ets." We laughed as she drew out the word.

"Why don't you girls go on into living room and let us guys handle getting dinner ready." Michael handed them both beers he had retrieved from the refrigerator.

The boys didn't get any argument from us.

We settled into the large black leather couch in the living room. The weather had cleared up during the day and we enjoyed watching the sun slowly set behind the mountain, the sky turning a flamboyant red and purple. Streams of pale light filtered in between the trees and a chill set in as the shadows deepened.

This was the reason I loved living in Mintock - being away from the hustle of a big city, running with the dogs along the lakeshore, and having my best friends close. Debi and I had met in high school in our home town of Torrance, in southern California. During the summers, I would come up to Mintock to stay with my aunt Ruth and met Don and his family. Debi started coming with me and fell in love with Don.

I loved this dear friend of mine, who had stood right with me through all the difficulties of my life, including my disastrous first marriage. She knew me better than most and I could always count on her to be in my court.

Debi's tortoise shell-colored eyes stared at me, as if to prompt me to dish.

I smiled and tucked my feet under me. "I'm feeling pretty spoiled right now."

Debi's round face nodded. "You *should* feel that way. I'm sure the man in that kitchen is planning to spoil you for the rest of your life. Now let's see the ring!"

I stuck out my left hand to her. "Isn't it beautiful?" The platinum ring had a two-carat, princess-cut center stone with matching channel-set diamonds and rows of pave' diamonds down the sides.

Debi's lips made a big 'O.' "You know that cost a small fortune. It is certainly very shiny and I'm jealous."

"Can you believe it, Debi? I'm pregnant, engaged, and my book is being made into a movie!" I marveled. "Michael is so happy about the baby, too. I was afraid to tell him."

"I don't know why - you know how much he loves kids. It's evident he cherishes you as well."

"I didn't think he'd want to start a whole new family. Now that Tammy and Katy are both in college, he had talked about traveling. In fact, he'll be up in Canada visiting the polar bears in March for several weeks. The project he's doing with the San Diego Zoo finally received approval from the Canadian government. I'm a little afraid that he'll feel tied down again with a new baby."

Our attention diverted to the dogs barking and a commotion in the kitchen. Don's parents had arrived. Frank was Mintock's police chief and Annie, an elder with the local Native American tribal counsel of the Pomo people, was my second mom. After my mother passed away several years ago, she had taken me under her wing.

She came out of the kitchen first, her arms wide open for a hug. Dressed in her jeans, cowboy boots, and denim shirt, her slim body moved quickly across the room. She hugged us together. I could see tears in her eyes as she looked at me, which, of course, started my own waterworks.

"Oh *Mija*! I am so happy for you and Michael," she said, hugging me even tighter. Even though I towered over her tiny five-foot frame, her hugs made me feel enveloped somehow. Her little nickname for me, meaning "daughter" in Spanish, was always special to me. Ever prepared, she produced a small packet of tissues from her pocket to dry my eyes. "I know your mother would have loved Michael. He will make you a good husband."

I nodded happily. Michael had won Annie over from their very first meeting, which was a remarkably difficult task. Considering everyone disliked my first husband, and what a catastrophe my marriage to him was, my future with Michael seemed especially bright.

Frank joined us in the living room. "Do you girls want to eat? Michael said it's all ready and I'm starving!"

I took Annie and Debi's hands. "Me too! Michael has been cooking all afternoon- the smells from the kitchen have been driving me crazy."

Debi laughed, "Nothing wrong with your appetite."

Laughing with her, I agreed. "You're right about that. I've been eating like a pig and will probably be a huge pregnant woman."

"You can stand to gain a few pounds, skinny girl," Don said, playfully squeezing my shoulder.

I winced as Don's hand inadvertently moved over the scar on my shoulder. The scar, the source of my nightmares, and the result of my ex-husband brutally attacking, and almost killing, me last Thanksgiving.

Frank's expression darkened. "I'm glad that son of a bitch is behind bars where he belongs."

I sighed deeply. "They still expect me to testify. It's not something I'm looking forward to."

Annie wrapped an arm around my waist. "Don't worry, *Mija.* We are all here for you. Kevin will get the justice he deserves."

"Elizabeth, I'm sorry, I keep forgetting about your shoulder," Don grimaced.

"No worries Don. I'm okay."

Michael placed the heaping tray of bubbling homemade macaroni and cheese on the table. "With your recovery from the injury, and your morning sickness, you've shed enough weight."

I laughed while approaching the table. "You keep cooking like this, and, like I said, I'm going to be a *huge* pregnant woman."

He leaned over and kissed my neck. "And I will love you forever, no matter what," he said as he nuzzled my ear.

Annie's eyes sparkled, again looking moist. She raised a champagne glass that Frank had been busy filling. "A toast to love. To new love, old love, the love of a wife, the love of a husband. The love of a mother, father, and of friends. May it always surround those who live in this house and who live in our hearts."

The clinking glasses made a merry sound as we toasted. My eyes were only on Michael after I took a sip of the cold sparkling apple juice. "I love you," I whispered.

"And I love you more," he whispered back to me…

ALSO BY C. J. CORBIN

The Destiny Series
Eagle's Destiny
Revealing Destiny
Protecting Destiny
Meeting Destiny
Choosing Destiny
Finding Destiny
Celebrating Destiny

The Crescent City Series
The Weekend (A prequel)

The Chronicles Series
Love is a Spell (A Prequel)

Anthologies
Storybook Pub
Storybook Pub Christmas Wishes
Storybook Pub 2
Caught Under the Mistletoe
Tricks, Treats, & Teasers
Heroes with Heat and Heart 3

ABOUT C. J. CORBIN

C. J. Corbin writes sizzling contemporary & paranormal romances which will leave you breathless!

She lives in Southern California with her cocker spaniel, Isabella. An avid wildlife conservationist, she donates a percentage of her book sales to animal conservancy projects.

C. J. relaxes by being SASSY at all times and blasting alternative rock music through her headset while feeding a shameless addiction to online shopping.

And she truly believes in happily-ever-after.

The latest news on her books can be found on her website CJCorbin.com

Friend on Facebook: http://www.facebook.com/christiane.corbin
Like Facebook author's page: http://www.facebook.com/cjcorbin00/
Follow on Twitter: http://twitter.com/CJCorbin00
Follow on Instagram: @CJCorbin00
Follow on Threads: @CJCorbin00

Made in the USA
Las Vegas, NV
25 July 2023

75211658R00207